## The Other Side of Midnight

"No one mixes romance, mystery, and that faint, spine-tingling sense of the supernatural, that curtain lifting in a breeze that isn't there, the hair prickling on the back of your neck, like Simone St. James. Her novels are the perfect combination of classic ghost story, historical fiction, and romantic suspense."
—Lauren Willig, author of the Pink Carnation series and *The Ashford Affair*

"With *The Other Side of Midnight*, Simone St. James has once again crafted a headily atmospheric and suspenseful mystery that kept me reading until the wee hours. Her command of the period is so immersive, and her characters so real and heartbreakingly broken, that I felt transported back to the hard, cold gray years after the Great War, when its legions of dead and missing were a ghostly and inescapable presence, and the bright lights of the Jazz Age were but a fleeting distraction for the privileged few."
—Jennifer Robson, author of *Somewhere in France* and *After the War Is Over*

"Simone St. James has created her own genre—historical gothic mystery romance, with more than a dash of the creepy. In *The Other Side of Midnight*, young psychic Ellie Winter and her partner, war-damaged veteran James Hawley, have terrific chemistry as they tackle the case of a rival medium's death in 1920s London. But what's truly haunting is how St. James uses the post–World War I period, and its poignant undercurrents of unresolved trauma and anxiety, to ground her story in real emotional resonance."
—Susan Elia MacNeal, *New York Times* bestselling author of the Maggie Hope Mysteries

## Silence for the Dead

"Kudos for Simone St. James. I was swept away by this atmospheric and truly spine-chilling page-turner, a riveting tale of dark suspense. . . . If you love a good ghost story, you will be entranced."
—Mary Sharratt, author of *Illuminations: A Novel of Hildegard von Bingen* and *Daughters of the Witching Hill*

"Vivid, eerie, and atmospheric. St. James's latest will simultaneously tug at your heartstrings and send chills down your spine. Absolutely riveting."
—Anna Lee Huber, author of the Lady Darby Mysteries

*continued . . .*

"Atmospheric. . . . St. James cleverly intertwines the story's paranormal elements with what is now called PTSD, crafting a pleasurably creepy tale about the haunting power of the unseen." —*Publishers Weekly*

"Aficionados of the classic gothic style in the tradition of Victoria Holt won't want to miss this atmospheric tale of romantic suspense." —*Library Journal*

## An Inquiry into Love and Death

"I thoroughly enjoyed it! I do like a good ghost story, and Simone clearly relishes and is steeped in the traditions of gothic fiction—in the best way. She conjures that secretive, hushed atmosphere perfectly, and the story kept me turning the pages from beginning to end." —Katherine Webb, author of *The Unseen*

"Another chilling story. . . . St. James delivers a quickly paced read that will satisfy both new and old fans." —*Publishers Weekly*

"A perfectly balanced combination of mystery, romance, ghost story, and history. Told in the first person, it conveys the lasting psychological and practical consequences of war movingly." —*RT Book Reviews* (Top Pick, 4½ Stars)

## The Haunting of Maddy Clare

**Winner of the RITA Award for
Best First Novel from Romance Writers of America**

**Winner of the RITA Award for Best Mainstream Novel with
Romantic Elements from Romance Writers of America**

**Winner of the Arthur Ellis Award
for Best First Novel from Crime Writers of Canada**

"Downright scary and atmospheric. I flew through the pages of this romantic and suspenseful period piece, where a naive city girl must brave a terrifying apparition in order to find justice and redemption for all."
—*New York Times* bestselling author Lisa Gardner

"An inventively dark gothic ghost story. Read it with the lights on. Simply spellbinding." —Susanna Kearsley, *New York Times* bestselling author of *The Winter Sea*

"A compelling read. With a strong setting, vivid supporting characters, and sympathetic protagonists, the book is a wonderful blend of romance, mystery, and pure creepiness." —Anne Stuart, *New York Times* bestselling author of *Shameless*

"A compelling and beautifully written debut full of mystery, emotion, and romance. . . . Great story, believable characters, wonderful writing—I couldn't put this down."

—Madeline Hunter, *New York Times* bestselling author of *The Surrender of Miss Fairbourne*

"This deliciously eerie, traditionally gothic ghost story grabbed me with its first sentence and didn't let go until the very last."

—Wendy Webb, author of *The Tale of Halcyon Crane*

"With a fresh, unique voice, Simone St. James creates an atmosphere that is deliciously creepy and a heroine you won't soon forget."

—Deanna Raybourn, author of the Lady Julia Grey series

"Chilling. . . . Fans of the modern gothic novel will enjoy filling up a few creepy hours."

—*Kirkus Reviews*

"Fast, fun, and gripping. Kept me up into the wee hours."

—C. S. Harris, author of the Sebastian St. Cyr Mystery series

"Compelling and deliciously unsettling, this is a story that begs to be read in one sitting. I couldn't put it down!"

—Megan Chance, national bestselling author of *City of Ash*

"An atmospheric and resoundingly old-fashioned ghost story that pulls you in from the first pages. . . . St. James's writing evokes the time period without pretension, the pacing is just right, the ghost story plausible, and the love story important but not all-consuming."

—*The Historical Novels Review*

"St. James deftly ratchets up the tension in this thrilling ghost story."

—*Publishers Weekly*

"Author Simone St. James has an entrancing voice that mesmerizes from beginning to end . . . filled with fascinating characters and unrivaled suspense in a gothic setting guaranteed to spellbind. This novel is a superb ghost-hunting story, unlike anything I've read in years. . . . Easily earns Romance Junkies' highest rating. Don't miss it!"

—Romance Junkies

Other Books by Simone St. James

*The Haunting of Maddy Clare*
*An Inquiry into Love and Death*
*Silence for the Dead*

# The OTHER SIDE of MIDNIGHT

# SIMONE ST. JAMES

 New American Library

New American Library
Published by the Penguin Group
Penguin Group (USA) LLC, 375 Hudson Street,
New York, New York 10014

USA | Canada | UK | Ireland | Australia | New Zealand | India | South Africa | China
penguin.com
A Penguin Random House Company

First published by New American Library,
a division of Penguin Group (USA) LLC

First Printing, April 2015

 REGISTERED TRADEMARK—MARCA REGISTRADA

LIBRARY OF CONGRESS CATALOGING-IN-PUBLICATION DATA:

St. James, Simone.
The other side of midnight/Simone St. James.
p. cm.
ISBN 978-0-451-41949-1 (paperback)
1. Women psychics—Fiction.   2. Murder—Investigation—Fiction.   3. Women
detectives—Fiction.   I. Title.
PR9199.4.S726O85   2015
813'.6—dc23      2014031006

Printed in the United States of America
10  9  8  7  6  5  4  3  2  1

Set in Adobe Garamond
Designed by Spring Hoteling

This book is dedicated to
the memory of author
Mary Stewart
(1916–2014)

# ACKNOWLEDGMENTS

Thanks to my editor, Ellen Edwards, for your enthusiasm, dedication to my work, and brilliant ability to make my books better. To the staff at New American Library, including art director Anthony Ramondo and the team who creates my beautiful covers, as well as the editorial, publicity, sales, and design teams, I appreciate everything you do. Thank you.

To my agent, Pam Hopkins, who is my partner in the crazy ups and downs of this business, thank you. Also my friends: Molly, Maureen, Tiffany, Julie, Michelle, you all know what you do for me. My mother, sister, and brother help me every single day. And Adam, who believed from the first that I could do it: There are no words for what you mean to me.

Good mediums are rare.

—Hereward Carrington,
*Psychical Phenomena and the War*, 1920

# The OTHER SIDE of MIDNIGHT

# CHAPTER ONE

The man who sat before me at seven o'clock on a Tuesday evening was lying.

He'd come with an impeccable reference from a barrister client of mine, and though he was barely thirty-five, the tailoring of his three-piece suit and the glint of his watch chain spoke of success. He wore power easily in his posture and the set of his shoulders, like a man accustomed to it, and yet the problem he set me was not only trifling; it was false.

He dropped his gaze to the table, where my fingers rested over his, and I took the opportunity to study his face undetected. Slender, clean shaven. Almost handsome, but not quite; something about the width of the temples was off, and an absolute seriousness marred his expression, suggesting no sense of humor. His brows were drawn down as though something weighed on him, and his mouth was pulled into a grim line, as if he was thinking of something terrible

and new. Whatever his true reason for consulting a psychic, he was
not giving it away.

I glanced at the clock on the mantel. We'd been here for an hour
already. I'd earned my shillings.

The man looked up at me, uncomfortable in my silence. "I wonder perhaps—"

"Hush," I said. "You must not interrupt."

It never occurred to him to obey. "It's just that—"

"Mr. Baker, if you cannot let me concentrate, I have no hope of
finding your sister's brooch." I gave him a stern look, the black beads
on my dress clacking. I was prolonging things needlessly now, but
he'd annoyed me, and I was admittedly peevish. "Please concentrate.
Picture the brooch in your head. See it in as much detail as you possibly can. Picture where you last saw it."

He sighed, shifting in his chair, as if it hadn't been he who'd
come to waste *my* time this evening. "I suppose I'll try again."

He would fail. The brooch he'd asked about did not exist; I'd
known as much as soon as I'd touched him. What I didn't know—
what his touch hadn't told me—was what he actually wanted from
me. And here I was, trapped at the little table in my sitting room,
hungry, my cold supper waiting for me in the kitchen. If this man
didn't want to be honest, then he could suffer in one of my hard chairs
a little bit longer.

I waited for a stretch of minutes, my eyes closed, as the clock
ticked on the mantel. "It really isn't coming very clearly," I said at last.

Mr. Baker, who was no more Mr. Baker than I was, squirmed
just a little. "Perhaps I should come again another time."

"No, truly, I can find it. Sometimes it takes a little while, that's
all, and you must concentrate harder. Just a little longer . . ."

"It's quite all right." He squirmed again, and from under my
lashes I saw the first evidence of a conscience. "I'm afraid I have another appointment."

I shook my head in a show of frustration and lifted my hands from his. "But of course. We've run out of time, haven't we? I'm sorry the brooch did not appear to me, Mr. Baker."

"No, no. You mustn't apologize. I insist." Now he seemed almost annoyed. His gaze wandered off and clouded over with disappointment, as if he'd expected something else entirely from this evening and was already forgetting my existence. "Perhaps I'll come and try again another time."

I stood, pushing my chair back coolly. "You could, but that wouldn't make an interesting story, would it?"

He frowned. "I beg pardon?"

"For your newspaper." My peevishness was fleeing now, leaving only tiredness behind. "I assume you write for one. 'Famous Psychic Debunked,' perhaps? Or 'Seer Bilks the Innocent of Money' may also work. Though I can't imagine why any newspaper would want yet another story about people like me."

"I don't know what you mean." His outrage was convincing. He pushed his chair back and stood as well, and though he was only slightly taller than I was, he somehow seemed much larger. "Do you honestly take me for a journalist?"

"Honestly? You don't look like one. You dress too well, and your demeanor is wrong. Honestly, Mr. *Baker*, I don't know what you are, but a journalist is the only kind of person who would go to elaborate lengths to get a referral, then come here and waste my time with a false story about a valuable brooch."

He went very still.

I looked at his face. "Of course I knew it was false. Though if you like, you can publish in your newspaper that I have found the toy soldiers you lost when you were eight. That's what you were really thinking about just now. Here it is: Your brother Tommy took them. He broke them in half and fed them to the dog while playing African Explorer."

There was a long beat of silence. I hadn't meant to say that, not exactly. It had just come so clearly to me—the crisp fall day, the little boy roaring as he pretended the dog was a man-eating tiger, eagerly snapping up Stanley and Livingstone. I wondered whether the dog had gotten indigestion from the enterprise. It seemed likely, though the vision didn't specify. A shadow crossed the vision of the boy, something foreboding, but I pushed it away.

Mr. Baker was looking at me with the shocked expression people wore when they first realized I was telling the truth. "There's no way you could know that," he said softly. "No way at all."

This was a telling moment. People came to me for answers, yet they were always knocked on their heels when I actually gave them. Some customers tittered nervously; others grew angry and defensive, accusing me of trickery or lying. Those were the dangerous ones. The truth, even one so small as the fate of a few wooden soldiers, affected everyone differently. You couldn't predict it. It was why I kept my client list so select.

But the look on Mr. Baker's face was one I hadn't seen before. He stared at me with a sort of profundity, as if I'd answered a question he hadn't even known he'd been asking. And yet the revelation seemed to strike him as a blow, and his look of desperate misery almost made me step back. It was the look of a man who has just seen proof of hell's existence, an answer to one of life's deepest questions, and not the answer he wanted to hear.

"Mr. Baker," I said, keeping my voice level, "I'm asking you to leave the premises."

He swallowed, and something indescribably sad crossed his features. "If only you'd let me explain."

"There's no need." My voice rose almost to shrillness. I wanted no part of the sadness and desperation on his face, none at all. "I'm well acquainted with the local constable. If you don't leave, I'll have no choice but to send for him."

It was a bluff—the local constable thought me a hussy, when he thought of me at all—but Mr. Baker only looked ashamed. He took an expensive handkerchief from his pocket. "I'm sorry," he said, dabbing his forehead and looking away. "Good night."

And then he was gone, without another word to me, my front door shutting on the back of his well-cut suit. I still had no idea why he'd come, what he'd wanted, or even why he'd left so quickly. I told myself the most important point was that he had gone. *You're a woman alone in this job,* my mother had taught me. *You must never take chances.*

I sighed into the lonely quiet of my sitting room. I looked around at the narrow chintz sofa, the heavy draperies over the front window, the plum velvet curtain hanging artfully over the door to the corridor. In the middle of the room was the session table, a simple square with a flowered tablecloth and wooden chairs on opposite sides. Every piece in the room had been picked out by my mother.

"At least he paid me in advance," I said to no one.

The room stared silently back at me. *Theatrical,* my mother had called the decor, *yet respectable. It's the sort of look that works best.*

The Fantastique. That was what my mother had called herself. It had made my father uneasy and the neighbors had never approved, but séances were a very lucrative business. For as long as I had memory, there had been a small hand-painted sign in the window next to our front door, a crystal ball with striped rays emanating from it. THE FANTASTIQUE, it read. PSYCHIC MEDIUM. SPIRIT COMMUNICATION. DO YOU HAVE A MESSAGE FROM THE DEAD? Everyone, it seemed, had someone dead they wanted to talk to.

"It looks a bit like a sunset," I'd said to my mother of that painted crystal ball when I'd been old enough to notice.

"It's theatrical, yet respectable," she'd replied. "It's the sort of look that works best."

Then my father died in the war, and my mother and I were left alone in our little house in St. John's Wood, my mother grieving and, eventually, sick. She taught me everything she knew. And when she died three years ago, what was I to do? Her clients still needed someone. The money was good enough, and steady. I was beholden to no one. Now The Fantastique was me.

But I meant to get the sign changed. The Fantastique now found lost things; that was her only offering. She didn't do séances anymore.

I left the sitting room through the velvet curtain and went up the small staircase to my bedroom on the first floor. I undid my dress—a custom creation, dripping in black jet beads, that had been my mother's—and set it carefully in the wardrobe. It was The Fantastique's only costume. I disposed of my stockings and heels and untied the black scarf wound in my hair. I brushed out my short waves with a silver-backed brush. Then I tied a silk wrapper over my underthings and went barefoot to the kitchen, making a stop in the lav to wash the makeup from my face.

Supper was set on the table, a dome placed over it. I removed the dome and looked at a chop, a potato, and cooked carrots. I had a daily woman who came, cleaned, prepared a few meals, and left again, always while I was working. She didn't mind me and I didn't mind her. I paid her on time and she ensured I had a bottle of wine uncorked by supper. It worked out well enough.

I sat and ate in silence. Work always made me ravenous, if it didn't give me headaches. I cleaned the plate of every crumb, trying not to think of Mr. Baker, of the sadness in his eyes. I wondered whether I should buy a gramophone to break the silence. But no, the image of a girl alone listening to a gramophone seemed a lonely one.

After supper, I poured myself my first glass of wine for the night and took up my cigarettes. It was the first week of September, with summer just beginning to let go, and the cold and dark not yet arrived. Night had fallen when I stepped into my tiny back garden, and there was no breath of heat on the breeze, but the stars were clear and the air that slid down the neck of my wrapper was warm enough to be soothing.

I lit a cigarette, and in the flare of the match I saw a man at the back gate.

I stilled. He stood in the lane that ran behind the row of houses, the wrought-iron fence barely reaching to his chest. He loomed as tall as he had in my sitting room.

"I'm sorry," said Mr. Baker.

I couldn't see him in the darkness after the match died, but I didn't hear him move any closer. "I can scream," I said, my voice curiously calm. "There are neighbors in every direction."

"I don't mean to frighten you," he said from his place in the dark. "Really I don't. You needn't scream."

I took a drag of my cigarette, thinking. I was still close to my back door, close enough to duck inside if he came at me. I hadn't been lying about the neighbors. I wasn't friends with any of them, but they would at least come to investigate if I screamed. I felt horribly vulnerable in my wrapper and bare feet, the makeup scrubbed from my face. "Look," I said. "Just leave. I don't know how else to make this clear. I'm not selling what you're buying."

"Dear God, it's nothing like that." Even through his desperation, he sounded disgusted. "I apologize for what happened . . . in there. I was rather shocked. I hadn't expected . . ."

"The truth? Of course you didn't."

"I can explain all of it," he said. "You're right—the brooch was a lie. I had a good reason. I had to see you for myself, see what kind of person you are. It was important."

I sipped my wine. I still wanted nothing to do with whatever drove him, but I was a little curious despite myself. Perhaps I'd find out why a powerful man had taken the trouble to come to a paid psychic on a Tuesday night. "And did I pass?"

He made a hoarse sound that was almost a laugh; it was unpracticed, as if it was a sound he'd never made before. "You find lost things," he said at last. "You really do."

"It's my specialty, yes."

"You knew what I was thinking. Exactly what—" He cut himself off, then made the hoarse sound again, only this time it sounded like grief. "Ellie Winter," he said. "You have to find my sister."

I shook my head, a senseless weight of dread filling my stomach. "No. Oh, no. I don't find people. I made that clear to you from the beginning. I make it clear to every customer."

"I know. You told me."

"No exceptions, Mr. Baker."

"My name isn't Baker," he said. "It's Sutter. George Sutter."

There was a long beat of silence in which I stared into the dark and hoped I was wrong and none of this was happening, not ever.

"My sister is—" The man at my gate stumbled over the words. "My sister was Gloria Sutter."

My cigarette fell to the ground. "Gloria is missing?"

"Gloria is dead."

My vision blurred, black circles overlapping black circles.

"She got herself murdered," he said. "But before it happened, she left me a note. It said, 'Tell Ellie Winter to find me.' Now, what do you think that means?"

I couldn't answer. I was lowering slowly to the paving stones in my garden, my knees giving way almost gracefully, the wineglass clinking to the ground and rolling away. George Sutter said something else, but I didn't hear it. I had raised my arms and locked my hands behind my head, squeezing my arms over my ears, blocking out the world and everything in it. I closed my eyes and felt the cool silk of my dressing gown against my cheek, and I never wanted to get up and feel anything else again.

# CHAPTER TWO

"I suppose I made a hash of this," said George Sutter as he stood awkwardly in my kitchen. "I didn't foresee that it would upset you quite so much."

I was seated at the table, where he'd ushered me to get us out of sight of the neighbors. I blinked my dry eyes and felt the world come slowly back into focus. "It was something of a shock," I said.

"You seemed quite distressed." He stayed standing, close to the door to the back garden, as if my emotion was contagious. And though his expression was as controlled as ever, I thought I saw a hint of disapproval. "I didn't know you were friends."

"We weren't."

He waited, but when I didn't elaborate, he said, "You were in the same business, and I know how competitive Gloria was. You were rivals?"

I looked up at him. "I find lost things," I said. "Gloria was a spirit medium, communicating with the dead from the other side."

"Soldiers, yes," he said.

"That is not the same business," I told him firmly. "Not at all."

He frowned. "If you say so. But you knew each other?"

"We were acquainted." I felt in control enough now to force the words through my lips. "When did she die?"

"Last night." He looked away, his lips thinning. "She was at one of her . . . sessions. A ghost hunt in a house."

I shook my head. "Gloria didn't do ghost hunts. She did *séances*. In the privacy of her own rooms. Are you saying she was on location?"

Now he looked confused. "She was at some sort of session, or so I was told."

"At a private home? With a group of others?"

"Yes."

I digested this. "And what happened?"

The misery I'd glimpsed in my sitting room came over his face again. "Someone stabbed her," he said, his voice flat. "A single wound to the heart. Then he dumped her body in a nearby pond."

I set my hands on the kitchen table, feeling the coolness of the wood on my palms. I took a shaky breath.

Sutter finally grasped the second kitchen chair, the one my mother had always sat in, and lowered himself onto it. "What about the note?" he asked me. " 'Tell Ellie Winter to find me.' What does that mean?"

I looked at him for a long moment. "You don't know much about what your sister did for a living, do you?"

He regarded me steadily back. "We weren't close."

"Gloria told me her family disowned her," I said. "After her other brothers died in the war."

His control had returned, and now I could tell he was choosing his words carefully. "There were three others, yes."

That explained the shadow I'd seen over the little boy with the soldiers. Three brothers, all of them dead in the mud of France. Gloria had almost never spoken of it. "You two were the only ones left, and you weren't speaking."

He showed no flicker of emotion. "My parents disowned Gloria when she took up her . . . profession during the war. Taking money from people and pretending to talk to their loved ones. It was ghoulish—she made a living from grief. It cut my parents to the bone. After our brothers died, it was too much for them to forgive." His tone implied he agreed with this wholeheartedly. "And, of course, she simply had to be so . . . *showy*. Going to wild parties with her lovers, getting her photograph in the papers. It was shameless. She never cared about the rest of the family, never cared about anything but herself. She never once asked our family for forgiveness. Having a good time was the only thing that mattered."

Perhaps he was right. I never did any of those kinds of things, of course. Not anymore. Not ever again.

George continued. "Last year our mother died, and our father is now in a hospital for the elderly. Age has taken his faculties. Neither one of them had spoken to Gloria in years."

I didn't give him the usual expression of sympathy; something told me it wouldn't be welcomed. "So now she's dead," I said, "and you're all that's left."

"In any meaningful sense, yes." His gaze rested sharply on me. "But you didn't answer my question. What does the note mean?"

I took a breath. "Finding people is what Gloria did," I said. "It is the term she used. You'd go to her to *find* your husband, *find* your son."

He looked at me in disbelief. "Among the dead," he said. "Find them on the other side."

"Yes. Those who died in the war were her specialty."

"Specialty."

"It takes effort," I explained. "The exact soul you're looking for may not be there, may not hear you calling. It may be wandering lost. In that case, Gloria would find it. And then she'd communicate with it."

"And you believe all of this?"

"Gloria," I said carefully, "had a great many satisfied customers."

George grunted. "And can you . . . do this thing? Can you *find* her?"

I felt a brief note of panic as I thought of the sign next to my front door. "Mr. Sutter, I told you. That is not what I do."

"And yet she seemed to think you could do it."

I rubbed my eyes, suddenly more exhausted than I could ever remember being. That wasn't who I was anymore. I had decided on that years ago, and if I hadn't exactly been happy since, at least my life had been quiet and peaceful. "Mr. Sutter, I'm very sorry for your loss, but your family disowned Gloria. You think she was a fraud of the worst kind. I'm not certain exactly what you want from me, and, frankly, I don't even know if I want to help you at all."

He seemed to think this over. He leaned back, crossed his arms over his chest, and regarded me. "Gloria and I had not spoken in seven years," he said. "I have a town house here in London, but it is under renovation, so I have been staying at a hotel. The hotel is called the King Richard. It is not the fanciest hotel in London, nor is it the lowest. It's modest and it's near where I need to be for work, which is why I chose it."

I raised my eyebrows and stared at him, waiting for him to continue.

"Gloria knew nothing of this, of course," he said. "And yet last night, when I arrived at my hotel after supper at my club, I found that note I speak of. It had been left for me at the front desk. Gloria's note. I'm a careful man, Miss Winter, and I've examined the note thoroughly. It is most definitely in her handwriting. The clerk at the front desk described her in every detail—Gloria was rather unforgettable, as you know. There is no chance of fraud in this case. Gloria knew where I was. She could have left a note for you directly, but she didn't. She left it for me, communicating with me for the first time in seven years. And six hours after she left that note, she was dead."

"And what of the people who were with her last night?" I said. "What of the police?"

"Scotland Yard is involved, yes. They have interviewed the people who were with her—low characters, all of them. A murder weapon has not been found, and an arrest has not been made. They claim they have no cause for an arrest as of yet."

"Then you should let them do their jobs."

"Gloria wanted *you* involved."

"No," I said, shaking my head. Everything was closing in on me. "No."

"I believe you'll find me a very persistent man, Miss Winter. And I have some connections in law and government that you may find unpleasant to deal with."

"What does that mean? What connections?"

"My meaning is clear enough, I think." He regarded me impassively. I wondered who he worked for, where he'd collected such power. I'd never broken a law in my life, but a pulse of unease went down my back. I didn't want complications; I wanted simplicity. Something told me that no matter what I did, I wasn't going to get my wish.

"Why did you come here?" I was almost trembling with a sudden spurt of anger. "Why did you pretend to be Mr. Baker? What did you think you would accomplish?"

He uncrossed his arms, frowning. "I had never heard of you before I received the note, of course." The "of course" was dismissive, as if it were ridiculous to think a man so important could have heard of me. "I checked into who you were and discovered that you are some kind of psychic. I assumed you were a fraud, as most psychics are. Before I involved you in my sister's case, I wanted to meet you for myself."

"And I just had to go and prove myself to you, didn't I?" I said bitterly. "I'm sorry to disappoint you, Mr. Sutter, but I will not help you. I do not find people on the other side. I do not speak to the dead. I won't do it for you, or for Gloria, or for anyone." I pushed back my chair and stood. "It's late. Please leave."

He sighed, as if my continued denial was a wearisome chore. "Miss Winter—"

"You may not have a reputation to protect, but I do," I said. "I can't have a man in my home this late. The neighbors only barely tolerate me as it is."

He looked surprised. "I have a wife and children, Miss Winter. You have nothing to fear from me."

"It doesn't matter." Despite my agitation, I tried to picture this man, so perfectly contained, siring children on any woman. I failed. "I only keep what reputation I have with great care. And so I am again asking you to leave."

He remained in his chair, looking up at me. "I have no wish to compromise you. I will leave on one condition."

"And what is that?"

"That you meet me tomorrow, after you've had the night to rest and think. I'll be in Trafalgar Square at ten o'clock. Surely there can be no impropriety in public at that hour."

I should have said no. I should have stayed firm. But I wavered. Perhaps it was because I wanted him to leave. Perhaps it wasn't.

"Miss Winter?" he said again, as inexorable as a schoolteacher.

I swallowed and nodded. His expression relaxed, almost imperceptibly, and he nodded in return.

"Good night, then."

I closed my eyes as the garden door shut behind him. Under my eyelids, black circles overlapped black circles again. It was a vortex, pulling, pulling. Gloria's vortex.

*Tell Ellie Winter to find me.*

Alone in my kitchen, I put my head in my hands.

# CHAPTER THREE

It was in the newspapers the next morning, of course. I read the headlines in the newsstands as I made my way to the tube to meet George Sutter, unable to stop myself from pausing. NOTORIOUS "PSYCHIC MEDIUM" FOUND DEAD, read one. And on another: SPIRIT MEDIUM MURDERED DURING SCANDALOUS SÉANCE. Gloria had been a favorite of the popular press, and everyone from the *Mirror* to the *Daily Mail* had splashed her death somewhere on the front page, complete with pictures and insinuations of outré behavior. The more staid and conservative *Times* stayed out of the muck, carrying headlines about a factory bombing in Manchester. TWO DEAD, BOMBER UNKNOWN, it read. NO OFFICIAL RESPONSIBILITY HAS BEEN CLAIMED. The *Times* had never been the paper for scandals.

The photo of Gloria most often printed was a studio portrait that looked to be recently done: Gloria in a bold-print wrap dress that accentuated her flawless narrow frame, her black hair bobbed and marcelled, curling almost sensuously over one ear. Her chin was

tilted, her dark-painted lips set in a mischievous smile, her big dark
eyes rendered black in cheap ink. She looked like the hoyden she was,
rebellious and full of glamour. I found myself mildly surprised she'd
sat for a studio portrait at all; Gloria did not like to sit still, even for
short periods.

Still, I bought three papers and read them as I sat on the train. The
stories were full of the usual misinformation and shaded truths that
always cropped up in stories about Gloria: lovers she'd never actually
had, parties never attended, rumors of everyone from the Church to
royalty on her client list. All Gloria had to do was appear in public,
innocently standing next to this person or that, and suddenly she was
written into legend as either the man's lover or his pet psychic. "My
God," she'd said to me once, when I'd shown her an article linking her
to the Earl of Craven. "I think not. His breath was positively *rotten.*"

As for the murder, the papers knew precious little. She'd been
working for a "private party" at an "undisclosed home" in the Kent
countryside when she'd been killed. One paper called the session a
ghost hunt; another called it a séance. Scotland Yard had questioned
all of the parties involved but had made no arrests. The other people
in attendance that night were not named.

Two of the three articles mentioned the now notorious report by
the New Society for the Furtherance of Psychical Research, uncovered by the *Mail* two months earlier, concluding that Gloria was the
only true spirit medium they had ever investigated. The articles
aimed derision at both the report and the Society itself, "an unusual
group of so-called scientists and untrustworthy researchers, mixed in
with wealthy eccentrics and curious artistic types, claiming to be on
a quest for the truth about the supernatural." I felt my jaw harden. I
had my own reasons for disliking the New Society, but the press's—
and the public's—attitude toward it was not new. It was easier for the
average factory foreman or bank clerk to dismiss the New Society as
fools than to face the possible alternative.

Not one article wondered what ghost Gloria had been seeking, or whether she had found it, or what it had said to her if she had. No one questioned why she was at a private home in the first place, something she had never done before.

Reporters, I thought, only ever wrote about the inconsequential details and never about the important things.

I threw down the newspapers in frustration as the train came to my stop, leaving them there for someone else to read.

In Trafalgar Square, I found a bench and sat with my hands in my lap, waiting. It was a crisp, warm September morning, the dome of St. Paul's looming bright against the cloudless blue sky, Nelson atop his column peering over all our heads into the distance. On the pedestal at the base could still be seen the marks of the victory bonfire that had burned there during the Armistice celebrations—several days of wild madness in the streets, or so I had read. I had stayed home on my mother's orders, staring at the walls and wondering madly what was going on.

I had deliberately dressed in deadly navy blue today, a suit of wool serge trimmed with silk braid, the hem just long enough, my heels just high enough. I had topped it with a felt cloche hat sporting a satin flower. I was a shopgirl, or a secretary who came to the City every morning and made awful tea in an electric kettle as she typed letters all day. Only my bright blond hair—natural, as it happened, though most people assumed I dosed it with platinum—gave away that I wasn't exactly a normal girl, but there was nothing I could do about it except bob it short and tuck it under my hat.

"Miss Winter."

I turned on my bench to address the voice behind me. "Mr. Sutter. You are almost late."

He gave me a look that said lateness was not in his repertoire. "It is ten o'clock exactly." He took a seat on the bench next to me, though he kept a respectable distance. He wore a dark three-piece suit much like the one he'd worn the night before. I pictured an entire wardrobe of similar suits, all kept cleaned and pressed by the mother of his children. "I take it you've thought further about our conversation last night?" he said to me now.

I looked away and idly watched a street performer, a man with a windup organ that played an out-of-key tune as the man made a marionette dance on its strings. "I don't understand exactly what it is you want me to do."

"Perhaps," George Sutter said, "I wasn't being clear."

The street performer put down his marionette and wound his music player again. "I read the papers," I said. "It seems that Scotland Yard is on the case."

I heard him sigh. "Miss Winter, what I am about to tell you is in confidence."

I turned and looked at him. His expression gave nothing away, as usual. He seemed to have regained his balance after the night before; here, in daylight in London's center of power, he was back in control. "Go on," I said. "I deal in confidences for a living."

"I have seen the coroner's report," he said. "It was released to the Yard this morning. It states that Gloria was hit in the face. Once, very hard, while she was still alive. Then a knife was inserted into her chest. She was stabbed, yes, but that word isn't quite accurate. What was done to Gloria was done slowly, precisely, and without passion. She had no defensive wounds on her hands. There is no bruising around the wound, as of a man punching the blade with force. The knife was inserted between her ribs and into the cavity of the heart, causing the heart to cease almost immediately. Death, the coroner states, would have come in seconds."

I looked down at my lap.

"So he hit her first," George said. "Once, hard enough to stun her. Then he put a knife into her and stopped her heart. Then he carried her body to the pond and dumped her in. She had told the others she wanted some air, and she was not immediately missed. Because the body was hidden in the pond, it was some time before she was discovered and anyone knew a murder had occurred."

I frowned. How could he know all of this?

He continued talking. "Scotland Yard has interviewed all of the people present that night, of course. You may have noticed that none of them are named in the papers. Most of the people in attendance were inconsequential; however, one of them was from a good family who wishes to keep things quiet. Suspicion falls on all of them, but the house was not exactly isolated. There are neighboring homes twenty minutes' walk in two directions, and the property backs onto woods in which there are well-trodden paths. The pond itself is in easy reach of at least two of those paths. A stranger or neighbor could have done this just as easily as one of the inner group—more easily, in fact, as the people inside the house are now alibis for one another."

"They could be covering for someone," I said, my words almost automatic. I had a suspicion about who the person "from a good family" was.

"I thought so as well," George replied, "but the Scotland Yard reports indicate that this was not a group of loyal friends. Far from it, in fact. They seem to have been a random group of pleasure seekers."

"The Scotland Yard reports?" I asked. "Gloria was murdered just over a day ago, and the papers say nothing. How have you seen the reports?"

"That's none of your concern," he said, turning away and looking out over the traffic passing in the square.

I tried to follow his gaze, taking a closer look around me. The spires of the Houses of Parliament were visible not very far away; Scotland Yard itself, though it couldn't be seen, was not far, either. Any number of government buildings, including Buckingham Palace, was within easy distance. My companion had approached me from behind, and I hadn't seen which direction he'd come from.

"Mr. Sutter, what exactly do you do for a living?"

He shook his head. "That is also not your concern, Miss Winter. Be assured my sources of information are valid. What I'm telling you is the truth. May I continue?"

I trained my gaze on a man sitting on another bench in the square, reading a newspaper propped in front of his face. MURDER! the headline shouted. NOTORIOUS PSYCHIC STABBED TO DEATH AT SÉANCE. And underneath it: WHO KILLED GLORIA SUTTER?

"Continue," I said.

"I'll put it bluntly. We may have been estranged, Miss Winter, but someone brutally killed my sister and dumped her body. I have no faith that Scotland Yard can solve this crime. There are too many possibilities."

"They've barely begun investigating," I said.

"It doesn't matter. I have no faith, Miss Winter. None at all. This is not unusual for me. Even in the smallest things, I never have faith that anything competent can be done unless I'm in charge. And this is, to me, very far from a small thing. They have not even found a murder weapon. I will not go home and wait for the official investigators to bungle this up. Do you understand?"

"Yes," I said. I did. To my left, I vaguely heard the marionette man playing his music again. The man reading the newspaper turned a page.

"I considered hiring an investigator, but the note Gloria left me made it simple. I came to see you instead, and you impressed me. You are not a con artist as I suspected. You are honest. You are, in fact, the ideal candidate. You knew Gloria. You can talk to her friends, her associates without suspicion. You can move in her world in a way that no one else can—especially me. And you specialize in finding lost things."

"I don't talk to the dead," I said, panic in my throat.

"Perhaps you don't, though I'm well aware that your mother did." He caught the look I gave him. "It's hardly private record, and I told you I researched you. Perhaps you're correct and Gloria's note was wrong. But you have a talent, a sensitivity. I may not understand it, but I don't have to in order to make use of it. *You* are my investigator, Miss Winter. *You* will find who killed her for me."

I leaned my head back, looked up at the sky. The usual London gloom had vanished, and I looked into a vista of cerulean blue punctuated by far-off clouds. The usual protests bubbled up in me: I wasn't trained as an investigator; it wasn't my profession; I would have no idea what I was doing; I already had a job. "I don't work for you," I told him, still staring up at the sky. "I have no access to coroner's reports or papers from Scotland Yard."

"You'll have what you need," he said.

Of course. I rubbed my nose, unladylike. "Did your research tell you that we were enemies, Gloria and I? Did it tell you what she did to my family? That I hadn't spoken to her in three years?"

"If that mattered, Miss Winter, you wouldn't be sitting here now."

I hated her. Or I had, at one point. But I thought about that knife, the cold dispassion of it. Someone had slipped it between her ribs and stopped her heart as easily as if they'd put a key in a lock. Someone who hadn't even cared enough to hate her.

Still I kept my head tilted back and I stared at the sky. It was beautiful, and endless, and uncaringly cold. Mysterious in its way. All the mysteries of the universe were just above us, if only we would look up. And yet we never did.

"Miss Winter?" George said. If he thought it strange that I sat on a bench in Trafalgar Square staring at the sky, he made no comment.

"The papers," I said at last. "Scotland Yard. No one is asking the right questions. No one."

He sounded almost relieved. "How many of your appointments did you cancel today?"

I finally lowered my gaze, righted my head, and looked at him. "All of them."

He nodded, and his eyes gleamed, whether from satisfaction or excitement I could not tell. "Exactly," he said.

# CHAPTER FOUR

My mother had been a spirit medium since before I was born. She'd been orphaned by age twenty, her parents of artistic vagabond stock, and she'd set up shop doing séances and performing spirit writing. It had been a better way to earn money than char work, she told me, as long as you were careful about it. And she had been good. Very, very good.

My father, a young postal clerk from a good family, had met her in a pastry shop and fallen in love with her. He didn't care what she did for a living. It was only after they'd married and settled in the house in St. John's Wood that my mother bought the beaded dress, had the sign painted for the window, and began business as The Fantastique. She stopped doing group séances, which had a taste of seediness to them, and replaced them with discreet one-on-one consultations. It was her stab at respectability, at trying to appease the neighborhood for my father's sake without giving up her work. I learned from my earliest years to be quiet when Mama was working.

And she did keep it respectable, remarkably so. Her client list was discreet and carefully chosen; as a child I watched well-dressed men and women of obvious class and money come and go from our little house. We got appointment requests from well-trained assistants and underlings. I became accustomed to the sight of a sleek carriage—or, increasingly, a motorcar—pulling up our lane, steered by a uniformed driver, stopping just long enough for a beautiful woman or gray-haired gentleman to alight before it pulled away again, reappearing only after the appointed hour.

It was all very civilized, if you didn't think about the things I witnessed in our little sitting room. The things I *saw*.

My own talent became evident by school age. I'd thought it would please her; I didn't know that having the powers I had made one a freak, a pariah. But my mother knew. She must have known, from very early on, what kind of life I would have. And so she gave me an education of a different sort.

I watched the birds alight on Nelson's statue, flitter off, and land again.

*You have a talent, a sensitivity.*

I smoothed my hand over my handbag, where I'd placed the envelope George Sutter had given me. It contained a small stack of banknotes—a retainer, he'd called it, to replace the business I'd lose during the investigation. I had just curled my fingers around it, preparing to rise, when the man on the bench across from me lowered his newspaper with its lurid headline and stood. He tossed the paper on the seat behind him, adjusted the brim of his hat, and came sauntering toward me, his hands in the pockets of his coat. My mouth went dry and everything stopped.

He paused in front of me, looking down at me, his knees almost touching mine. "Ellie Winter," he said.

For a second I was speechless. I could do nothing but stare. He was as strong as I remembered, his shoulders bulky under the fabric of his jacket. His dark suit fit him perfectly, the shirt beneath it crisp white. I knew that his hair beneath the hat was dark blond and kept shorter than the current fashion. When he put his hands in his pockets—an ungentlemanly pose—his arms flexed and curled, and he looked almost menacing, looming over me with a lazy grace. His blue-gray eyes flickered down over me and up again, disintegrating my respectable blue suit as if it were a wisp of cloth.

I stared back at him, trying not to let my cheeks flame. "An unusual group of so-called scientists and untrustworthy researchers," the papers had said about the New Society for the Furtherance of Psychical Research. I was looking at one of those untrustworthy researchers now. Its top researcher, in fact. The one who had, three years before, investigated both my mother and me.

"James Hawley," I managed, my throat tight. "What the hell do you want?"

He shook his head, not bothering to tut at my language. His voice was deep and smooth. "He's a ghost," he said, "that friend of yours. Sutter. Did you know that?"

"Pardon me?"

He lifted his gaze away from seeing through my clothes and looked around the square, taking in the surrounding buildings. "I can't find out who he works for," he said. "I've tried. No one is talking. I thought Scotland Yard at first, but now I'm not so certain. Now I think he may be MI5."

That was curious; I imagined that when James questioned people, they usually talked—women because he was so handsome, men because of the size of his arms. "Why are you here?" I asked him, suspicious. "Are you following me?"

"Actually, I was following Sutter. Or I was trying to. He's as slippery as a fish."

"Then why aren't you following him now?"

"Because you're more interesting than he is."

"Very funny." My cheeks flushed this time, and I couldn't stop it. I didn't want James Hawley's attention. I patted my handbag, looking fruitlessly for a cigarette. "I take it you're still working for the New Society."

"I am," he said, watching my hands. "And you're still in St. John's Wood, taking clients and staying respectable." He motioned at my handbag. "I don't think you have any cigs in that thing, though you do have the money Sutter gave you."

My gaze shot up to his. He was watching me carefully, his eyes shaded under the brim of his hat. "My money is my business, James," I said. "Though I know you don't agree."

He shoved his hands in his pockets again and let that one go. "It's just interesting," he said. "Gloria is dead. I follow her brother, and I find The Fantastique, of all people. The two of you have a little tête-à-tête and he gives you money. Now I'm curious." His blue-gray gaze caught mine, held it. "You know how I get when I'm curious."

My face burned. "I know very well," I said to him. "The results were in that paper you wrote for everyone to read. The one the *Daily Mail* resurrected two months ago." I dropped my hands from my handbag. "It was a three-year-old report, James. What was it doing in the newspaper?"

He caught my meaning. "It wasn't my doing," he replied. "I knew nothing about it. It was just some enterprising reporter looking to fill column inches. I'm surprised he dug up that old paper at all—I thought everyone had forgotten about it." He shrugged. The ridicule of being a psychical researcher didn't concern him; it never had. "But that doesn't answer my question. What were you doing with George Sutter?"

I took the easy answer, the bitter answer. "I'm conning him, of course. Taking his money for a lie."

"I don't think so."

"No?" I rubbed the bridge of my nose, suddenly tired of parrying him. Just looking at James, trying to read the expression behind his flawless, clean-shaven jaw and dark blond eyelashes, was sometimes exhausting. "And what do you think?"

"Whoever George Sutter works for, he's very powerful," James replied. "He's intelligent, educated. He wouldn't be an easy mark. He disowned Gloria years ago, so he doesn't believe in the supernatural. If George Sutter is meeting with The Fantastique, it's probably because he's making use of her."

"His sister was murdered," I conceded. "He's concerned."

"So am I," James said. "I can read behind the headlines, Ellie, just like you can. Something is rotten about this."

"Of course," I said, trying not to let the bite of jealousy enter my voice. "You and Gloria were close."

"I studied her for nearly ten months. I wrote a scientific paper on her. You can call that close if you want, but I certainly never wanted to see her killed."

He was still standing at my knees, and when I abruptly stood, my nose was nearly in the knot of his tie. I caught the brief scent of him before he took a step back. "If you want to trade places, I'll gladly take it," I said, trying not to let on that that brief second marked the closest I'd been to a real, physical man in years. "I didn't go to Sutter—he came to me. I'm certainly no investigator. But I'm going to do the best I can, and you would do well to stay out of my way."

I thought it sounded rather tough, but all he did was give me a smile that was almost reluctant, as if he knew it would make me angry. "In my line of work, I don't frighten very easily."

"Good-bye, James."

"I meant what I said about Sutter," he said as I made to leave. "I have no idea what he's up to or who he really is. Don't trust anything he tells you to do."

"I don't trust anyone," I said. "Especially not the man who ruined my mother's career and made Gloria Sutter his prize exhibit."

When I saw him flinch, I turned and walked away.

# CHAPTER FIVE

Gloria had lived in Soho, in a studio on the attic floor of a run-down house nearly a hundred years old. The street was lined with dim poverty-stricken artists' studios and ramshackle galleries, pawnshops, and booths of cheaply made crafts. A Home for Fallen Women had established itself on the corner sometime in the last century, and it still kept its polished double doors open to girls unwed and pregnant or just down on their luck. I was quite certain the middle-aged spirit medium on the ground floor of Gloria's house—who had a Liverpool accent when she wasn't working and only appeared during the intermittent times she could pay her back rent—had no idea that two floors above her was the great Gloria Sutter, who quietly let everyone from priests to politicians up the winding back stairs to her garret.

Gloria could have afforded better, of course. Her clientele was of the highest level, and her fees reflected it. But she liked the eccentricity of Soho, the strange collection of fringe people who never asked questions and took most things in stride. And she found the discreet back stairs of the building too useful to give up.

I had no key to Gloria's apartment. I did not need one. I climbed the front stairs, passed the shuttered rooms belonging to the Liverpool medium, and knocked on the door to the first-floor flat.

I knew the occupant wouldn't answer, so I didn't bother waiting. "Davies, it's me. Ellie Winter."

A shuffle, and a sullen thump. Then silence.

I knocked again. "Davies, please."

The lock clicked and the door opened just wide enough to reveal the homely face of a woman. She was twenty-five, and her reddish bobbed and marcelled hair stood up in an unkempt mess. Her eyes were red from weeping.

"Oh, God," she drawled. "It's you."

This was Davies—her first name was Violetta, but no one ever called her anything but Davies. She had been Gloria's personal secretary, living in the flat beneath hers, managing her mail, scheduling her appointments, and, most important, screening her clients. Anyone who wanted to see Gloria went through Davies first. She was homely, intelligent, rootless, and mostly without feeling except for her fierce dedication to her job and to Gloria Sutter.

"I need to come in," I said to her.

Even though she looked a mess, she was admirably managing to sound bored and superior. "I've talked to the police about everything already," she said. "Go away."

"I'm not the police."

Davies rolled her eyes. "Do tell."

"Davies, please. Just—please."

"I said go away." She made to close the door.

"A ghost hunt, for God's sake?" I said. "In an outside location? You let her go alone? And how in the world did you let Fitzroy Todd get involved?"

She blinked at me, then tossed the door open and turned her back, walking into the room. She was wearing a housedress of hideous plaid and a pair of heeled mules with bows on the tops. The mules clacked hollowly on the floor.

"I told her not to go," she said.

"That's not good enough." I shut the door behind me. "There should have been no séance in the first place. She should never have even heard about it, never been given the choice. You should have stopped it."

She flopped heavily on a sofa, her feet in their mules jutting out onto the scratched wood floor. Misery flinched across her face.

Anyone who had been in the spirit medium profession for any length of time had a set of rules. First, never agree to a séance with a group of unknown people; the dynamics were too risky, and the medium never knew whether a reporter or a skeptic was hiding undercover. Second, never do a session—of any kind—on client property. Every psychic needed to work within her own controlled environment.

And third, never go into such a situation alone, because most men saw us as easy women. Psychics and palm readers were everyday targets for robberies, passes, and worse. The setup in which Gloria died had been one only the most desperate amateur would agree to.

"I don't know why you care," Davies said sullenly. "How long has it been? Three years since you decided you were too good to associate with the likes of us?"

"I'd think it was the other way around," I replied. I walked into the messy sitting room and looked down at her. "I wasn't good enough, and neither was my mother. I think Gloria proved that rather conclusively, didn't she?"

Davies rolled her eyes. "You always did take things too seriously. It was just one of Gloria's whims. She'd forgotten about it in a week."

I bit back a retort. My mother died six months after the incident that ended my friendship with Gloria, but Davies wouldn't care about that. "Tell me about this séance," I said.

"I couldn't have stopped it," Davies answered me. She wound a lock of greasy hair around one finger and tucked it ineffectually under one of her haphazard hairpins. "It didn't go through me. It was Fitzroy's idea. He went directly to Gloria, and before I knew it, it was done."

I'd figured Fitzroy Todd would be involved, but still it sunk home to hear it confirmed. Fitzroy was an on-again, off-again lover of Gloria's, a rich do-nothing who found it amusing to slum with those of us in the lower classes. He'd been the first person I thought of when George Sutter had spoken of a "good family who wishes to keep things quiet." The Todds had kept more than one of Fitzroy's drunken exploits quiet over the years. He had a few nice clothes and a droll way of speaking, but I'd never understood what compelled Gloria's attraction to him.

"I thought she was finished with him," I said.

"She was," said Davies gloomily. "I was under strict instructions to put his letters in the trash. But he talked to her somehow, and the next thing I knew she told me she was going."

"He was certainly there? At the session?"

"Yes, and I hope the police have made him good and uncomfortable. I hear they questioned everyone. If he killed her, I'll wring his neck and save us all the trouble."

I took a seat in the lumpy, mismatched chair opposite her, trying to picture fatally lazy Fitzroy murdering someone, and failing. "Who else was there?"

"Besides Fitzroy and Gloria, the clients. A couple of rich how'd-you-dos named Dubbs, if you can believe it. I never met them myself." Davies opened a tin of tobacco and shook some out onto a paper, preparing to roll one of her awful cigarettes. She seemed primed to talk now. "They also brought in another psychic, a lightweight who calls herself Ramona. Strictly a skimmer, from what I hear, and a showgirl, too."

I nodded. This was the language, the inner slang that was as familiar to me as the alphabet, though I never spoke it anymore. A skimmer was a psychic with no real powers who went for the easy money: the elderly, the naive who would be taken in by crystal balls and outdated spirit cabinet tricks. A showgirl was a psychic who did stage shows for profit. A psychic with any class never did a stage show. Never.

"That's odd," I said. "The second psychic."

Davies lit her cigarette. "I know. I can't think of why Gloria agreed to it. It certainly wasn't the money. And I can't think of why Fitz was so keen."

"What did they want?" I asked, trying not to inhale the putrid smell of Davies's homemade cigarette. I didn't know where she got the habit—it wasn't from her employer, who had smoked only the finest. "The clients. What was their story?"

"Grieving parents," Davies said, waving dismissively. "Their only son died in the war. Felt a ghostly presence in the house and believed their son was returned to speak to them. Et cetera."

I propped an elbow on my chair and rubbed my bottom lip, thinking. It was a simple setup I'd heard myself a hundred times since the war; Gloria, who specialized in communicating with soldiers, would have heard it almost every day. She could have had the grieving couple come to her flat and make contact there, as she had with every other client. Nothing about this enlightened me.

"Look," Davies said. "I'm as torn up about this as anyone. Probably more. I loved her." The cigarette drooped, the pain flitted across her face again, and for a second the angry facade dropped and she looked lonely. "I'm not one of those girls, you know, but I *loved* her. And aside from that, what am I going to do now? Where am I supposed to go?" She gestured briefly down to the housedress, the mules. "I'm hardly a candidate for finishing school, and Valentino isn't going to sweep me away to the desert. I would do anything to go back in time. I mean it. But there was no stopping her when she set her mind to something." Her voice cracked. "She told me everything would be fine."

I looked down at my lap. She'd told Davies everything would be fine. And then she'd left George a note saying, *Tell Ellie Winter to find me.*

"Have you heard from Gloria's brother?" I asked her.

Davies snorted, her grief receding for the moment. "That tweed? No, and why should I?"

"He came to see me."

"To see you?" She shook her head. "It's more than Gloria ever got from him. From any of them. Not that she cared."

"What about James Hawley?"

Now her gaze sharpened. "Don't tell me he came to see you, too."

"Something like that. He seems to be investigating Gloria's death."

"Well, aren't you popular?" Davies took a drag of her cigarette, thinking. "I wonder what he's up to. I thought he only investigated psychics, not murders. I hear he drinks too much, or he used to. He's still doing his little experiments on psychics as far as I know, trying to disprove them."

"When did Gloria last see him?"

"Months. Years, perhaps. They didn't have much to do with each other after that paper he wrote about her." She shook her head. "They didn't even speak when that reporter dug it up again. Gloria laughed at that—some reporter digging up the 'only proven psychic' angle. Though she said that paper was better off buried." Her eyes shuttered, and she looked uneasily away.

So she did feel something about the incident with my mother. Perhaps even Davies had a conscience. "So, they weren't friends."

"God, no. They weren't even lovers, at least from what Gloria told me. He's handsome enough, but Gloria was hands-off for some reason. They were all business. Though if he's sniffing around now, in my opinion we should be asking where *he* was that night."

I frowned. If James had murdered Gloria, would he have resurfaced, claiming to be looking for her killer? He had never seemed the violent type to me, but I didn't trust him. I had learned that from bitter experience.

"Look," Davies said, stubbing out her cigarette. "I'd love to chat with you all day, even though I never liked you and you haven't been here in years. But why don't we get down to business? I assume you came to see Gloria's flat."

I hesitated. It was why I had come, of course, along with questioning Davies, but now I wasn't so certain. The idea of pawing through Gloria's personal things seemed suddenly distasteful. "It's rather soon. It needn't be today."

"I disagree." Davies raised her gaze to mine. She'd ditched her maudlin emotion, practically the only emotion I'd ever seen her evince, and now her look was steely. "I think it most definitely should be today."

This was why I avoided Davies. She wasn't a psychic, but she knew all of our secrets. She knew everything. What she was unmistakably telling me now was that I should go to Gloria's flat and use my abilities to pick up information. I was capable of it, and she knew it perfectly well.

I hadn't planned to use my abilities. I didn't want to. I was used to using my powers in my sitting room during appointments with approved clients, just as our rules dictated. Working within one's own place not only controlled the physical aspects of a session—the objects touched, the people present, the smells, the level of light—it controlled the supernatural ones as well. Controlling my abilities—so I wouldn't see the dead on every bus and street corner—was one of the first things my mother had taught me.

"Objects aren't my trick," I said. "I do my sessions by touching hands. You know that, Davies."

"You could do it if you tried," she said.

"Perhaps not." I gave her a look. "Perhaps I'm a skimmer."

Davies only shrugged. "I suppose you could be. I don't really know, do I? You have a pedigree, but we all know what happened to that. Perhaps your mother simply passed down her bag of tricks."

I felt a flash of unbidden anger at that, and she saw it. She smiled.

"You could be a skimmer," she continued, "but Gloria never paid attention to skimmers. She knew a skimmer—like that old fraud downstairs—the moment she saw one. And she thought you were the real thing. Though I don't suppose she liked you much, did she?"

"The feeling was mutual," I snapped. Davies always could provoke me. "What she did was dangerous. Talking to the dead isn't a game."

"Certainly not one you ever wanted to play," Davies said, rising from her couch and shuffling for the door, dropping the stub of her cigarette in an ashtray. "God, talent is wasted on some people. Come upstairs, Mary Pickford. I want to see if you'll play it now."

I watched her, my nerves tight and my temples beginning to throb, but she'd already opened the door and started up the stairs to Gloria's, her mules clacking softly on the worn, thin stair runner. There was nothing for it. I got up and followed.

# CHAPTER SIX

Gloria's was the attic flat, a studio consisting of a large single room under a varied ceiling. On either end the roof buckled under the slopes of the house's upper gables; in the center it was tall and high beamed, the wood a pretty honey brown color that was pleasantly rustic. A cramped gas stove, icebox, and sink crouched in one corner were the only evidence of a kitchen, and a beet red curtain had been hung on a rod with gaudy brass rings to separate off a messy square of bedroom. The rest of the flat was living space: mismatched furniture like Davies's in the flat below—probably cast off from a former occupant—scattered about, low bookshelves filled with volumes of poetry and Russian novels mixed with movie magazines, topped with an odd Chinese ornament or clay head of Buddha. The wallpaper was repellent, the electric lights cheaply installed in old gas jets and unreliable, yet the place somehow had a friendly, lived-in air.

At the center of the room was a large round table of dark cherry-wood, the most expensive item in the room by far, and the only one

Gloria had had made. It was circled with matching wood chairs, a runner matching the red curtain placed across its center. This was the heart of Gloria's business: the séance table.

A round table is best for séances, as it allows all participants to view one another at equal angles. A rectangular table with the medium at the head encourages everyone, naturally, to look at the medium throughout the session; in fact, the medium would rather the participants look at one another. My mother had reluctantly given up her round table when she'd married my father and agreed to stop doing group sessions. It's harder to pinpoint the source of knocks and raps at a round table, and it feels more intimate, the participants drawn into a tight knot from which their attention rarely wanders, making it simpler for the medium to set up her tricks in the background.

If, that is, the medium was employing tricks.

"The police have been here," Davies said, turning on the feeble electric light. "A good-looking one, too. I told him if he took anything of Gloria's, he'd have to answer to me."

I reluctantly pulled my gaze from the séance table. "I don't think you can prevent the police from taking anything they like."

"They can just try it," Davies said darkly.

I sighed and moved past the séance table, giving it a wide berth. I had never witnessed one of Gloria's séances; we had never watched each other work. But I knew there would be no false panels or hidden drawers, no hollow spots hiding ball bearings, no clever hinges to make the table tilt. James Hawley was an experienced psychical researcher, and he'd nearly taken Gloria's table apart piece by piece before he'd written his report. He'd found no tricks—which, of course, brought up the question of why Gloria had a round table in the first place if it wasn't to accommodate tricks. I wondered whether the question kept him awake at night.

The answer was simple, at least to me. People expected to see certain things at a séance, and Gloria gave them what they wanted. Illusions within tricks within illusions—the spirit medium's stock-in-trade.

Scattered around the rest of the room were pieces of Gloria's life. Postcards from traveling friends were tacked to the walls; a fringed scarf of dark blue and pink was draped over the china shade of a table lamp. Sunlight from the gabled windows pressed illuminated squares onto the worn secondhand rugs. A closet door stood half open, spilling out the arm of a wool winter coat and the tail of a belt from a fashionable bright green raincoat. A pair of pearly satin heels lay discarded next to one chair, toppled over each other in disarray. An ashtray on a low end table overflowed with cigarettes, many of them not even half smoked. Behind the bedroom curtain, the bed was unmade and a low shelf was cluttered with thick, fragrant face creams and half-used makeup. The place smelled like sun-warmed attic, Gloria's perfume underlaid with wood rot, and something gone bad in the neglected icebox.

I picked up the fringed scarf from the lamp shade and ran it gently through my hands. I slowly circled the room, feeling Davies's eyes on me. I ran the scarf over my palms, feeling the tickle of its satiny fringe. Psychometry, it was called. The process of receiving a psychic transmission by touching a physical object. James Hawley had written about it in one of the New Society's journals; the New Society itself claimed to be very interested in proving its existence. "It is unknown," James had written, "whether psychometry is initiated by the medium or the object, but it is proposed that the object's natural energy field, combined with the medium's sensitivity, produces the effect."

All I knew was that it wasn't my specialty.

"Well?" Davies said to me from the doorway, impatient.

My gaze caught on a painting hanging on one wall. Done in a rustic style of heavy lines and bright colors, it depicted a mermaid on a washed blue background, as if swimming through water. Her top half was unashamedly naked, her hair streaming behind her, her shimmering green tail waving as she swam.

My hands stilled on the scarf and my throat closed. I had a sudden memory of a similar image of a mermaid printed on a postcard.

Of turning that postcard over and over in my hands and reading the words written on it in a familiar bold scrawl.

"Bollocks," Davies said accusingly. "You're not going to do anything, are you? I should never have brought you up here."

I closed my eyes briefly, let the world fall away, and ran my fingers along the scarf in my hands. An image flared in my mind, as brief and vivid as a camera flash. I opened my eyes again.

"Gloria bought this for five pence in a secondhand stall on Carnaby Street," I said to Davies, holding up the scarf. "She was getting over a cold that day, and she'd just eaten a bowl of barley soup in a café."

Davies's homely face wrinkled in disgust. "For God's sake. I should have known you'd be no use."

"Did you think this scarf would tell me the name of her murderer?" I asked, suddenly angry. I shut my eyes and put the scarf to my forehead, as theatrical as any showgirl. "My God, I see everything! I have all the answers! It wasn't the butler or the Prince of Wales. It was you, Davies! In a fit of mad jealousy!"

"Fine," Davies said, clacking back toward the door. "I'm going back to my flat to have a smoke and another cry. And maybe I'll think about what to do with my worthless excuse for a life."

"Excuse me?" said a voice from the doorway.

We both froze. A woman stood in the gap made by the half-open door, one gloved hand on the doorknob. She was perhaps twenty-one, with marcelled hair of honey brown under her cloche hat. She wore a pretty lilac coat and matching heels, and her narrow face was ethereal, with high cheekbones and gray eyes. She seemed familiar, but I couldn't place her.

"I'm sorry," she said, her voice cracking. "I saw the newspapers. I couldn't believe it. I just—I had to—" A tear trickled down the side of her nose and she looked from one to the other of us, her expression crumpling in grief.

"Oh, dear God." Davies sounded even more disgusted, if that was possible, than when I had arrived. "Hello, Octavia."

It clicked then. Octavia Murtry. She had been the fiancée of Harry Sutter, one of Gloria's brothers who died in the war. An heiress, she had, according to the gossip columns, taken up with Gloria after Harry's death, dishonoring his memory at champagne parties and all-night suppers. I'd met her briefly only a few times during my heyday with Gloria; she had moved further into Gloria's circle in the days after I'd retreated into anonymity in St. John's Wood.

"Davies," Octavia said now, pushing away from the door and taking a step into the room. "Is she really gone? I didn't know where to go. I just can't believe it." Another tear slipped from one of her lovely eyes and down her face.

If Octavia thought one of us would jump to console her, she was mistaken. Davies only looked at her in hopeless distaste, and I dropped the scarf on a nearby sofa, where I caught sight of a small satin bag that had been tossed onto the cushions. The bag held the familiar hard square shape that unmistakably spoke of a flask inside it. I was instantly tempted.

"She really is gone," Davies said, her clumsy attempt to at least get Octavia to stop crying. "Did the police talk to you?"

"No." Octavia reached into her handbag and picked out a handkerchief, with which she dabbed her eyes. "They haven't. I wasn't with her that night. I haven't seen Gloria since—" She sniffed, her eyes scrunching almost convulsively, as if she was trying to regain control. "Since last Saturday. We went shopping. It was— Oh, my goodness! I'll never see her again."

More tears threatened and Octavia fought them down. Davies watched with an expression of patient dread. When neither of them was watching, I reached down to the sofa and slid the satin bag containing the flask into my handbag.

"I knew something would happen," Octavia said, dabbing her eyes again. "I just knew it. I don't have the power, you know, the way she did. But something was wrong. Those last few days, she just seemed so unbalanced."

Now Davies perked up. "What are you talking about?"

"Didn't you notice?" Octavia said. "Something was eating at her. She wasn't herself at all." She touched her gloved fingers to her mouth in an *Oh!* gesture. "Do you think I should tell that to the police? Do you think it's relevant to their case? Davies, what should I do?"

Davies was disgusted again, and her voice was flat. "I have no idea what you're talking about."

"Wait," Octavia said, now looking at me. "I recognize you, don't I? You're Ellie Winter, the psychic." Her eyes lit up, thoughts of the police forgotten. "Are you here to do a reading? Are you going to find her murderer? This place must be full of Gloria's psychic energy."

"Don't waste your breath," Davies told her. "I've already tried it. She's of no use at all. And she was just leaving."

"Ye of little faith," I said to Davies. "I've barely gotten started. And yes, I'm leaving, but not before I get some information."

Davies threw up her hands, as if at the end of her rope. "Do tell me how I can be of service, and then leave me alone."

"Where is Fitzroy Todd living these days?" I asked.

"With his parents, of course. The Belgravia town house. Don't tell me you're going to see him?"

"I might," I said. "What about Ramona, the skimmer? Where does she live?"

"How would I know?" Davies shouted. "I've never seen the woman."

"Streatham," Octavia said from her place at the door. She was watching me now, her tears forgotten. "Ramona lives in Streatham. I can show you where."

I looked at Octavia for a moment. She had calmed; her interest was focused exclusively on me, and I saw in her eyes, deep beneath the drama and the selfishness, a thin strip of steely fascination.

"Do you have transportation?" I asked her.

"My driver is right outside," she replied evenly. "Are you truly going to find Gloria's murderer?"

"She'd better," said Davies. "Now both of you get out of here."

I touched the hard surface that indicated the flask in my handbag. *If you want me to find you, Gloria,* I thought, *you owe me a drink.*

"This is grand of you, Octavia," I said to the girl in the doorway. "Let's go."

# CHAPTER SEVEN

Octavia's motorcar was a fast, stylish little roadster with a uniformed driver waiting stoically at the wheel. Octavia leaned forward from the backseat and gave him an address in Streatham as I folded my legs into the tiny space next to her and put my handbag on my lap.

I glanced at her profile as she leaned back again and patted her hat. Her face was a bit long, perhaps, not round and cherubic like the current fashion, but there was no doubt she was beautiful. Streatham, with its cheap cinemas and trashy ballrooms, was decidedly slumming for a girl like her—but for girls like her, slumming for an evening was sometimes an entertainment in itself.

Especially when the slumming involved spirit mediums and psychics.

She turned to me, her tears gone though her eyes were still red, a sweet smile on her lips. "Isn't this cozy?" she said. "It's so nice to see you again. It's terrific that I showed up when I did, isn't it? Just in time to take you where you wanted to go."

"Terrific," I agreed.

"Did we meet at the Jaclyn-Dunbar party? I can't recall."

"No," I replied. "I don't believe so."

"Oh, well," she said, smiling again. "There are so many parties, aren't there? It's impossible to keep track. And ever since I heard about Gloria, I've barely been able to put two thoughts together. It's positively mad that I can remember anything."

It struck me then—the thought I'd been pushing away since the moment she'd come to the door of Gloria's apartment. This girl had been my replacement. After Gloria and I split up, Octavia Murtry had become inseparable from her would-be sister-in-law. I studied her face for a moment, trying to see what Gloria had seen there. Octavia was prettier than me, perhaps, in her patrician way, but I had a hard time picturing her taking her shoes off and dancing a French cancan at two o'clock in the morning, as I had once done on one of Gloria's dares.

"You two were close," I said.

"I was engaged to Harry, you know," she said. She set her nervous hands on her lap for a moment and looked out the window. I waited. "He died in Flanders," she said after a pause. "It was the most horrid day of my life." She turned back to me. "I've heard that some people had dreams when their boys died—prophetic dreams or visions. They see the man beside their bed or something, and they get the telegram a few weeks later stating that he died at that very moment. Have you ever heard of that?"

"Yes," I said.

"I thought for a time that I should have seen him," Octavia said. Her voice was almost avid, but it had not quite lost its well-trained coolness. "That the bond between us should have *done* something. I should somehow have known. But I didn't see anything."

She seemed to want a response from me, but I could think of nothing adequate to say. "I'm sorry," I said at last. "Gloria didn't speak about her brothers much. I think it was too painful."

"Tommy went first," Octavia said bluntly. "That was a shell. Then Harry. Colin went last—that was almost near the end of the war. He nearly made it through. But of course he didn't."

"You knew them?" I asked, surprised. "Gloria's other brothers?"

"Harry talked about them all the time," she replied. "His brothers— and Gloria—were the most important thing to him. Even Colin, who he didn't get along with, and George, who was a few years older than the rest of them. I met them all eventually, at family functions and the like. Did you know Gloria's brothers?"

"No," I said.

"They were all so different." Octavia had warmed to her topic now, brightening a little as she remembered. "Tommy was the young-est and the sweetest. Harry adored him. George was older, so he was almost more of a father than a brother—he was a bit remote. He likely still is, though I haven't seen him since the war. Colin was what Harry called the future politician, always angry and on about something— he'd dampen the party by getting on his political hobbyhorse and we'd have to ignore him. And there was Harry himself, of course." She sighed. "Harry was gorgeous, like a movie star. There are times I still can't believe that all of them are dead, all those men I talked and laughed with. But they're all gone now, even Gloria. All of them dead except George."

"I'm sorry," I said again.

She didn't seem to hear me. "Harry was killed by a sniper while delivering a message. They think I'm too sheltered to know what that means, but I know perfectly well. It means he was shot in the head, most likely. Colin was taken by the Germans and died in a prison camp—they never got his body back. George never went to the front—he did some kind of top secret office role. Do you know, I've actually thought it was a shame that, of all of them, George would be the one to survive the war." She bit her lip. "It's such a horrible thing to think, I know. Do you think I'll go to hell?"

I opened my mouth, then closed it again. "I don't think so," I said finally, my voice a little strangled. "I don't think there's a hell."

She took my gloved hand in hers and squeezed it. "That's what Gloria always said. You're a medium like she was, aren't you? That means you *know.*"

I stared down at our linked hands. I had encountered this type of person before, both in my own line of work and in my days with Gloria. Octavia Murtry was what we called a fortune-petter, a person addicted to psychics and fortune-tellers of all kinds. Fortune-petters would sit through any session, pay any fee, try any cheap sham to get the answers they thought they wanted. It explained why Octavia knew who this Ramona was. It also explained why she'd found Gloria so intoxicating. For a fortune-petter, a medium of Gloria's power would have been like a strong drug.

"It's so wonderful that I met you," she said to me, squeezing my hand again. Now that Gloria was gone, I seemed to be her new best friend. "I have so many questions," she said. "We should arrange a session."

I shouldn't have done it. Even as I did it, part of me knew it was wrong. I told my clients I needed our hands touching, skin to skin, to get a reading, but in truth that was all for show. I could do a reading even through gloves. It took only a second for me to let the world fall away and do what I did best: see what my client was seeking.

It came to me in a flash, as it usually did, and I pulled my hand away. A strange sort of revulsion rose in me. "You asked Gloria for a séance," I said. "You wanted her to find Harry. To find her brothers. On the other side."

The motorcar had pulled to a stop just off the Streatham High Road, the driver sitting in the front seat as mute as Gloria's Buddha head. Octavia looked surprised. "Well, yes," she replied with a little coolness. "I wanted to find Harry, to find all of them. I still do."

"You wanted Gloria to contact her own dead brothers?"

"Harry and I were to be married!" she said. "He was taken from me without a good-bye. Is it so unusual?"

I swallowed and looked away. "I'm sorry to disappoint you, but I don't do spirit sessions."

"You can do them," Octavia said. "Your mother could, too."

I looked back at her. "I thought you didn't remember me."

"I remember you now," she said. "You were Gloria's friend for a time. I heard that your mother was a psychic, too. The Fantastique."

My throat was dry and the words tangled before I could speak them. What else had Gloria said about me? "Did she tell you what happened? To us?"

"I assume you had a falling-out," said this girl who had been my replacement. "Lots of people fell out with Gloria, or she with them. She was hard to get along with sometimes. But to me, she was family."

I felt a faint throb of pain in my head, the beginnings of a headache. I wanted to get away from her. "My mother was proven a fake, or didn't you hear?"

"I heard," she replied. "I don't put any stock in those kinds of reports. Some people simply don't believe."

I placed my hand on the door handle. "I won't find him for you, Octavia. I won't."

"They didn't even tell me what happened to him," she said as I pushed the door open and stood. "Not really. I don't know if he died fast or slow, or whether it hurt. Whether he thought of me before he went. Gloria wouldn't tell me."

I turned and looked down at her, sitting elegantly in her plush motorcar. "Then you aren't meant to know," I said, and shut the door.

# CHAPTER EIGHT

Octavia had dropped me on a winding street off of Streatham High Road. It featured a seedy café, its windows dirty, and a theatrical costume shop, the front window filled with faded wigs on the blank heads of mannequins. Before me, past a half-broken stoop, was a ramshackle building of inexpensive flats, one of a line of unappealing square buildings built sometime in the past fifty years to accommodate the single, unattached London worker. The flats weren't big enough for families, but on the stoop of a building next door a young woman with a tired face watched me as she rocked a sleeping baby in its pram, a second child playing quietly with a marble at her feet.

I ascended the uneven front steps and stood under the cornice, now dusky from the London smut, peering at the curling notices pinned next to the door. SMITHERS, IMPORTER OF CURIOSITIES, 3-B. NEEDLEMAN, FILMIC CASTING AGENCY & SEEKERS OF TALENT, 2-A. And, near the bottom, RAMONA, FORTUNES TOLD (NO SATURDAYS),

4-A. Perhaps this had been a working-class neighborhood when it was built, but now its inhabitants made money any way they could.

I pushed open the front door, crossed through an airless vestibule, and found myself in a front hall that admitted no light at all. I took a moment to adjust my eyes to the gloom. Ahead of me was a staircase with a thin rail leading to the upper floors. To my left was a lift, silent and empty. There was a strong musty smell, as of a disused library, underlaid with sour neglect. There was no sound. I wondered whether all the tenants were eerily quiet, or out, or whether the curious setup of this building muffled their furtive movements.

I pulled off my cloche hat and lifted my hair from my forehead. The headache was moving in now, pulsing from the base of my skull at the back of my neck, rolling gently over me like far-off thunder. It was becoming common for me to get these low-grade headaches when I exerted my powers too heavily or too quickly in succession, as I had just done in Gloria's flat and with Octavia Murtry.

I sighed and tugged my hat back on, wishing for a cigarette or a swig from the flask in my handbag. Something about this building was tiring and oppressive, like a funeral home, and for a moment I was painfully aware that I was alone, foolishly embarking on a quest that was doomed to fail. How could I hope to find Gloria's murderer on my own? I thought wistfully of what it would be like to have a companion, someone to talk to, someone who could help me pin down the frantic thoughts spinning through my mind. I saw James Hawley's gray-blue eyes. He hadn't been wearing a wedding ring. I pushed the thought away, disgusted that I'd even noticed.

On impulse, I decided to take the lift instead of the stairs to the fourth floor, though I regretted it the moment the diamond-grille door slid closed and I stood in the semidarkness, my hand on the lever. The lift shuddered reluctantly to life. The smell was even mustier in here, and the floor of the lift shook under my feet. I could have walked twenty stories in the time it took to rise four, or so it felt, and when the lift finally groaned to a stop, I flung back the sliding door and came gasping out into the corridor.

Only three doors opened from this hall. All were closed and silent. A single mullioned window shed the only light that came through, the sunlight far off and diluted by the clouds moving overhead, sending the light into eerie fragments that made me feel as if I was underwater.

I approached the door of 4-A and raised my hand to knock. Something stopped me for a moment—the absolute silence, perhaps, or a faint unidentifiable smell. But I shook off my misgivings and rapped on the door, once, twice, the sound muffled by the stale air.

There was no answer, and unlike at Davies's flat I heard no shuffled movements inside. I rapped again. *She's not here,* I thought, and then, unbidden: *She's dead. Someone killed her, and she's lying dead in there.*

The thought stopped me. Suddenly I could picture it, not through my powers, but through my overactive imagination. I could see a body splayed on the floor, arms sprawled, the bare feet strangely helpless, the back arched by the body's last desperate attempt to grab something, to rise. And the stillness, the clock ticking unheeded, the slow seeping of blood onto the floor.

My headache throbbed. I took one step back, and then another, and then I was descending the stairs, my heels clicking crisply on the risers. My pace quickened as I passed landing after landing. I saw and heard no one. The dust floated undisturbed in the beams of sunlight coming through the windows on the landings.

Finally I stepped out the front door onto the stoop, gulping the fresh September air. I was a superstitious fool. The woman had been out, that was all, shopping or visiting a friend. A practicing psychic might have been home seeing clients, but not if business was bad. I'd never had the power to see through closed doors; what I'd seen was imagination, nothing more.

A man stood on the front path waiting for me. I froze, taking in the familiar figure in dark suit and hat. James.

He reached up to the brim of his hat, tilting it back to get a better look at me. As always, he was in no hurry, as if he'd been standing there all day. His muscled shoulders were incongruous under the lines of his jacket.

"Trying to have your fortune told?" he said.

"Yes, of course," I managed. "That's very clever."

He glanced past my shoulder. "I take it Ramona wasn't home."

There was no point in lying. "No, she wasn't."

"What do you know about her?"

"Nothing," I replied. "Apparently she was there the night Gloria died." I took a step down, coming closer to him. "What do you know about her? Why are you here?"

"A lucky guess." He looked at me, curious. "Is something wrong?"

"No, of course not." I would rather die than admit how relieved I was to see him, to see anyone. "Everything is fine."

James pulled himself up a step. Level with me now, he looked down at me. He was close enough that I could smell shaving soap. He was almost ridiculously attractive, his features even, his eyes calm and intelligent, his lips a firm line. I'd seen that handsome face up close once before, smelled that familiar shaving soap, under circumstances that were rather humiliating. I didn't like to recall it, and I wondered whether he remembered it at all. With the luck I had with men—with James—he most likely remembered it perfectly. *Chin up, Ellie. He's just a man.*

James nodded toward the building behind me, the movement emphasizing the line of his jaw. "Do you know where she is?"

"How would I?" I replied.

He gave me half a smile at that. He was different from the man he'd been three years before, though I couldn't put my finger on how. A little sadder, perhaps. "Her real name is Joyce Gowther," he said.

"She's from Norfolk, twenty-nine years old. Her father owns a small brewery, though she hasn't seen him in years, since she came to London to take up acting."

I stared at him, openmouthed. He kept the smile, watching me, and didn't move away.

"Acting must not have worked out for her," he continued, "because a few years later she surfaced as Ramona, spirit medium and fortune-teller. She's never been married, doesn't seem to have many clients. She was at the séance with Gloria, as you heard, though I don't know why. The police questioned her until about eleven o'clock yesterday morning."

I bit my lip. "All right, that's useful. Thank you."

He leaned closer and I tried not to jump away. "Admit it," he said, his voice quiet. "We want the same thing, Ellie, and you could use a partner."

*I hear he drinks too much, or he used to,* Davies had said. Perhaps he did. I'd never seen any evidence of it, and since I'd first met him in a bar on Gerrard Street in which all of us were drunk except him, I had reason to know. James Hawley, the mystery. I raised my eyes to his.

"Why?" I asked him. "Gloria is gone. She's been nothing to you for years, and I never was anything to you at all. Why are you here?"

A frown crossed his forehead, but his expression gave nothing away. "Have luncheon with me," he said.

"Luncheon?"

He shrugged. "It's lunchtime. You're hungry."

I glanced behind me at Ramona's ramshackle building, its dirty stoop and blank windows. I *was* hungry; I hadn't eaten since I'd left the house that morning. I could practically hear Gloria's voice in my head. *Who gives a damn what happened three years ago? You can have luncheon with a man who melts your insides, or you can go off alone. Darling, sometimes you're an idiot.*

"Very well," I said finally. "Luncheon. You lead the way."

# CHAPTER NINE

James found us a place on the Streatham High Road, a restaurant smelling of freshly baked bread and coffee and populated with small tables and booths. It was half empty, and we took a seat at a booth by the front windows, looking out onto the street, the cracked leather of the seat threatening to snag the backs of my stockings as I adjusted my skirt.

"Be honest," I said to him as the waiter brought tea. "Do you know where Ramona is?"

"No," said James. He took off his hat and dropped it onto the seat next to him, briefly running a hand through his hair. It was dark blond, just as I remembered, and he'd kept the length shorter than most men did. It sat soft and sleek against his head, the temples pressed from his hat, and if he wore any hair cream, I couldn't detect it. "Though I'll have an answer of some kind tomorrow night at nine o'clock."

"What happens tomorrow at nine o'clock?"

He pulled a piece of paper from the breast pocket of his jacket and unfolded it. As he smoothed it over the table between us, he replied, "She either appears, or she doesn't, for this."

It was a playbill. CLAIRVOYANT EXTRAVAGANZA, it declared. COMMUNICATION WITH THE DEAD! FORTUNES TOLD FROM THE AUDIENCE! AMAZING PSYCHIC FEATS! And across the bottom: CONTACT YOUR LOST LOVED ONES! SEE THE TRUTH FOR YOURSELF!

On the bill for the evening were Ramona and another psychic. Next to Ramona's name was an ink drawing of a dark-eyed woman with black hair slicked down into a bob. The venue was the Gild Theatre, Streatham.

"I've never heard of this theater," I said.

"It's not far from here." James stirred his tea. "I've used some of my contacts to request an invitation to the private sitting she'll do after the show. If she hasn't fled the country and she actually appears, we'll get a chance to interview her."

"We?"

"You're solving this for George Sutter, are you not? Besides, you're an expert."

I gulped my tea, which was hot, thinking. For showgirls like Ramona, the theater performance was an opportunity to show off in front of an audience, but it wasn't particularly profitable. The theater would take the lion's share of the sales. The real money would come from the private sitting offered afterward, for which she would hopefully get takers impressed by what they had seen. This was the showgirl way of working, used when you didn't have a repeat client list. "I thought you were the expert," I said. "Is she one of your subjects?"

"If you mean did we test her, the answer is no," James said. "I think it's rather obvious she's a fraud, as is the other psychic on this bill."

The waiter came, and we ordered our luncheon. I managed to speak my order past the bitterness that had risen in my throat. When he had gone, I said, "That's still what you do, then, is it? Expose frauds like my mother and me?"

He went very still, and for a moment even the quiet noise of the café seemed to disappear.

"I don't suppose I ever apologized to you for that day?" he said softly.

I gaped at him, my bitterness stealing my speech. "No," I managed. "Never."

"Of course not." He ran a hand through his cropped hair again, his eyes dark and serious. "I always meant to. I certainly felt sorry enough. I suppose I just never got up the courage to do it." He looked at me, taking in the incredulous expression that must have been on my face. "I realize it's hard for you to believe, Ellie, but I do try to have some semblance of honor. And something about that day felt dishonorable, at least to me."

"It's very simple," I said. "The New Society did tests on my mother, and on me. To assess our psychic ability. We failed."

"No," said James. "I don't believe it was that simple. Not anymore. Though I'm damned if I know why."

Our luncheons came, and for a moment he cut his steak while I stirred my soup. Outside the window, the busy London crowd moved by—shoppers, nannies with children, workingmen, newsboys. I saw none of it. I could feel the disappointment of that day like a fresh wound—disappointment that we had failed the tests, yes, but also the piercing sense of failure that James Hawley thought me a skimmer, a fraud. Just like all the others. That particular sense of failure had dogged me for more long, sleepless nights alone than I wanted to admit.

I raised my gaze from my soup to see him looking at me again. "You know," he said, as if he'd read my mind, "I've thought about you quite a lot since that day."

My throat went dry. He was looking at me steadily, his face perfectly half lit in the light from the window, his eyes on mine. We'd never spoken since the day of the tests. He'd never contacted me; he had no reason to. I'd told myself a thousand times that it didn't matter to me how James Hawley had looked at me the first night we met, or that he now had the lowest opinion of me. But now something shifted in my chest, squeezed my blood in my veins. I looked at the firm, well-shaped line of his mouth. He had thought about me?

"What—what do you mean?" I managed.

He leaned forward over his plate, and for a second I thought he was bringing his face closer to mine, that he would bring up the night at the bar. "The tests we did," he said, his voice low and urgent. "The results we got. It doesn't feel right to me. It never has."

"I beg your pardon?"

"She shouldn't have failed," said James, still leaning forward. "Your mother. Every client we interviewed called her real. They told us stories that couldn't be faked. And you, Ellie." Still he stared at me, and I couldn't look away. "Your clients don't lie to me when they tell me what they've seen you do."

I sat up, my spoon clattering in my soup bowl. "My *clients*?"

"Yes, of course." He returned to his steak, cutting it gently. "They aren't very hard to find, you know."

"My client list is—"

"Private, I know. All I had to do was stand in a secluded spot across the street for three days, maybe four, and watch who came out the door. Those ones gave me the names of the rest. They refer each other. I don't think you're a candidate for MI5."

"You—you watched my house?"

"Place of business," James corrected, briefly holding up his fork. "There's a sign on the door, after all."

"But why?"

"I told you, I've been thinking about you since the day we did the tests on your mother. But when that journalist recently dragged up my old paper and put it in the newspaper, it brought all of it back. I have very good instincts. And I was curious."

*You know how I get when I'm curious.* Everything spun. I reached for my handbag and patted it, looking for cigarettes so I'd have an excuse not to look at him. He'd been investigating me. "It was a shock," I said, "that newspaper article. I thought it was over, that no one would ever read that paper again after my mother died. But there it was in the newspaper, all about how Gloria supposedly had proven psychic powers, and my mother did not. As for me, I escaped the reporter's notice, but I believe the term used in the original report was 'inconclusive and unproven.'"

"We thought we were being objective, Paul and I," James said. He was referring to Paul Golding, the head of the New Society.

"Objective," I said.

"Yes." He took a bite of steak. "That's the scientific method—pure objectivity. That has always been Paul's goal, to have the supernatural examined with the same objectivity brought to biology and chemistry and other forms of scientific study. We were certain, at the time, that we were being objective when we published those results. But now I'm not so sure."

"What in the world does that mean?"

His gaze traveled over me as it had in Trafalgar Square, frank and assessing and almost rude, except for the fact that it made me blush like a schoolgirl. "The results Paul and I had from Gloria were unprecedented, and we were rather excited about it. It was heady. I think now that we got carried away, allowed ourselves to be influenced by her opinions. We looked for the results we expected, which is a scientific sin." The half smile surfaced again, this time apologetic. "In short, Ellie, I think we underestimated you."

I stared at him. A rush of feeling came over me, gushing from some long-buried recess, and I struggled with it, suddenly blinking back tears.

James's smile faltered. "Is something wrong?"

I swallowed and bit back the feeling, regaining control. "No one has ever said that to me," I managed. "But at least you admit it. That you believed Gloria and not me."

He put his fork down. "I believed Gloria was a true psychic, yes. I still believe it. But Gloria never told the truth. Not completely. She hid what she didn't feel like revealing, or she fudged around essential facts. But you, Ellie—" His voice lowered, grew almost quiet. "You don't lie as easily. You don't like to lie at all. You hedge, or you deflect the conversation. When you're pushed into it, you just go silent rather than lie. It's really quite fascinating."

My hand rested on my handbag. I could feel Gloria's flask inside, and I wondered what it contained. Gin, perhaps. Whatever it was, I was looking forward to it.

"I have a theory," James said softly, "that you lied to us that day we did the tests. I don't know why, but you did. You've been at it quietly for years, haven't you? Taking clients, finding what they seek. No fanfare, no shows. No newspapers. I've investigated over two hundred claims of spiritualist powers since I came home from the war, but I now believe I'm sitting across from the second true psychic I've ever met."

A psychic, if she is to have a career, must deal with both skeptics and believers. They both bring their own set of problems—skeptics with their endless needling questions, believers with their suffocating faith. My mother taught me that, in the middle of the storm, the medium herself must have only one philosophy: *Believe, or don't believe. It is up to you.*

Most mediums hoped to convince their marks of their veracity, of course. But the true medium—the one who possesses powers, whether they are recognized or not—must walk away. Otherwise, my mother taught me, we are nothing better than circus acts, trying to create greater and greater feats in front of a disbelieving audience. And where is the peace in that?

Gloria herself never cared who believed in her; she was always right, and she always knew it. In my own way, I was the same. Until now.

This was James. Disappointing him, failing those tests, and having him see me as a liar had nearly crippled me three years earlier. I couldn't have said why. We don't always choose whose opinion matters to us. Sometimes there is no logic to it. Sometimes there is only faith.

I let go of my handbag and put my hands on the table, my palms up, my fingers cool. I looked him in the eye.

"James," I said. "Give me your hands."

# CHAPTER TEN

My hands lay on the table, between my emptied cup of tea and the shaker of salt. I'd removed my gloves when we'd sat down, and my palms were vulnerable and bare. Without a word, James lifted his hands and placed them in mine, his arms flexing under the sleeves of his coat. His palms were heavy, the sliding of his skin against mine sending sparks along the surface of my flesh.

I looked down at his hands. They were wide and masculine, the knuckles prominent, the thumbs strong. In a flash I remembered the feel of those hands sliding over my ankles, up my calves. They had been firm, certain, and warm. The memory sliced me like pain.

I wondered whether he had a girlfriend, whether those hands ever touched her, stroked her back, her breasts. I had no idea.

"What do I do?" he asked, his voice rough and uncertain.

"Just let your mind go," I said. "Let your thoughts come. Think of something you lost, something gone from you that you'd like to see again. Picture it. Picture how you lost it. Whatever floats to mind. Just let it come."

"How many people," he asked after a moment, "think of a lost dog?"

"Many," I said. "If you think of a lost dog, you'll believe I guessed it. So think of something else. Something only you would know."

He went quiet again. His hands were warm against mine, a fine charge of electricity moving between us. It was exciting and comforting at the same time. I closed my eyes. I had never done this in a public place before, outside my own sitting room, yet I shut out the world, the voices at the other tables, the clinking of china, the tinkle of a bell as the door opened, the sounds from the street. I let it all wash away. *You are in control, Ellie,* my mother always told me. *Manage your power. Train it. It can be made to follow your will.*

And it could. I could feel it, could feel my mind opening, could feel something at the edges of my thoughts, like an itch. It was something powerful, something—

"Ellie," James rasped.

"What is it?"

"I'm sorry," he said, and then I saw it.

A forest. The trunks black and narrow, the tops of the trees heavy, everything dappled black and white in the intermittent light. The wind whistling in a low voice, the ground hard and cold, shapes moving through the trees, running. The heavy tang of smoke, in the eyes, in the throat, pulled into the lungs, the taste of it everywhere. And the smell . . . dear God, the smell . . .

*Geben Sie es mir.*

*Give it to me.*

Someone was screaming.

*Geben Sie es mir.*

Pain as deep as a scalpel's blade, overwhelming. Something wet and warm. My vision blurring. Deadwood in the undergrowth next to me.

*Geben Sie es mir!*

Shaking against the ground, the soles of my boots rattling on the hard earth as my legs convulse and shiver. Reaching into the front of my tunic, smeared with blood, my eyes watering in the wind, groping with fingers gone numb with cold. The deadwood in the undergrowth—don't look at it. Don't. Just give it to him, and quickly.

Rifle shots crack through the trees. The German's face is suddenly clear, gray with fear, the pimples on his skin etched in ink. His chin and neck are red with cold, red from the rough shave he gave himself in the ice this morning with a dull blade and no mirror. His hand grasps my numb wrist and pulls the thing from my hand, and he backs away. The smell comes again, sickening. And in the undergrowth, where the ground is wet with gore, something moves—

I opened my eyes. My feet were pressing into the floor, pushing me back in my seat, my hands jerking away from James's and into my lap. I did nothing but gasp for a moment, my pulse beating hard in my neck, my mouth dry. James's dark-lashed eyes opened slowly and regarded me with a look that was utterly unfathomable.

"Why?" I managed, my voice strangled.

He blinked slowly, as if coming out of a dream.

The vision still lingered like smoke, but from the edges of perception I began to hear the everyday noises of the restaurant around us. "Why did he want your canteen?" I asked.

Shock rippled over his face. "What?" he said to me. "What did you just say?"

"Your canteen. Why did he want it? What could he possibly want it for? Was it a trophy?" I swallowed, pressed my hand to my face. "The smell—I think I might be sick. And there was something—something moving . . ."

His hand shot out and grabbed my upper arm, harsh and bruising. His face was utterly pale. "Ellie. *What did you just see?*"

"I saw what you saw!" His hand was icy on me. Something awful moved in the depths of his gaze, and suddenly I was appalled beyond measure that he had actually *lived* through what I had just seen—lived through that, and more. Weeks, months of it. How could anyone come through such a thing with his sanity intact? "They were dying in the woods," I said, knowing as I spoke that the words were inadequate, that everything was inadequate. "In the undergrowth. The man on the ground next to you was named Fenton, but I can't see what happened to him. It was something horrible, and he was screaming."

"My God," he said softly.

"The German took your canteen. After the battle, after you'd been injured. I don't know whether he was thirsty, or whether it was just a trophy. That's the belonging you were thinking about—the canteen. Wasn't it? A gift from your father. You lost it, and you wanted to know what happened to it." My throat felt as though lined with sandpaper. "He lived barely sixteen hours after he took it. His body fell in a ditch; no one found it. Not until after the war, and it was so—so decomposed, they—"

His grip tightened. "Stop it."

"They buried him in a graveyard with other unknown soldiers. I can't see the name of it. I don't know where it is. They knew it was an English canteen, but they buried him with it anyway. He's in the sixteenth row, the seventh grave from the right. He—"

"Stop it," he said again, louder.

People were looking at us now. I saw an older man, an apron tied around his waist, watching us with consternation and a trace of uncertainty, and I realized he must be the owner, wondering whether he should intervene. I pulled my arm gently, but James did not relinquish his grip.

"James," I begged softly.

He looked at his hand on my arm, his fingers disappeared into the fabric of my sleeve, and he let me go. He looked sick.

I nodded at the man in the apron. "It's all right," I said to him. "He's upset. I'm sorry."

The man gave James a narrow look and reluctantly turned away.

My headache loomed, insistent. I'd need to rest, and soon; I'd used my powers three times that day already, and this last vision was one of the strongest I'd ever encountered. "I don't know what to say," I said to James. "I'm sorry." I searched his face for something, anything, to indicate that it was all right, but I found nothing. "I've never seen anything like that." I was babbling now. "I can usually control it. The visions aren't usually so complete. The smells, and the cold, and the screaming . . ."

"Please go," said James.

His voice was soft, half choked the way a man's is when he is struggling to keep control. But it was stronger when he raised his eyes to mine, his jaw set, the words he spoke enunciated with unmistakable clarity: "You've proven yourself. It's done. Leave."

For a split second, I wanted to protest, to—what? Stay here and comfort him? Make it all better? I dropped my gaze to his hands, those hands I'd conjured in my memories, gripping the edges of the table, the fingers clenching, the knuckles white.

My heart sank. I was a stupid, stupid fool. I'd wanted to prove something to him—to make him see me as I really was, perhaps. To have him notice me, believe me. All I'd managed to do was humiliate him and cause him pain.

I stood, sliding out of our booth on unsteady knees, picking up my handbag. All around us was the quaint café with its peaceful patrons, the soft click of teacups, gentle swells of conversation, a simple English day under blue skies and early-autumn daylight. After what I had just seen, it all seemed unreal, as if the vision had been reality and what I saw before me now was the dream. The headache pulsed up the back of my skull.

As I turned to leave, I saw the owner glance at me, and an older couple sitting at a nearby table wordlessly watched my progress. When he caught my eye, the husband gave me a nod, soft and solemn. I didn't need psychic powers to know what he meant. *A soldier, yes, we understand.* Perhaps they had a son who had come home damaged, or who hadn't come home at all. They were the right age for it.

I blinked and looked back at James. He was staring down at the table, unmoving. *A soldier, yes.* I did not look at the couple again. Instead, I slipped out the door and let it fall shut behind me.

The dead don't walk among us, peering invisibly over our shoulders or watching us as we sleep. There are such things as hauntings, certainly, but they are confined to certain spaces, tied to a place and often with a purpose, though they are in fact rare. Most such cases are actually the product of a living person with an unrecognized, or uncontrolled, power. The true dead, if you wish to speak with them, must be called.

I saw my first ghost when I was seven years old. I was sitting in my accustomed space on the floor behind the plum curtain that separated the sitting room from the rest of the house, listening to my mother with a client. I knew my mother was wearing her black-beaded dress, the scarf tied in her reddish blond hair, but I had not seen the man who was her customer, only heard his voice. I flexed my toes as I listened to them, my legs sprawled out before me as I ate half a tea biscuit and tried not to spill the crumbs.

"Mother," the man was calling out as I licked my buttery fingers. "Mother! Please speak to me!"

My own mother's voice was a soft murmur. "Sometimes the spirits are reluctant. Sometimes they are far away and cannot hear. We must be patient."

"But I must speak to her," the man moaned. "Mother! Mother!"

"Mr. Carver—"

"Mother!"

I finished the tea biscuit and rubbed my fingers on my stockings. Something was bothering me, like an unpleasant itch in my brain. I pulled up my knees and hugged them.

"Mr. Carver, you must be silent," my mother said. Her voice

sounded weary. "The sound— I cannot— Too much noise interrupts the communication."

The itch grew worse. It was cold and somehow crawling. I rubbed my fingers along the back of my head, under the hair, rubbing my scalp, trying to make it go away. It persisted. The man's moans for his mother, and my own mother's protests, faded as I rubbed. Then I looked up, and the lady was there, standing in front of me.

She wore a heavy black dress adorned with thick braid, and her gray hair was pulled back from her face. Her hands hung limply at her sides, the gnarled fingers curled. Her skin was ghastly, mottled under the eyes and in the jowls. She stood just past the toes of my shoes, ignoring the voices beyond the curtain and staring down at me.

I couldn't move. I heard nothing but the heartbeat in my ears, felt nothing but the chilling throb in my skull. The woman's face was a mask of disapproval and anger as she stared at me, her eyes livid with fury.

"I feel something," I heard my mother say. Her voice was uncertain, a tone I'd never heard her use with a client before. "I don't—I don't exactly know. I think it's—"

"Mother, is it you?" Mr. Carver called. "Please tell me you forgive me!"

The lady made no acknowledgment, only stared at me, unmoved. Some awful sense radiated from her—misery perhaps, or just cold anger. I knew she was dead, that these were the clothes she'd been buried in. A rank smell wafted from her, a damp and clinging odor. I shrank back into the wall, pulling my knees tighter to my chest.

"Forgive me, Mother!" Mr. Carver cried.

I pointed at the curtain, trying to redirect her horrible attention. *Go away,* I thought in desperation, through the cold fog in my head. *You're dead. It's them that want you, not me.* My finger brushed the curtain and it rippled as if in a breeze.

"She is here!" Mr. Carver said. "The curtain is swaying!"

"I beg pardon?" my mother said, confused. "I don't—"

"Mother, are you here? Answer me!"

I pointed again. *Go away,* I thought at the woman again. *Please.*

For the first time, she moved. Her furious gaze left my face and crawled down to my pointing finger.

*Not here,* I thought, able to keep calm now that she wasn't looking at me. *There. Not me—them.*

She did not move like a living person; it was something like it, and yet nothing like it at all. Her chin seemed to angle one way, her eyes another; her shoulders turned, but her waist did not. Her legs did not walk, yet the hem of her skirt brushed the floor in cold silence. The curtain did not stir with the slightest breath as she vanished through it. And then she was gone.

"Wait," my mother said, and even through the aftermath of my horror I could hear the relief in her voice. "She is here. She is here! Speak, spirit! Speak to your loved ones!"

I didn't stay for the rest; I'd had more than enough. I left my crawl space on silent feet, the tea biscuit a lump in my stomach. The itch was leaving my brain in a slow trickle, an uncanny feeling that left a throb in its wake. I went to my room and curled up on my bed, even though it was three o'clock in the afternoon and I was supposed to be doing my lessons. I fell asleep almost instantly.

I awoke to find the sun setting and my mother in my room. She lowered herself onto the edge of my bed, as slow and exhausted as a woman a decade older than her thirty years. She was already untying the scarf from her hair.

"That was you, wasn't it?" she said to me without preamble.

I rolled to my side, facing her, and pulled my knees to my chest. I still had my shoes on, which was absolutely forbidden in bed, but my mother didn't seem to notice. I said nothing.

She sighed, as if I'd spoken. "I felt something. Dear God, I've always thought . . . I've always wondered—" Her words seemed to choke her and she dropped the scarf into her lap, her narrow shoulders drooping. "I never knew whether I would be happy or horrified if it was true."

"That I'm like you?" I asked.

I wanted badly for her to turn to me, to run her palm and her warm fingers over my cheek, to gently kiss my temple as she did when she put me to bed at night. But she stayed staring at nothing, her back turned to me as if she'd forgotten me. I stared at the line of her shoulders, the thin bones of her arms in the sleeves of the black dress, the mass of red-gold hair that she'd gathered at the nape of her neck.

"You mustn't tell your father," she said at last. She ran her hand over the scarf in her lap, smoothing it against her legs. Then she squared her shoulders a little. "I'll have to teach you. There are techniques you can learn. We can handle it at the end of your lessons, while your father is at work. You must not let on when he's home—you must be normal. I expect you to practice and to follow my directions exactly. You will have to watch my sessions from behind the curtain. I expect you to be observant and obedient, and you must not be afraid." She turned her head just enough to glance at me over her shoulder. "Do you understand?"

"Yes, Mother."

"This will not be easy for you, so do not expect it to be. I admit I've anticipated this possibility, which is why I did not put you in school. Now I see I was right. A girl of your abilities cannot go to school."

I blinked away tears. Who needed school, anyway? I didn't want the company of other girls, who would probably be mean and stupid. "Yes, Mother."

She looked away from me again, as if the sight of me, even from an angle, somehow pained her. "Once you begin to see the dead, Ellie, you must learn to maintain control. It is a doorway that has cracked ajar. The dead will take advantage of it; they cannot help it.

It is in their nature, especially if they are being called. But the dead are dead, and they cannot hurt you. Do you understand?"

"Yes, Mother," I said.

She nodded and stood. "Do not put your shoes on the bed again," she said, and left the room.

But I left my shoes where they were and stayed on the bed, listening to the clock ticking as twilight stole the light from the room. My mother loved me; I knew that without a doubt. It was because she loved me so much that she was concerned. It was because she loved me so much that she expected more of me. I could help her. She hadn't been able to call that old woman; I had. Perhaps she was tired, but I was not. I had been born with her talent, and instead of going to school I would learn to use it. The thought both excited and horrified me.

The next day, we began our lessons.

# CHAPTER ELEVEN

I sat in front of the vanity in my small bedroom, wearing my mother's dress and tying her scarf into my hair. I wore my blond hair bobbed, one of the many things I'd horrified her with just before she died; I'd cut it to follow a fad, but discovered I loved the style. Still, it was difficult to wind the scarf through hair so short.

*You must be normal.*

I'd come home the day before to find my disapproving neighbor, Mrs. Weller, at my door with news that a Scotland Yard inspector had come looking for me and questioning my neighbors. "He was dressed respectably enough, I suppose," Mrs. Weller had said, "but these policemen are low sorts. Not the kind of people we want in this neighborhood." She'd handed me a note left in her care for me and gone off home in a righteous huff.

The note sat on my vanity now, its dark, masculine handwriting mocking me:

*Please contact Inspector Merriken, Scotland Yard, at your most urgent convenience. Regards.*

The clock ticked softly from its place on the wall, where it rested against my mother's rose wallpaper. Outside my window, a bird sang in my small back garden. I looked at myself in the mirror. I was tired. I'd barely slept, and when I had, my dreams had been about mud and stark terror under a cold canopy of trees and a man named Fenton screaming beside me. It was possible that James Hawley would never speak to me again. Psychic mediums had only clients, not friends; displays like the one I'd shown James the day before drove people off—even psychical investigators. And so there I was, alone in my mother's room, with only the police interested in my whereabouts.

*You must be normal,* my mother had said.

I rose and left the bedroom, leaving the note behind on the vanity. My first appointment of the day was about to arrive. A girl has to make money, after all.

After seeing two clients—a lost wedding ring and the inevitable lost dog, respectively—I wrote a note to Fitzroy Todd, asking to see him. *It's urgent. You know what it's about.* By teatime I had a reply by messenger, along with a second note by post. Fitzroy was agreeable to see me at seven o'clock, if I wanted to come by the house where he was cadging off of his parents. The second note was from James Hawley. It said only: *Gild Theatre, Streatham, nine o'clock. Do not forget.*

I stood by my front window, reading the note more times than its brief message warranted. I lowered the paper and watched Mr. Bagwell, my elderly neighbor, walk his collie, Pickwick, down the street. Both man and dog made slow progress, their legs equally arthritic, though the dog had slightly more spring to his step than his master. The collie turned his head and looked adoringly up at the man as they walked, his long, beautiful fur rippling as he moved.

A man on a bicycle came into sight, headed for my door. It wasn't
my next client, who was due in half an hour. The man wore a uniform and cap; another messenger, then. He saw me in the window as
he dismounted and tipped his cap at me. I walked to the front door
and opened it.

"Miss Winter?" the fellow asked.

"Yes."

"Special message, miss." He handed me an envelope.

I opened it and read:

> *You are making appointments, not investigating. Was
> the fee insufficient? Please advise of progress. Messenger
> will await reply.*
>
> *Please report any new developments by telephoning
> Hampstead 1207. Messages left at that exchange will
> reach me.*
>
> *—G. Sutter.*

I frowned. Hampstead 1207. The exchange didn't mean that
George Sutter—whoever he worked for—was physically in Hampstead; it only meant he had someone answering the telephone for him
there. I glanced up at the messenger, who only shrugged. I'd get no
information from that particular source. Incensed, I took up a pencil
and wrote across the bottom of the note:

> *Does MI5 have nothing better to do than to watch
> people's houses?*
>
> *—E. Winter.*

I folded the note and gave the envelope back to the messenger.
After he left, I lit a cigarette, something I never did during the day,
trying to calm my nerves. How had anyone watched my house without

my noticing? Through the front window, Mr. Bagwell returned home from his walk, Pickwick following on his leash. By the time the cigarette was ash, I was reasonably calm again.

I walked to the telephone I'd had installed in the front hall. I took up the receiver, dialed the first exchange, and began to cancel appointments.

Fitzroy Todd's parental home, in Belgravia, was a narrow terraced town house of pale Georgian stone bordered by a wrought-iron fence. A maid admitted me into an elegant front hall, took my hat, and informed me that Mr. Todd was upstairs.

There seemed to be no one else home, and my heels made no noise on the thick carpeting of the corridor. "Up here," came a masculine voice. I ascended all the way to the upper floor, where I found Fitzroy standing in a tastefully decorated but utterly messy dressing room.

He stood before a mirror, in trousers, braces, and a white shirt, carefully combing back his dark hair. He swiveled in one easy movement and saw me in the doorway. "Ellie!" he exclaimed, taking my hands and kissing me on the cheek. "You look too ravishing. Your hair—my God, that color! I could write poetry. Come in; it's just an old dressing room. No need to be a prude." He smelled of cigarettes and cologne.

"It's nice to see you, too, Fitz," I said, making my way over the shirts and ties left in piles on the floor. There was a chair beneath a stack of jackets, and I gingerly moved them and made myself a seat.

"You don't mind, do you?" Fitz gestured around the room. "I know it's a screaming disaster. I need to get ready for supper with Niles and a few other fellows before we go to the club, and your note said it was urgent. Mum and Dad aren't home anyway, not that they'd mind."

"No, I suppose not." Fitz's wardrobe stood open, revealing a tumbled spill of expensive clothing. A painting on the wall featured a seminude woman bending over a well to fill a bucket of water, her

breasts visible through the thin cloth of her dress. Through the doorway I glimpsed his bedroom, the bed rumpled, a glass and bottle on
the night table. The air smelled oddly musty, like a stranger's body. I
didn't want to admit I'd never exactly been inside a man's private
rooms before; Fitz would only laugh at me. He'd been Gloria's lover,
and I wondered whether she had ever been here.

He returned to a gilt-framed mirror to straighten his collar.
"You're here about Gloria, of course," he said. "I'm ripped to pieces
about it, Ellie. Just gutted. You can't imagine."

I watched him study his handsome dark-eyed face in the mirror.
"What happened?" I asked him. "I mean, you were there. What in
the world happened?"

"Damned if I know." He looked over his dressing table and ran
his finger over a selection of ties. Many women thought Fitzroy Todd
extremely attractive; he was invited to parties everywhere and was often pictured in the gossip columns, usually with a few beautiful
women at his side. What the newspapers didn't cover was that he usually ended such nights being poured, incoherent with gin, into taxicabs by those same callous hangers-on. He was well-bred and almost
as tall as James Hawley, though not as muscled. As he selected a tie I
looked at his hands and wondered whether they were strong enough
to knock a woman out, stab her, and carry her to the lip of a pond.

"Just start from the beginning," I said to him.

"I already told the police everything," Fitz said, looking steadily
down at the ties and not at me. "I truly did. They had me for hours,
you know. It was horrid." He glanced at me in the mirror. "Not that
I wouldn't have gone through worse for Gloria's sake, of course. I
hope they catch the bastard, and soon."

I tugged off my hat and ran a hand over my hair. "Fitz, for God's
sake. It's me. I'm not the police. Don't give me that line."

He sighed. "Very well. I met a couple named Dubbs at a party
about a year ago. We hit it off—they're decent sorts, though they're a

bit older. They're fascinated by spiritualism. Their only son died in the war, and they never got over it." Fitz selected a tie and looped it under the collar of his shirt. He himself had been just a few years too young to fight. "Frankly, they were a bit of a bore, but they were persistent. They wanted Gloria to do a séance, and they wanted me to arrange it."

"Where did Ramona come in?" I asked.

"Who? Oh, the showgirl. God only knows. All I know is that she must have smelled money, because she latched onto the Dubbses like an unwanted puppy. She was a nuisance, and it was difficult enough to pull this off without going through that hideous dragon Davies."

"Davies told you no?"

"Of course. Gloria's dance card was full, and she was taking a higher sort of client, or so I heard. Do you like this jacket?" He lifted a black evening jacket off the back of the door and slid it over his shoulders. "Lesley and Roberts, Hanover Square."

"Fitz."

He sighed. "That blond hair, those perfect cheekbones, and those legs, yet you're all work and no play. You should come drink with me and some of the fellows. We love blonds. You used to be fun, you know."

"Fitz, Gloria is *dead*."

Fitz turned from the mirror and gave me the full force of his gaze. He was a man who gambled, borrowed money, did no work, and took on absolutely no responsibility, but he had a vital, low-life sort of charm. He used it now to look soulful, but the effect only made me feel uncomfortable and suspicious. "I'm well aware of that, Ellie. I loved her, you know. But we've all seen so much death. I think Gloria wouldn't want us to sit around like a group of old dowagers. I think she'd want us to get out and enjoy life any way we can."

"Just tell me what happened."

"Very well." Fitz patted around for cuff links. "I had been trying to get to Gloria for weeks. The Dubbses wanted to contact their son, Davey, and I *do* have a soul, you know. They were simply convinced Gloria was the only one who could help them. Then one night I ran into Gloria herself at the Gargoyle Club and I got to her myself to plead my case."

"What was she doing at the Gargoyle?" I asked.

He shrugged. "Drinking, of course. We all were. I told her about the Dubbses, and eventually she agreed. She wanted the Dubbses to come to her flat like the others, but the Dubbses wanted to do the séance at their home, and I convinced her to do it."

"Why did she agree?" I asked, shifting in my uncomfortable chair, the touch of one of Fitz's shirts on my ankle. "It was completely against her policy."

For the first time, he looked a little uneasy. "Well, I don't know. We're old friends. She simply said yes."

"No, she didn't," I replied. "Tell me the truth."

He scratched his chin, uncomfortable. "All right. I didn't tell the police this part, but I'll tell you, Ellie, because you're a straight one and you'll figure it out anyway. Frankly, the Dubbses were offering a bucket of money for Gloria to come to them, and if I arranged it I would get a slice of it."

I stared at him for a long moment, shocked despite myself. "You arranged access to Gloria for pay?"

"Not exactly. No, no. God, no." He looked away. "There was a lot of money on the table, Ellie. A lot."

"But Gloria didn't need money," I said.

"Is that what Davies told you?" He shrugged. "Interesting. But Gloria didn't tell Davies everything, Ellie. Especially about money. In fact, Gloria didn't trust Davies very far."

I had never heard this. "Fitz, what on earth are you talking about?"

"I don't know everything, but when Gloria and I were together, she mentioned some . . . irregularities. Problems with money not being where it should be. Gloria suspected Davies, though she never had enough evidence to come out and say it."

"You're making no sense," I said. Why I felt the need to defend the odious Davies, I had no idea. "Gloria was Davies's employer. She could have just sacked her. Why would she keep on someone she suspected of swindling? Not just for a short time, but for years?"

Fitz smiled down at me. He was fully dressed now, in clothes worth more than many people earned in a year, with more discarded on the floor like rags. "Ellie," he said, "you're a decent girl and I like you, but you can be awfully naive. Davies isn't exactly stable. Far from it, in fact. She has a temper that would put the fear of God into you, and Gloria was her entire life."

"What are you saying?"

"Gloria was a little afraid of Davies. Of what she might do if she was ever dismissed. Davies knows a lot of secrets, and if she felt wronged, she wouldn't be past making up a few more out of whole cloth. She could have done a lot of damage if Gloria ever cut her loose. So Gloria kept her on, where she could be controlled."

I stared up at him, wondering whether it was true, wondering what else I had missed. " 'Keep your friends close, but your enemies closer,' " I said.

"Exactly. Gloria was no fool. And more to the point, Gloria did need money. For what, I don't know. She didn't confide in me anymore." His voice grew almost bitter, and for a second his eyes were hard. "But I'll tell you, when I told her the number the Dubbses were offering, she agreed. It was the money, Ellie. That's what swayed her."

I dropped my gaze to my lap. *What were you into, Gloria? What did you need money for, so badly that you were willing to break your own rules?*

Fitz leaned back against the edge of his dressing table, his shoulders sagging a little in his expensive jacket. "And so I set it up," he said, the memory subduing his voice. "Ramona latched herself on— God only knows how. Perhaps through the Dubbses. So we all went off to Kent. It was a grand party, I tell you, all of us there to find Davey Dubbs."

But not, I thought, before Gloria had dropped a note at her brother's hotel, asking that I find her. I didn't mention this to Fitz. "What happened?" I asked, leaning forward in my uncomfortable chair, placing my elbows on my knees in an unladylike way. "Did Gloria find Davey?"

"She didn't get a chance to try," Fitz answered to my surprise. "It was a fiasco nearly from the moment the Dubbses collected us at the train station. Gloria had been drinking, and Ramona was being coarse and rude. The Dubbses were trying to keep a lid on things, to keep everyone calm—especially Gloria, who they begged to sober up. But the Dubbses weren't ready for a séance at all. They hadn't moved any furniture or prepared a table or anything. Mr. Dubbs disappeared into another room somewhere, and Mrs. Dubbs tried to serve us tea and cakes at nine o'clock at night. I had to instruct her how to set up for a proper séance. She was nice enough, but for a couple who wanted to see Gloria so badly, they were completely unprepared. Gloria was in a mood—something had gotten under her skin. She seemed angry and almost resigned at the same time, and she kept sipping from the flask she'd snuck in her pocket."

I thought of the flask I'd taken from Gloria's flat. It couldn't be the same one. Gloria must have had several, then. This didn't exactly surprise me.

"Finally," Fitz continued, "Gloria complained that she had a headache and needed some air. Then she got up and left the room."

Something about the story weighed on me, depressed me horribly, and I pressed my fingers to my forehead. "And no one went after her? No one at all?"

Fitz shrugged and ran a hand through his dark hair, messing its slicked-back style. "I don't see why we would, even when I think back on it. She just said she needed some air, like any girl might say."

*Gloria was not any girl*, I thought. Fitz caught my icy stare and looked away.

We were silent for a moment. Then I said, "None of it adds up. I can't figure who would want Gloria dead. Or who even knew where she was."

"It wasn't me, I can bloody well tell you." Fitz looked sullen. "I would have taken Gloria back if she'd ever thought to look at me. I've never had a girl to hold a match to her since." He looked at me. "If I were you, I'd be looking at that gorgon Davies. She knew where Gloria was, all right. Or perhaps the police should be looking at you?"

"Me?"

"You hated her, didn't you? That business with proving your mother a fraud and all that." Fitz pushed himself off the dressing table with one hip and straightened. "As it is, I can't even understand why you, of all people, want to find her killer."

I looked at him, at his eyes that seemed to sparkle yet were as impenetrable as a lizard's, and I knew I could never explain. "It matters," I said.

He shrugged, regaining his old demeanor now. "Suit yourself. But I wouldn't be surprised if you got a call from Scotland Yard."

*Because you gave them my name when they questioned you?* "I already have. I've been summoned by Inspector Merriken."

Fitz shuddered theatrically. "I wish you luck. I'd rather not encounter that fellow again, myself. He's far too canny for me. It's like he can see what you're thinking." He looked at me, sitting on his dressing room chair, and laughed his easy laugh. "Perhaps you should watch your back, Ellie. Now shove off. I've a dinner to attend."

# CHAPTER TWELVE

The Gild Theatre, which was to house Ramona's clairvoyant extravaganza, was nearly deserted at eight thirty. I stepped off the omnibus and looked up and down the street, noting a dim chop suey restaurant, a few tiny, smelly pubs, and the faint sounds of traffic from a nearby, busier thoroughfare. A thin rain had begun to fall, almost mist in the wet air, and the pavements were slick. This was not exactly the center of London's high-class entertainment.

The Gild was shabby, pushed right up against the street, only a dim electrical light glaring sickly from one of the street-level windows and shedding flimsy illumination over the peeling posters. So far, an evening of psychic stage demonstrations had not drawn an audience, and the weather wasn't helping.

"Ellie."

I turned. James detached himself from a pool of shadow and came toward me. He wore a dark overcoat against the damp, chill air, his hat pulled over his forehead. He raised an umbrella and opened it.

"You didn't come prepared," he said.

"I know." I pulled up my collar. I was most likely the only Londoner abroad tonight who had forgotten her umbrella, but I'd had a lot on my mind when I'd left the house. I glanced at James again, trying to see his face in the darkness. After what happened when we'd last seen each other, I couldn't guess what his attitude would be, and his voice gave nothing away.

He did not touch me, but moved me under the umbrella, his arm behind me. I could smell the damp wool of his coat. To any observer, we were huddled together as if we were a couple. Tension radiated from him like vibrations from a tuning fork.

"When was the last time you came to one of these?" he asked.

"It's been years," I admitted. "Gloria and I used to attend them sometimes."

He grunted. "Slumming."

"No," I said. "The ones we attended were always at better theaters than this."

"That isn't what I meant."

I supposed not. He meant that Gloria and I were two real psychics coming to watch a fake's stage show. "And when was the last time you attended a show like this?" I asked.

"Three weeks ago," he said.

"For one of your reports?"

"It's what I do," he replied. He turned his head, and for a brief second the lights reflected on the planes of his face. "You haven't missed much. The tricks haven't improved, from what I can see. I've bought our tickets."

"All right." I looked at the dreary facade of the Gild Theatre, slick now with rain. "Let's go see whether Ramona makes an appearance."

The theater was small, the proscenium low, the chairs hard and crowded close together. There was no heat, and already my toes were cold and damp inside my high-heeled shoes. A small crowd trickled in alongside us: older women, draped in heavy fabrics and cheap, elaborate hats; young people, visibly drunk and rowdy; single men, most of them older than forty, wearing graying shirts under jackets worn at the elbows. One man slept softly in his chair, snoring; I was fairly certain he'd bought a ticket just to get out of the rain.

We took seats near the back, and I unbuttoned my coat despite the chill. James slid down in his seat and our knees touched. I leaned away from him and scanned the audience again, trying to catalog everyone in more detail under the watery electric light.

"Ellie."

I turned to find James looking at me. He'd removed his hat, and under the light I could see that his jaw was tight, his eyes on me in an intense expression I couldn't read.

"About yesterday," he said.

I looked away again. "Stop," I said, forcing the words out. "I cannot apologize enough for yesterday. It was inexcusable." I blinked hard. "All I can say for myself is that I did not intend to be cruel."

"You are not cruel," he said softly after a long moment. "Look at me."

I turned back again. There was pain on his face now, bleak and vicious. I did not have to touch him to know that he was thinking of that black forest, the trees, the cold, the screaming. Just as I was.

"I am going to tell you this once and once only. Do you understand?"

I nodded, mute.

"What you saw yesterday, I have never told to anyone. And I never will. What happened in those woods, what happened to Fenton— you've seen some of it now, so there's no going back, but never ask me about it because I say now that *I will never, ever tell you*. Not ever. Is that clear?"

"Yes," I said through numb lips. I watched him turn away from me, run a hand quickly through his dark blond hair, watched a drop of rain make its way down the lapel of his coat. "Do you remember the first time we met?" I asked, the words a surprise even to me as they came from my mouth.

He paused, then nodded. "The Stavros Club on Gerrard Street," he said, but his expression calmed at the change of subject.

So he did remember. We had been drinking that night, Gloria and I. We'd been standing on the edge of the dance floor, mussed and a little sweaty, taking a breather while the orchestra members refreshed themselves at the bar. Gloria had bent to fix the buckle on her high heel, and when she went down I saw a man approaching us behind her, his hands in his coat pockets, striding fast through the crowd. His expression was angry and determined, but when he saw me—I was obviously a surprise—it changed. His gaze moved swiftly down me, taking everything in, sliding over my hips and my waist in a look so fiery I felt my skin flush hot under my clothes. When Gloria stood again he still stared at me, at my face and my mussed hair, my eyes. Finally he pulled his gaze from me and looked back to Gloria, getting angry again.

"Gloria," he said, his voice rough. "Get out of here and go home."

Gloria, laughing, had introduced him as James Hawley from the New Society, who was doing a top secret series of tests on her. Still not looking my way, James had reminded her that the stated tests were scheduled for eight o'clock the next morning, some seven hours away, and he'd appreciate it if his subject would sober up and get some rest. Gloria had told him to stop being a stick, and how had he found her, anyway?

I'd watched the entire exchange, speechless, my throat dry. I hadn't imagined that look. My body still felt it. When Gloria finally introduced us, I'd only nodded blankly at James, tongue-tied. He nodded at me formally, his gaze under control now, but still I saw the flare in his eyes.

I was more than a little bit drunk and the room was spinning and the air was close, but James Hawley, with his blond hair and

dark-lashed eyes and boxer's shoulders, had hit me like a blow. He
was the opposite of all of Gloria's other male acquaintances, who
were foppish and theatrical in comparison. When he'd told Gloria he
was going to order us a taxi and we'd damned well better get in it, he
gave me another glance, then disappeared into the crowd again. Gloria turned to me.

"He isn't always like that," she said. "He's just being beastly at
the moment. He can be rather nice."

"Oh," I said.

And suddenly Gloria was looking at me through the haze of all the
gin she'd imbibed, her eyes narrowing. "Ellie, darling, you like him."

"I didn't even talk to him," I said in a tone I thought was reasonable, my face going hot again.

"He's good-looking enough. I'll give you that," Gloria said as if I
hadn't spoken. "He looks rather stunning when he takes his jacket
off. But he's a difficult one. Moody and a little obsessive, like a tangle
of thorns. He'd probably be good for you, come to think of it. He
disapproves of drinking entirely."

"Oh," I'd said stupidly again, thinking that he must have noticed
I was drunk.

Gloria glanced at my face, then away again with an affected
shrug. "To each her own, but he isn't my type."

"What is your type?" I asked.

She took my arm. "Men I can manipulate," she said. "Let's go.
He's waiting."

I stared at James now, sitting next to me in the Gild Theatre three
years later, and thought about what had happened next. James had
put us into a taxi, as promised. He'd taken us back to Gloria's flat.
He'd dumped Gloria into bed, where she immediately started snoring.
And then he helped me, wobbling, onto Gloria's sofa, where he placed
an old chintz pillow for my head, and got me a blanket, and swung
my legs up as if fixing a mannequin. I don't know what I expected—I

had absolutely no experience of men—but I lay there beneath Gloria's mermaid painting, my eyes half closed as the ceiling spun above me, thinking I should say something clever and witty, something that would bring that look back, make him sit up and notice me. His hands had been strong and competent, holding my ankle as he un-buckled one shoe and slid it off, then the other. When I risked a glance at him, I saw he was looking down, his brow smooth, his expression blank. *It's not what you think,* I'd thought wildly as his palms touched my calves with impersonal care, moving my legs in place on the sofa. *I'm not what you think. I'm not.* But instead I bit the inside of my mouth until I tasted the tang of blood, and after a moment he stood in silence and left the flat, closing the door quietly behind him.

"I thought you didn't like me," I said to him now, thinking, *Moody and a little obsessive, like a tangle of thorns.* "When we met that night."

"Didn't like you?"

"It's part of the pattern, it seems," I admitted. "My making the worst possible impression on you."

He stilled, staring ahead at the empty stage, and he did not look at me. After a long pause, he spoke. "You can't tell a girl who's had too much to drink that she has nice legs," he said, choosing his words with care. "It makes you a cad."

I trained my own gaze on the stage, heat rising in my cheeks, and remembered his blank expression as he'd removed my shoes. I'd wanted to ask him if he knew who I was that night—knew *what* I was, whose daughter I was. But now I realized that the answer didn't matter.

"All right, then," I said. "Let's get to work, shall we?"

His shoulders relaxed visibly at that, his body settling almost im-perceptibly back into the chair. He looked around the theater, which had stopped filling at a quarter full. "Which one is the plant, do you suppose?"

"The fellow on the aisle," I said almost immediately, my cheeks cooling. I nodded toward a man, thirtyish, sitting alone in an aisle seat, running his fingers along the brim of the hat in his lap. A plant was someone hired by the onstage psychic to play into the fake reading, in order to convince everyone else in the audience. "Aisle seats are the best places for plants, and he looks respectable."

"Interesting, but no." James warmed to the topic, his expression losing its stiffness. "It's the old woman in the fourth row."

I stared at the woman's plump back, though I saw nothing unusual. "She's with her husband," I said. "That can't be right."

"That isn't her husband," James said calmly. "That's how I know."

"What are you talking about?"

"There are at least three inches of space between his shoulder and hers," James said. "He just reached down to pick up something he'd dropped, and he leaned away from her as if she had leprosy. Those two are acting, and not well."

I stared harder, more than aware that there was no space between James's shoulder and mine. "That would make two people in on the plant. It's risky."

"Perhaps," he replied. "But I've seen it before. No one suspects a nice old couple." He motioned toward a group of men moving single file down the aisle, wearing cloth caps and simple wool jackets— workmen, perhaps, from one of the factories nearby after the end.of a shift. "Those fellows have been drinking."

He was right; they wove unevenly and laughed at one another's jokes. I shook my head and tutted. "Drunks at a séance," I said. "There's nothing worse. I can almost feel sorry for her."

I glanced at James to find him smiling a little. I knew how he felt. I had the same sort of giddiness talking to someone who knew the business as well as I did. I took off my hat and tried to sop some of the remaining dampness from my hair. "I pick the fellow with the mustache," I said, eyeing a young man with hard eyes sitting alone. "He may as well have a sign."

"Single men don't make the best plants," James countered. "The audience tends to trust women more than men."

"I'm right," I said. "He doesn't belong."

The half smile didn't leave his lips. "We'll see," he said.

The lights flickered low and the stage lights came on. After a pedestrian warm-up act in which a man sweating through his pancake makeup released doves from his sleeves to the jeers of the sparse audience, a woman with a bust like a ship's prow took a seat at the piano in the orchestra and began to play a dramatic set of chords. Two technicians dragged wooden chairs onto the stage, angling them slightly together as if two people were to have a conversation. Then the lights dimmed again and came up, revealing a woman of forty-five standing on the stage, heavily made up and wearing a matching paisley dress and head scarf.

The woman raised her arms dramatically. "I am The Great Evelina!" she shouted. "I am here to speak to the dead!"

Someone hooted. The man sleeping in his seat snorted and changed position.

The Great Evelina swept her theatrical robes to one of the chairs and sat down. "This chair," she said, motioning toward the empty seat before her, "will contain the invisible spirit with which I speak. I tell you, a spirit shall sit here and converse with me!" She closed her eyes. "Who among the dead wishes to join me? Who among the dead has a message?"

Next to me, James sighed.

"Silence!" The Great Evelina shouted, as if she'd heard him. "The spirits are speaking! I am hearing something . . . a name. There is . . . a J. The name has a J."

"That's Jane!" The old woman who was with her faux husband sprang from her seat. "That's my daughter!"

The audience went quiet. "I should have bet you a pound," James murmured to me.

"Don't be cocky," I replied. "Two psychics, two plants."

"Jane!" The Great Evelina proclaimed from the stage, her eyes still closed. "Yes, Jane speaks to me. She uses me as her instrument to communicate with her beloved parents. I obey."

"Jane!" the old woman warbled, distressed. If she was acting, she was rather good.

"She speaks," said Evelina. "The voice is very strong. She says she died of influenza. It was quick and she did not suffer. She had brown hair. An innocent angel."

"It's true!" The old woman gasped. "My child! Oh, Jane, I miss you so much!"

The group of drunk men hooted again, bored of the sentimentality, while an elderly woman in the front row dabbed at her eyes with a handkerchief.

I felt James's shoulders lift and sag as he sighed again. "Do you have any premonitions?" he whispered in my ear.

"Yes," I said, ignoring the fact that I could feel his warm breath on my neck. "I predict that it's going to be a long evening."

"That sleeping fellow has the right idea," he replied, putting on his hat and pulling the brim over his eyes. "Wake me when Ramona comes on, if she ever does."

I glanced at him, at the relaxed line of his mouth under the hat brim, his muscular arms crossed over his chest, but I couldn't relax. I was jumpy with tension, with a sick feeling. Something about the entire display bothered me, and it wasn't just the terrible quality of The Great Evelina's act. It was the crassness of it, of the performer and the audience both—all of them using death for a night's cheap entertainment. I thought of the old woman I'd seen when I was seven, the horrible stench of her. I looked at the woman weeping quietly in the front row.

"This is wrong," I said softly.

Next to me, James shifted in his seat.

I watched Evelina continue her dreary, faked conversation with the imaginary Jane, using the empty chair as a prop, the girl's imaginary parents chiming in. "I can't stand it."

"I thought you said you'd seen shows like this before?" James's low voice came from beside me.

"I have. But it was with Gloria." I struggled with the memory, struggled with the words. "Everything was different with Gloria. This—this is just horrible."

"This," James said casually, "is why I hate people."

He reached up and tilted his hat back a little, fixing his gaze on the stage. Despite his careful pose, I saw he was not relaxed at all. There was something deadly serious and steely in his eyes, something I understood. "This is why you do what you do, isn't it?" I asked him. "You debunk people like this. People who cheapen all of the death you saw." He did not reply, and a chill of horror went down my back. "Did you ever equate me with this? Did you think this was me?"

For a moment I thought he wouldn't answer. "I didn't know," he finally admitted. "You have no idea how many liars I've met in my lifetime."

It threatened to close in on me again, the disappointment of failing him, but this time I fought it. "This is not me," I said, my voice fierce even to my own ears beneath the whisper of it. "This was never me."

Finally he looked at me. The steeliness left his expression, and the lines of his face were almost amused, almost relieved. "I know."

The lights dimmed again, and Evelina, finished with her show, tottered off. James sat up in his chair and took off his hat again, his attention evaporating like water. I was still giddy from the look he'd given me, but I felt my own pulse of excitement as I followed his gaze.

On the stage, a dark shadow appeared from the wings. It took its place in the center.

"Finally," James said. "Here comes a hell of a show."

The lights came up to reveal a woman with a sleek black bob in the distinctive style of Louise Brooks, dressed in a midnight black dress. Her eyes were lined with heavy kohl, but beneath the elegant fashion even I could see that her face had a haggardness to it, an age beyond her years. The hungry lines of her cheekbones and the sunken sockets of her eyes only made her look more commanding.

The chairs had been removed from the stage, and Ramona raised her arms from her sides, as if beckoning to us. "Death," she said in a husky, mannish voice that carried to the back of the auditorium, "is the final act. The final obscenity of our short, pointless lives. The brutality that ends it all. Or so we are told."

I felt James go very still.

"What have you been told?" Ramona lifted her chin. "That you must do good deeds, and you'll be rewarded in the afterlife? That angels watch over your soul? That you must pray to God, and read his book, to gain entry to heaven? That if"—her voice seemed to catch for a moment—"you went to war for your King and country, you would die a *good* death? A *proper* death? Is that it?"

The room was silent. I could hear James breathing.

Ramona lowered her hands again. She almost seemed to be swaying. "You have been lied to, all of you. By your country, by your religion. By your teachers, by your parents. By everyone. Death is not beautiful; it is brutal. Beyond life is only a wasteland, where souls wander in pain. The devil is coming for you. He is coming for me. He is coming for *everyone*."

There were a few quiet gasps in the audience, and one shocked sob.

"Get to the show!" one of the drunk men shouted. The tension cracked. I turned instinctively and looked at the hard-eyed man with the mustache, the one I'd guessed was a plant. He was frowning at the stage, but he sensed my gaze and looked at me. I looked away.

Beside me, James let out a breath. "Hell," he said. "This doesn't sound like a script. She's improvising."

I turned back to the stage. "Who disbelieves?" Ramona cried now, her raspy voice cracking. "Which of you fools still believes in a happy afterlife, in heaven and hell? That you'll be judged by your worth after death, that it is not just random biology that makes us who we are? Who here wants to summon the dead from their icy graves?"

The plant did not speak. Instead, a voice came from the other side of the theater.

"Take me!" it shouted. "Use me!"

It was one of the drunken men. He leapt from his seat, tears streaming down his leathered face. When Ramona blinked slowly at him, surprised, he called to her: "You're wrong, you cow. I know my Sam is happy. You call on him and you ask him, if you even can."

Ramona took a step and her gait wobbled. Perhaps she was upset, or perhaps she'd had a few drinks herself before the show. "Yes," she said to the man. "I can summon him. Just close your eyes and let me try."

I glanced at the mustached man again, but he was gone. The seat was empty.

The man in the audience closed his eyes, but his friends were jeering.

"Think of the person you wish to speak to," Ramona said over the noise. "Call to him. Give me your hands."

James flinched next to me. "What the hell?" he said.

"What?" I couldn't take my eyes from Ramona, wondering what she would do. "What is it?"

"That's how Gloria did it. In her séances. She would have people call to their loved ones while holding her hands."

I blinked. Ramona would never have attended Gloria's séances; Davies would never have allowed it. There was a faint noise somewhere up in the balcony, where no one was sitting. I twisted in my seat to look.

"Just think," Ramona said to the inebriated man again. She had approached the edge of the stage and held out her hands, but the man in the audience stayed where he was. "Let the one you love hear you calling and—"

Something flew through the air and landed on the stage. A man's shoe. It missed Ramona but caught the edge of her skirt on its downward arc, brushing the side of her leg and tumbling onto the stage.

Ramona broke her concentration and looked around, her gait stumbling again. There must have been a signal somewhere backstage, for just in that moment the curtain fell, the lights went down, and the houselights slowly came back up. The piano player was gone. All was silence.

There were a few jeers, but something about the finality of it affected the crowd. They rose from their seats and began to file from the room, some of them grumbling, some of them dazed.

James gave a low whistle. "Well," he said, still in his seat. "That wasn't bad. It was fake, but it wasn't bad." When I didn't respond, he said, "Ellie, what is it?"

"I don't know," I replied. I was still sitting turned in my chair, looking up into the balcony. The lights were on and the balcony was empty, just as it had been during the show.

But someone had been there. As the lights had come up unexpectedly, I'd glimpsed a shadow of someone exiting, a dark figure who slipped from the balcony in silence. Someone who had been watching the whole time.

# CHAPTER THIRTEEN

We made our way through the thickening rain, from the Gild Theatre—where the thin crowd, exiting, quickly dispersed—down a succession of side streets, our steps clicking softly on the empty pavements. James led the way. He had taken me under his umbrella again, and in the intermittent light of the passing lamps his face was in grim shadow beneath the brim of his hat. I leaned into his familiar scent of shaving soap and damp wool, relieved to have him with me in the dark.

He pulled a watch from his pocket with his free hand as we walked, tilting it under a lamp to check it. "The séance isn't scheduled to begin until eleven o'clock," he said, "but something tells me she'll be early."

I shuddered, and not just with damp cold. I didn't particularly want to attend one of Ramona's private séances, not after that show, which had left me both depressed and strangely frightened. But there was no help for it; we had agreed to see Ramona in person to try to question her. I needed to hear for myself her account of Gloria's death.

Soon we were on the street that I recognized as Ramona's. James stopped us under an awning, lowering the umbrella and checking his watch again. I turned and realized we stood in front of the wig shop I'd noticed on my first visit here. Dummy heads stared vacantly at me from the darkened window, adorned with Renaissance tresses, eighteenth-century Marie Antoinette curls, and modern pageboys. CLOSING PERMANENTLY, announced a sign on the door. I peered at the handwritten page attached beneath it and read:

> I am Retiring
> My only son died in the War and I have no one to
> take over the Shop
> Closing permanently end of month
> Thank You for your Patronage

"There are others waiting," came James's voice. "At the door to Ramona's block of flats. Let's go see who our fellow seekers are, shall we?"

I pulled myself reluctantly away and followed him. Four people huddled on the stoop where I'd stood two days before, a man and three women. James lifted the umbrella and nodded at the small knot of people as we approached. "Good evening," he said.

The man peered up at him. He was fortyish, with a face that sagged with premature age and, I thought, some saddening grief. "She hasn't let us in yet."

"When will she begin?" James asked.

"When she's recovered from that disgrace of a show," one of the women said.

The younger woman who was with her, obviously the woman's daughter, huddled under the umbrella and nodded her head. "It's always a challenge when disbelievers are present," she said. "I imagine she has to refocus herself in order to be able to contact the spirits."

"What show?" said the man. "I didn't know of any show. I just came here for the spirit session."

"I hope there are to be no more of us," the older woman said, ignoring him. She gave James and me a disapproving look. "Six is plenty. Any more would ruin the session."

Perhaps, but six paying customers was a half-decent take for an evening.

The young woman, who looked about nineteen, peered curiously at me through the rain. "What are you here for?"

"Hush," her mother said. "There should be no talking amongst the attendees."

"I'm paying my money," the saddened man said a little loudly. "I say I can talk to whomever I please."

"Do you want to ruin it all for us?" the woman hissed at him. "It upsets the spirits. She'll send us all home, and then where will we be?"

The man went silent and looked away.

The door opened and Ramona appeared. She had washed off her stage makeup and reapplied the kohl around her eyes. She was dressed in a silk wrapper, with strings of beads layered around her neck. She looked calm, as if the debacle at the stage show had never happened. She wasn't even wet from the rain. I wondered how she had traveled from the theater so quickly, and how we hadn't crossed her on our way. "Enter," she said, and turned away.

We followed her through the dreary vestibule and into the grim lobby. Ramona ascended the stairs, her wrapper luminous in the halflight, and I was glad we didn't have to take the elevator. The sad man ascended after her first, followed by the girl and her mother, and finally an elderly woman who had not yet spoken. I held back, James at my elbow.

"Are you all right?" he said softly.

The yawning shadows at the top of the stairs swallowed Ramona, and then the others, one by one.

"I'm fine," I said, and started after them.

Ramona's silk-clad form reached the fourth floor and opened the door to her flat, beckoning us all in. She was strikingly underdressed in the wrapper, her body narrow and bony beneath it, and up close her face was strangely haggard, yet attractive, under its makeup. Her gaze skimmed indifferently over me as I passed her, then fixed on James with considerably more prurient interest.

The flat was small, the electric light dim, and the main feature was a séance table—shabbier than Gloria's, perhaps, but undoubtedly meant for the same purpose. It was impossible to tell at first glance where the contraptions, strings, and pulleys were hidden, but I had no doubt they were there. A small kitchen with yellowed linoleum lay through one door, and a second closed door presumably led to the bedroom. I had a brief, disturbing memory of standing in the hallway outside the door to this flat the day before, listening to the silence and wondering whether Ramona was dead. I sat hurriedly at the séance table with the others and pushed the recollection away.

When we were seated, Ramona switched off the electric light and set a candle in the middle of the séance table. She struck a match and lit the candle, and when she lifted the match to her face to blow it out, I noticed her pupils were shrunk to small points. I gasped in a breath. Not drink, surely. Some kind of drug, perhaps?

She stood facing us in the candlelight, still on her feet. She seemed to look us over for a moment. I glanced around the circle: the young girl and her mother, the sad man, and the older woman. And James and me. We all sat quiet, waiting. The candle gave off a thick, smoky smell.

"The spirits shall come here tonight," Ramona said. When she wasn't shouting from a theater stage, her voice was low and husky, almost hypnotic. "We shall form a spirit circle. Join hands."

She held out her hands, palms facing the ceiling. The rest of us obeyed. To my right was the young girl; this close, I could see the ruffles on her ill-fitting silk blouse, the sullen turn of her lip, the blotches of acne on her chin and neck. Her hand was plump and clammy in mine.

On my left side was James. He slid his hand in mine with no discernible hesitation, as if unconcerned about what I might see. He did not look at me.

"Now close your eyes and concentrate," said Ramona. "Speak to the spirits. Listen. I am your conduit. I am nothing but a vessel, built between this world and the next. Send your messages through the circle, through me. The spirits will seek my power and come."

Everyone closed their eyes. Ramona lowered her lids and flung her head back, as if listening to a signal from the other side; it was a timeworn trick, and she did it well. A medium who closes her eyes and throws her head back can watch the table from under her lashes and gauge facial expressions and body language—the priceless currency of the sham artist.

I watched her for a moment, then closed my own eyes. If Ramona had any skill, she would identify me immediately as a threat and attempt to contain me, probably through the communication of the spirits. But if her brain was muddled by drugs, I had no idea what she would do.

I waited. The scent from the candle on the table was pungent and strange, and in a split second I suddenly knew that the young girl who held my hand was named Rose, and that she did not seek any spirit in particular. She had come here for answers, because she was dying. She had a sickness—some sort of family illness, the name of which did not come to me—that would kill her within a year. Something about the dark, the candle, the spirit circle made my powers receptive, and I focused on controlling them, on shutting out messages, especially from James on my left hand.

"The spirits are restless tonight," Ramona said.

The smell of the candle was strong in my nose. What sort of candle gave off a smell like that? If it was a trick, it was one I'd never heard of. Washes of emotion came to me from the circle—fear, anger, blackest grief. I inhaled a breath and sweat trickled down my back, cold and damp. *Keep it under control, Ellie.*

A low moan arose from the table, deep and eerie, barely a human sound. The hairs rose on the nape of my neck. I opened my eyes to see that Ramona had slackened in her chair, her head slumped back. I could see the whites of her eyes in the slits of her eyelids.

"*I have awoken,*" she said, her voice pitched at a low tenor, like a man's. "*Who has called me? Who calls?*"

Someone gasped. "What is your name?" This was Rose's mother, gripping her daughter's hand tightly and leaning forward into the circle. "Can you tell us?"

"*I remember not who I was in your world,*" Ramona replied in her spirit voice. "*I lived many thousands of years ago, under the hot desert sun far from here. My body is gone, but I remain. When my spirit guide calls, I awaken. I bring messages from the dead.*"

I calmed a little. I had never seen this particular trick up close before, though I had often heard of it. Many spirit mediums claimed to have a specific spirit they spoke to most often, who acted as their conduit to the other side. I'd heard of such spirits guised as ancient princesses, Indian chieftains, even aristocrats killed during the French Revolution. It sounded like this one was supposed to be from ancient Egypt, perhaps. James squeezed my fingers once, lightly and quickly, the equivalent of a wink. He'd likely seen this trick dozens of times.

"We wish to communicate," Rose's mother said, excitement in her voice. She had easily taken over the session, and I wondered briefly whether she was a plant. If so, her daughter was unaware of it. "We welcome you and your messages. We are listening."

"*There is a message from one who has departed and left his wife behind.*" Ramona moaned. "*He watches over her.*"

The silent old woman made a choked noise. That was an easy one, I thought: elderly woman, who attends alone. Very likely a widow, the spirit medium's bread and butter. The noise she'd just made had given away that Ramona was on the mark.

"*My good and faithful wife,*" Ramona said, pressing her advantage.

"*We will not be parted much longer. I will hold you in my arms again within the year.*"

"Oh," came a strangled sound from the old woman's throat. Her face sagged. I watched her expression closely in the candlelight. She looked stricken, but not surprised. Ramona was telling her something she already knew.

The smell of the candle, I thought, was positively putrid. Had no one else noticed? I breathed lightly through my mouth, but the smoky smell was so thick it almost had a taste. The emotions at the table roiled in my stomach like nausea.

"What other messages do you bring us tonight?" urged Rose's mother.

Ramona's head lolled back and she moaned as if in pain. I felt a breath of air on my neck, and from somewhere in the center of the table came three quick, staccato raps.

"Speak!" cried Rose's mother. "Oh, please, speak to us!"

The sad man, across from me, spoke up. "Oh, be quiet!" he said to her. "You're ruining it. What about me? I've been calling. I don't want to hear about some stranger's dead husband. I paid my money. What about me?"

My stomach turned again. My attention shifted to the man and I felt the familiar itch at the back of my skull. It was coming from him, grief and rage, like a smell. I pulled my gaze away from him and glanced at James. He was tensed in his chair, his body flexed, his face scowling as the argument grew louder. The light, flickering down the line of his throat, seemed to be sliding its fingers under his collar.

"Be quiet, you selfish man," Rose's mother said.

"Mama, please," whined Rose.

"I paid my money and I want answers," the man nearly shouted, making the old widow next to him jump. "I mean it. I want to see—"

"*Silence.*"

Ramona had straightened her shoulders, though her head was

still lolling against the back of her chair, her eyes still rolled back in her head. As we watched, startled, she shifted slowly, her head sliding like a half-animated thing until it rested sideways on one shoulder. She looked, in that position, uncannily like a woman whose neck had been snapped.

Still she used the low, mannish voice. *"There is one other at this table,"* she said, her lips the only part of her to move, *"who death comes for. Someone here will be dead before the year is out."*

There was a beat of silence. I felt Rose's fingers flinch in mine, her breath hitch. *"Death knocks,"* Ramona said, and as she spoke the raps sounded on the table again, hard and angry. *"Death comes for someone in this room, someone who will not escape it. The spirits warn me. Death has its hand on someone's throat."*

"Stop," I said.

There was a cold beat of silence and everyone looked at me— everyone except Ramona, who stayed unmoving in her uncanny position. If she'd heard me, she gave no sign of it.

Beside me, I could feel Rose quietly convulsing her breath, near to hysterical sobbing. "Just stop," I said to Ramona, though she gave no indication she knew I was there. "You're scaring—" I remembered I wasn't supposed to know that Rose was dying. "You're scaring all of us." I forced the words out. I took my hand from James's grip and ran it over my forehead, which was chilled with sweat. "You should leave, all of you," I said. "Someone is coming and I don't think I can stop it."

"What are you talking about?" said Rose's mother. She squinted hard at me. "Who are you?"

"Are you one of them?" The sad man was staring at me, his bottomless gaze devouring me in its pain. "You can call them, too, can't you? I can see it. Give me your hand." He dropped the hands he was holding and lunged across the table, grabbing for me, but another hand came down hard on his wrist, pinning it.

"I'd think twice about that," James said in a low, dangerous voice.

I leaned back in my chair, dropping Rose's hand. "Please," I said
to the man as his grief hit me again. Or perhaps it was the smell of
the candle; I could no longer tell. The itch was bad now, a crawling
sensation under my scalp. "You must leave. Sometimes, when they
come . . . it's better they didn't. Sometimes—"

But then the room dropped away, and there was only the dark,
and the pinpoint of candlelight, and my breath rasping in my lungs.
And sitting across from me was a woman.

She made no sound. She wore a high-necked blouse and skirt in
the fashion of ten years ago, her light hair tied back in a bun. She
looked perhaps twenty. She stared at me, her eyes large in her pale
dead face, her form flickering in the candlelight, yet somehow waxy
and real. She held a small child in her arms, its face pressed to her
chest, the delicate curls of its hair the same color as hers.

Voices carried on around me, far away. I stared at the gaunt curve
of the woman's cheek, the long fingers pressed into the baby's back.
Her gaze on me held a consuming hunger that made my stomach
turn again. The child's feet dangled past the curve of her elbow, slack
in their tiny shoes. It could have been a boy or a girl; it was so small,
in a simple baby's dress and a delicate dusting of curls, it was impossible to tell which. One of its arms rested against the waist of her
skirt, pinned between the child's body and hers. She held the small
body tightly to her, unmoving.

Behind me, a creak of wood. A rapping on the table. A breath of
air blowing. The other participants were shadows, their lips moving,
but I heard nothing. A slow, deep arch of pain made its way up the
back of my skull.

I mustered myself. *Go,* I said to the woman. *Go. Not now.*

She only stared at me, avid and wanting, the baby clutched to her.

*Go!* I commanded. It wasn't working, and my own power was
slipping from my grasp, like something warm and slimy and wet. I
had been trained since that day when I was seven to keep my power

under strict control, but all of that was gone now and I felt only monstrous panic as I tried harder and harder to grip it. *Go away!*

Her hands moved on the child, slid eerily over its back. It lay with its face buried in its mother's chest, unmoving and still. More raps sounded on the séance table and the draft on the back of my neck meant a door had moved. *This is the worst kind of visitation,* I heard my mother's voice say. *The kind that comes of its own volition, the kind that cannot be controlled by a medium. They are malignant and must not be allowed through.* This woman had no message to give, only pain that I felt like an echo through my body. Tears stung my eyes.

"It isn't going to move, is it?" I said. "The baby."

"What?" I heard the sad man's voice clearly over the rushing in my ears. "What did you say?"

I summoned my strength. The only way to get rid of a visitation like this was to convince it to leave if you could. "I'm sorry about your baby," I choked, a sob in my voice. "I'm sorry. Please leave."

*"What did you say?"*

"Come any closer," came James's voice, "and I'll lay you out. I mean it."

The woman did not seem to see anyone in the room; still she stared at me, and again her hands moved over the child's back. The expression in her waxy eyes seemed to shift, like ink that has had water spilled on it. Her mouth moved.

I jerked my hands up and jammed my palms over my ears. "No!" I shouted. "Please!"

*"Is that my Alice?"* the man cried, and the woman's lips opened, revealing a blurry set of awful teeth, a black pit of a mouth. She gripped her baby, her eyes gone mad, and screamed, a sound of unearthly agony that split through my brain. The stench was unbearable, the sound a high keen. I opened my mouth to scream over it, to drown it out, but the woman leaned over the table, her face gray and dead in mine, her baby dead in her arms, and then the candle went out.

The scream stopped. I sagged in my chair, my hands still over my ears. A strong hand gripped my upper arm in the dark, warm and certain.

"Ellie," came James's voice.

The rushing sound vanished, and through my hands I could hear a flurry of voices—outrage, confusion, fear. Rose was sobbing, her face pressed into her handkerchief, her shoulders heaving as her mother soothed her. The sad man was shouting, glaring at James. The old widow had pushed her chair back and was staggering from the room, ghastly and silent. And Ramona had come out of her trance and was laughing in a throaty voice, a sound vicious and heartless and utterly without humor. James stared into my face, his concern overlaid with a mask of pure horror as he looked at me. I dashed the tears from my eyes. The woman had gone, taken her dead child and vanished into whatever hellish place she had come from.

The séance was over.

# CHAPTER FOURTEEN

Ramona sat at her séance table, lighting a cigarette. The other guests had left and the electric lights had been turned on, highlighting the bleary pallor of her face under the makeup. "That was quite a show," she admitted to me in a tired voice. "I should have had them come see you instead. At least everyone paid me up front."

"Everyone always pays up front," I said automatically.

She raised a penciled eyebrow at me. I sat opposite her in one of the séance chairs as James prowled the room around us and poked and prodded the table legs. "You're in the business, then. Come to steal my clients, did you?"

"No." I reached across the table without asking and flicked open her cigarette holder. Ramona's cigarettes were a brand I didn't recognize, narrow and dark with a smoky smell. I picked up her matches and lit one as she watched.

"Have we met?" she said finally, her tone unimpressed.

I took a drag of the cigarette—it sent a plume of pungent flavor down the back of my throat—and shrugged. The horror of what I'd seen was slowly falling away from me and my professional armor was starting to work. The panicked sensation of my powers slipping away from me was fading, along with the headache. As long as I did not think about that woman's baby, I would be fine. "My name is Ellie Winter."

"The Fantastique?" Ramona rolled her eyes, angry and trying to hide it. She hunched her narrow shoulders farther forward under their flimsy wrap. "And what about your handsome friend here? He looks like police to me."

"I take offense to that," James said, straightening from the crouching position he'd assumed under the table. "I'm not nearly competent enough for the police. I'm from the New Society."

Ramona glared at him, her pinpointed pupils seething with sudden hatred. "You," she said to him, my presence forgotten. "You are utter scum."

"And you are a disappointment," James replied, placing one hand flat on the table and leaning forward. "Two of the table legs are hollow, you have a pedal under each foot, and there's an electric fan set up to be tripped by a switch over the doorway."

That explained the table knocks and the uncanny breeze. Ramona spat at him like a cat. "I'm just trying to make a living. Go away and get out of my business."

"Not until you answer some questions," James replied.

"About what?"

"Gloria Sutter," I broke in.

Ramona turned at the sound of my voice and I watched her try to think through her chemical haze. Emotions crossed her face, frustration and anger and some kind of choking fear. "You think I killed her?"

I held her gaze. "Did you?"

She took a drag of her cigarette, and I admired how she summoned her composure. "I hated her, of course," she said. She lifted her gaze to me. "But then, so did you. Everyone knew you were rivals."

I blinked, surprised, and then I glanced at James. He shook his head. "Where did you hear that?" I asked her. "Did Gloria tell you?"

Ramona rolled her eyes. "Darling, I've been in this business longer than you think. I hear things. All about The Fantastique, and Gloria Sutter, and how they used to be friends cutting up London. How Gloria had your mother declared a fraud. How you've hated each other ever since. Which means I cannot figure out why—no matter how good-looking he is—you would associate with the likes of *him*." She gestured violently toward James with her ashy cigarette.

"I'm irresistible," James said easily.

"You prey on the likes of me," Ramona shot back. "You have no mercy."

"I have as much mercy as you had for those poor grieving people tonight," James said, "as well as everyone in the audience at your stage show."

"How much money did you lose?" I asked her as she furiously ground out the stub of her smoke. I doused my own, half smoked. "I assume the theater wouldn't give you your share of the ticket take after that display."

"Philistines," Ramona said in disgust.

"What happened that night?" James pressed her. "At the Dubbses'. What did you see?"

Ramona sat sullen for a moment, and when she spoke, her voice was bitter. "Not much. None of them wanted me there, but that was just too bad. I went anyway. We waited around—the marks seemed to be waiting for something. I got drunk as quickly as I could. The marks were clueless—I almost felt sorry for them, except they were shady types themselves."

I sat up. I hadn't heard this before. "The Dubbses were shady?"

"It's a feeling you get, you know?" Ramona shrugged and looked away. "It takes one to know one, I suppose. All I know is that something about that house was all wrong. I would have backed out, but by then I was drunk and there was no way home."

"All right," James said. "So you didn't like the Dubbses. And you were drinking. Then what happened?"

Ramona closed her eyes briefly and touched her fingertips to her forehead. "God," she said. "I told the police everything, over and over, but they wouldn't leave me alone. This is a bloody nightmare." She dropped her hand and shifted in her chair, uncomfortable. "You two have to leave."

I glanced at James, but he stood unmoving. He did not speak.

Ramona looked at us for another moment, then threw up her hands dramatically, the sleeves of her wrapper flapping. "God, I don't know. Gloria said she had to get some air, and she left."

"If you weren't invited, how did you know the séance was happening?" I asked.

"Figure it out if you can," she said, baring her teeth at me in a grin. "You just try it, darling—try not being able to pay the rent, wondering where the next meal is coming from. Try living on the few pennies I scrounge up and see whether you wait for a polite invitation. My guess is that you'll follow the money, just like I did. I was sick of hearing about the great Gloria Sutter, the irreplaceable Gloria Sutter. I wanted a piece of her, and I would have done anything to get it."

James had rounded the séance table while she was speaking, and now he looked down at her, his gaze on the pinpoint pupils of her eyes. "It isn't food you need," he said, almost gently. "It's money for your next fix. The stage shows and the séances don't earn enough to buy what you're taking. Where do you get the money, Ramona?"

She only smiled up at him, and in that moment I could see the girl who had run away from home only to see her dreams of becoming an actress fall apart in bitter failure. Ramona was a survivor, even if the act of surviving was itself grim, and she no longer knew what she did it for. "Are you asking if I'm for sale?" she asked. "Name a price, handsome, and I'll consider it."

I pushed my chair back and rose. My head was throbbing and I couldn't stand it anymore in this awful little flat, with its close air and shabby furniture. "There's no point, James," I said. "Let's go."

I had just reached the door when Ramona stopped me, leaning a hand on the doorframe. Up close, under the electric light, I saw that her forehead was damp. A single bead of sweat trickled down her throat to the neck of her wrapper. Her body sagged slightly, as if she fought off pain. "You," she said to me. "You saw something tonight, something real. Don't lie to me."

I shrugged, not wanting her to get her teeth into how it had upset me. "Perhaps."

"Such power," she said softly, and even through the ache of craving her next fix, her voice carried a note of wonder. "You're truly The Fantastique, then. You can see the dead, just like she could."

I put my hand on the arm that blocked me; it was chilled through the thin fabric of her sleeve. "Let me leave."

"It isn't going to help you, you know," Ramona said, and for a second I saw the woman I'd seen onstage, eerily commanding and pitiful at the same time. Her bleary eyes were half mad with fear, and for a second they reminded me of the inkblot eyes of the dead woman I'd seen. "Your power. It won't help you—not with this. You have no idea what you're dealing with."

"Then tell me," I said.

She only laughed and pulled her arm away from the door. "The devil is coming," she called after us as we retreated down the hallway to the stairs. "He's coming for you. He's coming for me. He's coming for all of us."

I sat on the front stoop of Ramona's building, the night's chill seeping through the layers of my skirt and coat. The rain had stopped and the darkened street looked slick as a mirror, the few streetlights reflecting in yellow pools. It was late and the street was empty. I tilted my head back, breathing in the damp air and the pungent smell of rainy pavement.

James lowered himself next to me, his body large beside mine. He set his forearms on his knees. He moved with a grace that was physically uncanny; I wouldn't have been surprised if he could climb walls.

"What exactly did you see in there?" he asked.

I sighed. "James Hawley," I said, letting the name circle on my tongue. "James Hawley wants to know what I saw."

"He does," James agreed.

"Will this go into a report for the New Society?"

He looked away, his jaw tightening. "I thought we'd moved past that."

*I cannot figure out,* Ramona had said, *why you would associate with the likes of him.* Perhaps she was right, and he couldn't be trusted. The problem was that I could think of no one else to tell.

"The man at the séance," I said. "His child died. And his wife . . ." I slid my arms around my knees and hugged them. "She killed herself, I think. At least, it's possible. It's difficult to tell."

He was very still, and turned toward me. I knew he was looking at me but I could not look back. "What is it like?" he said at last. "Seeing the dead."

An old woman walked by, huddled into a thick coat, her footsteps splashing through the reflected lamplight on the street. "Like plunging your hand into a bucket of worms in the dark," I said. "Except it's inside your mind. It's repellent, and cold, and you don't know what you're touching because you can't see—you don't know what it looks like, and you don't want to know."

"Jesus, Ellie," James said. I turned to him to find his face stark in the harsh lamplight. "Gloria did that for a living."

"So did my mother," I said.

*So do I.*

He looked tired, but a curious light lit his eyes. "I have so many questions."

"I have no answers. At least, no one ever gave them to me." I watched the shaky reflections of light on the street as I spoke. It was far past midnight, I realized. "I don't know why I have the powers I have, or what they mean. I don't know if there is anyone else like me anywhere else in the world right now—or how many there have been in history."

"None," James interjected flatly. "Not in this country, at least, except for Gloria. I can tell you that firsthand."

I shrugged. "I only know who I am, and that with my mother and Gloria dead I'm alone."

He seemed to ponder this, picking through the questions he wanted to ask. "Can you see the future?"

"No. My mother taught me that seeing the future isn't possible, that no one can do it. She never told me how she knew." I fought down the lump in my throat. "There were a lot of things she didn't tell me, a lot of things I didn't ask."

"When you see the dead, do they see you?"

"Yes." I chose my words, tried to explain it. "I think they see me only vaguely, through a veil. But yes, they see something."

"Do they speak?"

I thought of the woman screaming, and suppressed a shudder. "Not exactly. There is usually some strong emotion, which I pick up. And I pick up words, images. But they don't speak in sentences." I was tired myself, and I didn't want to talk about this anymore. "There's something I want to know about what happened in there."

"All right."

"The old woman. How did Ramona know she was dying?"

James raised an eyebrow. "Are you asking if Ramona is psychic?"

"No, though I admit her act is a good one. If I didn't know better, I'd be fooled." It mustn't have been easy to hold the pose with her head bent to her shoulder for so long; it would take practice and determination. "But if we agree that Ramona is a skimmer, how did she know that the widow will be dead within a year? She was right—I could see it on the woman's face."

"So could I. All Ramona needed was the woman's name and a little advance notice. Then she would have her plant find whatever he could. He could have found out about the illness by following her to the doctor's, or going through her handbag in a café and finding a prescription, or overhearing her at the chemist's. I knew one skimmer who found out everything she needed about her clients by going through their trash bins every week before the dustman came."

It was disgusting, but I could see how it could work. "But the second prediction—when she said someone else in the room was going to die. What about that one?"

James shook his head. "Come now, Ellie. It's the oldest trick in the book—a vague prediction that gets a shock. She may as well have said that someone will cross water, or meet the love of their life." He looked more closely at me. "Are you saying she was right?"

"It must have been a lucky guess."

"The girl," he said, his quick mind putting it together. "She was very upset. I thought you couldn't see the future."

"I didn't have to. She's sick," I replied. "I was holding her hand. I felt it."

"Well, then, Ramona had a lucky shot. I've seen it before." He rubbed a hand over his face. "I have the frustrating feeling we're no further ahead than we were before, and it's one o'clock in the morning."

I was giddy with exhaustion, but it was almost freeing. I had spent three years going to bed at exactly ten o'clock every night, whether I slept or not, atoning in some way for all of the late nights with Gloria. I hadn't seen one o'clock in the morning on the streets of London for a long time. "I didn't choose this line of work," I said to James, almost musing to myself. "But you did."

"In a roundabout way. I was supposed to read for the bar."

I raised my brows, trying to picture it. "A barrister?"

"Yes. It was what my parents wanted, and it was what I wanted; it all lined up. It was the only career I'd thought of having. I was going to be a young, smashing success." He shrugged, his shoulders flexing under his jacket. "Then the war came. Afterward nothing worked the way it was supposed to, including me. When I came back, the law seemed stupid. I was . . . broken." He gazed down the darkened street. "I drank myself into oblivion for a long time. It was a sickness, like a fever. The war didn't leave my head unless I was drunk. My parents disowned me. They expected a barrister son—war or not—not a drunk. And then I was at the veterans' office one day for one of their health tests, and in the waiting room I met Paul."

"The president of the New Society," I said.

"Yes. He'd been an officer, like I had. He took one look at me and said that the New Society needed men like me to help, and he offered me a job."

"Why?" I asked.

"I don't know," he replied. "He says it was because he saw what kind of man I could be once I dried out. Maybe he just saw my desperation and pitied me. I don't think I'll ever know."

I watched his face, and suddenly I was terribly lonely. I wished he would touch me, put his arms around me, with a longing that was almost a physical ache. I wished he would look at me the way he had when he first saw me, the way he had in Trafalgar Square. I wished he would make my blood pulse, make my skin come alive, make me warm. I had spent three years buried, fossilized, feeling nothing. To feel things was painful and terrible, but it was better than being dead. "It's impossible to know, isn't it," I said, "what people see in you?"

He turned his gaze on me, and his understanding slid through my ribs and stabbed my heart. "She liked you, Ellie," he said. "She just didn't exactly know how to show it. Gloria didn't like very many people."

I stood up, brushing at my coat. "That's an interesting theory."

"I'm right."

"I didn't know you were an expert."

"Do I have to be an expert to understand your friendship with Gloria?"

I descended the steps to the street, my feet icy in my shoes. "Who says it was a friendship?"

"Both of you," James said to my back. "Stop fighting it, Ellie."

"I'm going home." I walked down the darkened street, heading for the Streatham High Road to find a taxi. It was too much to feel after three years of being numb: regret, longing, lust, shame, anger. I pulled my coat tighter around me. James did not call after me again, nor did he follow me. He was wrong. Gloria and I had not been friends; we had never been friends.

*Tell Ellie Winter to find me.*

The grief hit me again, as solid as a punch, just as it had that first night in my garden when George Sutter told me she was dead. I made a strange little gasping sound, but I kept walking. My heels clicked on the pavement. And I kept walking until the world had receded into nothing behind me, until all of it was gone.

# CHAPTER FIFTEEN

I first met Gloria Sutter in early 1919, a few months after the war ended. It was still frigid winter, and I was on a train home from Bournemouth, sound asleep in my seat in a compartment by myself.

My mother had given me a few precious days off to visit distant relatives of my father's. My father died in Gallipoli in 1916, and I thought that visiting his relatives would bring me some kind of peace. My mother had known better; still deep in mourning, she had refused to accompany me. I'd made the trip only to find my father's relatives cold, unfriendly, and deep in blame that my father had ever married my mother at all. The entire thing was exhausting and depressing, and almost as soon as I'd embarked on the trip home, the train swaying rhythmically, I'd pulled my muffler up around my neck and fallen asleep.

When I opened my eyes, there was a girl sitting across from me, watching me.

She was about nineteen, my own age, and the first thing I noticed, almost with a pang of dismay, was that she was utterly beautiful. Her black raven's wing hair was cut in a marcelled bob, a new fashion my own mother had strictly forbidden, and her big dark eyes were ringed with skillfully applied makeup. The effect of her was sophisticated and roughly sensual at the same time, and when she saw my eyes open she gave me a sly smile, as if I'd just done something clever.

"Oh, hullo," she said.

I rubbed my eyes, taking in her pretty kidskin gloves and the expensive fur collar of her coat. "Sorry," I said, the word automatic and pointless in my mouth, not feeling clever at all.

The girl shrugged knowingly, as if I'd made a joke, the smile still twisting her lips. "Would you like a cigarette?"

Another thing I'd never been allowed. "No, thank you."

"Come on, now." The girl had taken two cigarettes from a case and she held one out to me. "I hate to smoke alone."

I sat up. The girl's eyes were hypnotically dark, almost black, and I had my first premonition that she was, in some way, not quite normal. "I'm not allowed."

"Under Daddy's thumb, are you?" she said.

I flushed and took the cigarette. The girl lit a match for me, and I took a drag, trying not to cough in front of her. I waved a hand through the smoke in the air as an unfamiliar feeling buzzed through my brain, as if someone was rubbing my scalp. "My father is dead," I said, trying to sound worldly and casual.

"Jolly good," said the girl. "That just means more freedom." She rose and went to the door of the compartment, opening it a crack and peeking out as she took another effortless drag on her cig. Her legs, I noticed, were long and elegant under her dress. "Did you see the dark-haired man a few compartments down? The one in the cashmere coat?"

I was still numbly working through the fact that she'd said my father's death was jolly good. "What?"

"I think he noticed me."

Since she wasn't looking at me, I dropped my pretense with the cigarette and just stared at her. I was starting to feel as if someone had spun me in circles. I frowned, recalling the man she was talking about. "He's thirty, at least! And he had a pipe!"

"Men with cashmere coats and pipes have money," the girl said. She glanced at my shocked face and rolled her eyes. "I don't mean *that*, you know. Even though he's passably good-looking. I meant that men with money make good clients."

"Clients?"

She shut the compartment door and leaned a shoulder casually on it, putting the cigarette to her lips again, and said nothing.

"What?" I said, growing more alarmed as the silence stretched. "What is it?"

"Hush," the girl replied, the corner of her mouth curving. "I'm enjoying this."

"Enjoying what?" I was starting to think fondly of the chilly nap I'd just taken.

"Watching you work it out. It's all over your face, you know. The word 'client' has thrown you off. Am I one of those bad girls your mother warned you about, do you think? Or does the word 'client' mean something else?"

I swallowed in bewilderment. Of course the word "client" had meaning for me; it was part of my profession. What was this girl getting at? "I don't—"

"Oh, come now." She noticed the cigarette still in her fingers, took a last drag, and smothered it in an ashtray. "I know you just woke up, but think a little harder. Do you know who I am? Because I know who *you* are. It took me a moment to figure it out, but I saw the name when I looked into the compartment." She pointed to my valise, which I had placed on the seat next to me, clearly marked in my mother's careful hand with the word WINTER. "You look like her," the girl said, "and I know she has a daughter."

"Who has a daughter?"

"The Fantastique, of course." She took in the expression on my face and smiled again.

"All right," I said. "I'll play along. I'm Ellie Winter. Who are you?"

"Gloria Sutter," she said, holding out a gloved hand. "We're in the same business."

I had never heard the name and I didn't know what she meant, but in an automatic reaction I took her hand in mine. And in that second, even though we were both wearing gloves, I knew.

Something extraordinary crossed the depths of Gloria Sutter's eyes when our hands touched. For a long moment, her air of sophistication disappeared, and her expression was raw and almost hungry. Then she let out a long breath and a sound that was almost a laugh, a shrill exclamation of excitement that exactly mirrored the feeling that was jumping through my body.

"My God," she said. "This just got interesting. When this train stops, we're going for a drink."

I wasn't supposed to do it, of course. My mother was expecting me home. But after I'd felt what I felt when I took Gloria's hand, I could no more have walked away from her than I could have walked on the moon. After a lifetime of being strange, of being alienated from everyone except for my mother, I had met someone who *knew*.

I found myself in Soho, following Gloria to her studio flat. I eyed the Home for Fallen Women on the corner half in suspicion, wondering whether it swallowed up girls who didn't do what their mothers told them, girls who followed other girls they'd just met into seedy London neighborhoods.

The ground-floor psychic's shop was shuttered; this was the woman, Gloria told me, who only inhabited the place when she came up with money to pay the rent. OUR PRECIOUS BOYS DO NOT DIE, a hand-lettered sign in the window read. THEY WISH TO SPEAK TO US. I

forced my gaze away; my mother and I had been inundated with
mourning women for the past four years. Widows and bereaved
mothers were a medium's largest pool of clients, and the war had
created a boom. *Tell me my son is happy. Tell me he did not suffer. Tell
me he thought of his mother before he died. Tell me. Tell me.*

At the first-floor landing, Gloria put a finger to her lips and motioned for me to be quiet, as if she wished to avoid someone. It didn't
work. As we passed, the first-floor door popped open and a mannish
woman poked her head out. "You're late," she said, turning her suspicious eyes on me. "Who's this?"

"Davies, dear, this is a friend of mine."

The woman's look of shock was unmistakable. "The hell she is.
Who is she really?"

"A bosom sister," replied Gloria. "A fly in my web. A deadly rival.
I'm in love with her and I've decided to give up men."

Davies's eyes narrowed as I gaped at Gloria in openmouthed
shock. "Am I supposed to pick one of those?" she grumbled. "Or
none of them?"

"Whatever you like."

"God, you're being difficult again. Is it your time of month?"

Again, I stared openmouthed.

"Perhaps, sweetheart," Gloria said. "You'd know better than I,
wouldn't you? You keep the schedule, after all."

"Fine." Davies threw her hands in the air in frustration. "I can't
deal with you when you're in this mood. I'm only trying to tell you
that Number Thirty-One wants to see you at seven."

"Tell Number Thirty-One I am indisposed." Gloria hefted her
valise and turned to continue up the stairs, her legs flashing before
me as I scrambled to follow. "Ellie and I have things to discuss."

Once in her flat, Gloria dropped her handbag and coat in a mess
and disappeared behind the thin curtain of her bedroom. I stared at
my surroundings, at the clothes spilling from the wardrobe, the

mermaid painting on the wall. She lived alone here, I realized. No mother, no flatmates. Gloriously alone, like a man. I eyed the séance table. "Who is Number Thirty-One?"

"A client," came Gloria's voice from behind the curtain. "They expect complete privacy, so Davies and I assign them numbers, just in case."

"You really do this for a living?" I asked, tugging off a glove and touching the séance table. It vibrated under my hand, as if attached to an electrical wire. I pulled my hand away.

A hand came up and pulled the bedroom curtain aside. Gloria had shed her skirt and blouse and now wore a sleeveless dress of midnight black, belted just above the hips. Her body was long, sleek, and slender, with a narrow waist and breasts that sat high and round under the bodice. The hem of the dress swept down just past the knee, and I could see her stockings and high heels. It was a shocking length for 1919. Over the next few years, I would watch Gloria's hemlines rise even faster than London fashion allowed.

"Darling," she said, something steely flashing across her eyes, "I not only do this for a living, but I'm the best there is."

"And you know my mother?"

"Not personally, no. But I know who she is, just like I know about every skimmer and showgirl between here and Calais. I make it my business to know about my competition."

The idea of my mother, who almost never left the house, competing with this girl made me laugh out loud. "What did you do, hire an investigator to look in our windows? You can't possibly be serious."

Gloria's eyes narrowed and she raised one penciled eyebrow, an extraordinary expression that was both witty and menacing. "I assure you, I'm serious," she replied. "It isn't personal, but I'm afraid I'm rather competitive. Even that hag on the ground floor is competition. I steal most of her clients, by the way. That's why she can't pay the rent."

I rubbed the palms of my hands together, trying to get rid of the lingering sensation from the séance table. "All right. It just seems rather bloodthirsty to me."

"I'm a girl on my own, darling. I pay the bills myself, and I keep myself in lipstick and heels. Are you telling me that The Fantastique isn't in business to make money?"

"Of course she is," I said. "If she didn't take clients, she'd be doing char work, especially since my father died. But people are grieving, and there are frauds everywhere. We— My mother means to help people."

"How noble." Gloria moved to a side table, picked up her cigarette case, and turned it over in the long fingers of one hand, the silver glinting in the dim electric light. "Nothing I do helps people. It only makes them worse." She raised her eyes to me. "How surprised do you think I am that The Fantastique has passed her talents on to her daughter?"

I thought of the sensation I felt when we'd shaken hands, and my cheeks flushed. Even though I lived with my mother, there was so much I didn't know, so much I couldn't ask her. I was desperate for answers. "How long have you known?" I asked Gloria. "About yourself, I mean. How early did you know what you could do?"

"Almost from the beginning," she said. "My family hates me. If I lived four hundred years ago, I'd be burned already. As it is, my family thinks I'm a liar and a tart."

She said the words with such calmness that my heart jumped in my throat, and I asked the question that burned inside me, that kept me awake at night. "Doesn't it bother you?" I asked her. "Seeing the dead? Don't you ever want to stop?"

Gloria tilted her head. "And do what?"

"Tell fortunes. Read palms," I said. Both were impossible, and therefore a lie—according to my mother—but sometimes I thought that lying would be better than telling those grieving women the truth. "Anything but endure those visions—the dead."

Gloria's gaze had gone curiously still as she looked at me, and I could tell she was calculating something. I'd said too much, perhaps, though in my distress I couldn't fathom what I'd said wrong. "It bothers you, then?" she said almost softly. "The visions?"

"How can you ask that?" My voice cracked, and I fought to keep control. My emotions were tumbling out of me of their own accord. "This power means I'm a circus freak. A witch—you said it yourself. A girl who will never have a normal life."

Gloria arched an eyebrow again. She put a hand on one hip and regarded me for a long moment. Then she walked to the door and slipped on her coat with its beautiful fur collar again.

"I've never wanted a normal life," she said to me, "so I can't help you with that. But it seems to me that your problem is that you have no life at all. Come with me, darling. Let's get drunk and see what we can do about it."

# CHAPTER SIXTEEN

When I finally arrived home from Ramona's disastrous séance, my street in St. John's Wood was as dark and quiet as if the world had ended. My heels clicked shallowly on the front walk and my key seemed to echo as it slid into its lock.

I tossed my handbag aside and dragged myself back to the kitchen, the silence deafening in my ears. It suddenly seemed that I had heard nothing but silence since my mother died; I'd been swaddled in cotton, the world muffled outside the confines of my head. Those last few years of my mother's life, after I met Gloria, had not been quiet in this house. There had been arguments about hemlines and hairstyles, and tense fights when I came home in the middle of the night, and one particularly shrill confrontation when my mother caught me smoking. Then there was the drama of my mother's scandalous retirement, and her moans of pain after she'd grown sick. And then all had been silence.

A tray covered with a dome sat on the kitchen table. My daily woman had come and gone as always, dutifully leaving me supper even though I was not in the house. What did she think of me? She never said. She had worked for my mother, and after my mother died we'd had a brief conversation in which she'd stated she'd like to stay on if I'd have her. She had offered no condolences, and I had asked for none.

I pulled the dome from the tray and looked down at the cold supper beneath it. This was how I lived: With the ghost of my mother, whose name I had taken, whose dress I wore every day in atonement. With the ghost of the daily woman, who hadn't mourned my mother and would never mourn me. With the ghost of Gloria Sutter, who had haunted me long before she died.

I hadn't gotten drunk that first night, despite Gloria's proclamation. I'd never been drunk in my life, and I was far too terrified to let even Gloria have her way. She had taken me to supper at a tiny club with plush red chairs, no windows, and a wizened proprietor who spoke nothing but Russian and communicated with his patrons chiefly in mime. Gloria had downed a bottle of wine over the meal, let me pay the bill with my last few coins, and then taken me out into the night.

There had been taxicabs and clubs, and almost-beautiful women in expensive dresses and fur coats, and men who poured drinks and whose comments seemed to insult you and compliment you at the same time. It was bitterly cold, the slush on the streets wet and nearly frozen, our breath pluming in the air as we went from a taxicab to a doorway and back out again. It was hectic and exhilarating and exhausting. Everyone knew Gloria; everyone loved her and referred to her as "darling" or "simply too much," but even I could see the wariness in their eyes beneath it all, the way none of them touched her.

Now, in my silent kitchen, I took off my high heels and rubbed my feet. My brain hurt and my eyes felt as if sand had been rubbed into them. Still, I made the journey back to the front hall to retrieve my handbag and pull out the little satin bag I'd taken from Gloria's flat the day before. I'd carried it with me like a talisman, never certain when I would need a bolt of gin. That moment seemed to be now.

I slid the little flask from its pouch and admired it briefly. It was well made, chosen with Gloria's impeccable taste, slender and feminine. When I touched the empty satin bag again, I heard a telltale crinkle, and when I slid my fingers inside, to my amazement I pulled out a few folded pieces of paper.

I opened the first one and held it under the light.

> *Dear Mrs. Sutter,*
> *It is with great sadness that we inform you that your son, Harry Sutter, died 19 March 1916, valiantly in defense of his country . . .*

There were three of these letters, telegrams, each of them as well-worn as lace. Tommy, the sweet one; Colin, the sour politician; Harry, the handsome one. Gloria hadn't spoken much about her brothers, but she'd quietly carried these letters with her everywhere she went. I set them aside, careful not to damage them.

Alongside the telegrams were three photographs, each perhaps two inches long. Each was a portrait of a man in uniform, from the neck upward, looking carefully toward the camera. They were going-to-war portraits, the same kind tens of thousands of men had had taken all over the country before leaving their families. I put them on the table and rearranged them.

One face was youthful, the hair possibly a light brown; this was Tommy, whom Octavia said was the youngest. Next to him I put a face so outrageously handsome it could only be Harry, whom Octavia had described as gorgeous, like a movie star. He had thick black hair and eyes of inky soulfulness, as well as a strong, soft mouth and a beautiful jaw. Movie star, indeed. Finally, at the end I placed the third photograph, this one of a man slightly older than the other two, his dark hair slicked down like Valentino's, his gaze serious. This was likely Colin, described as the future politician. What struck me about him was that, aside from the fact that he was obviously a man, his resemblance to Gloria was much closer than that of the other two. He had her straight nose, the dark, intelligent slashes of her brows. It was disturbingly like looking at two portraits somehow overlapped.

One more sheet of paper had been folded into the silk bag, this one crisp and much newer than the telegrams. I read from the top:

*4: 1500 44 2100 214*
*5: 1700 107*

I stared at Gloria's cramped handwriting. As codes went, it was hardly the most difficult to figure out: This was Gloria's daily schedule, tucked into her flask bag so she could handily remind herself. The first number was the date, followed by a time on the twenty-four-hour clock. The next number referred to a client. *Number Thirty-One wants to see you at seven*, Davies had said on that first day. The numbers *44, 214, 107* . . . those were all codes for clients. This, then, was Gloria's professional schedule for the last week before she died.

I scanned down the page, pausing to uncap the flask. I swallowed a bolt of gin—of course it was gin—and felt it burn from my stomach to the top of my head, turning to cinders the thought that Gloria's killer could well be listed on the page I held in my hands.

The schedule continued:

*7: [number blacked out] #321B!!!*
*8: 277 Kent collect UP FRONT*

I rubbed my forehead. On Sunday, the day before Gloria was killed, she'd blacked out her appointment and written in something else—a number in a different format, followed by exclamation points.

Monday, the day she died, she had written in the Dubbses' code number—277—followed by a note to herself to collect up front. *Everyone always pays up front*, I thought, but usually Davies handled those details. Gloria was reminding herself, because this time she'd bypassed Davies entirely.

My gaze traveled back to the line, this past Sunday, where Gloria had changed her own schedule and written something else in. Only one person could help me figure this out, of course. Davies would know what all of the code numbers meant. She would know about the schedule change the day before Gloria died. Davies, who, according to Fitzroy Todd, Gloria had not trusted, and neither should I.

And what about the police? They must have asked Davies for Gloria's schedule in her last days. Had Davies given it to them already? If I handed these sheets to the mysterious Inspector Merriken, would he know what they meant?

I tossed the page down and took another slug of gin.

That first night Gloria and I had gone out on the town, at about two o'clock in the morning my exhausted brain remembered that my mother was at home, waiting. I had never in my life been out so late—had never gone anywhere without her knowledge and approval. I was suddenly crushed with guilt that I'd disobeyed all of my mother's rules. She would be frantic.

"I have to leave," I'd said to Gloria as I worriedly patted my coat pockets, looking for my pocketbook. "I have to go home."

"Do you?" Gloria drawled. We were in a small, strange, drafty bar, lit only with dim wall sconces, featuring heavy velvet drapes across the walls. The place didn't seem to have a name. Two couples we had somehow picked up were dancing drowsily to the exhausted four-piece band, the girls leaning heavily on the men and smearing makeup on their jackets, while Gloria and I watched from an uncomfortable booth in the corner. Gloria was slouched against the wall with a cigarette in her fingers, her dark hair tousled in a sensual mess, wearing a fur coat that wasn't hers. I had no idea what had happened to the coat with the fur collar.

"My mother!" I said.

Gloria took a drag, unimpressed. "Yes, of course."

My mind spun. I'd had a valise with me on the train—what had I done with it? I remembered carrying it up the stairs to Gloria's flat, but that was it. I'd always been so obedient, so conscientious; it was as if Gloria Sutter had put a spell on me, or slipped me some kind of drug. I fought down the panic in my chest and glared at her. "You're enjoying this, aren't you?" I said. "Keeping The Fantastique up at night worrying."

She arched an eyebrow and I knew I was right, but I also knew there was something more to it that I couldn't see. "If you're asking whether I enjoy getting my hands on her progeny, yes, I do. I like to watch the chick toddling out of the nest."

It stung. She thought me stupid, naive, a child—or so she'd have me believe. Already I was learning never to quite trust that Gloria was telling the truth. "She worries about me," I said. "And I— We have clients coming tomorrow."

"Do you?" She put a slight emphasis on the second word, her gaze calculating. Then she leaned her head back against the wall as if it was too heavy to hold up anymore, her half-closed eyes suggesting I was no longer worth looking at. "God, this band is horrid," she said, and she raised one elegant hand and tossed the still-lit end of her cigarette in a perfect arc onto the dance floor.

It was the coarsest, most unladylike gesture I had ever seen, and I stood mesmerized by it. There was something so darkly sensual about her, so unafraid. I was aware of a vein of pure, black longing within me. I wanted to be free enough to do something like that, effortlessly and without thought, a gesture that would horrify my mother, horrify myself. Much of what Gloria did and said was an act, but with an ache in my chest I knew that throwing her cigarette in that moment was not one of them. It was not staged in order to shock. She had simply wanted to get rid of her cigarette, and that was the fastest way.

I wanted to ask her—something. I knew not what. Everything. Instead, I said, "Does drinking stop the visions?"

Gloria blinked slowly at me, her eyes dark and unreadable as she considered the question. "I drink because I like to be drunk, darling," she said finally. "And nothing stops the visions but sheer willpower."

I swallowed and my gaze flicked down to her hand resting on the table. I wanted to touch it, to feel her power, to feel that connection with her, with someone, with anyone. With Gloria Sutter. I pulled my coat tighter around me and took a step away. "I have to go."

"Let me ask you something," Gloria said, as if we'd never stopped talking. She leaned slightly forward over the table. "Your precious mother. What happens to you when she's gone?"

"Gone?" I said stupidly. "My mother is in perfect health. She isn't going anywhere."

Her voice turned harsh and almost amused. "Have you learned nothing? We're all going somewhere. The question is where."

The words hit me like slaps. I thought of the old woman I'd seen as a child, all the hideous dead I'd seen since. I could not—would not—think of my mother in the same way. "Be quiet."

"Do you think you'll get married?" Gloria pressed on. "What exactly do you plan to tell your husband? That you've spent your life staring into the eyes of corpses, but never mind, darling, I'm perfectly fine? You'll never find a man to take you unless you lie to him—do you know that? Besides, the men all went to war and didn't come home. I talk to those dead soldiers, and sometimes I think, 'There's another one. Another man no girl can marry.'"

I turned to leave, but Gloria was faster. Her hand shot out and gripped mine, cold and hard. I hadn't yet put on my gloves.

The feeling was stronger this time, fueled by alcohol and exhaustion.

It had taken me years to learn to fully control the power I'd been born with, but Gloria's power dwarfed mine easily. How she dealt with it, how she controlled it, what it cost her, I could not fathom. I could only gasp as the seedy nightclub fell away and the world went quiet and there was only Gloria, me, and the sharp electric current between us. Then she let me go. The next thing I knew, I was sitting in a taxi, shivering and inexplicably near tears. I *would* never marry; she was right. I was too freakish. And someday my mother *would* be gone.

I came home to find The Fantastique half mad with worry, moments away from calling the police. We had our first row that night, tearful and dramatic. I begged her forgiveness even as I bit back a resentment toward her I'd never felt before. I told her I'd made a new friend on the train home and we'd lost track of time.

I told her my new friend was named Florence. It sounded like a nice enough name. And through all the rows, that night and afterward, I never mentioned Gloria Sutter.

# CHAPTER SEVENTEEN

Despite the restless night I'd spent after drinking Gloria's gin, I was out of the house early the next morning. The silence in my sitting room was too much for me, the walls narrowing in. The bustle of London's morning streets numbed my mind. I told myself I was wandering with no fixed purpose, but by the time I took the tube to Aldwych station, I admitted that was a lie. Aldwych was only a few streets from the offices of the New Society for the Furtherance of Psychical Research.

The tube doors slid open and I made my way, along with a smattering of suited men and important-looking women, up to the street. The pavements were still damp from the last evening's rain, and a bank of gray clouds lowered over the city, threatening another round. My temples throbbed already. I was hungry and thirsty for some tea.

I had just paused at the doorway of a small café, considering a stop alone for breakfast, when a long black motorcar pulled up to the curb next to me and a man unfolded himself from the backseat.

I blinked at him in shock. It was George Sutter.

"Good morning, Miss Winter," Sutter said, touching the brim of his hat. "Join me for coffee, will you?"

He gently rested one hand on my elbow, and I automatically let him steer me through the door and to a seat at a small table. "Just tea," I managed to correct him after he ordered on my behalf—tea and a scone for me, black coffee for himself. Then he turned to face me, crossing one leg over the other.

He was dressed in one of his well-cut slender suits and an overcoat, a hat, and an unassuming tie. A folded umbrella sat in the crook of one arm. A businessman just like any other on a London morning, except that his air of power sent the waiter scrambling with extra speed to fetch his coffee. And I'd accompanied him at his request without question, like a servant.

Before he could speak, I asked the obvious. "How did you find me?"

"How do you think?"

I allowed a feeling of shock to move through me. "You have someone watching me? For how long? How did he follow me through the tube?"

"Does it matter, Miss Winter?"

His look told me it was a foolish question, which made me angry. "I never agreed to be followed day and night," I said, thinking about where I'd been the night before. Had George Sutter's man been watching? Had he seen James? "Besides, I don't understand. If you have enough manpower at your fingertips to follow a woman through the tube, then why do you need me in this investigation at all?"

The waiter returned with our order, and Sutter didn't answer. I could see little of Gloria in his smooth, impassive face—a little in the eyes, perhaps, but he had none of her sensual openness. He looked older than she ever had, older than she would ever now grow to be.

"I didn't intend to anger you," he said when we were alone again. "I wanted to speak with you privately, and I didn't think you'd agree

to see me. I prefer to speak in person rather than over the telephone."
He sipped his coffee and put the cup down on the saucer with a soft
click. "I did try to send you a letter."

"Your letter was rude," I informed him, still irked. "My reply was
warranted. I hope you don't often have to charm people in MI5."

"I have never told you I work for MI5."

No, that had been James Hawley's idea. "Then who do you work for?"

Sutter's demeanor didn't crack. "You can parry me all you like,
Miss Winter, but it doesn't change the fact that I require a progress
report. You've accepted my fee and, according to my sources, you've
been investigating. What have you found?"

I set down my tea. He was infuriating and I didn't quite trust
him, but I reminded myself that he wanted the same thing I did: to
find Gloria's killer. Still, I took a bite of my scone and made him wait
before I answered. "There isn't much yet," I admitted. "I've talked to
Gloria's assistant, Davies. The séance was the idea of Fitzroy Todd,
who talked Gloria into it."

Sutter nodded, sipping his coffee. "Go on."

"Fitzroy says the idea was the clients'—that is, Mr. and Mrs.
Dubbs. They offered him money to get Gloria to agree to the séance.
Fitzroy always needs money, so he took it."

"That isn't in Scotland Yard's reports," Sutter said. "The money,
that is."

"No, it wouldn't be. Fitzroy didn't tell them. He probably thinks
it paints him as a suspect, and he's out to save his own skin."

"And is he, in your opinion?" Sutter asked. "Is he a suspect?"

"I don't know. Fitzroy is without use, but he isn't violent. He could
have done it, however. He was there, and I believe he's strong enough."

Sutter thought this over. "Go on," he said again.

"I spent last night with Ramona, the spirit medium." I didn't
bother mentioning what exactly had happened at the séance. "She's a
fraud, and she was an opportunist trying to latch onto Gloria, but I
think she knows more than she's telling me."

Sutter evinced no emotion, but his gaze fixed on me and did not waver. "What exactly do you think she knows?"

I shook my head. It was a feeling I had—she had been so strange, so angry, and she had known so much about Gloria and me. But mostly it was the look in her eyes when she'd stopped me at her door. "She was afraid," I said. "Terrified."

"The police questioned her," Sutter said. "She had nothing useful to say. It seems a great many people are lying to the police in this investigation. Which is why I need you."

"I'll try talking to her again," I said. "Perhaps she'll be more reasonable in daylight." And after she'd had her fix for the day.

"If she was jealous of Gloria, don't you think that would be a motive for murder?"

I looked at Sutter. He was watching me carefully, as always, his features humorless and still. "Perhaps," I said. "But Ramona isn't stupid, only desperate. She would be better served to use the occasion to steal Gloria's clients, rather than risking murder." I crumbled a piece of scone in my fingers, thinking. "Besides, Ramona is a drug addict. Her brain is addled most of the time, and she isn't particularly healthy. I'm not sure she's strong enough to subdue Gloria and carry her to the water. And I think a drug addict would commit a crime of opportunity, not something carefully planned."

Sutter's eyes gleamed. "You're saying this was planned?"

I nodded, relieved to speak the thoughts that had gone around in my mind all night. "I'm starting to think it. I don't have proof. But the more I look at this, the more it seems to me that Gloria was lured and set up. Someone didn't just happen by and kill her. Someone quite deliberately, I think, wanted her dead."

Sutter looked out the window at the busy street for a long moment, his coffee cooling in its cup. "Well," he said finally. "That is very well-done, Miss Winter. You did almost as well as Scotland Yard."

I leaned toward him. "What have they found?"

"I'll admit they've surprised me." Sutter uncrossed and recrossed his legs, frowning. "The inspector there, Merriken, is smarter than I gave the Yard credit for. I have the impression that nothing much gets past him."

"He's asked to see me," I said.

Sutter nodded. "He has noted that he wants to question you."

I swallowed, my throat dry. "Am I a suspect?" I asked him. "Your information must say something."

"The problem with Gloria's murder is that there are too many suspects to choose from, not too few. Her life was full of shady characters, rivals, former lovers, and frauds. And those are only the people we know about."

"You forgot clients," I said. "Gloria's client list was supposedly powerful. It was certainly top secret. Any one of those people could have had her killed."

"Inspector Merriken has already covered that ground," Sutter said. "He's interviewed a number of Gloria's clients—with admirable discretion, I might add."

I stared at him, amazed. "Are you saying Davies actually gave him a list of Gloria's clients?"

"It seems she was rather reluctant. The note in the file includes the word 'unpleasant.' However, Inspector Merriken can be persuasive, and he tracked down some of the names himself. He's also spoken to your friend from the New Society."

"James Hawley?"

Sutter sat back in his chair. "Don't look so surprised, Miss Winter. I presume you're on your way to the offices of the New Society to see him right now."

He was right, of course, although I did not admit it. "Is James a suspect?"

"As I've mentioned, there are too many suspects at the moment. However, except for the fact that this James Hawley wrote an article about Gloria that gained him some ridicule in his profession, there isn't much motive for murder."

"That article was years ago. They haven't seen each other since."

"And yet it was revived by a journalist rather recently, it seems. He may have been subjected to a new round of disbelief in the scientific community."

"You don't know him," I said. "He doesn't give a fig about that. James is no murderer."

Sutter raised his brows at my avid defense. "I'm only trying to assist you. The article mentions you as well and is hardly a ringing endorsement of your powers. You mustn't trust too easily, Miss Winter. You don't know who is involved in this."

I gave him a pointed look. "I don't trust anyone—believe me." When he did not quaver in the least, I admitted, "I may contact the Dubbses next, ask them some questions."

"That would be covering ground already covered by Scotland Yard," Sutter countered. "Do you truly think that would be the best use of your time? I need you to talk to the people who won't tell the truth to the police. It's why I hired you. People like this Ramona." The disgust with which her name rolled off his tongue was audible. "If you feel there is more than what she's said already, it's best if you interview her again."

"And my powers, of course," I said. "You also hired me because of my powers."

He looked out the window again, as if the mention of my powers made him uneasy, though his face gave nothing away. "I admit your powers are of interest to me," he said. "Substantial interest, in fact. But you have as much as told me that you will not use them to contact my sister." He looked back at me. "Are you saying you've changed your mind?"

I thought of how my powers had slipped away from me the night before, how I'd seen that horrible woman and her baby. I shook my head. "That offer is not on the table, Mr. Sutter." I said the words with conviction, but they felt strangely dry in my mouth. I did not take the time to ponder why.

"Then I'm afraid I have a great many things to attend to." Sutter pushed back his chair and stood, placing several coins on the table. He bowed briefly, a formal gesture I watched with surprise. "Good day, Miss Winter." He paused in the doorway. "Be careful," he said to me, and then he was gone, vanishing into the London crowds as if he'd never been.

The New Society for the Furtherance of Psychical Research occupied a small set of offices in a building off the Strand, up a musty set of stairs and past doors advertising various low-rent solicitors, accountants, and even a small poetry magazine. I hadn't been here since the day they'd tested the powers of my mother and me, and yet I remembered it perfectly, as if I'd seen it yesterday.

My knock on the office door was answered by a huge bear of a man, bearded, wearing an ill-fitting suit and carrying an umbrella, apparently on his way out.

His eyebrows shot upward when he saw me. "My goodness!" he said. "Miss Ellie Winter." He turned and shouted at someone in the office behind him. "Sadie, do we have an appointment with Miss Winter?"

"No," came a voice at the same time I said to him, "No."

The man turned back and looked at me. He was pale, his light brown hair and beard threaded with gray. He had one of those faces that is impossible to age accurately, and he could have been anywhere from forty to sixty-five. He exuded intelligent vitality, and his eyes glinted at me from behind his glasses. This was Paul Golding, the president of the New Society. "A lovely surprise, then," he said, backing away from the doorway. "Do come in."

The main office contained three mismatched scarred desks, at one of which sat a stick-thin woman of fifty who was giving me a suspicious look. A door led to a second office, this one darkened, and a second passage led to a larger back room where, I knew, the Society conducted its tests on psychics. The wall behind the woman was lined with wooden filing cabinets, their tops stacked with files, papers, and books, and more papers sat piled on the floor in front of the cabinets. A single window looked out onto the street and gave a view of the graying sky, the dimmed light making the entire office rather gloomy.

"I hope you remember me?" Golding said, his eyebrows rising again.

"Yes, of course," I said softly. I hadn't expected a strange wash of emotion to come over me at the sight of these offices. I had been there only once before, and at the time I had been so hurt, so angry, it had seemed like the end of the world. Now I realized it had been nothing close.

"I surmised it," Golding said, "but one must be polite. Would you like a seat?" He turned to the stick-thin woman. "Sadie, fetch us some tea."

"I'm not staying long," I said as the woman, unmoving, sent me a deadly glare. "Please don't bother."

Still, Golding ushered me to the darkened office, obviously his, where he removed his hat and set down his umbrella. I followed, mostly to get away from the glare of the unaccountably hostile Sadie. "I've interrupted you," I said in apology. "You were on your way somewhere."

"Somewhere!" Golding said, as if I was joking. He pulled out the chair behind his desk and lowered his large bulk into it with a creak. "Just to the doctor's, where he'll lecture me yet again about my heart. He worries about that organ more than I do. No—" He sat back and laced his hands across his rather sizable stomach. "An unexpected visit from The Fantastique trumps all."

I quickly ran my mind over what I knew about Paul Golding. It wasn't much. He'd been president of the New Society since the war ended; before that, according to what James had told me, he'd served as an officer in the war. The papers, when they mentioned him at all,

dismissed him as an eccentric or a fraud, an attitude I was well familiar with. And he had run the tests that labeled my mother a fake and
my own powers "inconclusive and unproven."

"I hope this isn't about the newspaper article," Golding said to
me. "We had nothing to do with that."

"I understand," I said. "I'm here about—" I hadn't realized what
I was there for, really, until I'd already arrived. "I'm here about Gloria
Sutter."

Paul Golding's features lost their joviality, and it was no act.
"That girl," he said. "That poor, wonderful, irreplaceable girl." He
swallowed. "I thought you two were not on speaking terms."

I shook my head, not willing to explain it to a stranger. "You
must have spent a lot of time with her," I said. "You knew her well."

"I was well acquainted with her, but James is my researcher. He
had more contact with her than I did." A hint of humor crossed his
expression again. "He isn't here, by the way. In fact, he hasn't reported to work in several days. I believe he's been spending most of
that time with you."

I frowned at him. "Not exactly."

"That's not what he says." Golding shrugged. "I'd reprimand
him if not for the fact that I don't pay him much, and his job comes
with an utter lack of respect and heaps of abuse. And I know better
than to try to rein him in. Gloria's death seems to have awakened his
Galahad instincts."

I had questions to ask about Gloria, but I couldn't help myself.
"What do you mean, you know better than to rein him in?"

"James is independent," Golding replied. "We gave him his own
desk at first, but we soon discovered he didn't much like to use it. He
likes to work alone, in his own flat or out on investigation. He's the
best investigator I've ever seen—quite simply splendid. He's investigated hundreds of supernatural claims firsthand, and his skill in fer-
reting out frauds is unmatched in this country or any other." He

smiled a little, unashamed of the effusive praise. "Frankly, he should be doing something that brings him renown, not ridicule, but I can't convince him of that. And until I do, I get the benefit of his investigative brain."

James had been wrong about me, of course, and about my mother. *I've thought a lot about that day,* he'd said. *Something was not quite right.*

"As for you," Golding said, "I see you're still in business."

I was no longer angry, but it galled me still that these people thought me a liar. I recalled what my mother had taught me about attempting greater and greater feats for a disbelieving audience. She was right: There was no peace in it. "When was the last time you saw Gloria?" I asked him.

"Last year," Golding replied. "I went to one of her séances, in fact. I had seen her in our testing environment any number of times, but I felt the need to see her work in her own space. She knew who I was and why I was there. I made no attempt to keep it secret."

"But the article James wrote was already years old by then," I said.

"Yes, I know. I was going through a—well, you could call it a crisis of faith, I suppose, though not of the religious kind. We had launched a large project asking the public to write us their experiences with the supernormal—a psychical census, of sorts. We'd been inundated with letters, but it seemed they were all frauds, misconceptions, delusions, dreams, or outright lies." The corners of his eyes relaxed, and his expression grew distant and a little tired. "Humanity is sometimes terrible, desperate, and sad. I felt a need to see Gloria Sutter in action again, to be reminded of what it is like to be in the presence of a true spirit medium."

"You still believe she was a real medium?" I asked.

"Yes. Gloria Sutter was the most incredibly talented medium I've ever seen. She was a phenomenon of nature, and her loss is a permanent tragedy to the future of scientific study of the supernormal."

*And to me.* The words almost tripped out of my mouth before I could stop them. *It is a permanent tragedy to me.* But I only looked at him in silence as the pieces clicked in my head and I came to a realization. This man had admired Gloria, and he had appreciated her worth to science, but he hadn't loved her. I was starting to think that except for me and possibly Davies, no one had.

Paul Golding raised his eyebrows politely, taking in my silence. "Miss Winter?"

"I'm going to find her murderer," I said to him.

He took this in with barely a blink. "Indeed. And this is what James has been helping you with?"

"Yes."

"I knew he was looking into it, but I thought it was for his own satisfaction. He feels he owes her a debt." Golding took a piece of paper from his desk and uncapped a pen. "I have no faith in the police, Miss Winter, and you and I have something of a checkered past. However"—now he was writing quickly, with a flourish—"I do have faith in James Hawley." He handed me the paper, on which was written an address. "Please make good use of him and return him to me in one piece. You'll find him at his flat, I believe."

I took the paper and put it in my handbag. *To hell with it,* I thought, and held out my hand. "Thank you for your help."

He looked surprised, but he shook my hand. His grip was huge and strong. "Good day."

I stood. It had been easy this time, even with gloves on. "It's at the back of your drawer."

"I beg your pardon?"

"Your watch. You don't wear it every day because it's expensive and it was your father's and you're afraid of losing it. After the last time you wore it, you put it in the back of your drawer, thinking it was a good hiding place. But then you forgot your own hiding place when you decided you wanted to wear the watch this morning."

There was a brief silence. Then Paul Golding tilted his head, his gaze on me changing in a way I could not read. His voice was very careful. "Miss Winter, you surprise me."

I shook my head. It had been a stupid impulse, petty and vain, wanting to prove something to this man. Still, I couldn't quite be sorry I'd done it. I turned to go.

"As it happens," Golding called after me, "you are correct."

With my hand on the knob of the office door, I turned to face him again. "Sorry?"

He reached into his pocket and pulled out an antique watch on a chain. "I found it this morning, after nearly an hour's search," he said. "Perhaps we underestimated you, Miss Winter."

I stared at the watch, hiding the waves of shock that were breaking over me like a fever. I swallowed and forced myself to shrug. "That's up to you," I said, my voice cracking. "Good day." I walked breathlessly through the outer office, past the eternal glare of Sadie, and hurried down the stairs, nearly running by the time I got out the front door and onto the street.

He'd *found* it. He'd found the bloody watch already. I made my way through the crowds on the Strand, looking at no one, seeing nothing. The vision had been quick, and so very clear.

And yet he'd already found it. This had never happened to me before. I'd never been wrong. Or nearly wrong. For a second, panic gripped me so hard I nearly stopped breathing. I tried to calm myself. It was a simple slip, purely human to be wrong from time to time. But my powers had never failed me—not ever. And if they could be wrong this time, could they be wrong again? Had they been wrong before? How many times? What else had I seen that wasn't true?

If my powers could be wrong, then who was I?

Someone bumped my shoulder, and a woman with a pram nearly nicked my shin. Raucous laughter came from a window somewhere. I took a breath, and then another.

I wouldn't think about it now; I had other things to worry about. It must have been a random mistake, wires crossed over what Paul Golding had been thinking about at the moment I touched him. It was just one of those things.

In the meantime, Gloria's killer was still free, and I needed help. I knew where to find it.

I fished the address from my handbag and headed for the nearest stop to catch an omnibus.

# CHAPTER EIGHTEEN

According to Paul Golding's paper, James lived in Brixton. I boarded a bus going east, then got off and boarded another going north. I sat with my gloved hands folded in my lap, my eyes trained ahead as I tried to note everyone around me. What did George Sutter's man look like? Was he the fiftyish gentleman trying to relight his dampened pipe? The man in the houndstooth jacket reading a copy of the *Daily Mail*? The stout man wiping his forehead with a handkerchief? Had I seen any of these men before? I didn't remember.

I entered my third bus and sat on the second deck, looking down at the streets below. What if it was a woman following me? I had no idea whether MI5 even employed women, other than as secretaries or typists. George Sutter knew who James was, and could presumably find his address, but the thought of being followed bothered me in a way I couldn't explain. I remembered the hard-eyed, mustached man I'd seen at Ramona's disastrous stage show. I'd assumed he was Ramona's plant, but now I wondered.

I circled for a while, until I was tired of buses and certain I hadn't seen anyone twice, and then I went to Brixton. After disembarking, I turned up one street, then ducked through a likely alley and came out on another. I zigzagged the best I could, past washing lines and through tiny back lots with bedraggled kitchen gardens and bemused cats watching me from the damp tops of garden walls.

I finally arrived at James's street address. It was a three-story brick home that had long ago been turned into flats, like much of Brixton. The front stoop was sooty and the walk hadn't been swept in ages, but a single pot of geraniums stood well tended by the door, vainly hoping for sunlight. I approached the door, raising my hand to knock, and the corner of my gaze caught something familiar. A houndstooth pattern. I turned to see a man in a familiar jacket cross the street a block away and turn a corner. He did not hurry, and he did not look at me.

So much for losing my pursuer.

A woman of at least eighty greeted my knock, her knobbed hands almost silvery pale in the cloudy light.

"Third floor. The door is right off the landing," she said when I asked for James. She eyed me swiftly up and down, but made no comment. I wondered how often girls came here asking for James Hawley.

I climbed the windowless staircase—it smelled vaguely of gravy—and knocked on the door.

The door swung open and James stared at me. He wore trousers and a white shirt open at the throat, his braces hanging loose. His hair was mussed, and when I dropped my gaze I couldn't help but notice his feet were bare. My first thought was that I was happy to see him. My second thought, as I looked into his face, was that the feeling was not mutual.

"Oh, good God," he said.

I swallowed. "I went to the New Society," I managed. "They sent me here."

Wild surmise crossed his expression, and a flicker of panicked dread. "Paul sent you?" he said. "Paul sent you *here?*"

"This is a bad time, isn't it?" I babbled. "I'm sorry. I—"

"Wait, wait." I took a step back, but James reached out and grasped my elbow. His features looked harsh in the dim light. I wondered in horror whether there was a woman in the flat with him, a woman who had woken up with him. The thought stung, and I tugged on my arm, wanting to get away.

We stood in silence for a moment, his hand on my elbow, I pulling back from his grip, ready to run. I could hear him breathing.

"It's all right," he said at last. "Come in."

He pulled gently, and I followed the pull, my body slackening. I smelled shaving soap as I passed him in the doorway. I could not look in his eyes as I passed him.

It was a sizable flat for the top floor of such a small house. Two mullioned windows looked over the back garden with its high wall and the houses behind, and the cloudy light they let in illuminated all corners of the room. It was a simple bachelor's flat, unfurnished except for the barest of necessities, with a tiny kitchen in one corner and a doorway that led, presumably, to the bedroom. A desk sat before the windows, placed advantageously to catch the light, its surface covered thickly with books and papers. More books and papers stood in wobbling stacks around the foot of the desk, the papers sliding off one another and onto the floor, and against the wall stood three hefty cloth sacks with folded envelopes spilling from their tops.

"Don't say it," James said to me as he disappeared through the door to the bedroom. "There's a method to it, I swear. Just give me a moment and I'll make you some tea."

"You don't—," I started, but he was already gone. I stood awkwardly in the middle of the room, smelling the strange, intimate scent of a man's bachelor quarters—burnt coffee, dusty papers, laundry soap, male skin. A flush heated my cheeks. I pulled off my hat and my gloves, determined not to look at the doorway as he moved about in the next room.

I set down my hat and my gloves and wandered restlessly to the desk. I picked up the top letter from one of the mail sacks and slid it open.

> *Dear Sirs.*
>
> *In response to your request in the* Times *of 24 July. I do apologize for the tardiness of this response as my wife sometimes does keep the newspapers in her sewing basket and neglects to give them to me in a timely manner. However I had an experience I do not often speak of.*
>
> *In the early part of 1916, that is 22 February to be exact, at five twenty in the morning I awoke for a reason I could not determine. At this time it was still dark. I descended the stairs and as I approached the kitchen door I saw the figure of my son, Alan. He stood next to the table where he'd always sat for supper before he left for war. It sounds strange but I do swear I saw him as clear as if he'd been in the brightest daylight, though the room was dark. He was in uniform, and he stood looking at me as if he could see me, though he did not speak.*
>
> *I called his name. I thought that by some wild chance he had come home on leave without telling us, but something about his appearance told me it was not so. When I spoke his name, he disappeared.*
>
> *I did not speak of this even to my wife, for she had been depressed in spirits since our son went to war and I did not wish to upset her. I thought I may have imagined Alan's appearance, the thought of which distressed me not a little as I have always been a logical man. As*

*it happened, we received a telegram three days later*
*stating that my son, Alan, had been hit in the head with*
*shrapnel and had died of wounds in a field hospital on*
*the morning of 22 February.*

*I do not claim to explain this. I do not speak of it to*
*anyone. I do not know whether it was a communica-*
*tion from Alan or the product of my own distressed*
*brain, and I do not ask that question. If you ask these*
*questions, dear sirs, then you are braver than I, and as*
*of this moment I pass this letter to you and from this*
*day will think on this incident no more.*

*Regards,*
*Samuel W. Eustace*

"A deathbed vision," James said.

I turned to find him standing at my shoulder. I inhaled in surprise; I hadn't felt him approach.

He'd combed his hair and put on his braces, but the top buttons of his white shirt were still undone. *He looks rather stunning when he takes his jacket off,* Gloria had said. She was right. He made the flat seem smaller. He put his hands in his pockets and nodded toward the letter. "A sighting of the dead at the moment of passing. They're called deathbed visions. You'd be surprised how common they are."

"Paul Golding mentioned something about this," I said. "Asking people to write letters."

"The Society put an ad in the *Times*," James replied. "Paul has a vision of some kind of countrywide census of the supernatural, I think. My job is to sift through the responses and weed out the mad ones."

I looked at the bags of mail. "Are these all deathbed visions?"

"No. People write us about all sorts of things—hauntings, boggarts, even garden pixies. But deathbed visions are especially numerous since the war."

"My God," I said. There were hundreds of letters here, thousands. "This seems insurmountable."

"You should be used to it," James said, taking the letter from my hand. "Bereaved parents, bereaved widows, fatherless children. England is full of them, it seems. An endless parade."

His voice was harsh, and he turned away from me. There was no sign this morning of the James who had confided in me the night before—or, for that matter, the James who had disintegrated my clothing with a single look in Trafalgar Square. This James was angry, exhausted, and I didn't know why. It seemed he would ever be a cipher to me. *Moody, like a tangle of thorns.*

"I've come at a bad time," I said. "I should leave."

"It isn't that." James dropped the letter back onto the desk and paced away, moving like a cat. He did not glance at me again. "Paul shouldn't have sent you here, to see this—to see how I live. I never have women here. You can see why." He pulled a kettle from the cupboard and turned on the water in the tiny sink.

"There's nothing wrong with you," I said.

He made a noise that was not quite a laugh. "There's plenty wrong with me, Ellie."

"Fine, then," I said, suddenly angry. "There's plenty wrong with me, too. There's plenty wrong with everyone since the war ended. Everyone who's still alive, that is."

He put the kettle on the stove, unlit, and paused, his back to me. He put his hands on the counter, his shoulders hunched, his head down, and there was a long moment of silence. When he spoke, his voice was calm again, but the pain in it had not abated. "Do you ever feel like you're living someone else's life?" he asked suddenly.

"Yes," I answered, thinking of living in my mother's house, wearing my mother's dress.

Still he did not move, did not turn. "Some days I wonder if I'm going to wake from a dream and find myself in the trenches again. If everything that has happened since the war has happened to a stranger, a man I don't know." He seemed to be forcing the words out, and I watched him, entranced. "The war," he said slowly, "is my most vivid memory. Do you know that? More vivid than my child-hood, more vivid than law school, more vivid than any woman. How is that fair? I tried to blot it out with drink for the first few years, until Paul found me, though it never worked. Every time I closed my eyes, I saw my men in those woods." His knuckles went white on the edge of the counter, his arms flexed, his head bowed. Every line of his body spoke of pain.

"Tell me," I said softly.

"I was an officer," he said, though I thought perhaps he would have spoken even if I hadn't asked. "I was in charge of those men. We were ordered to take the woods, to clear them out—it was tactical. So we advanced. But no one knew there was a machine gunner." He lifted one hand and rubbed it over his face. "My men were mowed down. All of them. It took maybe ten seconds. I saw it happen, and I will never unsee it."

"Fenton," I said.

James shook his head. "There was nothing special about Fenton, not before that day. He was just one of my men. He was the only one besides me who made it alive past the tree line, that's all. We didn't make it far into the woods before we fell. I was only shot behind the knee, while the rest of them were dead in the grass. Except Fenton, who died on the ground next to me. He'd been ripped open, nearly split in half. It was a miracle that he ran as far as he did."

And then the German had come for his souvenir. I was chilled, shocked—but not as chilled and shocked as I should have been. Part of me had seen it, smelled it. Part of me had lain on the ground, lis-tening to the screaming. I *knew*.

James straightened, ran a hand through his hair. Finally he turned and looked at me, his features etched in the cloudy light from the window. "When Paul found me, I realized, what did it matter? All the drink in the world couldn't make the war go away. Why not face it head-on, then? Talk to the grieving, the mad, the deluded. Why not look for the answers to life and death? It wasn't like I had anything better to do. I threw myself into it. I exposed the liars, the ones who prey on the families of the men who were butchered just like my men were. It was satisfying, a little like I was avenging my men in the only way I knew."

"And then Gloria came along," I said.

James shook his head. "No. Gloria's power was amazing, it's true, but finding her was a little like an astronomer claiming to discover the North Star. It was incredibly obvious to me, as experienced as I was, that I was dealing with the real thing, almost from the first moment. The one who bothered me—the one who still bothers me—is you."

"We've been over this, James."

He pushed away from the counter and came toward me. "It wasn't just that I was fooled, that there was a true medium under my nose and I didn't see it. It was that it had to be you." He came close and brushed his fingertips over my cheek, his gaze taking me in. I held my breath. "I knew perfectly well that you were awake that night, you know, when I put you to bed on the sofa. I knew it all along." When I sighed, he smiled. "I've told you, you're a terrible liar."

*You'll never find a man to take you unless you lie to him—do you know that?* said Gloria's voice in my head. "I was drunk," I told James, "and rather pathetic. I wanted you to like me."

"It always bothered me, what happened," he said softly. "I told you that. But I tried not to think about it. And then Gloria died, and there you were in Trafalgar Square, and I was reminded . . ." His fingers traveled to my hair, touched the blond ends where they curled over my ear. "I spotted you right away. I told you it was a lucky guess that I found you at Ramona's, but I lied. I followed you. I didn't even know why, not really—it was just instinct. I knew that whatever was

going to happen, I only had to wait. And then you had that vision."
He looked into my eyes and his gaze cleared. He was so close I could
feel his breath on my cheek, see the warm shadows in the hollow of
his throat. I could smell his familiar shaving soap. "What did you
come here for, Ellie?" he asked me.

Words tumbled through my disordered mind, but I couldn't
speak them. I could only look at him for a long moment. He was
right—I was a terrible liar, and all the longing I felt must have shown
in my face. I curled my fingers over his wrist, pressed my fingers into
the warm pad at the base of his thumb.

"I want to meet the Dubbses," I said.

He raised his eyebrows a little and waited, not moving away.

I took a step back, though reluctantly. "I want to interview them,"
I said, my voice admirably calm, I thought. "And I want to see where
they had the séance. Where Gloria died."

James dropped his hand, his wrist leaving my grip, but the gesture was leisurely. "It's an interesting idea."

"They've been strangely quiet, don't you think?" I said. "There's
barely a line about them in the papers. You'd think a reporter would
have gotten to them by now, but that doesn't seem to be the case."

"Then you should probably talk to Scotland Yard."

"George Sutter says you already did."

James shrugged. He sat on the edge of the radiator next to the
window and began to pull on his shoes and socks. "They interviewed
me yesterday afternoon," he admitted. He seemed to be recovering
from his dark mood, training his thoughts back to the case. "An inspector called Merriken. He didn't think much of either me or my
profession, and he didn't bother being polite about it. Not that it
mattered to me." He looked up at me. "There's nothing to tell, Ellie."

"If you were the Dubbses," I said to him, "who would you be
more likely to talk to? The police, or the New Society, who can help
you contact your dead son?"

He pushed himself off the radiator and thought it over. "Fine. I'll see what I can dig up, and we'll bypass the Yard for now. And what are you going to do?"

I thought about the coded schedule I'd found in Gloria's flask bag, and I sighed. "There's nothing else for it," I said. "I'll have to talk to Davies again."

# CHAPTER NINETEEN

When I heard a dog barking, I opened my eyes. It took a frantic moment of disorientation before I remembered where I was.

I was home in St. John's Wood. I'd called on Davies after leaving James, but she hadn't been home at her flat. I'd waited for nearly half an hour, beset by a strangely frantic feeling—if Davies ever had social engagements, I was unaware of them—but she hadn't returned. By then I had a roaring headache that made the darkened streets seem as bright as the Sahara and nearly made the world buckle before my eyes. I had gone home, the sound of the tube enormous in my head, and sent my daily woman away. If I was being followed by the man in the houndstooth jacket, I was in too much pain to notice. I'd made a cup of tea and sat in a chair in the sitting room, as shaky as an old woman, absorbing the silence like a sponge. The clock ticked on the mantel, sullen rain spattered the window, and I drifted off.

Now I sat up groggy and confused, my eyes heavy, my head

spinning. The headache had drained away. I rubbed my neck and looked at my watch. Three o'clock in the afternoon.

The dog barked again, and again. I realized the sound was high pitched and frantic.

I stood and went to the front window, pulling back the curtain. My neighbor's collie, Pickwick, was standing in the street. His leash lay forgotten on the ground.

I frowned and went to the front door, opening it. "Pickwick!" I called into the damp, brisk air; the rain had moved off, but left its breath behind. "Where is Mr. Bagwell?"

Pickwick spared me only the quickest glance before returning his gaze to something down the street. His tail was low, his ears back. He barked again and again, the sound high and unhappy.

The street was deserted. I took a step outside and stopped, awareness trickling up my spine. Pickwick's long coat was soft and vivid in the afternoon light, orange and russet brown, short and dark over his sleek, intelligent head. His tail was set so low that its long brush of fur touched the ground, and I thought incongruously that Mr. Bagwell, who adored Pickwick and kept him meticulously, would likely tut over the dirt when he saw it.

I took another step toward the street. The wind touched my sleep-heated cheeks, cleared my head. Pickwick crouched lower, still barking, his back legs digging into the ground. I had approached him and bent to take up his leash before I realized I felt a telltale tickle at the back of my neck.

"Pickwick," I said. I picked up the loop of his leash and straightened again. I followed his gaze down the street.

Mr. Bagwell stood down the lane, almost at the corner. He was wearing his usual brown trousers and matching jacket, a cloth cap on his bald head. He stood facing us, his hands at his sides. *Oh, dear,* I thought at first. *I've interrupted a training exercise of some kind.* I had the urge to rub the skin at the back of my neck, scratch under my hair. If Mr. Bagwell was training Pickwick to stay, it was strange that he'd do it in the middle of the road. We had motorcars come through here every day.

Pickwick made a whine deep in his throat and lowered his haunches farther, his toenails scrabbling against the cobbles. He was trembling, and he wasn't pulling on the leash I held. His gaze was locked on his master, his look almost desperate. A faintly putrid smell wafted to my nose through the rain-fresh air.

"No," I said, my voice low and thick. "Please, no."

Under the lip of his cloth cap I could see Mr. Bagwell's eyes, their gaze fixed on the dog. He did not seem to have noticed me. I felt Pickwick's body shake.

"Please, no," I said again, but my voice was flat, hopeless.

Mr. Bagwell lifted one hand and held it palm out. Pickwick raised himself up, as if he would lunge; then he lowered himself again and whined. Mr. Bagwell's hand stayed level, the gesture unmistakable. It was the dog master's universal gesture of *Stay*.

Pickwick stayed. But a sound came from his throat, low and awful, unlike any sound I'd heard from a dog—mournful and angry and confused. A howl, but the dog swallowed it, tamped it down to please his master. His ears were back, flattened to his silky head. Dog and man locked gazes, and their look was so despairing, so intimate, that I moaned softly myself. *Don't go,* I thought. *Wait, please, please—*

A hand grabbed my arm, turned me roughly. It was Mrs. Campbell, my neighbor of two doors down, her hair askew and her face flushed with anger.

"What is the matter with you?" she cried, furious.

I stared at her in shock. The itching drained away, the throbbing in my head, and for the first time I noticed a knot of people gathered in the street behind her. "What?"

"Are you blind, or just stupid?" she nearly shouted. "Can't you see what's happened? Don't you even care?"

Inside the knot of people, a man was bent over something on the road. A van turned the corner and stopped, two men in uniforms jumping out. The man bent over moved aside and I glimpsed the familiar brown suit, the legs of Mr. Bagwell prone on the road, unmoving.

I turned and looked back at the corner, my mind clear. The spot where Mr. Bagwell had stood was empty.

"I didn't know," I said to Mrs. Campbell as Pickwick put his nose to the ground. He did not look at the body of his master. "I didn't—"

"Some neighbor you are," she spat at me. "Turn your back on a man while he dies on the road."

*I didn't turn my back on him,* I opened my mouth to say, but she had already moved away and was helping the ambulance men with the body. "His heart stopped," came the murmurs from the crowd. "Just like that, sudden-like. No one saw it coming."

More people drifted from their homes and up the street to watch the spectacle. A policeman in uniform approached me as they put the body in the back of the van and asked if this was Mr. Bagwell's dog.

"Yes," I said, my grip on the leash tightening instinctively. "This is Pickwick. I'll take him home with me."

He took down my information, told me someone would contact me with instructions for the dog once the relatives had been informed. Mr. Bagwell was a widower, and his grown children had long since moved away; even I knew that. I moved closer to Pickwick, leaning my shins against his trembling rib cage. When I had finished with the policeman, I tugged gently on the lead and the dog followed me back into the house. He had stopped shaking, and he did not look at me. He curled up obediently at my feet as I sat at the table in the kitchen. I watched him lay his nose on the linoleum and sigh.

"I'm sorry," I said aloud to him, my voice ringing in the quiet kitchen. "That was awful. I'm so sorry for you, sweetheart."

Pickwick made no move.

My chest felt tight. I kicked off my shoes and slid from the chair, going to my knees in my stockings on the kitchen floor. I bent over Pickwick, running my hands over the short fur of his forehead, the luxurious ruff of his neck. He didn't respond, but I sat there anyway, stroking him for a long time. He seemed to need no words; the action consoled me as much as it consoled him, I was sure. I lifted his chin and looked into his eyes, so sweet and soulful, eyes that had seen what I had seen. Eyes that understood.

Deathbed visions, James had called them, though it seemed cruel to call it that when a man had died so far from his bed before he'd even grown old. Yet I also thought that hadn't been exactly what it was. That *had been* Mr. Bagwell, not just an echo or a shadow of him. It had really been the man, telling his beloved dog to stay as he went where his companion couldn't follow. It had been just like all of the visions I'd called for my mother, only this time, like the previous night, I hadn't called it at all. My grip on my powers was loosening, and the dead could come whether I willed it or not.

I dug my hands into the dog's warm fur and waited for the terror to subside.

"Davies," I said into the telephone that sat in my front hall. "It's Ellie."

"What now?" she said. "I thought I was free of you, Mary Pickford."

I sighed. Mary Pickford, the name of the ringleted, golden-haired movie star, was Davies's epithet for me, her attempt at the kind of wit Gloria had wielded so easily. "I came to see you earlier."

"I was out."

Doing what? "Yes, I know. I need to talk to you."

She snorted. "Did you have fun with Octavia Murtry, that little fortune-petter, the other day?"

"Not really, no."

"Useless, isn't she? The only reason Gloria put up with her was because of Harry, though God knows what Harry saw in her. I was glad to see you have to put up with her for once. My guess is you'll have a hard time getting rid of her."

I was starting to feel steady, the nightmarish event with Mr. Bagwell fading from my mind. Pickwick was asleep on the kitchen floor. "She wants to contact Gloria's brothers," I said.

"She never had half a chance," Davies replied. "Gloria would never do it. She always said she could bear to look at other people's dead, but she had no desire to contact her own. Those boys dying ripped her to pieces."

She seemed talkative, so I pushed her further. "Did you know Gloria's brothers?"

"No, but Gloria had photographs. I only saw them once, because she never showed them around."

"She carried them with her. All three of them. Along with their notification telegrams."

There was a pause, and I realized I'd thrown Davies for a loop. "How the hell did you know that?"

She hadn't known, then. I rubbed my hand on my forehead. She'd be resentful now that I knew something about Gloria that she didn't; it would be an insult in her book. "I took her flask bag," I said, trying to sound apologetic. "When I was at her flat. It was all in there."

"You took her flask bag from under my nose? When I let you in and everything?"

"I didn't plan it." I tried to sound remorseful. "An impulse, that's all. I'm sorry, Davies."

"Some people have no manners," she said.

"Look, the letters and photographs weren't the only things tucked in there. She'd written out her schedule as well."

"*I* kept her schedule."

God, Davies was a monster of ego. "Yes, I know. This is in her handwriting—she jotted it down and carried it with her so she wouldn't forget. A reminder note, that sort of thing. I assume you gave a copy of her last week's schedule to Scotland Yard?"

"I didn't have any bloody choice, did I? One of those toffs could be the one who killed her."

"Yes, I know. I agree. The thing is—Davies, in Gloria's own schedule, she's crossed out one of the appointments and written something else in. Something I can't decode."

The line went very quiet.

"Davies?" I said.

Her voice was low, almost hurt. "She wouldn't have done that. Gloria wouldn't have."

"Maybe something important came up," I said.

"If it was important, it would have gone through me."

For a second I felt for her; Gloria's schedule had been Davies's entire life, her reason for existence. But this was Davies, after all, and my sympathy was short-lived. "Maybe you know what this means. It says—"

"Stop! Don't say it." Davies's voice lowered. "I won't discuss it over the telephone. It could be secret. You never know who is listening in on these things."

"Oh, please. That's ridiculous."

"No. It was Gloria's own policy—never discuss business on the telephone. Meet me at Marlatt's Café at six o'clock, and I'll look at this code, whatever it is."

"Davies, I don't have time for this. It's really a very simple question."

"Are you thick? That's my offer, Goldilocks."

I gritted my teeth. "Fine. I'll be there."

"Make sure of it," she said, and hung up.

# CHAPTER TWENTY

Itelephoned my daily woman—to say she was shocked to hear from me would be an understatement—and explained, omitting the supernatural elements, what had happened to Mr. Bagwell and his dog. She agreed to come by and check on Pickwick, let him out in the garden, and walk him if he needed it. I wanted to warn her that the dog was dejected, but it seemed a strange thing to discuss. She'd see for herself soon enough.

I found some tinned meat and put it down for him. He glanced at it from his spot under the kitchen table, then put his head on the floor again. "I'm going out," I told him, running my hand over his head. "I'm not sure when I'll be back, but you won't be alone. You should eat something." He made no reply.

I put on my coat and hat and was just tying the belt at the waist of my coat when someone knocked at my front door.

I thought it might be Mrs. Campbell or one of my other neighbors, come to check on the dog. But I opened the door to an unfamiliar man, tall and dark, his overcoat hanging ominously from his broad shoulders. He removed his hat and I saw a handsome face, its features serious and intelligent. "Miss Winter," he said. "I've found you at last."

I stared at him as the cool September breeze snaked past me through the doorway and a child on a bicycle pedaled by on the street behind him.

The man reached into his breast pocket and handed me a card. "I'm Inspector Merriken, from Scotland Yard. May we speak?"

I took the card in fingers gone numb. "I'm on my way out to meet someone."

His gaze traveled over me, missing nothing. "Anyone I know?"

"No," I lied.

"That's a shame," he said. "Still, I'm certain you can take a few minutes."

"I can't." I looked past him, but his large frame with its wide shoulders and long dark coat blocked the door. "I have somewhere to be."

"In London?"

"Yes, of course."

"Perfect," the inspector said smoothly. "I happen to have a motorcar here. We can talk at the Yard, and then I'll drop you wherever you like."

At the Yard? Panic squeezed me. I rubbed my throat, as if massaging the air through it. I'd never been to Scotland Yard before—I'd never had any reason to. What did it mean that he wanted to take me there now?

Inspector Merriken read my face like a book. "Don't worry," he said, his voice as smooth as cold water over river stones. "I'm not in the habit of eating women alive at the Yard, only questioning them. Especially women who pop up all over my murder investigations, then avoid me."

I stared up at him, my hand still on my throat. "I'm not going to get rid of you, am I?"

He raised an eyebrow. "Honestly, no, you're not. Persistence is a virtue of mine. Shall we go?"

He didn't speak to me on the drive to the Yard, and I didn't speak, either. I sat in the backseat, twisting my hands in my lap. Damn George Sutter. I'd asked him whether the Yard thought me a suspect and he'd neatly avoided the question. If he had access to Inspector Merriken's files, he must have known. Now I was on my way to Scotland Yard and I had no idea of the situation I was walking into.

I looked out the window at London passing by and tried to plan how I would play my cards. Did Inspector Merriken know that George Sutter somehow had access to his files? Had the man who followed me that morning seen me leave with the inspector? If so, then George Sutter would learn any minute that I was on my way to the Yard. In any case, if it got out that I was somehow aligned with the police, no one I needed would ever talk to me again, and any hope of my finding Gloria's killer would disappear.

Scotland Yard was smaller than I'd imagined, an intimate warren smelling of ink and smoke, half the desks empty. "It's getting late," Inspector Merriken said to me as he led me down a corridor, though I hadn't voiced a question. "Most of the others are either out on an investigation or have gone home."

"I see," I said.

"I'm just in here. Have a seat." He showed me into an odd-shaped cubbyhole containing only a desk and two wooden chairs. Stacks of paper teetered on the desktop, and blots of ink had soaked into the aged wood. It could have been an accountant's office except for the newspaper clippings about Gloria's murder on the desk, the file marked SOMERSHAM STABBING half pulled from the stack of papers, and the large map of London pinned to the wall.

I pulled up a chair and sat, glancing at my watch. Half an hour and I'd be late meeting Davies. I pulled off my gloves and laid them in my lap.

Inspector Merriken shed his coat and lowered his tall frame into the chair behind the desk. "You needn't calculate so obviously," he said. "All I want is information."

"About what?"

"What do you think?" he said. "So far, in my interviews over this murder, one name has persistently popped up. Miss Davies, Fitzroy Todd, James Hawley, even Paul Golding. Every single one of them, somewhere in the conversation, has eventually mentioned you."

I stared at him aghast.

"It seems you're very well-known in certain circles," Inspector Merriken went on. "And yet my journalist sources know almost nothing about you, even though you're a practicing psychic. You manage to stay out of the public eye. Yet everyone in these certain circles knows about your association with Gloria. How the two of you were great friends for a while, and how it ended. Paul Golding himself told us about how his tests debunked your mother's powers, and how the tests were Gloria's idea. But he didn't need to tell us about it really; we'd already read the article ourselves. It was recently in the newspapers, after all. Even Ramona—or Joyce Gowther, as she should be known—was eager to tell us about it."

I sat speechless. They had talked about me? Paul Golding had talked about me? *I hear things,* Ramona had said. *All about The Fantastique, and Gloria Sutter, and how they used to be friends cutting up London.*

Inspector Merriken seemed to need no reply. "Hawley claimed he hadn't seen you in years, that you likely hated him. He'd been part of the tests on your mother. And yet"—the inspector leaned forward, and for the first time a flicker of frustration crossed his impassive face—"there the two of you were at the Gild Theatre last night, thick as thieves. The man I've got watching Ramona saw you plain as I see you now."

My mind raced. The man with the mustache—the man I'd thought was a plant. Was he working for Scotland Yard? What about the person I'd glimpsed leaving the balcony?

*He didn't think much of either me or my profession,* James had said.

"James Hawley has nothing to do with this," I said.

The inspector looked at me. "James Hawley threw away a law career, by all accounts, in order to be a drunk. Then he dried out and started investigating psychics. His employer, Paul Golding, recently wrote a forty-page journal article about fairy photography. I'd give a limb for a credible source in this case."

"You don't know anything about it," I said, my voice shaking. "You're hearing all the wrong stories. James had no reason to kill her. Neither did I."

He leaned back again and let out a disgusted sigh. "I'll admit you don't seem likely. Murderers tend to be rather impulsive, and the tests on your mother happened three years ago. What's more, you've had a thriving business ever since, and Gloria's actions didn't threaten your livelihood."

I flushed. They *had* threatened our livelihood; my mother's career had been finished. We'd paid the bills only because I'd officially stepped in and taken over. But I saw no need to disabuse the inspector.

"And yet," I said, my voice trembling, "I make a living as a psychic, so I must be a liar. I'm not one of your credible sources. That is what you assume, isn't it, Inspector? That is why I'm on your list. Let's get to the heart of it, shall we?"

He drummed his fingers on the stack of papers on the desk, looking at me thoughtfully, and said nothing.

"I could tell you where I was on Monday night," I said. "I was home alone, just as I always am every night of my life. But you haven't asked me that, because there's no point, is there? I'm a liar, and any answer I give to your questions must automatically be a lie."

"It may not be a lie," he said easily. "It's just possible. Your neighbors didn't see you leaving."

I gripped the arms of my chair, my fingers squeezing so hard they began to go numb. "You questioned my neighbors?"

"Yes, for the fat lot of good it did me." He pushed back his own chair and stood, and I saw how much frustration was leashed inside his large frame, cloaked in the elegant way he handled his body but still informing his every movement. "Do you want to get to the heart of the matter?" he said. "Very well, then. Let's. By all indications, this should be an open-and-shut case. I've got witnesses, or close enough. A victim who was a popular public figure, distinctive and easily recognizable. A murder that happened out in the open for anyone to see. I have Gloria Sutter's client list, her schedule, her every movement for her final week. I know who she saw, how much she charged—I even know who she slept with, which was no one, at least not for the last few months. Everyone I've interviewed has been more than happy to talk my ear off, yet no one has given me an inkling of information that can actually lead me to her killer." He said the last word as he thumped one large, well-formed hand on the desk in front of me, leaning on it and looking down at me. "*That* is the heart of the matter."

I stared up at him, biting my lip. I knew then, from the honest frustration on his face, that Inspector Merriken had no idea that George Sutter—whoever he was, whoever he worked for—was reading his reports. If I told him now, it would unbalance everything. And I *needed* George Sutter if I was to get to Gloria's killer. However, I needed Scotland Yard as well.

"All right," I said. "Do you want to hear what I think?"

The inspector made a sound I couldn't interpret and walked to a sideboard where a pitcher of water stood next to several cups.

"You're looking in the wrong place," I said. He turned and glared at me, but I gathered my courage and plunged on. "Clients, rivals, lovers—none of those things matter to her death. It's all misdirection, like the card tricksters use. Gloria's entire life was a misdirection. She was a master at it."

Inspector Merriken poured one glass of water, and then a second. "You'd be surprised who some of her clients were. I know I was."

"I wouldn't," I said. "But what does it matter? What powerful man is going to be afraid of a psychic? I could go to the newspapers and say I had psychic information about the prime minister, or the King, and they'd just laugh at me. Some politician's petty affairs are not the reason she was murdered."

"Then pray tell, where should I be looking?"

"I keep coming back to the murder itself," I said as he took one of the cups of water and handed it to me. "It didn't fit Gloria's usual pattern. She never did sessions outside of her own flat. The only reason she did the session for the Dubbses was for money."

Inspector Merriken took a sip of his water and waited for me to continue.

"The Dubbses paid Fitz to get access to Gloria," I said. "And then they paid Gloria. Do you have any idea how much money that must have been?"

"Wait a minute." The inspector frowned at me. "Fitzroy Todd never told me he'd been paid."

"That's because he's a liar who would sell his own mother to suit his ends. Trust me, Fitz needed money, and whatever the Dubbses offered him was well worth the risk. Then whatever they offered Gloria was worth her abandoning her own rules to solve her money problems. Both of them had expensive tastes, especially Fitz. Neither one would have agreed for less than a princely sum. So exactly how rich are the Dubbses?"

Inspector Merriken sipped his water and frowned. "The house in Kent was rather nice," he said. "But nothing about them suggested they were wealthy."

"Look again," I said. "Look for where the money came from, and then look for why."

"Miss Winter," he said slowly, his voice a low drawl, "what exactly are you suggesting?"

"It wasn't a random act," I said. "It was a lure, a setup. Someone put it together very deliberately because someone wanted her dead."

"Are you saying that the Dubbses killed her?"

"I wish I knew," I said. "To me it doesn't seem likely that if you want to kill a girl, you invite her to your house and do it right on the property. But then, I know less about murder than you do."

Still he stood by the water pitcher, frowning, idly swirling his water glass. "It bears examining, I suppose. We looked at the Dubbses from the first, because we looked at everyone in attendance that night. But they seemed a normal couple. He works in the city, where they have a flat he uses during the week, while they spend weekends at the house. Affluent, but not too rich. No surviving children. The house has three servants, none of whom live in, and all of them had been given the night off. Everything they told us seemed to fit." He frowned. "Except for one thing, now that I think of it. Ramona told us that when she and Fitzroy Todd appeared with Gloria at the train station, the Dubbses were upset and tried to send them home. But both Todd and the Dubbses denied it, so we assumed Ramona was lying."

"Why would she lie?"

"Why not? Why would Todd and the Dubbses lie?" He looked at me. "If it wasn't the Dubbses themselves orchestrating the murder, that means they were somehow being used. You know that you're suggesting something with large implications?"

I set my water glass down on the desk, untouched, thinking about George Sutter, how he'd given me confidential documents from the first.

"You don't seem surprised," Inspector Merriken said.

"May I go now?" I asked.

His gaze sharpened on me. He didn't reply, but instead said, "Are you truly psychic?"

I sighed. "Why ask? You're not going to believe my answer."

"You'd be surprised at what I believe, Miss Winter."

My gaze rose to his. There was a hint of something, deep in his eyes, that made me wonder what exactly had happened to Inspector Merriken to make him ask that question. But I wasn't ready to reveal myself to the relentless scrutiny of Scotland Yard.

I lifted my chin. "You have a fiancée," I said, "and you're on your way to see her tonight."

The inspector went very still.

"Here's how I know," I continued. "There is a clock on the wall behind my right shoulder. I can hear it ticking. You've glanced over my right shoulder exactly six times during this interview, which tells me you have somewhere to go. It's past five thirty at night, and Gloria died four days ago. You've likely put in long hours since her murder. If you're looking at the clock, you're likely expecting your first evening off since her death. And you're doing something you're very much looking forward to."

He opened his mouth to speak, but I interrupted him and went on. "You aren't going out with friends for a pint, or going home alone. You're going to see someone important, someone who matters. That means a woman." I nodded toward his left hand. "You don't wear a wedding ring, so you haven't married her, at least not yet. But she isn't a casual girlfriend, either, judging by your anticipation. That leaves a fiancée." I looked into his eyes again. "Does that answer your question?"

His expression had gone very hard and his jaw was flexing. "Very well," he said tightly. "You may go."

I pushed my chair back and stood, but as I turned to leave he spoke to me again.

"Miss Winter. Did Gloria have contact with her family that you know of?"

I turned back to him. The tightness in his jaw was gone, but his expression gave nothing away.

"No," I replied.

"How many brothers did she have?"

"Four. Three died in the war."

"And her parents?"

He must have known this already. "Her mother is dead and her father is in a home. He's lost his faculties."

"What were her brothers' names?"

"Harry, Colin, and Tommy. George is still alive."

"And what is the name of my fiancée?"

"Jillian."

We both stopped. The air in the room seemed to turn itself inside out, become something unbreathable.

"Very interesting," Inspector Merriken said.

Anger flushed through me and I stood frozen, staring at him.

"Misdirection," he said softly. "A useful trick. If you can use it, then so can I."

"Am I right?"

"You know you are." He shook his head. His voice carried a hint of admiration, but no wonder or shock, and again I was curious about exactly how he had come across the paranormal before. I suspected it was an interesting story. "You almost had me, you know. That was a clever move, making me angry."

I hesitated. "The glass of water," I admitted. "It came to me when you handed it to me."

His fingertip had barely touched mine, and yet it had come so clear, like a rush of water. No pain, just a flow of information, my powers working just as they always had. And they had been *right*.

He seemed to accept my explanation. "Did you get anything else?"

"She has dark hair," I said. "And she drives you crazy, and the last time you kissed her she tasted like apples. As for the rest of what you're thinking about, I'll only say it's a good thing you're going to marry her." I watched his expression and shrugged. "It was in your mind—sorry. I can't always help what I pick up."

"I'll be damned," he said softly. "That's a very good trick. But for God's sake, please don't repeat any of that."

"I never do," I said, and turned and left to meet Davies.

# CHAPTER TWENTY-ONE

B y the time I arrived at Marlatt's Café, out of breath and my hat askew, I was thirteen minutes late. It wasn't much, but I didn't trust Davies to wait.

The café was a little closet-size spot in the warren of streets and alleys of Soho, run by a tiny man with nut brown skin whom everyone assumed was Marlatt. The place specialized in coffee that was painfully strong, served in an atmosphere in which you practically rubbed knees with the person at the table next to you, and there was a blue-tinged fug of cigarette smoke that never dissipated day or night. Gloria had loved the coffee here, but she'd said the place was like a great-grandmother's closet, and smelled worse.

I pushed open the frosted door, nearly bumping into the back of an old man who sat smoking at one of the tables, and squinted into the gloom. At the counter in the back corner stood Marlatt. He was wiping it down with an oily rag and did not look up at my entrance.

I looked around frantically. The old man I'd almost collided with was the only patron in the place. Davies was nowhere to be seen. My stomach sank. She had left—if she had ever kept her word and come here at all.

Marlatt was looking at me now, his dark eyes incurious. He was Turkish, we thought, something over fifty, his black hair combed back and slicked down on his head. He picked up a teacup and slowly polished it with his rag.

"Excuse me," I said as politely as I could, considering how hard my heart was thumping in my chest. I stepped to the back counter. "Was Miss Davies just here?"

Marlatt frowned at me and shrugged, uncaring.

"Please," I said. "I'm looking for her urgently. She was supposed to meet me. Was she here?"

"Sure," Marlatt told me, though grudgingly. "Just a minute ago."

"What happened?" I tried not to sound shrill. "Where did she go? Did she go home?"

"How do I know? I didn't follow her."

"Did she say anything? Please, it's important."

Marlatt shrugged again. "She didn't say. I assume because she was following the fellow."

I went cold.

"Fellow?"

"The fellow who came in here. Talked to her a few minutes only. Then they left."

"Who was he? What did he look like?"

"How do I know?" Marlatt said again, annoyed now. Behind me, the door opened and someone else entered. "He looked like all the other fellows."

"But have you seen him before? Was he—?"

"I didn't know him," Marlatt said, shooing me with his hands. "Now go away."

"If you're asking, I didn't know him, either."

I turned and saw the old man I'd almost bumped into, still sitting at a table by the door. He wore a rumpled suit and held a cigarette between two tobacco-stained fingers. He regarded me from under gray-white eyebrows of astonishing length.

"Please," I said, turning away from Marlatt and approaching his table. "My friend was supposed to meet me here. It isn't like her to go walking off with strange men. Can you tell me what he looked like?"

The old man looked me up and down and shrugged. "Can't say I got a close look at the chap. Slim. Dark suit, black coat, black hat. Respectable. Spoke softly."

"His face?"

The man shrugged again.

"Was he dark haired or light haired?"

"Dark haired, from what I could see."

So it wasn't James, then. It couldn't be. "Did she seem to know him?"

The man took a drag of his cigarette, enjoying the attention, likely the only he'd had all day. "Well, she gave him a glare when he approached her, though she's always got a sour face, that one. Argued with him a bit at first. But then she got real quiet while he talked, and the next thing I saw she followed him out of here without a word."

"Did you hear them?"

"Miss, I haven't heard right since about '13. I have no idea what they said."

"Which way did they go?"

"That way." The man pointed.

The opposite direction from her flat, then. I thanked him and hurried back into the street. The rain had long stopped, but dusk was just beginning to fall, the sky turning lavender-blue. I hurried down the sidewalk, looking for Davies's rumpled hat and mismatched jacket, her patented slouch as she walked alongside a nondescript dark-haired man. I pushed through the suppertime crowd, dodging elbows and handbags and puffs of cigarette smoke.

By the time I pushed my way out into the crowds on Shaftesbury Avenue, I had to give it up in despair. Davies and her mysterious man could have gone anywhere, ducked into a shop, taken a taxi or a bus. I was nearly at the roar of Piccadilly Circus, where I had no hope of finding them, even if they had come this way.

Davies never went off with strange men.

Never.

Perhaps she knew him. It was probably nothing.

It wasn't nothing.

*She got real quiet while he talked, and the next thing I saw she followed him out of here without a word.*

What could a man—any man—have said to Davies to make her follow him in silence?

"Damn it," I said under my breath, the curse feeling satisfying on my tongue. I tried it a little louder. *"Damn it."*

"Watch your language, young lady," a woman said disapprovingly as she passed me. She turned and tutted to her companion. "Girls today."

"Damn it," I said to her back, and walked toward Piccadilly Circus.

I suppose it was inevitable that things would fall apart after I met Gloria Sutter. I'm convinced that she had some of it planned, possibly from the moment she recognized who I was while I was sleeping on that train. But sometimes I wondered whether even she was fully in control of what she'd set in motion. The problem with Gloria, as always, was sorting out the truth from the lie.

My mother believed in my new friend Florence for nearly two years. The incredible stretch of time I kept my mother's suspicions at bay both relieved me and utterly shamed me. In my occasional "nights over" at "Florence's" house, my mother was never given the burden of knowing exactly what I was up to. But her credulousness came from her belief in me, in my honesty and my loyalty, none of which I earned.

I didn't see Gloria every day, of course, or even every week. But a month would pass, or possibly two, and I'd get a note in Gloria's distinctive handwriting, the words toppling over one another like children's blocks, inviting me to Soho. Perhaps she missed my company, or perhaps she was simply bored; I never knew which, and I never cared. I'd pack my valise, tell Mother I was off to visit Florence, and we'd go out on the town.

Those are some of the longest nights of my memory, stretching until three or four o'clock in the morning. We went to nightclubs and late-night supper clubs; we danced with people we didn't know; we mixed gin with champagne. I grew used to the sophistication of Gloria's social circle, their shallow jokes and ridiculous pretensions, and though the experiences were foolish and ultimately meaningless, they had one salient quality: They were fun. We were young, the war was over, and we dealt in death day after day, the faces of the dead haunting both our waking lives and our dreams. So fun was its own reward, a virtue in and of itself. And although we were usually in a crowd, I always felt that between Gloria and me alone there was something different, some recognition and understanding of the desperate need we had for those endless riotous nights.

And then one night I stupidly took a taxi home instead of sleeping on Gloria's horrible sofa, arriving home drunk at three o'clock in the morning and waking my mother out of bed.

It was a moving scene, straight from a stage melodrama or a two-reel film. My mother was bewildered, then tearful, then angry; I was sullen, rebellious, and finally sick. Before I passed out, my head already aching, I confessed that Florence was a hoax, and I gave my mother Gloria's name.

The next day, as I alternated between moping in the kitchen and lying prostrate on my bed, my mother called off her afternoon's appointments and marched out the door, handbag in hand. Through my fog I was able to feel the sheer, horrified embarrassment that my mother was going to Soho. She came home two hours later, white faced and unspeaking.

I stared at my mother over our silent supper that night, watching her pick at her food. "What is it?" I managed, overcoming the shame that had kept me silent. "What did Gloria say to you?"

She set down her fork and looked at me. She wore a faded day dress under a black cardigan, her hair tied at the nape of her neck, and in that moment she looked like any other housewife on our street, a woman who had seen a war and buried a husband and raised a daughter. The anger had faded from her eyes, but something else had replaced it, something deep and terribly torn.

"Why didn't you tell me about her?" she asked.

I swallowed. "I thought you'd disapprove."

"The drinking? The strange men?" She shook her head. "Of *course* I disapprove."

My cheeks heated. "I don't do anything with strange men."

"Well, there's that, at least." She sounded weary. "But that isn't what I meant. Why didn't you tell me about *her*? About Gloria?"

She meant Gloria's powers; she'd almost certainly sensed them from the first moment, just as I had. What had happened when they met? What had they talked about? Had they discussed me? I was seized with jealousy, sharp and overwhelming. I hadn't told anyone about Gloria because Gloria was *mine*.

"I don't know," I managed, sullen.

My mother put an elbow on the table and pressed her fingers to her chin, her gaze leaving me. She had long, elegant hands, the fingers tapered, the nails oval. I'd only partially inherited those hands; mine were nice enough, but my mother's had a beauty I'd always envied. Now she sat thoughtful, the thin circle of her wedding ring dull in the evening light.

"I feel sorry for that girl," she said at last.

I gaped at her. "Sorry for her? She's beautiful and rich."

"She's lonely," my mother said. "This is a lonely business. Do you know she actually offered to contact your father for me?"

"What?"

"Oh, yes. It was a clever offer, you know. Contacting one's own family . . . It's unthinkable. I could never have done it myself, though I've thought about it more times than I can count."

I swallowed. "You've thought about contacting Father?"

"Every day. Don't look so shocked, Ellie. Someday, when you have a husband, you'll understand what the cost is to lose him."

She looked tired again, and I closed my mouth. She almost never talked about my father, who died in the war. A shell hit him in Gallipoli, and he never came home. My father had always been kind and loving to me, but the center of his life had been my mother—a sentiment I understood, because she was the center of my life, too. My own grief at his death had been suffered in silence, subsumed by the fact that my mother had nearly fallen apart. My parents had never been showy or romantic; it was only after the loss of my father that I began to understand how truly in love they had been, in their quiet way.

"Gloria Sutter," my mother had said, "knew within seconds just what to offer me, and she had no second thoughts about speaking of it. She called it an offer to atone for how the two of you deceived me. I turned her down, but I won't lie—I was horribly tempted. I considered it more seriously than I'd like to admit before I said no." Her gaze focused on me again, and she sighed. "I'm still angry with you, and perhaps this is stupid, but I'm not going to forbid you to see her again. You don't have very many friends your own age—possibly the two of you can help each other in some way. But I don't want you drinking in public. And stay away from any of the men she introduces you to."

It was generous, but I defied her, even in that. It was 1921, and hedonism was the height of fashion in London. I stayed out late dancing; I had my hair bobbed. We had another fearful row. I continued to see Gloria, and I continued to follow her into anything she told me was fun. I kissed a few different men who seemed to want me to, but they tasted like alcohol and cigarettes, and the thought of taking off my clothes for them was humiliating. Still, I tried the kissing at least, and we laughed about it afterward. Something about me was jagged and off-kilter; I felt like a stranger inside my own skin, a person I didn't recognize. And somewhere in that fog of late nights and arguments, the stranger I had become met James Hawley, and watched from under her lashes as he removed her shoes, her heart squeezing in her chest in longing and disappointment as the room spun.

My mother and I did sessions during the day as we always had, with Mother in her beaded dress and scarf in the sitting room and I behind the plum curtain with my eyes closed, the back of my neck itching, summoning the dead. They always came. My mother grew tired more often, and sometimes she went to bed after supper and slept without pause until I roused her in the morning. I watched her grow paler, the smudges under her eyes becoming larger, and something inside me wanted to climb into bed with her at night and curl up next to her as I'd done as a child. But I never did.

One day, after our last appointment had left, I found her sitting in the kitchen, still wearing her dress and scarf. She held a letter in her hand.

"I've made an appointment," she said. "For a test."

I stared at her. She couldn't be sick—she couldn't possibly be. "A medical test?"

"No." She put the letter on the kitchen table. "A test for the New Society for the Furtherance of Psychical Research."

I blinked at her. It was early spring, the air raw and damp, and I pulled my oversize cardigan closer over my chest. "What are you talking about? Are you mad?"

Her lips thinned and she didn't answer me.

I pulled back a kitchen chair, the legs scraping loud in the silence, and dropped into it. "Gloria has done tests for them for a year," I said, trying not to think of James Hawley. "She laughs about it. It's a lark to her. The tests she describes are horrible—demeaning and useless."

My mother raised her gaze to mine. Outside, the sky darkened as the supper hour approached, the faint, dismal gray that had lingered over the day finally fading. "It was Gloria who asked me to participate."

"What?"

"She wrote me." My mother traced one long, beautiful finger along the edge of the letter on the table. "She told me the work was important, that the New Society was fighting for recognition for people like us. She said it would mean a lot to her if I'd submit."

"And you believed her?"

"Of course not. I may not know her as you do, Ellie, but I know enough. She wants something, or she thinks she does. I think she believes that by convincing me to do this, she's winning some sort of game."

*It isn't personal,* Gloria had said the first day she met me, *but I'm afraid I'm rather competitive.* In all those drunken evenings, I'd never confessed to her that it was I who managed all of my mother's séances. Part of me had always known better. I'd had no idea she was planning something like this, and I couldn't fathom why; I was only glad, for the moment, that I wasn't the one in her sights. "You shouldn't go," I told my mother, panic in my voice. "Say no."

"I could," she said, "but I won't."

"Mother, you *can't.*"

She leaned toward me, her eyes tired as they always were now. "My sweet girl," she said so softly that tears sprang unbidden to my eyes. "My sweetling, my precious one. What do I have to prove to anyone anymore?"

"Fine." I swiped the tears from my eyes, letting them soak into the sleeve of my cardigan. "Suit yourself. Go ahead—I don't care."

"But, darling, you're coming with me."

I stared at her, her face breaking into stars through the tears on my lashes. "What?"

"They want both of us," my mother said. "Gloria requested specifically that you be part of the test."

She knew. That was the only thing it could mean. She *knew.*

"Mother, we can't," I protested.

But The Fantastique smiled at me, the jet beads on her dress clicking softly. "Oh, yes," she said, her voice low. "We can."

W e did the tests, and it went worse than I could have imagined. We were taken to the back room of the offices of the New Society. There were three chairs in the middle of the room and three more chairs lined along the wall. "Our simplest experiment," Paul Golding told us. "No gadgets, no tricks. You need do nothing except answer our questions. However," he continued as two men came into the room, "it is sometimes customary for a psychic to have an accomplice giving her signals and signs. For the experiment to be pure, we have to ensure there is no chance of it. Please take a seat, Mrs. Winter, Miss Winter. This is Mr. James Hawley, my assistant."

He was even more handsome than I remembered, now that I saw him in plain light, not in the dimness of a bar or the darkness of Gloria's flat. He wore no hat and his short, dark blond hair was neatly groomed. He moved with the grace I recalled, even in a jacket and tie, and he nodded formally at me as if he'd never met me, his blue-gray eyes shuttered. I realized, with a shock, that he was carrying ropes and a blindfold in his hands.

Mother and I sat in two of the chairs in the center of the room placed back-to-back. I watched in dismayed silence as James Hawley knelt before me—without a word to me—and tied my ankles to the legs of my chair, the motion pushing my knees apart. His hands were warm and competent. I flushed, watching the strong column of the back of his neck as he bent to his work between my knees, the neat line where his hair ended against the skin. I felt shame and dread and a creeping, self-loathing outrage as his fingers brushed the backs of my calves, just as they had on that night that now seemed a million years ago.

"What is this?" I finally choked.

He moved upward, gently taking my hands and tying them to-gether at the wrists. Behind me, I could hear the other man tying my mother in a similar fashion. "No foot taps," James said softly, his voice low and familiar from my many heated daydreams. "No hand signals. No body signals at all. We have to make certain."

"Then just send me from the room," I pleaded, my blood pump-ing, to my horror, as his fingers grasped my wrists.

He shook his head. "This is part of the experiment."

My throat closed in panic. I was part of the experiment. They thought it was *me* summoning the dead. The only person who could have told them was Gloria.

"Did you pay her?" I asked him, my voice a vindictive hiss. "Don't tell me she did this for you for free."

But he only shook his head again, rising and sliding the blindfold through his large, supple hands. The sound of the cloth against his palms made me shake in fear.

He paused for only a moment. "This won't take long," he said. I searched for the sound of apology in his voice, and found none. "Just hold still." And he slipped the blindfold over my eyes.

He lied; it did take long. It took hours and hours, Mother and I tied to our chairs, blindfolded, while Paul Golding sat in the third chair and James and two others observed from the side of the room. The tests themselves, I learned, were the most basic ones they gave to people with supposed psychic powers. *What is printed on the card I'm holding? What word have I just written on this piece of paper? What name am I thinking of right now? Can you move an object in this room? Take your time, Mrs. Winter.*

She failed, of course. Sometimes she guessed wrongly; other times she sat wordless, or whispered, "*I don't know.*" I seethed with silent anger in the darkness in my chair. She had made me promise. On the journey here, she had made me swear, to the bottom of my love and loyalty to her, not to help her with the tests. She had told me, quiet and confident, that she wanted to do them on her own. If I helped her, she said, she would never forgive me. There was nothing I could do; she was all I had. And so I sat there, in an agony of humiliation suffused by a red wave of anger, and listened to her fail.

Inevitably, they asked me the same questions, but by then it was obvious that The Fantastique, who had been in business for decades, could not perform even the simplest psychic task. To use my powers and answer correctly—the ones I could answer, since it was absurd to think a psychic could tell you what card you were holding—would only expose her further. And so, when they asked me their questions, I had no choice but to grit my teeth, follow her lead, and say I didn't know.

My fury burned itself out sometime in the second hour, and by the time they took the blindfold off, it was wet with tears. I could have shouted at all of them, shouted that The Fantastique was not a liar, the tests were unfair, and my mother was tired. But I said nothing. She wanted no defense; she wanted only to do the tests on her own terms, pass or fail them as she would, though I did not know why. When James untied my hands and feet at last, I jumped from my chair and faced all of them, the tears smearing my cheeks.

"This is finished," I said, taking my mother's hand in mine. She was unresisting, her skin cool and clammy. "You've bullied and humiliated two women for an afternoon, and you've done enough. We're going home. Do not contact my mother again."

In the taxi, I looked at her exhausted face and said only, *"Why?"*

To my amazement, she smiled. "It's over," she said. "It's over. After all these years—all of my life—it's finally over."

"They'll write about it," I said, my voice still tight with anger. "They'll write that we're liars, frauds. And then where will we be?"

I felt her stroke the back of my hand with her beautiful fingers. "I'd have you live a different life if I could. Do you understand? This isn't a good life—the right life—for a girl. Sometimes I think I should have done it years ago."

"But this is our livelihood," I replied, fighting panic. "This is what keeps us independent. That's what you've always taught me."

She shook her head, and I thought she would say something else, but instead she closed her eyes. "I'm so tired," she said. After a moment she leaned into me, her head on my shoulder like a child. I put my arm around her and held her tight for the rest of the ride home, my anger forgotten, my mind spinning. I had never known, never suspected, that my mother wanted to be free.

She never worked again. She grew sicker and sicker—cancer, the doctors finally admitted. By the time the New Society's report came out, neither of us cared about losing clients. She was too sick to work, and I was too busy caring for her, and too grief-stricken, to take over. The months went by and the money dwindled. A numbness came over me, growing around me like a shell. The world disappeared.

Five months after the tests, she was dead. I held her hand in those last moments, all of our arguments forgotten. And when she was gone, and I sat hollow and empty and helpless, I had no luxury to take up another life as she'd wished. I salvaged what clients I could and I found new ones—there are always people looking for answers who have never read obscure reports—and I started up business as The Fantastique. I stopped doing séances and I consoled myself with the fact that, despite how badly Gloria had wanted it, she'd never proven that I had been the power behind my mother's curtain. My mother and I had won that much dignity, at least.

*It isn't personal,* Gloria had told me.

But it was. It was.

# CHAPTER TWENTY-TWO

Davies's disappearance had left me at loose ends, unsure of what to do. It had also left me, I soon realized, in the company of George Sutter's agent, the man in the houndstooth jacket.

I glimpsed him briefly in the reflection on a shop window as I wandered the crowds of Piccadilly Circus. He vanished into a doorway across the street, but before he disappeared I noticed his jacket and almost got a good look at him. He was tall, narrow shouldered, built very thin, wearing a hat that was the worse for wear. He did not have a mustache, which eliminated him from being the man I'd seen at the Gild Theatre.

If he was an MI5 agent, he wasn't overly discreet, especially in his distinctive choice of jacket pattern. If MI5 had employed women, I would have dressed more blandly and done a much better job. However, it was likely that he saw me, a blithely unaware girl, as the easiest—and possibly most demeaning—of assignments, and my futile attempt at escape that morning had done nothing to alter his impression. It had been obvious that I'd been carted away from my home by a Scotland Yard detective, for example, and it would have been a simple matter to linger outside the Yard and wait for me to leave. And now here I was, oblivious again.

It chafed me. Men underestimated me at every turn—Paul Golding, Inspector Merriken, even James Hawley, though at least he had apologized. Certainly George Sutter seemed to think me nothing but a pawn for some mysterious end of his. All right, then—he could find me.

I continued to stare into the shop window like a dunce. I adjusted the set of my hat in the reflection in the glass. Then I looked in the next shop window, and the next, for all the world like a silly girl going shopping, a girl who has forgotten that she is in the middle of a murder investigation because she's spotted a nice pair of shoes.

At the entrance to the Piccadilly Circus tube station, I ducked inside, bought a ticket, and hurried down the stairs. It took him exactly sixty seconds to follow me; I knew because I watched him from behind a set of scaffolding, covered by a canvas tarp, that was set up near the entrances to the platforms. The station was under construction, thank God. This time, from my vantage point, I got a clear look at his face. I watched Mr. Houndstooth look this way and that, then move through the gates, his eyes scanning the crowds. I turned to find two construction workers staring at me, one of them with a cigarette in hand. The other one waggled his eyebrows at me.

"Old boyfriend," I said to them, making my tone brassy. "He's the last bloke I want to see!"

Their laughter followed me up the stairs and out into the street.

Perhaps it would work, I thought as I quickly boarded a passing omnibus. Or perhaps it wouldn't. At the very least, it would buy me some time. At least I knew now where to go next. George Sutter had suggested I interview Ramona again, and despite myself, I agreed. I would get off this bus after several more stops and use George's money to take a taxi to Streatham.

. . .

Dusk was falling when I arrived, the light fading from the bruised sky. I paid the taxi driver and hesitated in front of Ramona's building. As before, there was no sign of life. I glanced across the street at the soon to be shuttered wig shop, thinking of how I had stood under its awning in the rain waiting for Ramona's séance. I didn't want to think about the séance, and I certainly didn't want to go back into Ramona's awful block of flats. But there was nothing for it, so I plunged ahead.

The vestibule and the hall were as dark as I remembered, and the grimy smell was the same. Since the previous night, however, a thin rope had been strung across the entrance to the stairwell, a simple handwritten paper sign over it: OUT OF ORDER.

I approached the rope and peered up the dark stairwell. How could a flight of stairs be out of order? I waited and listened, but heard no sounds of ongoing work. Perhaps some of the stairs had caved in, or a section of ceiling had fallen. If so, any workers that had been hired to fix it must have left for the day.

That meant only the horrible old elevator could get me to the fourth floor. I gritted my teeth and slid open the diamond grille, pulling at the door and stepping into the yawning black space inside. Only a small eye-level window in the door lit the interior of the elevator, letting in the fading gloom. There had been a light in here last time I'd used it, but it must have broken. I fumbled in the dark for a long moment, looking for the lever. Outside the window, nothing moved and no one came or went.

There was a distinct smell in there, as of someone who hadn't washed in weeks, underlaid with a more sinister odor. I breathed shallowly and slid my gloved hands over the controls, no sound but my own breathing in my ears. I was about to give up and try the hazardous stairs when I finally pressed the lever the right way and the elevator began its shuddering ascent.

It seemed, if possible, even slower than the last time. Something creaked high overhead as we passed the second story, and the floor juddered under my feet; I grasped the wall with one hand, wondering whether I would have to burn my gloves. I wasn't certain I wanted to look at them in the light once I was out of here.

The third story passed by slowly out the window. I slid into the bored stupor of the elevator captive, staring out the window and waiting for my floor. Then the fourth floor came into view and I froze, the hairs on the back of my neck on end.

On the other side of the tiny window, Ramona stood in the hallway.

She was in front of the door to her flat, barefoot, facing me. She watched as the elevator finished its climb and my face appeared in the window. She was wearing only a brightly patterned dressing gown in the Chinese style, its pink and blue muddy in the dim light of the hallway, the belt tied loosely around her waist, the top gaping open to reveal the bony center of her small chest. Her dark hair was untidy, her makeup smeared.

The elevator stopped with a lurch. Silence fell, complete and stifling. Ramona stared at me.

The back of my neck roared into life, an itching crawling from the base of my skull, and a nauseating smell overpowered me.

"No," I said softly.

I reached one gloved hand to the handle of the elevator door. Ramona shook her head, the motion slow and eerie, the dim light from the high window glowing pale on the high skin of her forehead.

"No," I said again.

She raised one white hand, palm out. Her arm shimmered in the air, and the movement was uncanny, like the imperfect imagination of how a human might move. I had seen too many dead in my life to misunderstand, yet part of me refused to believe it. I had just left her the night before.

She held her hand out to me, and I recognized Mr. Bagwell's

gesture. *Stay.* Only this time it was directed at me. I remembered the first time I had come here and knocked on her door, how I'd seen a vision of her lying dead on the floor of her flat. She shook her head again.

My heart flipped in my chest and I backed mindlessly away until I hit the wall of the elevator chamber. A strangled sob came from my throat. *Someone has murdered her,* I thought, *and he is still in there.*

And he must have heard the elevator move.

I fumbled in the dim darkness for the lever again, my hands slick inside my gloves. The elevator started with a sound so loud to my ears that I gasped out a whispered scream. *She can't be dead,* I thought in high-pitched disbelief. *First Davies gone, now Ramona dead. Is Davies dead, too? Am I too late for everyone?* Pulleys creaked, the cab juddered again, and I began to lower. I backed against the wall as I watched Ramona disappear through the window, first her head, then her wasted body in its awful dressing gown. When her feet vanished past the top of the window, she still had not moved.

He would hear me. He would have to—everyone in the building would have been able to hear this execrable elevator. Had he heard my ascent? Had he—whoever he was—stood just inside the door of Ramona's flat, waiting for me to exit the elevator and come to the door?

I pounded the wall with the heel of one hand, the strangled sob emerging from my throat again. *Move!* The killer, if he heard me, had no need to wait for the ancient elevator to come back. He only needed to step past the rope closing off the stairs to beat me to the hall and meet me there.

The car creaked patiently to the ground floor, and I peered out the window. The front hall was empty. When the elevator had stopped and silence fell again, I hesitated for only a moment, weighing the possibility that the murderer was waiting in a spot I couldn't see against the possibility that he had not yet come down the stairs. In either case, it was impossible to stand in this stinking car any longer, waiting to be killed. I gripped the door handle and pulled it back, sliding the metal grate with my other hand.

The door creaked with a sound like a scream. I slid out into the hall before it was all the way open and ran to the building's front entrance, my heels clicking on the tile. From upstairs came the sound of unhurried footsteps descending the stairs.

I burst out onto the front walk, gasping. The street was empty, darkness falling in pillowy folds. A thin, misty rain was beginning. I looked left to right and for a horrifying second my body froze in the most paralyzing, utter indecision I had ever experienced. *I should run from the murderer behind me. I have nowhere to hide from him. I should turn and identify him.* I gasped another breath, wasting time, before self-preservation asserted itself and won out. I darted around the side of the building, ducking into the narrow alley that separated it from its neighbor.

I moved as quietly as I could, the walls of the two houses nearly brushing my shoulders in the dim, narrow space. At the end of the alley, I braced myself against the corner and glanced behind me. There was no sign of movement, but the hairs standing upright on the back of my neck prompted me to keep running.

The alley emptied into a ragged back garden, its few paving stones overgrown with weeds, a pot of dying flowers in one corner. I crossed the space quickly, thought about exiting by the open back gate, then changed direction and ducked around the other side of the building. In the alley on this side, just as narrow as the other, stood two large dustbins smelling of old rot. I slid behind one of them, crouched low to the ground, and waited.

It didn't take long. Footsteps came from the alley into the back garden. They stepped forward once, twice, and stopped.

I closed my eyes. I could hear my own breathing inside my rib cage. I pressed my back to the brick wall, trying not to move.

Another footstep came from the garden, unhurried.

I pressed a hand over my mouth. For the first time, it fully bloomed in my mind what a deadly game I was playing. The rope on the stairs with the sign—why had I not seen it before? It had been a sham, a ruse calmly set up by a murderer going about his business. Put up a rope and a sign, and anyone who approaches during your deadly work would have to take the noisy lift. Just as I had.

And when he had heard the clatter of the lift, indicating he had an intruder, he had calmly finished his killing and started down the stairs after me. Even now he was in no hurry, his footsteps measured in the back garden.

Passionless and planned—just as Gloria's murder had been. What had I thought of when George Sutter first told me of it? *Someone who hadn't even cared enough to hate her.*

Two more steps sounded; they seemed to aim for the back garden gate, which I remembered stood open. A careless neighbor, perhaps, or one of the residents leaving by the back way and not bothering to close the gate. Outside the gate was a lane that ran between the backs of the two sets of buildings, a convenient path to quickly get from building to building or out to the street. It would have been a logical assumption that I'd fled that way—in fact, it would have been the smartest route if I'd been thinking properly, instead of hiding behind dustbins six feet away. If I'd had the presence of mind to flee out the back gate, I'd be hidden in the crowds on the Streatham High Road by now.

Decided, the steps now fully approached the gate. My hand still pressed to my mouth, my breath still heavy in my chest, I shifted carefully on my numbed, squatting haunches and leaned forward. One inch, two. I looked past the edge of the dustbin.

The man stood at the garden gate, his back to me. He was not tall, though taller than me; not bulky, though of average size for a man; not fat, nor thin. Something about his very blankness frightened me. He wore a black overcoat that fell without a flaw from his shoulders to the middle of his calves, beneath which I glimpsed black trousers and expensive shoes. His hat was also black, as if he were dressed for a funeral, its shadows smeared in the rainy, darkening light of early evening. As I watched, he put one black-gloved hand on the open gate and looked out into the lane, one way and then the other.

I pressed my hand tighter to my mouth and did not breathe.

Still, he did not turn. He reached into his overcoat pockets, as unhurried as a man taking a leisurely break, and removed a cigarette case. His back still to me, he raised a cigarette to his unseen lips, and I heard the scrape of a match. He tilted his head as the flame briefly lit the side of his face, and I glimpsed an ear below the brim of the hat, a tuft of dark hair combed neatly behind it, a smooth temple and the knob of the back of his jaw. Then he righted his head again and his face retreated into the shadows under his hat brim.

He stood for a long moment, smoking. Watching the lane, the yards and streets beyond it. Waiting for movement or sound. Contemplating me, who I was, where I had gone, what I had seen. Weighing, perhaps, whether I would telephone someone, thinking where he might find me.

He did not rush through the gate, hot in pursuit. He did not search the back garden, thrashing me from my hiding place. He simply stood and smoked, and as the silence stretched on, my nerves frayed and I felt the wild impulse to jump up, to scream—anything. I became wildly convinced that he knew exactly where I was, that he was only playing with me. That I should give myself away and end it now. He did not rush after me—not because he was fooled, but because he would find me eventually. There was no need to hurry after someone who was already dead.

He smoked the entire cigarette while standing there at the back gate. I watched him finish and then I watched him lower the lit stub, watched him raise one elegant foot, watched him douse the embers of the cigarette on the sole of his shoe. He straightened again and dropped the stub into the pocket of his overcoat in a smooth, deliberate movement. As the last tendrils of smoke drifted away in the wet air, he turned and walked away, back the way he'd come.

I didn't see his face in the darkness. I only heard his footsteps, easy and measured, as they retreated down the other alley. I swallowed, dropped my hand, leaned back against the wall again. I was more terrified now than I'd ever been, more even than when I had seen Ramona's dead face outside the window of the elevator door.

He had pocketed the cigarette.

He had not thrown it away; he had not ground it out underfoot and left it. He had doused it out very carefully on the damp sole of his shoe, placed it in the pocket of his expensive overcoat. As if a cigarette stub were an object of great value.

Because it was.

I thought of myself standing in Gloria's flat with Davies, running one of Gloria's scarves through my hands. Psychometry, it was called. James had written about it in one of his papers. It wasn't my specialty. But I could do it. There was a chance—though not a guarantee—that I could pick up the stub of a man's cigarette and get a picture of him, images, thoughts, even a name. And somehow—God, I didn't know how—he knew it. He knew who he was dealing with, and he knew what I could do.

He knew me.

Too afraid to move, I waited as the rain began to fall softly. What if I walked to the front of the building and the man was still there, waiting for me? In the abject darkness of my terror, it didn't matter that I was in public, that he wasn't likely to assault a woman screaming in the middle of the street. All that mattered was the blackness of the shadow over his face and that stub of cigarette, his unhurried assurance that I was already his.

And so I sat there, my feet numb in their heels, my thighs aching from squatting, as I inhaled the stink of the dustbins and growing damp, even after I heard someone enter the front door of the building, even after I heard someone—probably the same person—throw up the sash of a window on the third floor. *The devil is coming,*

Ramona had said. *He is coming for you. He is coming for me. He is coming for everyone.*

When I finally got the courage to move, I didn't take the alley to the front of the building. I pushed myself away from the wall and tottered into the back garden on cramping legs. I stood for a moment where the man had been. Then I forced myself through the gate and into the lane, nearly stumbling as I made my way back to the crowded streets of London.

# CHAPTER TWENTY-THREE

I walked. I walked as the sky darkened, as the rain spattered the streets in fits, as the wind gusted against my damp skin with the first breaths of cold autumn. I walked through the sounds and smells of London, motorcars and shouts and clanging bells and laughter and the heavy, oily scent of wet pavement, the tang of cigar smoke, the smoggy London itch at the back of my throat. I walked in crowds, the larger the better, so I would not be alone. I walked without knowing where I was going, without looking around me, without seeing anything, my feet vaguely hurting in their heels, my hands in the pockets of my coat. A knot of young men in cloth caps catcalled at me—blond hair always being a magnet for catcalls, the sound of it as meaningless as a how-do-you-do?—and as I brushed past them, jolting one of them with my shoulder, I discovered that the abject terror I'd been under had dissipated, replaced with a hot, low-grade anger.

Without my realizing it, while I had walked, my terror-numbed mind had pondered the question of the man in the houndstooth jacket.

The man I had seen at Ramona's flat was, without a shadow of a doubt in my mind, Gloria's killer. I needed no evidence to know it, no psychic vision. I had been within twenty feet of him, watched him smoke a cigarette, and I had done it after finally dodging my unwanted pursuer, the houndstooth gentleman. What if things had gone differently? What if I had failed to dodge him, and he'd been there when I'd encountered the murderer? Would he have helped? Made an arrest? Would he have done anything at all, or were his orders simply to watch and report?

Report what? My movements? Or my death?

Suspicion, I discovered, works like a lens. Once you have looked through it, and seen everything you thought you knew in a different way, its version of the truth does not recede. Once you can see through that lens, you can no longer ignore it.

I pushed into a telephone box as the rain splashed the pavements again, and closed the familiar red door behind me. Outside, the crowds still flowed by, silent now beyond the windows of the box. It smelled pungently of cigarette smoke in there, as if the last caller had smoked his entire supply. I stared at the telephone for a long time, my mind moving back and forth like a rocking horse, going over the same ground again and again. Rain splashed the glass. My feet were cold and sore. Finally, I picked up the receiver and had the operator connect me to the exchange George Sutter had given me: Hampstead 1207.

The woman who picked up the line was nasal, businesslike, obviously a secretary of some kind. She did not speak a greeting. "To whom am I speaking?" she said in my ear.

"My name is Ellie Winter," I replied, my voice croaking. I had not spoken for hours. "I have a message for George Sutter."

The woman made no comment. "What is your message?"

"Where is he?" I asked her, knowing I would get no answer.

"What is your message?" the woman asked again.

I closed my eyes. I smelled the cigarette smoke, the damp, close air of the telephone box. I listened to water patter on the roof. I was speaking to a stranger I couldn't see, sending my message down the lines to a woman who did not know me, did not care if I lived or died. No, I was no longer afraid. I was angry.

" 'You missed him,' " I said, each word lifting off me like a weight. " 'Ramona is dead.' " I thought it over, and added, " 'I resign.' That is the message." Then I hung up.

There was a hard rap on the glass door, and I jumped. I turned to see a fortyish man in a heavy mackintosh holding an umbrella over his head, knocking on the door and gesturing impatiently for me to get on with it. I blew out a breath, then gestured back at him.

"Go away," I called through the glass, and picked up the receiver to make my next telephone call.

It was raining fully by the time James found me at the Saratoga Hotel. I had taken a seat on one of the plush chairs at the back of the lobby, next to a luxurious fern placed in the corner. My shoes were slowly drying by then, and I'd taken off my dripping hat. A drink sat untouched on the table before me.

James wore a coat of dark gray, his umbrella folded under his arm. He dropped into the seat across from me without a word. I watched his strong, easy movements, smelled the cool, rain-scented air he brought with him, ran my gaze along the shadow of blond stubble on his jaw. He looked at me for a long time as people flowed past behind him and laughter came from a group exiting the elevator and heading out into the night.

"All right," he said finally. "It's done. I went past there myself. They've taken away the body, and the crowd of neighbors is starting to disperse."

I licked my lip. "Thank you."

He sighed and took off his damp hat, tossing it onto the seat next to him. "Of all the telephone calls, that one was the least expected."

He nodded toward the drink in front of me. "Are you going to drink that?"

"I couldn't leave her there," I said. "Just leave her—like that. You know I couldn't. I had to know that someone had found her."

"Well, it looks like Sutter got your message and called the police. Or, more likely, had a lackey do it." He picked up my drink and took a swallow, the strong muscles of his throat working. He caught my glance and the smile he gave me was bitter. "Don't worry. I'm not a drunk anymore. I've just had a hell of a day."

"What about Davies?" I said. I'd asked him to check on her, to see whether she had ever come home. Then I had sat here, waiting for him as the centuries ticked by, knowing deep down what the answer would be.

James leaned his sleek bulk back in his chair and shook his head. "She hasn't come home. I even checked with that fake skimmer who rents the shop on the ground floor. She hasn't heard anyone come or go, and she's been taking clients since four o'clock."

"There was time," I said, the words tumbling out of me, though I didn't move. My body felt frozen in place, my legs stiff. "I've been thinking about it while I've been sitting here, waiting for you. There was just time for the same man to have taken Davies and killed Ramona. If he was—if he was quick with Davies . . . If he disposed of her somewhere . . ."

"Stop it," he said, his voice hard.

"I failed them." The words seemed to crack me open. "I failed them both. I could have been half an hour earlier. Twenty minutes. When I stood on Ramona's front step, I could have turned around and waited for him and screamed."

"You'd have had a knife in the ribs for your trouble," James said. "Quick and quiet. This man is no amateur, Ellie. He's no madman running around the streets speaking in tongues. He's some sort of professional. Your best action was to run."

"I keep coming back to the rope." I leaned forward now, put my elbows on my knees. A man in an evening jacket passed us, looked me up and down, and carried on. "The rope and the sign that said the stairs were out of order. He'd set it up. He knew the layout of Ramona's building. He knew when she'd be home, how to get her to let him into her flat. He knew how much time he needed. He knew the lift made a lot of noise. He took the time to bring *supplies* with him. What kind of man does that?"

"Jesus, Ellie." James leaned forward, took my hands in his. He gripped me hard, his fingertips pressing into my wrists past the edges of my gloves, and in the middle of everything I reveled almost painfully in that touch, enjoyed the fire it set in my veins with a fierceness I did not recognize. "Shut up, will you? It's driving me insane, just thinking of how close you came."

"George Sutter has been having me followed," I told him. "But I'd lost him by then. So I have no other witnesses, no one who saw."

James's grip grew even harder on my wrists. "What did you say?"

So I told him about the man in the houndstooth jacket, how he had followed me to James's flat that morning—it felt like decades ago—and to Piccadilly Circus, and how I'd lost him. James stared at me for a long minute when I finished, his gaze on me. His mood was as wild as mine, I realized, and the thought made my heart thump and my blood sing crazily.

"That conniving bastard." James dropped my wrists and leaned back in his chair. "Bloody hell. He's been manipulating you. Manipulating us."

"I've been going over and over it," I said. "Why would he contact me, hire me, if he's already two steps ahead of me?"

"Don't you know why?"

He waited for me to answer. I wished I could swear like a man, like a sailor, but my mother's training was too ingrained. "It's one thing to know who the murderer is," I said, "but it's another thing to know *where* he is, isn't it? I was bait." I rubbed my hands roughly over my temples. "James, the killer knows who I am. He knows. He wasn't in a hurry, didn't need to rush. How does he know everything?"

"Ellie," James said, "the Dubbses have left England."

I dropped my hands. "What?"

"I tried to set up an interview today. I couldn't reach anyone, and I finally found their occasional housekeeper. They packed up and left for the continent. They've gone."

"So they were in on it," I said.

"Or they've been threatened, and they're afraid."

"How easy for them," I said. I grabbed my coat and stood. "I have to go."

As I crossed the lobby, my heels ringing hollowly on the marble tile, I knew he was following me. I felt his presence like a solid mass behind me, watching me, not letting me go. The hotel doormen were assisting well-dressed couples into taxis waiting on the street outside, men in evening coats and tails, women in silk gowns and jewels. Through the glass doors to my right I could see the hotel bar, could hear laughter and the clink of glasses and the soft tinkle of a piano. A Friday evening in London. The man who killed Gloria was out there somewhere. I pushed past a doorman and out into the rain.

The water was icy on my neck. Water splashed through my shoes and up the backs of my stockings. I pushed through the crowds of people headed for Charing Cross. Behind me, Waterloo Bridge loomed low over the Thames, the river hurling angrily at the base of its arches.

An arm came around my shoulders and I was pulled against a hard, familiar body. An umbrella snapped open overhead. "This way," he said, his voice rough.

He steered me down a side street, his arm heavy around me. I smelled wet pavement and damp wool and James. My skin sang, even through the layers of clothing, and there was water on my cheeks. He swung me into the notch of a church doorway, out of the rain, my back against the brick. He closed and dropped the umbrella and his face was stark in the light from a far-off streetlamp.

"Come here," he said, and kissed me.

It was harsh and gentle at the same time. He was warm against my cold lips, and his big hands came up and cradled my head, his thumbs against my cheeks. He tasted like salt and gin and rain. There was a rushing in my ears, darkness before my eyes, and in a prickling explosion of sensation nothing existed but James. He pressed my shoulders hard into the cold brick and his stubble scraped my skin.

My reaction was instantaneous. I grasped the lapels of his coat and pulled him closer, kissing him harder. He pushed back, gripping my shoulders, and I moaned, biting his lip. He used the opportunity to open my mouth and slide his tongue along the inside of my upper lip, tasting me, raw with anger and emotion and his own bottomless need, and as lights seemed to go off in my brain I fell harder in that moment than I had ever thought possible for any man.

My hands hurt from my desperate grip on his coat. Part of me knew that I was cold and damp and that the bricks behind me were rough, but none of it mattered. He lowered his hands and I slid my arms around his neck, feeling the strength of his shoulders under the coat. He put his hands on my hips and kissed his way down my neck, behind my ear, his skin prickling mine. He bit my earlobe, and when I gasped at the sensation, he kissed me again. I couldn't breathe; I didn't want to breathe. I only wanted it never, ever to stop.

When he finally broke the kiss, his hands still on my hips, I let my head tilt back against the wall, the rainy air vivid against my flushed skin. "Why did you wait so long?" I asked, catching my breath.

He leaned in and I felt his breath against my ear. "You hated me until three days ago," he said. "I was biding my time."

"I've forgiven you for that," I said.

"Good." He took his hands from my hips and placed them against the wall on either side of me, blocking me in, his unbuttoned coat falling open. His gaze held mine, dark and possessive. He seemed to be searching for something in my face, his breath coming hard. I felt his heat. I dropped my hands.

"I want to go to your flat," I told him. "I have something to show you."

He smiled a little, raw need overlaid with humor. "Interesting," he replied. "I think that's my line."

"What— Oh!" My cheeks flushed. It was ridiculous that I would feel embarrassed in front of a man I'd just kissed like that, but there it was. I wished fiercely that I was more sophisticated with men, but there was nothing to be done about it now. "I don't mean that. I mean—"

"I know." He slid a finger just under the collar of my dress, traced it along the skin of my neck and my collarbone almost wistfully before dropping his hand. "I've waited this long. I can wait a little longer. I'll get us a taxi."

# CHAPTER TWENTY-FOUR

"No, no, no," James said. "None of this works. Let's try again."
He put his elbows on his knees and thrust his hands through his hair. We were at his flat, where we'd been for hours, going over the codes in Gloria's handwritten schedule. He was in his shirtsleeves, the button at the throat of his shirt undone. Outside the rain had not abated; it had only grown heavier, and rolls of thunder weighed heavily over the rooftops.

I dropped into the other chair and looked again at the sheet of paper we'd used for our latest attempt at a cipher. "My daily woman says she can keep Pickwick for the night," I said. I'd gone down the hall to use the boardinghouse's only telephone.

James shook his head, staring down at the paper. "God knows how you picked up a dog."

"It doesn't matter how," I said, not wanting to think about Mr. Bagwell. "But I've been a dog owner for less than a day, and already I've fallen down on the job." I motioned to the paper, which was on the table next to the three telegrams and the three photographs, which I'd also shared with James. "I thought that last one would work."

"Bloody hell. It doesn't."

I was quiet for a moment, rubbing my stockinged feet. Despite everything—the fear, the uncertainty, Ramona's murder, the fact that it had almost been my murder, too—part of me was humming with excitement at being here, alone with James in his little flat. I liked watching him work. I liked what the rainy light did to his handsome, intelligent face. After that scorching kiss in the doorway, I wasn't certain I'd be able to concentrate. But we had quickly become immersed in the puzzle of Gloria's final week, working together as easily as if we'd done it for years, the seriousness of it doing nothing to diminish the quiet pulse of excitement in my veins.

James gazed down at the desktop, unseeing, his head still in his hands. "It's the three-digit sequence that makes no sense," I said. "Except for '44,' which is two digits."

We'd tried everything to figure out what the numbers meant, marrying numbers to letters in a code. We knew which client the Dubbses were—277—and we had tried to work backward, cracking the other names from there. We'd tried master code words—guessed, of course—used as a key, numeric patterns, mathematical algorithms, everything we could think of. It made sense that a combination of either two or three letters would represent a set of initials: first name, last name, and a third letter for the middle name inserted whenever there was a possibility of duplicates. But it seemed that what made sense was obviously not the case.

What mattered most to us, of course, was not the week's schedule, but the number Gloria herself had written in—321B—on the day before she died. If we could crack her code, we could figure out where she'd gone that day, the appointment so secret that even Davies hadn't known about it.

"It can't possibly be a simple list, can it?" James asked. "A simple list of names in order, with every new client given a number?"

"The highest number on that list is 321," I replied. "Even if that entry isn't part of the same code, the second highest number is 277. That means that Gloria knew some three hundred names, associated with their random numbers, in her head." I raised an eyebrow at him. "Tell me, did you *meet* Gloria?"

"I know, I know," he said. "It doesn't seem likely. And if she had a written codebook marrying the names to the numbers, then there would have been no reason to have a code at all in the first place." He lifted his head and leaned back in his chair again. "There's nothing for it. I'm going to have to ask Merriken at Scotland Yard."

I bit my lip. Davies had supposedly given the inspector Gloria's schedule, so if we got the information in turn, we could use it to map the code for the missing name. "He's going to want to know why. That means we have to show him this paper with the unknown name."

"So we show it to him," James said. "He's the police, after all. What do we have to lose?"

If Inspector Merriken saw the paper with Gloria's unknown appointment on it, he'd write it up in his files. And that meant George Sutter would see it. And George Sutter would get no more information from me. "I don't want to."

"Ellie, this could be the key. Gloria went somewhere the day before she died, and she didn't tell anyone. Then she left a note for her brother saying, 'Tell Ellie Winter to find me.' There must be a connection. There simply must be."

"The number sign," I said, changing the subject. "Before the mystery number. None of the others has a number sign, but the mystery number says '#321B.' That looks like an address to me. Maybe it isn't part of the other code at all."

James ran a hand over his jaw. I could hear the rasp of his stubble. It was a light shadow, blond mixed with caramel brown, and the sound of his hand traveling over it reminded me of its rough feel on my skin. "That is a possibility, yes."

"Then there's no point telling the inspector about it, because the information Davies gave him can't help us."

He sighed. He picked up the near-empty bottle of wine, filled my glass, slid it toward me on the desk. He'd had very little wine, I noticed—barely half a glass. Since there was no one else here, I supposed I must have drunk the rest of it. Against the wall, the sacks of mail—the deathbed visions, the accounts of fairies and pixies and poltergeists—hulked in the shadows. "All right, Ellie. You win. Keep your secrets."

I opened my mouth to deny it, then shut it again. There was no point in lying to him.

"It isn't because I don't trust *you*," I said finally.

He shrugged. He'd folded back the sleeves of his white shirt, and I watched the strong, fine bones of his wrist, the faint trace of blue veins through the warm skin. "Of course not. It's just that you want me to help you without giving me all of your information."

"James, I simply don't *know*," I said, pushing back my chair and standing. I picked up my wineglass and took it with me as I started to pace again. All I had were theories about who George Sutter worked for; if I talked to James about George, was I putting him in danger? "I haven't put all of it together myself. Besides, I don't think you've told me everything, either."

"Ellie, I've told you everything. I'm an open book."

"You haven't told me why you're so dedicated to investigating this." I sipped the wine; it was rather good. James kept good wine for a bachelor who never had company, and my head was pleasantly spinning, my thoughts loose and full of possibilities. "You knew her and you feel badly that she was killed, yes. But there's more to it than that. Do you want to know what I think?"

He watched me pace, his expression closed. "Go ahead."

"You're the one who wrote the article about her for the New Society," I said. "I think that, deep down, you are wondering whether somehow that paper, the work you did with her, is the reason for her murder."

He was silent.

I turned on my heel and looked at him. "Am I right?"

He dropped his gaze. "All right. I always felt a little sorry for Gloria. I think she was used by everyone she knew, myself included. Everyone except, possibly, you." He raised his eyes to mine again. "But yes, part of me thinks it's possible. Her death was so soon after the story in the newspapers. If I'm somehow responsible, I want to know."

Our gazes locked for a long moment as a gust of wind blew up and threw rain at the windows. I lowered my glass to my side. "How could that be?" I asked softly.

"I don't know," he admitted. "I don't know what I wrote that would make someone want to murder her. I just feel . . ." He shrugged. "I can't rest until I know for certain that I didn't contribute to this."

"Did your tests include spirit sessions?" I asked him.

"At least a dozen."

"Perhaps it has to do with someone she found on the other side. Something she learned." I thought it over. "My mother and I learned a lot of family secrets in the spirit medium business. Things people take to their graves." We had spoken once to a woman who had died giving herself an abortion, though the fact was kept from her grieving husband. We had heard about infidelity, and babies given away for adoption, and money stashed in places where the heirs would never find it.

James looked thoughtful. "I don't recall any shocking revelations offhand. It's a possibility, I suppose, but it's a distant one. If Gloria died because she uncovered secrets, then she could have uncovered those secrets during her regular business. That means hundreds of clients, hundreds of suspects. And Scotland Yard is already covering that."

"It would be someone recent," I said, thinking of Inspector

Merriken saying, *Murderers tend to be impulsive.* "Someone from the past few weeks. Perhaps someone on this schedule is a client because they read the article."

"Or perhaps he's just a madman who likes killing spirit mediums."

A shiver of cold fear went down my spine. "In which case, James, your article is blameless."

"Except that it gave her publicity in the news."

"Gloria made her own publicity. And Ramona's name was never in the papers, so why did she die?"

"It's a gut feeling, Ellie. None of which tells me why you don't want to pass information to Scotland Yard."

I sighed. I was exhausted, but since my experience that afternoon, a part of me felt more awake than I could ever recall. "I suppose it doesn't matter, but if you get carted away in a black van and interrogated in a windowless room somewhere, please don't blame me."

"Ellie, what in God's name are you talking about?"

"George Sutter," I said. "You told me in Trafalgar Square that you don't know who he works for."

"No, and I still don't."

"Neither do I," I said. "But whoever it is, it's an office that has full access to every report Inspector Merriken submits regarding this case."

James blinked, then shoved back his chair and stood. "And you know this how?"

"Because he told me when he hired me. He said he'd give me everything I need from Scotland Yard's reports. And he has."

I told James everything I knew that hadn't been in the papers, or anywhere else—that she'd been hit once in the face, very hard, to subdue her, and then she'd been stabbed calmly through the heart and dumped in the pond. I told him what George had said of the layout of the property, the possibility of neighbors, the paths the killer could have taken to and from the Dubbses' house.

"The damned coroner's report and everything," James said when I finished. "You waited a hell of a long time to tell me, Ellie." His voice was rough, and he was starting to use profanities, which meant he was tired.

"I'm sorry," I said.

He dropped onto his single narrow sofa, his body graceful even in exhaustion. "Did Sutter tell you the Dubbses had left town? Did you already know that?"

"No."

"Perhaps he didn't know. The Yard may not know, either—I got the information from my own channels." He looked up at me, standing in the middle of the floor in my stockinged feet, holding my forgotten wineglass. "What is it?"

"What do you mean?" I asked.

"I mean the look you're giving me. What is it?"

I gathered my scattered nerves, took a breath. I felt jumpy, terrified and strangely free at the same time. "I'm going out there," I said to him. "To the Dubbses' property. I don't care that they're not there. I'm going myself."

He watched me from his lazy pose on the sofa. "And what do you expect to find there?"

"Answers. Courage, perhaps." I swallowed. "I'm going to do what Gloria asked of me, what George wants of me. I'm going to find her on the other side. I think that if I'm there, in the place where she died, I may have the backbone to do it. And I have to do it soon."

James was quiet, his face in shadows. "All right," he said at last.

"There's more," I said. "I'm going to travel in daylight. No hiding. Let whoever wishes to follow me follow me."

"Ellie."

"I can draw him out, James," I said. "If he wants me, he'll be able to find me. At least this time I'll be ready."

"For what? Are you going to tackle him to the ground, then? Arrest him?"

"No. But the police can, if we have Inspector Merriken on our side."

James looked at me for a long moment, then shook his head. "He'll never go for it. Never."

"He already has."

"What are you talking about?"

"When I used the telephone in the hall to call my daily woman, I tracked down the inspector as well. I told him I had reason to believe the killer will come after me next. And that our best chance of success is to have me draw him out of London."

"And he believed all of that? With no evidence?"

That had struck me as well. I hadn't wanted to tell the inspector about my close brush with Ramona's murderer, because he'd want to bring me into the Yard for questioning. "I think he has his own reasons for believing it. Certainly Ramona's murder creates a pattern of dead spirit mediums, as you pointed out. He may know that Davies is missing as well."

James's expression had drawn tight; I could tell he didn't like the plan. "So you're to go to Kent tomorrow, and the police will follow you. That's what the two of you cooked up?"

"He's moving fast, James," I said, meaning the killer. "If he's going to get rid of me, he'll move as quickly as he can. He's proven he can kill with impunity when he can fade into the city crowds. In the country, he'll be more visible, less able to hide."

"He did a good job of killing with impunity in Kent, it seems to me."

"Because the police didn't expect him." I put down my glass and walked toward him, my voice softening. "I'll be fine. The inspector is going to call on the local police for extra men. All I have to do is take the train to Kent, then hire a motorcar. Inspector Merriken and his men will already be there, watching the roads—there are only so many roads one can take in that part of the country. The killer has evaded everyone so far, but he's just a man. He has to transport himself somehow."

He raised his gaze to me, still unconvinced. "And George Sutter. You think he won't hear about this plan?"

"If he wants to send men from MI5, so much the better. I'm sure the inspector could use the help."

I watched him wrestle with himself. He wanted nothing more than to accompany me to Kent, to guard me, to keep me safe. But his presence would be the ruin of the entire plan. "I'm coming with you," he said finally. "I'll go to Merriken first thing in the morning. I won't get underfoot with his men, but I'm going to be there." He sighed. "It doesn't matter how safe you think you are. You're going to be in danger, Ellie."

"I know." I stepped close, unable to stop myself. "I don't care. I want to stop him. I have to. I've done nothing with my life for the past three years, and now I want to do what's right, no matter the cost. I don't care if he puts his hands around my neck and—"

"Stop it."

I had reached the sofa, and I lightly hiked up the hem of my skirt and straddled him, sitting on his long, hard thighs. He smelled clean and pleasantly pungent, a man who had put in a long day. He did not move beneath me, but his gaze darkened and his expression went blank with careful control.

"But you won't let that happen to me," I said, my voice a whisper. "I know it. You won't."

His shoulders were tense under the palms of my hands, his skin hot through his shirt. He took a harsh breath and gripped my hips, his hands strong and surprising, and then he slowly let his palms slide upward to my waist, pulling at the fabric of my dress.

I leaned toward him and rubbed my cheek against the rasp of his, the sensation setting fire to everything inside me. I was wild in a way that had nothing to do with the wine and everything to do with being on a sofa with James Hawley, with the rain outside and the two of us the only people in the world. "I saw the way you looked at me,"

I said to him. "The first night you met me. And when you saw me in Trafalgar Square."

His hands twitched a little on my waist, then gripped me tighter. "I've been very patient."

"I know." I rubbed my cheek against him again.

His breath seemed to grow heavier. "What changed?"

"I grew up," I said, knowing as I spoke the words that they were true.

His hands slid up my rib cage, his thumbs running along my torso and the undersides of my breasts, and I nearly gasped.

"You're agreeable?" he said, his breath harsh in my ear.

"Yes."

He put his hands to my face, as he had earlier that night, and looked into my eyes. The shadows played with his brows and his cheekbones, the fine line of his mouth, the column of his neck. He was staring at me with the intensity I recognized. "Do you see anything?" he asked, seeming to push the words from his throat. "When I touch you like this?"

It took a pathetic second for me to understand what he meant, and I shook my head. "No. Nothing."

His gaze flickered, his thoughts dark behind his eyes. His thumbs moved across my cheekbones. "Whatever it is about you," he said, "I'm damned if I know."

"The feeling is mutual," I breathed, and he pulled me in and kissed me.

In the bedroom, he unbuttoned my dress and let it slide to the floor. He knelt before me as I sat on the edge of the bed and unfastened my garters from my stockings. I looked down at his dark blond head and the bunched line of his shoulders, feeling his fingers moving between the fabric and my skin. I had never done this before, and he probably knew it. I was supposed to be afraid, and I was supposed to be ashamed, but somehow I couldn't make myself feel either. All I knew was that I could have died that day without ever having felt this kind of pleasure, pure and so intense it was nearly painful. When he rolled down my stocking and pressed a kiss to the inside of my thigh, I couldn't breathe.

He rose and pulled off his shirt, his skin supple in the watery light.

As night moved through its darkest hours, I learned several things. That I liked being touched extensively, and in a certain way. That James Hawley had a length of scarred skin on the side and back of one thigh. And that when he twined his fingers with mine and pinned my arms over my head, both of us gripping the headboard—and when his body came over mine, musky and heavy—I no longer cared about what I was supposed to do and who I was supposed to be, and everything else was washed away.

"I want to tell you something," I said to him in the dark, hours later. I rolled over, tucked my chin into the crook of his neck. "The answer to a riddle."

He moved sleepily, crooked a hand behind his head as he lay on his back. "Go ahead."

I sighed a breath and closed my eyes, letting the secret lift from me like a burden. "My mother was a true psychic," I said. "There is no doubt of it. If you'd tested her when I was a child, you would have been amazed."

He was quiet, awake now and listening.

"When I was sixteen, my mother told me she no longer wanted to do spirit sittings. I had developed my own powers by then, and she had trained me to use them. My father was gone, and there was no reason for us to pretend anymore. She told me that she got no pleasure from the sittings and she wanted to stop. She didn't tell me the truth, which was that she couldn't do it anymore."

"Ellie, are you saying—?"

"Yes. It took me a long time to figure it out, I suppose. I didn't question it, and I just wanted to help. She didn't want to do the sessions anymore, but she was The Fantastique and I was just a girl. She was the one the clients came to see. So she did the sessions, and I sat behind a curtain and summoned the messages from the dead." I traced a finger idly on his chest as I spoke, touching the springy hair there and feeling his heartbeat. "But she didn't stop because she chose to. Do you see? She stopped because she had to. Because her power disappeared."

"Of course," he said softly. "It explains why we heard so many accounts of her powers. It could have been a natural function of age."

"That day you did the tests on us." I rolled over on my back, looked at the dark ceiling. "I always asked myself why she agreed. Gloria asked her to do it, fed her a line about how important it was to her that the New Society complete their research."

Far from offended, James made a derisive sound. "Gloria didn't care about the New Society. She liked the attention our tests gave her, and she liked to show off. But mostly she did it because we paid her for every test we did. Rather handsomely, too, by the end."

"I know. My mother knew it, too. Gloria suspected from the first that it was me doing the sessions, and she wanted proof of it. She wanted to win; it was just her way. So I couldn't understand, at first, why my mother would agree at all to a session that was set up expressly to humiliate her."

"That wasn't the intent on my part," James said.

"That's because you didn't know what the outcome would be. But we all knew it, my mother most of all."

He seemed to think this over. He rolled to his side, propped himself on one elbow, and looked down at me. "So why did she do it?"

"She was tired," I said. "She was sick by then, although she hadn't seen a doctor yet. She didn't want to lie anymore. I think that, instead of admitting that her powers were gone and she'd been lying, it was just easier to let herself be officially exposed."

"And it kept you out of it."

I shrugged against the pillows. I hadn't thought of that. "Perhaps."

He ran one finger along my collarbone. I tried not to shiver. "You've left out one part of the riddle. What about you, that day of the tests? We saw no trace of your powers, either. And yet yours are strong."

I thought back on that day, sitting tied to the chair, helpless and angry. "I could have tried," I admitted slowly, "if I had calmed myself down, made myself focus. It wouldn't have been easy in that situation, but I could have done *something*. But—" He traced my collarbone again, and I lost my train of thought. "She asked me not to. She made me promise. She told me that if I helped her that day, she would never forgive me."

"Jesus, Ellie. I had no idea."

"I know," I said. "I know you didn't. You couldn't have. I was angry at you for so long, even though I wished you'd noticed me at the same time."

"I did notice you."

I blushed in the dark. "It was embarrassing, yes. But you didn't force my mother to agree to it—no one did. You didn't know what else was going on. You didn't know that my mother was using you, using the Society, to get what she'd wanted for a long time. But there's something else."

"What is it?"

I swallowed. "When I went to the New Society office to look for you, I spoke to Paul Golding. I wanted to prove something to him—childish, I know, but there it was. I told him where he'd left his favorite watch, which he'd thought he'd lost. And he pulled it out of his pocket and told me he'd already found it." I turned and looked up at James's face in the dark. "That has never happened to me before, James. Never. In all the sessions I've done, finding lost items for clients, I've never once found an item that had already been found."

He took a soft breath. "You think—"

"Yes. I've been having headaches, getting tired. Sometimes my powers go out of control, like at Ramona's séance. Other times they don't work. I could fool myself, I suppose, since much of the time they work as they always have." I thought of the messages I'd received when Inspector Merriken had brushed my hand, coming as easy as water. "But the truth is that things are changing. Perhaps my powers won't be gone next year, or the next. But I think they're leaving me."

"My God," he said, putting the pieces together. "Gloria."

"That schedule of hers is too light; it was never like that when I knew her. Gloria could handle three or four appointments a day, and she usually did. Four appointments in a week? Five? It didn't hit me at first, but it isn't the kind of schedule she used to handle. And, James, she needed money."

He ran a hand through his hair, rumpling it. "It explains why she took the job with the Dubbses. If she was having problems with her powers, she was funding her own retirement."

My heart was racing in my chest. I had never put the thought into words before, that my powers could leave me. It was terrifying, unfamiliar—and yet part of it was so exciting I could barely begin to fathom it. What would I be if I was not The Fantastique? What would I do if I couldn't see the dead? I couldn't be normal—I could never be normal. And yet . . .

"I suppose," I said slowly, "you're going to miss your chance. To do tests on me. If you want to do tests on me, that is."

"Is that an offer?" he asked. But then he shook his head. "Don't answer that. I'm not going to test you, Ellie. I don't think I'm going to do that work ever again." He leaned over me and his scent came to me like a drug, clean male sweat and faint laundry soap from the sheets we'd rumpled. "I suppose I should spend the rest of the night trying to convince you to abandon this plan, that you shouldn't put yourself in danger, that you're a defenseless female and you should let us manly types take care of this sort of business."

I took in a luxurious breath of him. "And I should spend the rest of the night asking how many girls you've brought here and whether they were pretty, and wondering if I'm special."

He made a sound and the bed shook for a second; I realized it was the quiet vibration of laughter. James Hawley was laughing. "You're not really going to ask that, are you?"

I thought it over. "No."

"How brave and modern of you." He leaned over me further and kissed me just behind the ear, slow and soft, his breath warm on my skin. It was gentle, and it sent a shock straight down my body. "The answers are none, no, and yes, you are. Fine, then. We'll do it your way. I'm coming with you tomorrow," he said.

"I know," I replied, sliding an arm around his neck. "Now hush." And we did not talk for a long, long time.

# CHAPTER TWENTY-FIVE

My street in St. John's Wood was quiet when I arrived home the next morning. The rain had moved off at dawn, leaving the pavements soaked and empty, the clouds breaking up in ragged pieces. The husbands on my street had gone off to work in the city, and the wives were home behind their curtains, doubtlessly staring in disapproving curiosity at the guest who waited on my doorstep.

Fitzroy Todd wore an impeccably tailored evening jacket, now rumpled and damp. His tie was undone, the top buttons of his shirt open. Dark stubble shadowed his jaw. He lounged on my front doorstep as if he owned the street, his dark-clad legs sprawled over the cobblestones of my front walk, his feet in their once shined shoes crossed negligently at the ankles. His hair was messy and he looked as if he'd spent the night in a sewer. And yet when he saw me, he laughed.

"Well, good morning!" he said.

I came up my front walk and stood by his feet. "What do you want?"

He laughed at me again, and he didn't move. "Ellie Winter," he said. "I do believe you've been out *all night*."

"God, are you still drunk? It's nine o'clock in the morning."

"And I was drinking until six. It will wear off soon, darling." He looked me up and down, assessing, a half grin on his face. "You've done a good job of cleaning up, I must admit, but unless I'm very much mistaken you're wearing yesterday's clothes. I can always tell when a girl is wearing yesterday's clothes."

I tilted my head, surprised to find I wasn't the least bit embarrassed. A night as good as the one I'd had seemed to have its benefits. "I didn't take you for a prude."

"God, I couldn't be happier. You'll get no judgment from me."

I looked down the street. Three doors down, a curtain twitched in a window. "Come inside," I told him. "My neighbors hate me already."

He followed me into the house. "This is very nice, in a bourgeois sort of way."

"Shut it, you snob," I said. "You can sit in the kitchen, but if you think I'm making you coffee, you can think again."

"Ellie!" he cried, pleased. "That's the girl I remember. That sharp tongue, and always a lot of jazz in her. We missed you, you know."

"I was always the wet blanket, and you know it perfectly," I replied. Pickwick was in the kitchen; my daily woman must have dropped him off early. He looked rested and well fed, but I opened the door and let him out into the back garden just in case. "Now sit on that chair there and stop trying to flatter me. What do you want?"

Fitz made no comment about the dog—he was too caught up in his own problems, as usual. He sat at the table, and I had to admit that in the harsh morning light his years of dissolution didn't sit on him very well. His face looked lined and pale from too many dark nightclubs, and, even more surprisingly, there seemed to be a smell about him, as if he'd passed out in something awful. The Fitz I knew may have been somewhat—all right, terribly—flawed, but he had always been impeccably groomed.

He put his hands on the table, his jocular manner draining away. "Well, Ellie, I suppose I'll get to it." He rubbed a hand up and down his face. "I seem to be in a small spot of trouble."

I looked through my cupboards, trying to find something to put out in case Pickwick was hungry. "What is it?"

"I suppose you may have heard—Ramona died. She was murdered."

Some of the good feeling from the night before evaporated. I took a tin of meat from the cupboard with numb fingers. "Yes. I heard."

"Someone choked her. I heard it was a—a *garrote*, you know, some sort of wire."

I turned and looked at him. James hadn't told me exactly how Ramona had died, and I hadn't asked. *He's some sort of professional,* James had said. I pictured the body on the floor, the way I'd seen it in my mind when I'd knocked on her door that day, so still, the arms reaching.

I looked more closely at Fitz. Sweat was beading on his brow. He and Ramona had both been in attendance at the séance when Gloria died, so they had at least been acquainted. But he looked torn now, and strangely guilty, and some of the missing pieces fell into place. "You knew her," I said. "You were the one who invited her to Gloria's séance."

"I didn't invite her," he protested. "I swear it. But when I told her about it, she was adamant. She wanted to go. She wanted to see Gloria in action, she said, and she wanted a chance at such a rich client." He breathed out, rubbed his face again, that strange smell wafting from him as he moved. "She needed the chance, she said, and she was going to take it whether I allowed it or not."

"You were lovers." It all made sense now—how Ramona knew so much about Gloria, about me. How she'd known what Gloria did in her séances. Why she'd hated Gloria so bitterly. *I was sick of hearing about the great Gloria Sutter, the irreplaceable Gloria Sutter.* "You were trying to replace Gloria with her."

He shrugged, and then he laughed mirthlessly. "Gloria wouldn't take me back."

Ramona with her glossy black bob, her kohl-rimmed eyes. She'd looked nothing like Gloria, but she'd done her best to try. Ramona with her savage will for survival, her pinpointed pupils. "And the drugs?" I asked him. "What about the drugs?"

A flicker of surprise crossed his face that he didn't bother to hide. He'd had no idea I knew. "I tried to get her off them, but she wouldn't listen."

I stared at him. "That's a lie," I said, suddenly certain. "You gave them to her. You supplied them. You're the only one who had the money."

*Are you asking if I'm for sale? Name a price, handsome, and I'll consider it.* She'd practically told us everything that night, if only I'd opened my eyes to see it. How could I have been so stupid?

"Ellie, you don't understand." Fitz was nearly pleading with me. "The drugs had a hold on her. I wanted to get her clean. I did. What was I supposed to do?"

"Why are you here, Fitz?" I said to him. "Why have you come to my house for the first time? What do you want from me?"

He was silent for a moment, and I heard a polite scratching at the back door. I let Pickwick in, then worked on putting down some food and water for him. Even if my daily woman had already fed him, I still wanted to do it myself, as an offering. He gave me a placid look and a single thump of his tail in thanks.

"All right," Fitz said, as if we'd had some sort of argument that had exhausted him. "You're right—there's no point in going over everything. What's past is past. The fact is, Ellie, I'm in a spot and I need a loaner of a little bit of money."

"What?" The request was so outrageous that if I hadn't had a creeping feeling of wrongness climbing my spine and the back of my neck, I would have laughed. "You want *money*? What for?"

"Just to get out of London for a little while. Take a little trip, you know."

"And you don't have your own money for this?" His dinner jacket alone, which he seemed to have rubbed in garbage, cost more than a month's earnings for me.

"I'm a little out of pocket right now."

"Then go to your parents."

He looked away. "They won't give me anything. My allowance is gone, and Father says he's finished handing me money."

I pulled out a kitchen chair. "What about the fee you got from the Dubbses?"

Still he looked away. He really did look awful, his skin pouching under his eyes. I'd never seen him look like this before, even after he'd been on a multiday bender. "It's gone," he replied finally, seeming to grit the words out. He turned back to me. "Ellie, I have to get out of London, and quickly. Ramona is dead. Do you understand?"

"And you think you could be next," I said. "Why?"

He didn't answer me. I looked into his bloodshot eyes, and suddenly I felt a strange, slow jolt of panic, a pulse of it injecting itself heartbeat by heartbeat into my veins. It felt as if something was crawling up my back on invisible insect legs, and a telltale itch was beginning at the base of my skull. And the smell . . . the smell . . .

"Fitz," I said, trying to keep my voice under control, trying not to scream. "What did you do?"

"I didn't do anything," he said. "Ellie, I swear I didn't."

*Someone is here,* I thought, the words a certainty in my mind. I glanced at Pickwick and saw him sitting next to his bowl, his food half eaten, his ears pricked up. "Fitz, *what did you do?*"

"Nothing!" His shout was hoarse. "A few weeks ago a fellow came to me. He said he knew about Ramona, about the drugs. He knew I was selling them to supplement my allowance. I don't know how he knew, but he did. He told me the only way I could stay out of prison was to do as he asked."

"And what was that?"

"To go to Gloria and ask her to do this one job. This one séance, for these clients, the Dubbses. To convince her to do it."

"So the Dubbses weren't friends of yours," I said. "You didn't meet them at a party. They didn't wear you down with requests to meet with Gloria. All of that was a lie."

"It was the cover he gave me," Fitz said. "The man. He made me memorize it. It's the story I gave the police, the story I gave you when you visited me, and the story I gave Davies. Davies said no—that part was true. But I couldn't leave it, or my parents would find out and I'd go to jail. So I followed Gloria around for a few days, you know, and I got her alone."

"And what did she say?"

"She laughed at me." Even in his extreme state, Fitz managed a flash of hurt outrage. "She told me to go to hell. She was in one of her wild moods. But she came to me two days later to ask how much money was in it, and I knew I had her."

I pressed my hands to my forehead. "Oh, my God, Gloria," I said softly. "You walked into a trap."

"I didn't think anyone would hurt her!" Fitz nearly shouted. "I swear, if I'd known, I wouldn't have—"

"Wouldn't you?" I said, and he drew back, silent. "So Ramona was telling the truth when she said the Dubbses didn't want either of you there. When she said they wanted both of you to turn back and go home when they saw you at the train station. You were never invited along at all. They wanted Gloria *alone.*"

"I wanted to be there," he protested. "In case she needed protection."

"No, you wanted to be there because you saw a potential mark with money, just like Gloria did." I leaned back in my chair. "This man—the one who came to you. Who was he?"

Fitz shook his head. "I don't know. He didn't give his name."

"What did he look like?"

"Like a fellow—any fellow. Brownish hair, not too tall. Tony accent, but not too upper, if you know what I mean. His suit was decent, but I didn't recognize it." He leaned forward. "He knew everything about what I was . . . into, Ellie. Everything. I thought maybe he was from the Yard at first, but what would they want with Gloria?"

The man who had abducted Davies had been dark haired and nondescript. The man who had killed Ramona had looked the same. I felt suddenly overwhelmed by the number of nondescript men in England. "You're saying you think he was higher up," I said to Fitz.

"What else could it be?" he said.

I looked around the room. I was still chilled, and Pickwick still sat quiet, his ears pricked. *Go away,* I thought at whoever it was. *Don't show yourself.*

"What is it?" Fitz was following my gaze around the room. "Do you think someone is listening?"

"Why Ramona?" I said to him. "If whoever it was got what they wanted, if you led them to Gloria and he killed her, then why kill Ramona after the fact?" I searched his face. "Tell me."

"She saw something," he said. "At least, I think she did. It was an accident. The séance was going nowhere, and Gloria had walked out, saying she needed air. Ramona needed a hit, so we went out into the trees." He looked at my face, hardened his jaw. "She saw something— over my shoulder. I could tell. She got very quiet, said only that she wanted to go back into the house. I thought about it when we discovered Gloria had been killed, but there was so much chaos that I didn't ask her about it, and of course I didn't tell the police. I didn't think about it again until she was killed. I swear to you I didn't. But that's why she was killed—it must be. And what if the man who did it doesn't believe I know nothing?"

"Fitz, you have to go to the police. You have to. The Yard is working under all the wrong information. If they knew about the setup—"

He laughed. "And tell them exactly what I've been up to? What I was doing outside in the trees? Do you think I'm out of my mind? My father would disown me. I won't do it."

"You'd rather be killed?"

"I won't be killed if you loan me the money to get out of London. Just for a little while, until all of this cools down."

I opened my mouth to reply to him, to reason with him, and then I stopped.

Ramona stood behind Fitz's shoulder, her face a white smear in the shadows of the kitchen. Her dark-rimmed eyes were fixed on him, and she did not look at me. I could see through the shadows that she wore the dressing gown she'd had on when she'd warned me away from the door of her flat.

I forced my gaze back to Fitz, who was still talking. My headache lit up as if someone had touched a match to it, a lick of pain that traveled up from the base of my skull. *Go away,* I tried to tell her through the fog, but from the corner of my eye I could still see her there, standing in the shadows, watching.

"God, it's been horrible," Fitz was saying to me. He was oblivious to the figure behind him in the corner. "I had to tell lies to the police, to you, to everyone. I've barely been able to hold it together, and sometimes I feel like I'm about to go mad. The only thing that makes me sleep is alcohol, and last night . . . last night I only had nightmares."

I stared at him, and through the pain pounding my brain I could feel no pity. I'd always known that Fitzroy Todd was shallow and somehow hard, but I'd never really understood the extent of it. I'd never seen a spirit follow a living person before, though I'd dealt enough years with the dead to know it was possible. The dead I'd seen were tied to old emotions, to things left undone. I rubbed my forehead, which did nothing to ease the pain, and a sudden idea occurred to me. I took a gamble.

"Fitz," I said, "what do the numbers 321B mean to you?"

He broke off his lament, confused. "I beg pardon?"

"The numbers 321B," I repeated patiently. "Just think about it. Do they have any meaning to you?"

"Do you mean like a puzzle? I'm no good at these things, Ellie. What about my problem?"

"It could be an address," I persisted.

He frowned. "Well, Octavia Murtry lives at Harriet Walk, number 321B." His gaze hardened, suddenly curious. "Why do you ask?"

Octavia Murtry. *My God.* "I saw it written down somewhere."

"Really? Where?"

My mind spun. It must have been Octavia that Gloria had seen the day before she died. But I didn't trust the man across from me, so I made something up. "It was—written on the blotter on Inspector Merriken's desk when he interviewed me yesterday."

Fitz assessed that, his bloodshot gaze traveling over me. "Well, I don't know what they'd want with Octavia. She wasn't there that night."

"Neither was I, but they interviewed me."

He shrugged, accepting it at last. Behind his shoulder, Ramona moved, a strange sliding motion. She was coming closer to him, inch by inch. Suddenly I felt sick, my stomach rebelling at the fear and the horrible sight and the awful smell of her, at the pain that kept her here in my kitchen, at the throbbing pain in my head. I wanted to stand up and scream. In an overwhelming rush, it suddenly seemed I'd spent so much of my life in the company of the dead that I'd never lived much of a life.

"I can't help you," I said to both of them.

It was Fitz who answered, of course. "Ellie, for God's sake. Haven't you been listening to me?"

"I've advised you already," I said. "I think you should go to the police. Perhaps you're in danger, or perhaps not, but they're the only ones who can help you."

"Ellie—"

I flicked my gaze to Ramona. "I can't help you. I've tried. I have. But I simply can't." She gave no indication that she'd heard me; her gaze stayed fixed on Fitz.

"I'm wasting my time here, aren't I?" Fitz pushed back his chair and stood, angry and convincingly hurt. "I should have known better than to ask you for help. Don't disturb Ellie's quiet little life—that's the rule, isn't it?"

I looked back at him, tired of him, tired of everything. "You have no idea."

"If I'm dead, it's your fault," he said sullenly, like a child, and then he was gone.

I pressed my hands to my temples. Ramona had vanished, but a lingering smell remained. When I heard the front door slam, I got up, reluctantly walked into my sitting room, and peered around the edge of the curtain. Fitz was shambling off down my street, his hands in his pockets. I saw no ghosts.

I sat at the window for a long moment, invisible from the street, looking past the curtain, watching. I saw nothing move, saw no one pass. The houses facing me across the street were still and quiet. And yet I felt certain that someone was watching the house; why not? It could be George Sutter's man, or Inspector Merriken's man. It could be the man who had killed Ramona and sent her into her hellish half existence, watching my doorway and waiting for his chance.

The pain in my temples throbbed, lighter now. I left the window and went upstairs, where I washed, changed my clothes, and put a few belongings into an old messenger bag of my father's. I chose one of my older dresses to wear, a soft shirtdress with a lace collar and a narrow belt. When I'd finished, I looked around my bedroom—the room that had been my mother's bedroom and now was mine. I looked at the dressing table, the mirror, the silver-backed hairbrush. I opened the closet door and looked at The Fantastique's beaded dress hanging there, waiting for my next session. I ran my fingers gently down the sleeve of the dress, feeling its cool perfection, listening to the faint sound it made. I took the head scarf from its hook on the back of the closet door and wound it around the hanger, letting its ends dangle over the dress, and then I closed the door.

Pickwick waited for me in the front hall, sitting up, his ears alert. He was not exactly exuberant, but he watched me with a bright, calm expression, his intelligent brown eyes following me. Again he thumped his tail once, a gesture that seemed to say, *Yes, here we are. You're not my master, but at least you're something.* It was an improvement over his dejection of yesterday.

"I should leave you here," I said to him, shouldering my bag. "I should call my daily woman again. I have no need for a dog, and this way you'd be out of danger."

Pickwick made no move, and in my imagination he chided me. He was a collie, after all, bred to run through fields and herd livestock, not to sit decoratively in a London sitting room. I looked around at the silent, ordered house I had lived in for three years now without moving or changing a single piece of furniture.

"Are you a guard dog?" I said to him, thinking of the danger I would face today.

Thumps of the tail, and a patient expression.

I sighed and took up his leash, which my daily woman had left by the door. "All right, then, but don't blame me if you get tired. I suppose I'll put up with you." When I bent to attach his leash, he pressed his nose to the inside of my elbow, as if he knew perfectly well that I was relieved to have him along, that the vision of his master that we'd both seen made me feel like kin to him. "We're going to Kent," I told him conversationally, "but we're making a stop at

Harriet Walk first. I have questions for Octavia Murtry. The police are coming to Kent as well, and so is James, but we won't see them because they'll be out of sight. So don't let on, all right?"

Pickwick seemed to be in agreement. I took a deep breath, gathered my courage, and left my house for what felt like the last time.

# CHAPTER TWENTY-SIX

"I have no time to talk," Octavia Murtry said to me. "The taxi is leaving."

It wasn't exactly true; the taxi was idling in front of the row house on Harriet Walk, and a burly hired man was working on transporting a trunk and a valise from the door to the back of the cab. Octavia stood on the walk in a beautiful forest green coat, her honey brown hair tucked under a matching hat, as she watched the man work with a vaguely tired expression.

"It's just a few questions," I said. I had put on a belted wool coat over my shirtdress, as well as a soft cloche hat and the comfortable buttoned shoes I usually wore only to the grocer's. It wasn't exactly fashionable—the dismissive glance Octavia gave my ensemble confirmed that—but I found I didn't quite care. I was comfortable, and aside from the aches from the night before, my body felt newly awake, aware of itself.

"I'm in a hurry," Octavia complained, though she quite obviously wasn't doing anything except watch someone else work. "I'm leaving for Paris today, and Lausanne after that. Father says I'm to go to the Continent for at least a month, if not longer."

"Why?"

She sighed, put upon. "He says I need to find a new influence since Gloria has died. He also thinks I'll meet a man and forget all about Harry." She slid me a sidelong look. "I'm sorry we won't have time for a proper séance, like I'd hoped, but perhaps I'll find someone who can help me in Paris."

"I wish you well," I said, almost meaning it. "But I have one question before you go."

"Very well."

"Why did Gloria come to see you the day before she died?"

Octavia's expression went very still.

"You said you hadn't seen her since you went shopping with her last Saturday," I said. "That was a lie, wasn't it? She came to see you on Sunday, the day before she died. No one knew about it, not even Davies, and you didn't tell the police. Why?"

Octavia had gone ghostly white under her powder. "How could you know that? How could you?"

I shrugged, and her eyes widened. If she thought I'd used my powers, all the better.

She shifted and looked away. "I didn't want to tell anyone," she said. "In fact, I never wanted to think of it again."

She paused, so I prompted her. "Start from the beginning."

"I'd been asking her to do a special reading for me. Like you said, you know, when we met the other day. I wanted her to contact her brothers, but she always said no." She glanced at me; I gave her no reaction, only waited. "On Sunday," she continued, "she telephoned me. She told me she'd changed her mind, that she wanted to contact Harry and Tommy and Colin. She'd canceled her other appointment for the day, and she hadn't even told Davies. She wanted money for it—it was a little insulting, because we were practically family and the sum was so large. But I wasn't about to say no, so I agreed. I was supposed to have tea with my grandmother, but I canceled everything and cleared my schedule."

"What happened?" I asked.

"She came here. God, she looked awful, like she hadn't been sleeping, like she'd been drinking. She said she had a headache. I can only imagine how much she'd had to drink to make her look like that."

I dropped my gaze to the top of Pickwick's head where he sat at my feet, my own headache pulsing, left over from Ramona's appearance. Pickwick's tail slid over my ankles as if he knew what I was thinking. "Go on."

"I told you before—there was something wrong with her in those last days. She never did sessions outside of her own flat. But she said she'd been home alone, trying to contact her brothers and unable to do it. She said she had to get out of there, that she needed me. That because I'd been engaged to Harry, contact with me would help her do it. She seemed almost panicked. I have to say, it was tasteless of her to ask me for money when she already wanted to contact her brothers herself, but there was nothing I could do at that point. You know what she was like when her mind was made up about something."

*I can't listen,* I thought. *I can't.* I pictured Gloria, her powers fading, knowing that her final chance to speak to her beloved dead brothers was slipping away forever. That Octavia would always have money, but Gloria's only source of wealth was about to dry up. My mother had had me to cover for the fact that her powers were fading, but Gloria had no one. And neither did I.

"Did she do the reading?" I asked.

Octavia was silent for a moment, until I finally raised my gaze and looked at her. She had gone even paler than before, and though she was looking at me, she seemed to be staring at something far away that I could not see. "Tell me," she said after a moment. "When the dead communicate with you, do you always tell your clients everything they say?"

"This isn't about me," I replied, thinking of suicidal abortions and anonymous babies. "Tell me what happened when you did the reading."

The hired man had finished loading the taxi and now he leaned on a lamppost, taking a break to light a cigarette as the taxi idled. "At first there was nothing," Octavia said. "I thought it was the headache interfering, because she was quite obviously in pain. And then I felt something." She blinked, still staring at whatever it was behind her eyes. "The air was electric, and there was a sort of smell. Faint and almost bad. And I felt something brush the back of my neck." She touched a gloved hand to the back of her neck as she recalled it. "I know some would say it was the power of suggestion, but I know what I felt. I've been to a great many séances, and I've seen tables move and doors open—I've heard knocks and seen messages spelled with a Ouija board. But just sitting at a little table in my dressing room with Gloria, I felt something so real I almost couldn't comprehend it." She blinked, seemed to notice me, and shrugged, her previous shallowness reappearing. "It sounds mad, but I think you understand."

"Yes," I managed.

Her brow furrowed. A man, quite obviously her father, had appeared at the front doorway of the house and watched us impatiently. "I looked at Gloria," Octavia continued, "and her eyes were wide. She was breathing hard, almost as if she was afraid, and she was sweating. Then she looked at something over my shoulder." Octavia leaned toward me, uninterested in her father's impatient stance behind us. "She *saw* something, don't you see? I begged and begged her to tell me. 'Is it Harry? What does he look like? What does he say?' But she wouldn't answer. She looked like she'd had some sort of shock. She said, 'I had no idea,' and tears came down her face. She was *weeping*."

I blinked at that; I couldn't picture Gloria weeping any more than Octavia could. "That was all she said?"

"No, not all. She closed her eyes, as if listening to something. I begged her again to tell me what was going on, but she didn't seem to hear me. She said, 'Good-bye, darling,' and then she said it again, softer: 'Good-bye, darling.' And then she opened her eyes, just like that. She pushed back her chair and stumbled out of it and said she had to leave."

"She didn't tell you what had happened?"

"It wasn't *fair*." Now real anger crept into Octavia's voice. Her father waved at us, and she made an impatient gesture ordering him to wait. "She wouldn't say. You have no idea how I pleaded with her. I was the customer. I had *paid*. Harry had been in the room; I felt it the same way I know you're standing here now. And she wouldn't tell me what he'd *said*." She sounded like a petulant child, and though it wasn't flattering on her, I couldn't help but feel empathy. "I was *so close*, don't you see? I deserve to know. You don't understand—you take it for granted, this power you have. You get to see things, to know things, that the rest of us go to our graves wondering about. It isn't *fair*."

I stared at her. "And that's what Gloria did," I said. "The next day. She went to her grave, and now you'll never know."

Octavia patted her cheeks briefly with her gloved hands and straightened her shoulders, collecting herself. "I simply couldn't believe it. I came to her apartment that day I ran into you there because I had to know if she'd left a diary, a note—anything. I was in such shock. I'm still not over it. I think Europe will be good for my nerves."

"But you didn't tell the police any of this."

"I saw no need for it," she said crisply. "It was a personal matter. What if the murderer was caught and I was required to testify in some sort of courtroom? I couldn't help but suspect that her murder had something to do with our session. And I was afraid, because Gloria was afraid, and Gloria was *never* afraid."

She turned away and started toward her father, who was saying something to her. She put a hand on the brim of her cloche hat and turned briefly back to me. "Good-bye, Ellie," she said. "If you speak to Gloria on the other side, tell her—" She stopped, and a look of pain and raw confusion crossed her face.

"I won't," I told her. "I have no plans to. Not ever."

She nodded and turned back to her father, who ushered her into the waiting taxi.

I felt the brush of a tail over my ankles again. "Sometimes you have to lie, Pickwick," I confessed to the dog. "Sometimes it's for the best."

As the taxi drove away, Octavia's father turned and stared at me, his expression dark and forbidding. He looked at me for a long moment before he walked back to the house.

I retreated, tugging on Pickwick's leash. I'd never seen the man before, but his expression was a familiar one. He wasn't just a father sending a troublesome dependent to the Continent. When Mr. Murtry looked at me, he was afraid.

The plan was simple. I was to board the 10:47 train from Victoria Station, alighting at Charing, in Kent, from which I was to travel to the Dubbs residence. I was to act normal—that is, oblivious—in case anyone followed me. Inspector Merriken and his men would already be in place in Kent, waiting to see whether Gloria's killer would show himself.

"And what will you do if Inspector Merriken refuses to bring you with him?" I'd asked James as I dressed that morning. "Go on foot?"

James had crooked an arm behind his head, watching me from the sofa. He was washed and dressed already—he was an early riser, I'd discovered—but he had not yet put on his jacket, and he was sprawled deliciously in his white shirtsleeves. "Ellie, did I ever tell you of how I tracked three German horse guards over fourteen miles of terrain in 1916?"

"You know you didn't," I said, tucking my hair behind my ears so I could put on my hat. "Are you saying you're some sort of tracking genius? And if you are, what are you going to do with it in the wilds of Kent?"

"I'm no genius, but I spent most of the war trying not to be seen by the enemy. I'd expect the police to know the same."

"You're not even armed." I reached for my hat, unwilling to admit that my own plans were giving me misgivings, that I was putting his life in danger. "I'd be happier if I knew you had—I don't know—some way to defend yourself."

He'd laughed at that, and I'd had to pause for a moment, appreciating the sight of it in daylight. "I don't intend to go around shooting people. But I do intend to keep you safe, with or without the police."

I wasn't exactly certain what that meant, and in the moment, I hadn't the courage to ask. I knew James's strength, his quickness, his intelligence. I knew he'd have expert help. I knew he'd spent several years fighting, experiencing things I couldn't bear to imagine before coming home. And now he was relentlessly focused—on me. It would have to be enough. We had no better plan.

"Ellie." James had gentled his voice, as if he'd followed my thoughts. "Just worry about yourself. Stay alert and don't take chances. I'll handle Merriken. We'll be there."

"And when we get to the house? If no one has come forward? If nothing has happened?"

"Then we do a séance, as you planned. See what Gloria has to tell us." His brow furrowed as he looked at me. "You're going to be all right, aren't you?"

I'd assured him I would, that I could do the séance, that I felt well enough. But my head was already aching as I stood in line at the Victoria Station ticket counter, the heavy smell and sound of the crowds beating in time with my heart.

"You can't take a dog in third class," the ticket seller said to me, noting the leash looped around my wrist, the patient collie at my feet. "It isn't allowed."

"But—"

"You'll have to buy a first-class ticket if you want to bring a dog. Those are the rules."

I swallowed. I couldn't resist a glance around me, through the dim light and crowds, before turning back to the ticket booth. I didn't see anyone I recognized, anyone lingering near. I was supposed to stay visible. In the privacy of a first-class compartment, it would take Gloria's killer only minutes to kill me.

"My sister can't afford a first-class ticket," I said, knowing that by looking at my clothes the ticket seller would never believe I was out of funds myself. "This is her dog. I'm taking him to her because she's sick and wants him back. She's devoted to him. We're meeting in third class. I'll never see her if I'm in first class. He's a quiet dog. He's the most well-behaved dog you've ever seen."

The ticket seller, distracted and sweaty, scratched his bald head and glanced at Pickwick, and then he shrugged. "Very well. It's nothing to me. But if he makes trouble and you're tossed off, you've no one to blame but yourself."

I bought my ticket, nearly sick with relief, and made my way to the platform. I boarded the third-class carriage, the conductor barely giving Pickwick a second look, and made my way to a seat. I sat with my knees together, my hands folded on my lap, my dog curled again at my feet, lying down now and preparing to nap. A plump woman who smelled of mint settled next to me, and other passengers filled the car, talking, laughing, one man ostentatiously pulling out a thick novel and leaning into the corner of his seat.

Still I did not see any man who seemed to be following me, anyone I recognized. My shoulders were wrung as tight as laundry in a wringer, and cold sweat beaded under my arms and down the back of my neck.

The train began to move, the station pulled away from the window, and I stared out, unseeing, waiting for it all to begin.

# CHAPTER TWENTY-SEVEN

After my mother died, I got a single letter from Gloria Sutter. It was a card, hand printed on thick paper, the ink expensive and beautiful. On the front of the card was a drawing of a mermaid perched on a rock, her black hair flowing down her body and into the water. She was pebbled with inky scales, the forks of her tail drawn long and narrow. Her torso, bare and white, was turned toward the viewer, her hair covering her breasts, but the dip of her navel was visible above the line of her fishy waist. She held her arms out, palms up, as if making a deliberate gesture, and her expression was peaceful and almost sad.

On the inside of the card was written only: *I am sorry. G.*

I knew whose handwriting it was. When I touched the card I knew that Gloria had written it while sitting in a café somewhere on the banks of the Thames, watching the boats go by in the blistering summer heat. I knew that she looked as beautiful as ever, her shoulders pale in a sleeveless white dress, a scarf wound in her hair, her big dark eyes thoughtful for once.

A peace offering, then, if only a small one.

I looked at the front of the card again. Gloria had a painting of a mermaid in her flat, and I'd never had to ask her about it. We both knew. The mermaid, beautiful and freakish, a human woman yet not, a woman unable ever to live a normal human life. The mermaid, who lives her existence as the only one of her kind.

I tore up the card and threw it away, and then I went back to mourning my mother.

I jerked out of a momentary, uneasy doze. The woman who smelled of mint was gone, and I was alone in my seat. The other passengers in the third-class car to Kent were quiet, many of them sleeping.

The memory of the mermaid card had surfaced, vivid and entire, and I sat horrified at myself. I'd been so angry, so furiously shaken by my mother's disgrace, her sickness and her death. I'd been nearly choked with grief, the blind unfairness of how my life had been pulled out from under me. How could I have known? How could I have been aware that the people around us, no matter how we feel about them, can be taken from us in the amount of time it takes to thrust a knife through the ribs? After all I'd been through, after all I'd seen, how could I *not* have known?

I pressed my hands to my eyes, fighting back tears. I took them away and noticed the girl across the aisle from me.

She was dressed smartly in a navy blue coat and hat, and she was in the depths of reading a movie magazine. The magazine hid most of her profile, but I could see the ends of a sleek black bob curling over her ears from under the brim of her hat. She crossed her legs, swinging one leg over the other.

I must have made some sort of sound because she lowered the magazine and looked at me. I swallowed. The girl was thirty-five at least, with a sizable nose and slightly crooked teeth. The eyebrows over her pale eyes were heavy and unkempt.

She caught me staring, and must have seen the shocked look on my face. "Well?" she said sharply, annoyed.

"Sorry," I mumbled. I dropped my gaze and noticed that someone had left a newspaper on the seat next to me, where the minty woman had been sitting. UNKNOWN BOMBER STRIKES AGAIN, the headline read. FOUR DEAD AT GUILDFORD AIRPLANE FACTORY. And beneath that: HAVE BOLSHEVIKS INFILTRATED ENGLAND?

I vaguely recalled seeing similar headlines over the past weeks. There had been a string of bombings of factories and such, but I had been too wrapped up in my own problems to pay attention. I looked away from the newspaper and reached into my messenger bag— trying not to create enough movement to disturb Pickwick, who was slumbering on my feet—and pulled out the three telegrams I'd found in Gloria's flask bag. I unfolded them and shook out the three small photographs, spreading them on my knees.

I studied the three faces, thinking of what Octavia had said about that final séance. I concluded, just as Octavia had, that Gloria had seen at least one of her brothers—if not all of them—that afternoon. I traced my fingers along the edges of the photographs, wondering. Which of them had she seen? Tommy, with his sweet, open face? Harry, with his dark beauty? Colin, with his bold, inscrutable features, so like Gloria's own? What did the words *I had no idea* mean? To whom had she said, *Good-bye, darling*? And why had she been crying?

I sighed and flipped over the newspaper on the seat next to me. I looked for anything written about Ramona's murder, but the sordid death of a cut-rate morphine-addict psychic was not news. Instead, the pages were dominated by the mysterious bombings; there had been four in all, all of them unsolved, with no group taking responsibility. The authorities were awash in theories. Anarchists? Labour fanatics? Fascists? Communists? Germans? Irish Republicans? Did the fact that two of the targets were factories mean that unions or

Bolsheviks were involved? No one knew, and in the meantime each successive bombing claimed a handful of lives.

I picked up the paper and used it as a cover to take a surreptitious glance around the train car, wondering whether I had a pursuer looking at me right then. If so, he was looking only at a girl reading a newspaper on a train car, as concerned as any other Londoner about whether there were Bolsheviks in her midst.

I glanced down at the photographs again, Gloria's three brothers looking up at me. Something about them bothered me, twigged something in my mind that I couldn't quite place. But before I could think too much on it, the conductor announced Charing, and the journey was nearly over.

I disembarked along with an elderly couple and a woman with two small children. I inquired at the station about hiring a motorcar, and the route to the Dubbses' house. The stationmaster told me that the only driver available—the only driver ever available—had just suffered a breakdown of his motorcar not an hour before and wouldn't be going anywhere today. However, if I really needed to get somewhere, I could rent a bicycle for a reasonable fee.

I hesitated. I hadn't expected something so important to go wrong so early. It was tempting to panic—the plan had me driving to the Dubbses' in a motorcar. Besides, I wasn't very experienced in bicycle riding, and my dress and stockings were hardly appropriate cycling wear. And what about Pickwick? On the other hand, I could simply bicycle up the same road I'd intended to drive. What should I do?

For a second I wished myself home, in my mother's bedroom with the curtains closed, far out of sight of Gloria's murderer. What I was attempting seemed insane. But the plan was already in motion, the police already in place. I had no hope of ever finding the man I sought, a man who came and murdered and left again without being seen. My only choice was to make him come to me. *You can do this, Ellie.*

"I'll take the bicycle," I said.

It was a sturdy contraption with wide handlebars and a low seat. I had hoped for a basket to put Pickwick in, but I had no such luck. I need not have worried, because as I awkwardly wheeled the bicycle away from the station, Pickwick, well rested, picked up his tail and pranced alongside me, eagerly sniffing the greenery and tugging on his leash. The countryside seemed to revive him. I promised him that I wouldn't cycle too fast—as if there were a chance of that—so that he wouldn't tire.

I mounted up and began. It took some getting used to, and I banged my ankles sharply against the body of the bicycle more than once, but as I left Charing and made my way out into the countryside, I began to find a rhythm. I slung my bag backward against the small of my back and pedaled. Pickwick trotted alongside me, and after a while I dismounted and unhooked him from his leash as he showed no inclination to run away. He wasn't a young dog, but my cycling skills weren't much of a challenge, and as we went along together I was reminded of how happy I was to have him with me.

The countryside was in full early-autumn glow, the grass still a gentle green but the trees beginning to turn red, yellow, and orange, like a painter playing with his palette. The sky was chalky white, the air warm, and I passed brick red houses with pretty terraces and cottages with thatched roofs. Hedgerows lined the road in places, and I cycled up and down a few gentle slopes. Kent may have been outside of London—and so a foreign country to a great many Londoners— but it was hardly wild; instead, it was a pretty patchwork of farms and cottages, churches and bridges, like a great garden. It didn't seem the place where anyone could be murdered. But my shoulders stayed tense and the back of my neck felt raw, as if someone had flayed the skin off. I was almost certain I was being watched.

After a while I stopped at the top of a hill, pretending that I was not gasping for breath, that sweat was not soaking my back between my shoulder blades. I put my feet on the ground and looked around me,

letting the teasing breeze cool my skin. Pickwick circled back to me
from the bushes at the side of the road and waited for me, a polite
question in his eyes. I twisted in my position and looked behind
me, wondering where my guardians might be. Around that farm-
house over there? Behind that stone wall, those hedgerows? Beneath
that bridge, or in that clump of trees, or behind the long wooden
fence to the left? Which roads were they watching, and how were
they staying hidden? The peaceful Kent countryside seemed to have
an infinite number of spots where a man could crouch unseen. No
one could jump out and garrote me in daylight on a bicycle, at least,
but I worried for James. Where was he? Had my lure worked? Was the
man from Ramona's apartment watching me even now?

There was nothing for it. I got back on the bicycle and pushed
the pedals, deliberately forcing my mind away. Instead, I thought of
the last time I'd seen Gloria.

It was November 1923, over a year after my mother's death. I'd
been standing in Fortnum and Mason, staring at a display of teas,
when I heard a familiar voice over my shoulder.

"Hello, darling."

Gloria was wearing a tweed jacket and matching hat that made
her look like a rich man's spoiled young wife on a shopping trip. She
wore lipstick so dark it was almost mulberry purple, the shade star-
tling against her pale skin, and I immediately felt the impulse to yank
out my handkerchief and blot it off.

She raised an eyebrow at me. "Doing a bit of shopping?"

I didn't need any tea, but I'd been desperate to leave the silence of
the house. "Yes," I replied, trying to sound sophisticated, casual.
"And you?"

She gave me a knowing twist of that dark mouth, and I wondered why I had even tried to fool her. Gloria always knew when I
was lying. "Darling, tea doesn't interest me. If it doesn't have gin in it,
I don't drink it."

No, Gloria never shopped for tea, and she never shopped in

Fortnum and Mason. She was standing there because she'd seen me; that was the only reason. And suddenly, past my grief and my anger, I was so pathetically glad to see her that I had to look away. "How have you been, Gloria?"

"Here's what I think," she said, ignoring my question. "You'll either take a walk with me, or you won't. Part of you wants to, and part of you wants me to walk away. The question is, which part of you will win?"

They were bold words, confident and challenging, but I knew better. I knew by the underlying quaver in her voice—undetectable by anyone who didn't know her as I did—that it was a question, an invitation. That she didn't know whether I would say yes. And that, in some part of her, it mattered.

It crumbled all of my defenses, that small quaver in her voice. Ever since my mother had died, since I'd torn up the beautiful mermaid card and thrown it out, I had been suffocatingly lonely in a way that had almost shocked me. I had been a cipher even to myself, an invisible woman. With Gloria's small overture, a year of anger, which I had fought so desperately to hang on to, slipped away. It hurt, but I felt something like relief, too.

I managed a shrug. "Yes," I said.

The day was chilled, the sun fighting to escape from behind a bank of clouds. We headed down Piccadilly, away from Piccadilly Circus, moving through the crowds, not speaking. Gloria walked half a step ahead of me, the shoulder of her tweed jacket aligned with my collarbone. I could see the white column of her neck under the bobbed edge of her hair and her cloche hat, the winking movement of an earring. I could smell her perfume. I had followed her into any number of restaurants and clubs this way, just at her shoulder, watching the gaze of every man in the room land on her before traveling idly to me. It was the natural order of things, bruisingly familiar.

I followed her into the calm of Green Park and we took one of the paths, the disintegrating leaves blowing like dust under our footsteps, the tall trees indifferent overhead. Even in November, Green Park was busy, Londoners taking the chance to stroll this stretch of relative quiet as the chill wind blew.

We stopped at Constitution Hill, and Gloria leaned on the wrought-iron fence, fishing in her pocket for a cigarette case. I crossed my arms over my chest and watched her.

"Thank you for the card," I managed at last.

She crooked a penciled eyebrow at me and searched her pocket again.

I sighed. "Do you want me to stay angry at you or not?"

Gloria found the cigarette case and straightened. "She wanted to quit, Ellie. I only provided the excuse."

"Ah, so that's why you arranged it, then? From the goodness of your heart?"

"No, of course not. I told you from the first that I don't like competition."

"You've taken care of it very nicely, then."

"Not exactly." She placed an unlit cigarette between her lips and watched me, her eyes hooded. She dropped the case back into her pocket and pulled out her matches. I had the urge, as I often did with Gloria, to put my hand on her. To feel the energy that came from her like heat. "The Fantastique is still in business, after all. But she doesn't do séances anymore."

"No."

"Finding lost things, is it? Interesting, I suppose." She shrugged. She knew what I was doing—of course she knew. She always made it her business. "I wondered what you would do once you were free of her."

"*Free* of her?" My skin stung as if I'd been slapped. My own guilt rushed over me. I *was* free of her—free of having to please her, free of having to do the séances. Free of caring for her in those last months. "I didn't want to be free of her."

Something flashed across Gloria's eyes. "For God's sake, Ellie. You still think that what I did was all about your mother, don't you? That she was the target."

"What are you talking about?"

"I did it because it needed to end," she said bluntly. "The lies, the foolishness. You living half an existence, sitting behind a curtain, helping her. You with a power you've been made to feel ashamed of, living nothing of a life." She pushed herself off the fence and took a drag off her cigarette. "Have you ever thought, Ellie, that we've been given the greatest insight into life and death in the history of mankind? The answers weren't given to a philosopher, or a religious leader, or a great scholar, or even a man. It was given to two *girls*, flappers who everyone sees as silly nuisances, cartoons, figures of fun. Girls who can't even vote." She tapped one finger against her temple through the cloth of her hat with a ruby-polished nail. "All of the secrets of the universe, of life and death, are sitting right here. A hundred people have walked past us on the street, and not a single one of them knows it."

I shook my head. "You're the one who enjoys the power, Gloria. It was never me."

"I don't enjoy it," she corrected me. She dropped her cigarette to the ground and stepped on it. "I simply refuse to feel ashamed of it, to feel ashamed of anything. I'm supposed to feel ashamed of how I look, how I dress, the language I use, the makeup I wear. For staying out late, for dancing, for making money, for thinking things and being angry and asking questions. For letting a man go to bed with me, when he can just button up his pants and never feel a lick of shame for the rest of his life. And I say all of it can go to hell."

My blood was pounding in my head, my cheeks flushing. I was powerfully angry, I realized, and it wasn't at her. "Stop it."

"Most of all, I'm supposed to be ashamed of my power," she continued, as if I hadn't spoken. "For being born with something the world has never seen. And I was ashamed of it—I never told you that, but I was. Until my brothers died, and George disowned me. That broke me, Ellie, in a way that you cannot imagine, but it also freed me. Because I suddenly realized: What is the point? Why waste your life being ashamed when you're going to be dead anyway? So I make money and I drink too much gin and I fall in with worthless men and my family hates me. I have headaches and nightmares that would ice the skin off you. But I'm living my life, Ellie, and I make no apologies for it. Can you say the same?"

Overhead, two birds called to each other, back and forth, a quick trill of notes. A couple strolled by, oblivious of us, her hand on his arm, his shoulder leaning into hers as he spoke something in her ear. I sighed, willing my heartbeat back to normal. "Give me a cigarette," I said.

She did, and lit it for me. "Well?"

I took a drag, my anger still simmering alongside my guilt. "My mother left me the house and a little bit of money," I said, "but not enough that I don't have to earn. I don't know how to type, and I'm too freakish for any man to marry me. And even though I can't stomach the thought of doing séances again, I really only have one talent." I looked at her and shrugged. "So here I am. The Fantastique finds lost things, but she doesn't talk to the dead anymore—I managed that much. I'll live in the house, take clients, and live a quiet life. I won't pretend I'm normal, but I also won't hide behind the curtain."

"And that's what you want?" she said.

"Yes, it is." It *was* what I wanted, in that moment. Just peace and quiet, a daily routine, a life where I knew what was expected of me. I'd had to build it myself, but now I had built it and I would live it. I had never had her courage, after all.

She crossed her arms and looked at me. Gloria Sutter, long legged and radiant even in a tweed suit on a cloudy November day, her eyes knowing and her lips dark. "Very well," she said at last. "I'll say this much. We had some good times, and now we're quits, as they say. But you know where I am, and you know how to find me."

She'd turned and walked away without another word, back toward Piccadilly. "I'll think about it," I'd called to her retreating back, but she gave no indication that she'd heard me. I could think things over, I thought. Perhaps something would change, something I couldn't foresee. Perhaps someday I'd want to talk to the only other person in the world who was made the same way I was. There would be time. If there was one thing I was certain of, it was that there was an endless supply of time.

But there hadn't been.

I rounded a turn in the lane on my bicycle. I was truly sweating now and my legs were hurting, but according to the map in my mind I had just under two miles to go. I was a different woman than I had been that day in Green Park. I was alive. I was ready. I was no longer ashamed. How right Gloria had been, about everything. I was who I was, and I would no longer make any apologies.

Pickwick barked, once, sharply. His ears flattened, and he disappeared beneath a hedgerow.

"Pickwick?" I said.

And then a sharp crack sounded through the trees, and something hit my bicycle. The handlebars shook under my hands, the wheels veered of their own accord, and in the next second I hit the ground, the blackness coming up to meet me.

# CHAPTER TWENTY-EIGHT

I landed on my shoulder, a jolt of pain traveling up my neck and into the back of my head. My legs tangled in the bicycle pedals, and the entire thing came down on top of me, scraping my legs and pushing me out of balance. I slid on the side of the dirt road and into the ditch by the roadside, breaking my fall with the palms of my hands as I scraped the dirt and the thin layer of rotted leaves.

I lay in the damp mulch in the bottom of the ditch, trying to push the twisted bicycle off me. Overhead, a rook cried from a treetop somewhere, and Pickwick barked again. I had just enough time to wonder whether there would be a second shot when I heard his toenails scrabble on the road above me.

The sound filled me with panic. "No, Pickwick!" I cried, pulling my legs beneath me—my stockings were shredded, one knee wet with blood—and crawling to the edge of the ditch. The dog was watching me, waiting for me to get up. "Go back!" I begged him, gesturing toward the hedgerow. "Now! Go!" My brain seemed to have detached, and all I could think in that moment was, *Please, don't let my dog get shot.* From somewhere ahead of me, through the trees, I heard a man's shout, and then another, but no second shot came.

Pickwick curled his tail to his haunches and crouched, not sure of what I was asking him to do. I held my breath and hesitated, on my hands and knees on the edge of the ditch, listening for a moment that likely lasted seconds but felt like a year. My hat had fallen off, the palms of my gloves had shredded, and my chest ached. I could not stay where I was. Whoever had shot at me—and I knew by instinct who it was, of course—could either shoot at me again or come closer to finish the job. I had to run.

I crawled out of the ditch, my hands and knees stinging, keeping low to the ground. I had just gotten my feet under me, ready to run in a crouch, when I saw the figure in the trees.

It was a man, tall and thin, far back in the green shadows. He was looking at me, but as I raised my gaze he turned away, and I saw only the brim of his hat, the sleeve of his jacket. Pickwick had gone still, his ears pricked, watching. He did not growl.

I wondered wildly, at first, whether it was a policeman. But the figure moved off through the shadows, smooth and uncanny, making no sound. From the trees came a whiff of an awful smell.

"*Oh, God,*" I whispered.

I forced my feet into motion. I half ran into the cover of the trees, out of the sunlight, into the cool shadows. A breeze cheerfully ruffled the leaves overhead, the scent of early autumn mixing with the blatant smell of death. An ache began in my head. Someone was dead. That much I knew: Someone was dead, and I'd seen his ghost.

From far off, a motor sounded, receding, but there was no sign of anyone on the road. If I was being pursued, if anyone nearby had heard the shot, they gave no indication. If James had heard, he did not come.

*James.*

It hadn't been him; it hadn't. The figure had been too tall, too unfamiliar. I would have known if it had been James; I would have recognized him even in death. Still, the possibility felt like a punch in the stomach, and I fought to regain control of myself. *You are alone, Ellie, and there is no one to help you. What will you do?*

Pickwick made my decision. He brushed past me, loping on quiet feet in the direction of the dead figure. His tail was up, his body alert. In seconds he had vanished into the bushes.

I followed, limping because of my bad knee. I had somehow kept my messenger bag strapped across my body, and I now tucked the bag behind me as I walked. The trees weren't thick here; they grew in small belts between properties and stretches of unused road and farmland. I followed the dog and the unseen figure, vanished now, across the soft ground, through the dappled light. Soon we climbed a rise and the trees thinned abruptly, and I stood on a bright hill of emerald green looking over the landscape of hills and valleys, changing to the warm colors of autumn between the dotted homes and barns below.

Sprawled on the hillside was the body of a man.

He lay facedown, angled down the hill, as if he'd been struck while descending. He wore a suit of chocolate brown, the back of the jacket flung upward over his back, left where it had folded when he fell. His arms were pinned beneath him, his legs sprawled. His hat had fallen off. Far below, at the bottom of the hill, parked at the side of the dirt road and partly under the cover of a thick stand of bushes at the edge of the trees, was a motorcar. Probably his.

I stopped, panting, and made a strangled noise. There was no movement, no sound; the man's body lay still, an unnatural part of the scenery. No one passed on the road below. It was as if the Kent countryside, in that moment, was deserted except for me, my dog, and the dead man. I gathered my courage and stepped closer.

His head was slightly turned, his eyes half open and glazed in death. The pretty grass beneath his neck was soaked in blood, the ground dark with it, droplets clinging to the blades of greenery. He showed no other mark; something very sharp had gone very deep into his neck, killing him quickly and effectively before his body had been left to fall. I recognized his thin build—I had seen it disappear into a doorway in Piccadilly Circus, and I had also glimpsed his face in the underground. It was the man in the houndstooth jacket.

I blinked hard, taking in the coppery scent of damp blood, and ran a hand over my face. I realized I was still wearing my torn gloves, the palms reduced to threads. I absently pulled them off and threw them to the ground, as if that would accomplish something. There had been a man's cry shortly after I'd been shot off my bicycle. Two of them, one after the other, quick. The sound of the man in the houndstooth jacket, dying.

Five minutes ago? Ten?

The grass where I stood at the top of the hill had been flattened, as if by feet. I stepped onto the flattened portion, peering for footprints I had no idea how to identify. Pickwick remained near the tree line a few feet away, sitting quietly, his tongue lolling as he panted. I saw nothing until I raised my eyes, looked back the way I had come. And then I understood.

From there I could see curling before me the road I had cycled down. I could see the bend I had taken, the ditch I had fallen into. I could even glimpse the wreckage of my bicycle beneath the leaves. This was where the killer had stood, aiming his rifle as I had come down the road.

I closed my eyes. A familiar feeling tickled the back of my neck, the base of my skull. He was still here, then, the man in the houndstooth jacket. I had seen his deathbed vision, and part of me called him even now.

I turned to find him standing six feet away, looking at me.

I took a breath. For the first time in a long while, I did not tell the dead to go away, to return where he had come from. I did not flinch at the smell, or at the sight of him, and I did not recoil in fear.

I did not try to harness my power. Not this time. Instead, I looked straight into his ghastly, uncanny face.

"Speak to me," I said.

W hen I told James that the dead do not speak in sentences, I had spoken the truth. I had also spoken the truth when I said it felt like plunging a hand into a bucket of worms in the dark. I plunged my hand now with the man in the houndstooth jacket, the chill of it freezing my spine and roiling in my stomach.

He was sadness and anger, frustration and overarching grief. I closed my eyes and saw things that had been left undone: a wife who had left him, to whom he had never apologized; a friend he had betrayed long before, though I could not see how; a brother he had not spoken to in years. I saw flashes of things I should not have seen— private memories, sensations: a woman sliding the straps of her brassiere off her shoulders and reaching for him; his mother weeping in unremitting pain in the last days of her life. Usually these were memories I pushed away, because they were unbearable, but now I let them wash through me, let their raw emotion fill me. I smelled late-autumn leaves burning and rich coffee, felt the sting as a long-ago teacher slapped his cheek, and then I saw the hillside, the last moments of the man's life.

He had parked the car and come up the hill, his gaze on the slender figure, its back to him as it aimed the rifle. The images were jumbled. The man with the rifle had been smoking a cigarette, its smell pungent in the autumn air. He wore a cloth cap and a simple farmer's jacket and trousers, but he was no simple farmer. The rifle was held rigid on his shoulder, its aim precise, and as he pulled the trigger the *crack* of it barely shifted his body, the recoil entirely controlled. The man in the houndstooth jacket had shouted, pulling a handgun from his pocket, thinking, *Black dog, black dog,* as the other man slid the bolt back on the rifle, ready to fire again, and the man had turned and lowered the rifle and—

I groaned, pressing my bare hands to my face. The sensations were furious now, too fast, and I had to stop them. Everything was out of order; I could make no sense of it. I pushed back, shutting the images out one by one, forcing down a rigid control. I opened my eyes and told him to leave, that it was over, that he should go and rest. The images slowed, trickled, stopped. I staggered, nauseated. The smell was gone, and so was the man in the houndstooth jacket.

With careful deliberation, I fell to my knees in the grass. That was it, then: He had saved my life, and he had died. If he hadn't come up the hill, shouting and drawing his gun, the man with the rifle would have taken another shot at me as I'd lain in the ditch, and he would not have missed. I remembered hearing the shouts, and I also remembered hearing the sound of a motor as I'd gone through the woods. The killer had taken care of his witness, then, and driven off in his own vehicle, even as I'd followed the dead man here. I glanced at the body again, unmoving in its bloody spot in the grass. The gun he had drawn, I guessed, was in one of his hands, pinned under his body; he'd had no chance to fire it, so quick had his killer been. *Black dog*, the man had thought, but there had been no black dog in the images I'd seen, and Pickwick did not seem alarmed.

I went back and forth through the pictures in my mind, shuffling through them like a stack of grisly photographs, trying to make sense of them. Coming up the hill; the man with the rifle . . . He had turned, and I'd seen the shadow of a face, but that did not matter. Something else mattered—something important. I was light-headed and terrified, but I had gone too far to stop now. The man who had saved my life had left me something I was meant to see.

I took a breath, calming myself, and went through the images again. That last moment before death. The man with the rifle had turned and—

I laughed aloud, my legs folding under me until I was sitting in the grass and staring at nothing, looking at the pictures in my mind. It was just possible—only just.

The man with the rifle had been smoking a cigarette, and when he'd turned in surprise, it had fallen into the grass.

I shifted on my bleeding knee, began sorting through the flattened vegetation with my scraped hands. The pain in my head was like a living thing, red and sodden in my skull, and the pulse of sunlight overhead felt as if it was scraping my brain, but still I continued. "Psychometry," I said to Pickwick. I was babbling, but the sound of my own voice seemed to calm the agony in my head. "It isn't my specialty, Pickwick, but I can do it. At least, I may be able to. I don't really know anymore, do I?" I kept searching, my face close to the ground, beyond caring how mad I looked. "If he even dropped it, it may give me nothing. I may see that he enjoys cottage pie, or that he wore brown socks instead of black this morning. I may learn something that isn't true, or nothing at all. If he even dropped it."

He had. I found the burned end of an abandoned cigarette alone in the grass, gone out now, not even a smell of ash coming from it. I looked at it for a long moment, thinking of how carefully Gloria's killer had put out his cigarette after he'd murdered Ramona and possibly Davies, too, how neatly he'd tamped it out and slid it in his pocket. I was looking at one mistake, one single mistake, the only one he'd ever made as he'd gone about killing people.

Maybe it wouldn't work. I was just a girl, after all, and he was an assassin of some kind, a professional killer. He was one step ahead of everyone—the police, George Sutter, MI5, and the man in the houndstooth jacket—calmly taking lives and walking away like a man who didn't exist. I was just a flapper who found lost dogs for money. There was no reason it would work.

Then Gloria's words came back to me, from the last time I had ever seen her, when I hadn't told her I was sorry or that I loved her no matter what. When I'd let her walk away.

"I was born with something the world has never seen," I said, and I picked up the cigarette.

# CHAPTER TWENTY-NINE

At first there was nothing. I was too tired, my head hurt, I had done too much already, the sun was too bright. My powers were fading. Despite what I so desperately wanted to believe, a single cigarette wasn't going to tell me anything.

And then I saw a motorcycle with a sidecar, clear as day. I thought, *Just a farmhand traveling the countryside on his motorcycle. No one will look twice.* That was what he was dressed as, the black suit and hat of London traded for thick boots, rough clothes, and a cloth cap. No reason for anyone to look at what he carried in the sidecar. None at all.

The vision faded, and I was on my knees on the hilltop again, but I gave a crow of triumph at my success so far that made Pickwick open his eyes. He was lying in the grass, having dozed a little after his long run, watching me calmly.

I ran a hand through my hair, rubbed the top of my head. A cloud covered the sun, and the countryside lapsed into pleasant shadow, the breeze cool and fragrant. My power didn't seem to be fading now; it was painful but almost jaggedly strong, as if joyous that I'd finally set it free. "Again," I said aloud, and I closed my eyes.

This time I saw the darkened outer wall of a factory at night, a window broken, a suitcase thrown through. A train schedule. Four men at a small table, talking quietly, and I approached them and sat down and spoke to them in a language I did not recognize, watching their eyes go wide in recognition. All of it disjointed, brief, frustrating. I opened my eyes again.

I shifted off my knees and lay back in the grass, like a girl enjoying a lazy day. I held up the cigarette and stared at it beneath the clouded sky. My head thumped, my stomach turned, and then I was ready. "Again," I repeated.

A woman. Lovely, dark haired. Sitting in a bleak room somewhere, black circles under her eyes. Looking up at me with hopeless dread. *No, no.* Thinking of her when I throw the suitcase. Thinking of her when the train stops at the border and I show my false papers, calm and unconcerned. Thinking of her when I shave with my straight razor, looking at the blade and wondering how quick I could be, but no, I will not do it, because of her. And then the telephone shrills and I know I'll pick it up and two words will crackle down the line at me, *Black dog,* and I will be given a set of coordinates. And I look up into the mirror and—

The shock of his identity made everything fuzzy after that. I dropped the cigarette; it was no good to me anymore. I must have picked myself up off the ground, though later I recalled nothing but the stinging in my knee and the wet blood on my shin. I must have staggered down the hill and toward the road, through the trees, Pickwick following me. I saw only the woman, the images I had seen, the feelings they had given me. I was in someone else's head, living someone else's life. The shaving razor. The face in the mirror.

I started up the road toward the Dubbses' house. He knew I would go there; he had put together what I wanted and why. He would go there as certainly as a bird goes to his nest, unable to stay away, unable not to finish the job. There was the possibility that, after the failed attempt with the rifle, I would turn around and go home, but he didn't think I would do it. I was supposed to be dead—quick, clean, no chance of getting caught, as usual—but the man in the houndstooth jacket had surprised him, and now he had something of a problem. Still, nothing he couldn't clean up quickly, as long as I was out of the way. Once I was dead, he could vanish, just as he had before. A man who didn't exist.

The hum of a motor approached on the road behind me. A thick, heavy sound, not that of a motorcycle. I rubbed my eyes.

It drew up beside me, and the motor idled as I heard the door open. "Jesus God," someone said. James's voice. Confusing, because James did not own a motorcar. Where had he gotten a motorcar?

And then his hands were on me, an arm beneath my knees and another behind my shoulders, picking me up swift and easy without even a grunt. "What the bloody hell," he said, his voice short with fury. I smelled the tangy scent of him, felt myself being placed gently in the motorcar.

"My dog," I cried.

I needn't have worried. Pickwick bounded into the car after me, uninvited, scrabbling on the seat. I put my arm around him. We were in the backseat, and someone in a dark hat was up front driving. James circled the car and slid in next to me, his weight making the seat sag. He slammed the door, said, "Drive," shortly to the man in front, and took my face in his hands as the vehicle began to move.

"Are you all right?" he said to me, brushing my cheeks with his thumbs. I looked into his face, the other vision finally clearing away. He looked more wonderful than anything I'd ever seen. I opened my mouth to tell him so, but he didn't let me speak.

"Jesus, Ellie," he said. "Where have you been? We found the bicycle—I nearly went mad. Are you hurt?"

"My head hurts," I rasped, "but he didn't hit me. Where were you?"

James glanced at the back of the driver's head, fury in his eyes. "I was doing my best to protect you, despite our mutual friend here."

"That was my chief inspector, you idiot," came the reply from the front seat. "For the last time."

"Inspector Merriken?" I said.

"The Yard took me in for questioning," James told me through gritted teeth. "For Gloria's murder. And the order to send men out here was delayed."

For the first time I felt a thin strain of hysteria. "You weren't there? Neither of you? Not on the train, not on the roads, not anywhere?" It had been the thought of the police watching from shouting distance that had given me courage. Instead, I'd been alone the entire time?

"No," James said, running his hands gently down my shoulders, over my arms, looking for injuries. "Because the Yard is full of oafs who don't know what they're doing—"

"I was the one who got you *out* of there," said Inspector Merriken.

"—and wouldn't know a suspect if he popped right out of their asses and said hello."

"There's no respect for the police in this country," Merriken complained, his voice deceptively mild.

"I came for you as soon as I could. It was him, wasn't it?" said James to me. "He found you. Ellie, your knee is bleeding. We'll have to— What did he do?"

I ran a hand through my hair, keeping the other arm around Pickwick, who was leaning into my side. He was trembling, unused to the motorcar, and I pulled him closer to me. "A rifle shot from a hilltop," I said. "He knocked me right off my bicycle."

The car was deadly silent as both men forgot their argument. James went positively gray.

"I'll never forgive myself," he said softly.

From the driver's seat, Inspector Merriken's voice was subdued. "I'm sorry that happened to you, Miss Winter, and I'm glad you're all right. If you can tell me exactly how it happened, I can have some of my men search the area for his vantage point."

"I already found it," I said, not ready to talk about the figure in the woods who had led me there. "I already searched it."

"Ah." The inspector's voice was gentle. "Good. With all due respect, Miss Winter, we still need to go over the scene for shell casings and the like. I don't suppose you found any shell casings?"

"No. But your men will have to go back there anyway, because he left the body of the man who stopped him." I swallowed. "And he left a cigarette." I turned and looked at James, who was regarding me with an expression I couldn't read. "I saw him," I said. "I know who he is."

# CHAPTER THIRTY

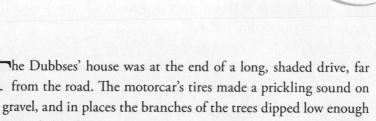

The Dubbses' house was at the end of a long, shaded drive, far from the road. The motorcar's tires made a prickling sound on the gravel, and in places the branches of the trees dipped low enough to scrape the roof. By the time Inspector Merriken pulled the motorcar to a stop in front of the house, it felt as if we had descended into a hidden pocket of the country, a place where no one could see us.

The house itself was of red brick, with a thatched roof and a thick patch of ivy, already half russet, climbing the walls. A door of fresh-painted white showed like a tooth from its nest of ivy, and the mullioned windows winked in the sunlight as the sun began to lower in the afternoon sky. It was a house that had stood for a hundred years, the picture of bucolic English gentility, and it was easy to picture an old gentleman smoking his pipe while his wife puttered in the garden. The very last thing it looked like was a house that needed a séance.

"This is it?" I said, staring at it as James helped me out of the car. "This is where they live?"

"In a manner of speaking." Inspector Merriken slammed the driver's door and patted his pockets, anger and disgust written on his face.

"What does that mean?" I asked.

"It turns out the Dubbses are something of a cipher," said James.

"That's putting it mildly," said the inspector.

I frowned, looking at the quiet house, the well-kept garden. "They're gone to the Continent, you said."

"Farther than that," said James. "They've vanished."

Inspector Merriken stopped patting his pockets and looked at me. "Do you recall our interview, Miss Winter?"

"Yes, of course."

"You suggested I take another look at the Dubbses, specifically at their finances, as they paid both Gloria and Fitzroy Todd presumably high sums. Perhaps this will surprise you, but I took your advice. And what do you think I found?"

I shook my head, bewildered.

"Nothing," the inspector said. "This house you see here is registered as owned by a Martin Dubbs, and that is all. Martin Dubbs has no birth record, no marriage record. His son has no birth record. He claimed to work for Barclays Bank in London, where he mostly lives, but when I checked, they had never heard of him. In short, Miss Winter, Martin Dubbs, and presumably his wife, are fakes." Anger flushed red on his handsome cheekbones. "And I missed it."

"But his identification?" I said.

"I inspected it when we questioned them, yes, and so did one of my men. I'm trained to look for false papers—I've seen dozens of them in my career, from the amateur to the professional. What the Dubbses showed us looked perfect to me. That means that, assuming what I inspected was fake, they had the very highest talent create their papers. One would have to be extremely well connected, and extremely deep in the pocket, to get work like that done."

"Unless," said James, "the papers were created by the government itself."

"What do you mean?"

Inspector Merriken patted his pocket again and pulled out a thin stick of metal. He turned toward the Dubbses' front door. "While I was investigating, Mr. Hawley here was doing some searching of his own. It seems he contacted the War Office, looking for the record of one Davey Dubbs, whose spirit Gloria was supposed to call on the night she was murdered. The War Office must have alerted someone. When Mr. Hawley turned up at the Yard this morning, asking to see me so that he could convince me to let him come on this operation, he was taken for questioning—in person—by my chief inspector. At the same time, I was told that my request for men to cover the roads in Kent this morning was delayed. It goes completely against protocol for my CI to interview a subject in my murder investigation without me while at the same time altering my plans. I'd like to know what the hell is going on."

"He kept me for two hours," James said. "I told him I had to leave, that I had to meet you because I was afraid Gloria's killer would go after you, but still he detained me."

Inspector Merriken regarded the Dubbses' front door. "When I heard what inquiry Mr. Hawley had made that had him detained, I picked up the phone and called the War Office myself. And do you know what I was told? 'Classified.' *Classified!*" He glanced at my bewildered face, as if I should have known what outraged him so. "My own evidence, in my own murder investigation, classified. No, I don't think that will do at all. I had no choice but to interrupt the interview, claiming I needed to question Mr. Hawley about new information I'd received." He reached down and twitched his trouser legs in an immaculate fall before crouching before the door and inserting the black pick into the lock. "We had no choice but to leave the Yard without backup—it was either that or continue to delay. In the meantime, since the Dubbses apparently aren't home and aren't even real people, I have no problem entering their premises for another look."

"You can pick locks?" I said.

James came next to my shoulder, his hands in his pockets, and watched alongside me. "Makes you feel safe as a citizen, doesn't it?"

"Sod off," said the inspector.

"You told him about George Sutter, didn't you?" I said to James.

"Yes," he replied. "It's made him rather angry."

"There is nothing I hate worse," Merriken clarified as the lock mechanism clicked, "than people who meddle in my murder cases. Except possibly ghosts. Don't ever talk to me about ghosts."

He had the door open in less than a minute, and we followed him inside. The front hall was tidy, the sitting room opening from it snugly furnished, with lace-trimmed curtains on the windows and a rustic clock on the mantel. I hesitated, Pickwick at my heels, before following the two men into the house. This felt like a home. How did it fit with the nonexistent Dubbses?

James and Inspector Merriken had already moved to the back of the house, past the narrow staircase leading to the upstairs bedrooms, to the snug kitchen, which was tidy and featured a large kitchen table. "This is where the séance was supposed to happen," the inspector said as he began opening cupboards and gently rifling through their contents. "Or so I was told, the night I interviewed them and they lied about nearly everything."

"Fitz told me the Dubbses weren't ready for a séance," I said. "That they seemed clueless about how to even go about it. Ramona said the same thing."

"Neither one of them told me that," said the inspector, continuing his search.

"According to Ramona, the Dubbses didn't want either of them there—either Fitz or Ramona. They were unhappy about it and wanted both of them to go home, as if they wanted Gloria alone." I rubbed a finger over my forehead, trying to remember everything through the fog of pain. "Also, Fitz lied to you about how he convinced Gloria to come here and do the session. He's been selling narcotics, to Ramona as well as others, and a man approached him and blackmailed him to get Gloria to show up, or else."

Inspector Merriken glanced at me. "We knew about the drugs. One look at Ramona and it was obvious she'd been taking—and that night. As for Fitzroy Todd, he isn't particularly bright, and he's never been discreet. He's not much of a master criminal. But his family is powerful, and none of our charges ever stick. He's become one of those nuisances we all know about but we have to put up with. I suspected his story was full of holes. I just couldn't figure out where they were."

"I keep coming back to the fact that they wanted Gloria alone out here," James said. "Do you think this couple, whoever they really are, is behind this?"

"It's a shell game," the inspector mused. "Set up an intermediary, make contact with someone close to the target who has something to lose—in this case, Fitzroy Todd. Blackmail him into bringing your target to the intended place. When it's all over, disappear again. The question is, what did they want her for?" He closed the cupboard he was peering into and turned to me. "I have my own theories. But first, Miss Winter, please have a seat and tell me what you know."

There was no refusing him. I pulled out a chair at the kitchen table and sat. If this had indeed been intended as the séance table, it was a terrible choice; it was too long, the feel of it too utilitarian, like a work-bench. And the cheery, sunlit kitchen was not a good place to summon the dead. James went to the kitchen sink, where he quickly found a rag and soaked it in cold water. He pulled out a chair next to me and placed the rag on my knee. Pickwick curled up in a corner of the kitchen, put his nose into his tail, and promptly fell asleep, exhausted.

I pulled my messenger bag off my shoulder, wincing as my sore muscles moved, and set it on the table. I opened it and slid out Gloria's three telegrams, in which I'd once again folded the three photographs after studying them on the train. Gloria's three brothers looked up at me from the wooden surface, their faces forever frozen in time. I bypassed Tommy and Harry, put my finger on the edge of Colin's photograph, and slid it into the middle of the table.

"It's him," I said. "This is the man you want."

"And who is that?" asked the inspector, angling his tall body down to inspect the photograph.

"Colin Sutter."

"*Colin Sutter?*" James stopped pressing the cloth to my knee and stared at me. "Colin Sutter is dead."

Inspector Merriken's quick brain calculated behind his eyes. "One of Gloria's brothers who died in the war?"

"He's not dead," I said. "He shot at me this afternoon. He killed Gloria and Ramona, and George Sutter's man." I looked at both of them, for the first time wondering whether they would believe me. "I saw it. I saw *him*. I saw his face in the mirror."

"Ellie." James put his hand on my leg, looked at me. "I know you," he said. "I know. So I'll only ask this once. Are you absolutely certain of what you saw?"

I blinked. "He's wearing an outfit that looks like a farmhand's, with a cloth cap. He's driving a motorcycle with a sidecar and taking back roads. I don't know how he was reported dead in the war—I didn't see that, didn't see how he survived. I saw something about a woman, and a few other things I didn't understand. But it was him." I dropped my gaze to the photo, to Colin's dark good looks, so much like Gloria's. The politician, his family had called him. Always so serious, so reserved. I thought of the razor blade I'd seen in the vision. "He wanted to die at one point," I said, "but he didn't do it. There was something he had to accomplish."

"What?" the inspector asked.

I looked up at him. "It's very vague, you understand. I don't get words, sentences, explanations. I get images. And I saw an empty factory, and I saw him throw a suitcase through a broken window."

Inspector Merriken straightened as if I'd slapped him. "The

bomber?" he said, and for the first time his unshakable composure broke and amazement crossed his face. "You're saying that Colin Sutter, who died in the war, is the bomber?"

Both men stared at me. I thought of the headlines I'd seen in the newspapers on the train: UNKNOWN BOMBER STRIKES AGAIN. FOUR DEAD AT GUILDFORD AIRPLANE FACTORY. I'd given the articles only a cursory read, using the newspaper as a cover. Now I wished I'd read everything in depth. "I told you, I don't know all the answers," I said, unable to help the defensiveness in my voice. "I only know what I saw."

Inspector Merriken turned away, pacing the kitchen. "Miss Winter, this is too much."

"Now wait, Merriken," said James. "You have to at least consider it. If you'd ever seen Ellie in action, you'd know—"

"I have," the inspector said. "I have seen her in action. For God's sake, I wouldn't have followed both of you this far if I thought she was a fake. But you have to see it from my position—this leaves me almost nothing to work with. I can't go back to the Yard and tell my chief inspector that England's mysterious bomber is Gloria Sutter's dead brother, and the only evidence I have is the vision of a psychic—and not just any psychic, but one who has been officially debunked by the New Society."

James removed his hat and ran his hands through his short hair. "Are the bombings your case?"

Merriken shook his head. "Terror acts don't fall to the Murder Squad. I'd have to involve the police, the Home Office, the War Office—all the way up the line. It wouldn't end. And it would take about a half hour before I'd be staring at some terrifying, cold-blooded fellow from MI5."

We were all silent, the air thunderous and still.

"George Sutter," said James.

"Wait." Inspector Merriken held up his hands. He pulled off his hat and dropped it on the sideboard, pacing again, his long dark coat flapping as he moved. "We have to stop right now. I'm trying to do police work here—proper police work, not speculate like madmen."

"George Sutter can't have known about it," I said. My voice was almost shrill with panic, and I took a breath. "He can't have. Why would he have come to me—why would he have recruited me, if he already knew about Colin?"

James touched my neck, briefly. "We already know why he needed you, Ellie."

"As bait?" My voice went shrill again, and again I tried to stay calm. "It makes no sense. How would he have known from the first that Colin would come for me? And what was Gloria, then? Was she bait as well?"

Inspector Merriken shook his head. "This whole setup," he said, gesturing to the house around us. "It's too elaborate. To recruit Fitz-roy Todd, the fake Dubbses, all of it, to get Gloria to come to the countryside so that Colin—if indeed it's Colin he's after—will follow her? It's completely impractical. No. This setup was for Gloria's bene-fit, but it was for a different purpose."

"And what could that possibly be?" I asked him.

The inspector sighed. "I can't believe I'm lending any credence to this, but if I had to guess, I'd say the purpose was to recruit her."

I stared at him, aghast. "Into MI5?"

"Possibly, yes."

I couldn't help it; I laughed.

James raised his eyebrows, but Inspector Merriken looked faintly thunderous. "What is so amusing?" he asked.

"Gloria would never have worked for MI5," I said. "Never. If that's what all of this was, they were wasting their time. Gloria would have told them to go to hell."

"Are you sure?" James asked me. "We both know Gloria liked money, and we know for a fact that she needed it. She could have dangled MI5 along and made herself a profit."

I shook my head. "Gloria didn't work for the government, or the prime minister, or anyone else. She certainly wouldn't have worked for the brother who disowned her as a liar and a fraud. Gloria worked for herself, and only herself."

"That may be, or it may not," Inspector Merriken said, his logic grating on me. "But first things first. I'm not pursuing a dead man unless I have evidence he's not dead. I'm going to make some telephone calls. I'm likely in very deep waters with my chief inspector right now, but I'll see if I can get some backup sent out here after all, to deal with the attempt on Miss Winter if nothing else. And I'll try to get Colin Sutter's records from the War Office."

"Hasn't the War Office already shut you out?" James pointed out. "The last time you asked them for information, they told you it was classified."

"Those were official channels. This time I won't go through the front door. As it happens, I have a contact at the War Office who owes me a favor."

James leaned back in his chair, his gaze speculating. "A woman? Just a wild guess."

"Leave it, Hawley." Merriken's face grew very, very still and dangerous.

James grinned. "Don't worry, old fellow. I'm a closed book."

"I'm warning you." Merriken pointed a finger at him. "Leave off. Try to make yourself useful, for the first time in your life, rather than pursuing pixies or fairies, or whatever it is you do." He turned and left the room.

I looked at James. "Were you *trying* to rile him?"

"I didn't think it would be that easy," he admitted. "But the shot about the pixies and fairies was a good one, I admit."

"Well, now you've offended him," I said, thinking of Merriken's fiancée, Jillian. There was no way he was unfaithful to her; that much I knew. Perhaps the contact at the War Office was a leftover from his pre-Jillian days. "I'll see if I can smooth it over when he gets off the telephone."

James turned to me. The humor had left his face. "Smooth it over, will you? That's interesting. I'd like very much to know what the two of you talked about."

I might have been working with two bulls butting heads; no one had ever taught me how to manage two independent, riled-up men. "Don't worry—he's taken. Quite comprehensively so."

Something flickered across James's eyes, and he leaned forward and kissed me, quick and hard. "So are you," he said. "Now sit and rest for a minute. I'm going to search the house."

"What for?"

"Anything," he said, and left the room.

The pain in my head had receded to a dull pounding, and James had cleaned most of the blood from my knee. My stockings were ruined, of course; looking down at my legs, I found myself in the strange position of wondering whether it was better to wear torn stockings or to remove them and not wear stockings at all. It was perplexing, the kind of etiquette question one's mother never covers. I gave up pondering it and limped to the sink, where I splashed water on my face and drank a glassful, suddenly dying of thirst. Pickwick lifted his head and thumped his tail hopefully at me; I put water in a bowl, gave it to him, and searched the cupboards for something to feed him as he gratefully inhaled his drink.

The Dubbses may not have been real people, but someone or other had lived here. There were a few tinned items, sardines and the like, and a smattering of mismatched dishes in the cupboards. The drawers contained eating utensils, and pots and pans hung from the walls. A kettle, a tin of tea on the counter. Who lived here, then, if not the Dubbses? What was this house used for? Where were the occupants? I gave Pickwick a tin of meat and began my own quiet search, unwilling to sit still despite my pain and exhaustion. From the sitting room I could hear the low rumble of Inspector Merriken's voice as he spoke on the telephone.

I had just started up the stairs, noting that there wasn't a single picture on the walls, when I heard James's exclamation of triumph. I found him in the master bedroom, which was as neatly kept as the rest of the house, with a handmade quilt smoothed on the bed. James was standing in front of a tall cabinet, its doors flung open, its lock discarded on the floor.

"Oh, my goodness," I said, looking over his shoulder.

"The Dubbses," he said to me, "are nicely stocked—whoever they are."

The cabinet held firearms, at least six of them by my count. Two were long rifles, one a thick shotgun of some kind, and the rest handguns. They'd been carefully placed in the cabinet, metal gleaming from the shadows. On the shelves beneath the guns themselves were boxes of gunpowder and ammunition, clearly labeled and neatly stacked.

Inspector Merriken entered the room behind us and gave a low whistle. "Well, well."

James picked up one of the rifles, turned it over in his hands. "Lee-Enfield," he said. "Standard issue, perfect condition. Well maintained." He lifted the bolt and retracted it, peering down. "Unloaded. Clean as a whistle."

"Recently fired?" asked the inspector, and I glanced at him. Did he think one of these was used to shoot at me?

"Not this one," James replied. It was strange, watching him with a rifle in his hands. He handled it capably, and I had to remember he had likely carried one of these every day while he was at war. I blinked; it was like looking at two men at the same time.

"Check the others," the inspector said, but James was already moving, picking each gun up and inspecting it. His face was unbearably handsome in its concentration. He picked up the shotgun last, his brow frowning slightly. "This is a lot of firepower."

"It looks like the Dubbses were rather dangerous," Inspector Merriken agreed. "Or at least Mr. Dubbs was."

"I wouldn't discount Mrs. Dubbs, either," James countered. "If they were government agents, she was as well trained as he was. In any case, I'm glad they left their cabinet stocked." He picked up one of the rifles again and ran his fingers over the boxes of ammunition, looking for the right kind. "That bastard, whoever he is, will get a surprise if he goes for Ellie again."

Inspector Merriken sighed. He had taken off his coat downstairs while on the telephone, and now he crossed his arms in their shirt-sleeves over his buttoned-up waistcoat. "Those guns may be government property, you know."

"You can arrest me later." James loaded the gun and clicked it shut, the sound cracking up my spine. I clenched my hands into fists at my sides.

Inspector Merriken hesitated, then uncrossed his arms and held out a hand. "Fine. Give me one."

"Rifle or handgun?"

"One of each."

James deftly loaded the weapons and handed them over. Merriken put the handgun in his waistband and carried the rifle at ease at his side. He had likely served at war just as James had.

James was obviously thinking the same thing. "Did you use a Lee-Enfield in France?"

"Not exactly," Merriken replied. "I was RAF."

"Ah. A high flier."

"Something like that. Still, I know which end is the business end. They taught us that much." He turned to me. "As it happens, Miss Winter, Colin Sutter's war records aren't classified at all. He enlisted as an officer in 1915, was captured by the Germans in August 1916, and spent six months as a prisoner of war, after which he died. Cause of death was listed as pneumonia. The Germans issued an official death certificate, which the War Office has in the file."

"His body never came home," I said. "There may have been a death certificate, but his body never came home."

Merriken blinked at me. "He was interred in the prison camp, yes. How did you know?"

"Gloria told me, of course."

From his position by the gun cabinet, James said, "If there's a German death certificate, that means he isn't a British agent, doesn't it?"

"Actually," Inspector Merriken corrected, "it means that he's dead."

I turned to James. "If he defected to the Germans—if they somehow recruited him while he was a prisoner—then the German authorities could have issued the certificate."

"If it originated high enough, I don't see why not," James answered me. "A man like that would be a valuable agent, because he's native British. No one here would suspect him. It would be worth it to them to kill his old identity, complete with paperwork, and give him a new one, if he was willing. The question is, why was he willing to betray his country?"

"This is pure madness," said Inspector Merriken.

"The newspapers," I said to James, ignoring the interruption. "They say that no group has claimed responsibility for the bombings. Not fascists, or socialists, or Bolsheviks. Would the Germans simply recruit a man to sabotage random targets?"

James looked thoughtful. "It's possible, perhaps. Germany has been in chaos since the Armistice and Versailles. But an agent like that wouldn't serve the government's purpose. It could be one of the smaller revolutionary factions, which are growing in Germany like weeds." He shrugged. "It's an effective way to seed terror, if you think about it. The speculation, the scramble to find a pattern, is almost as effective in creating fear as the bombings themselves."

"I wish I knew more about him," I said. "Gloria didn't like to talk about her brothers—it was too painful. I know that Colin was difficult and rather distant. But she carried the telegram notification of his death, along with the others, everywhere she went. And she carried his photo, just as she carried those of Tommy and Harry." I shook my head. "She loved him—perhaps not perfectly, but she loved him. And he killed her."

James's gaze settled on me, something about it sad and very cold. "War changes a man, Ellie. In ways you can't imagine."

I looked at him holding a rifle—likely the same kind that had almost killed me hours before—in his hands, at Inspector Merriken holding his own rifle, and I swallowed. "I'm going for a walk," I said. "I need to see where Gloria died before the sun goes down."

James closed the cabinet. "You're not going alone."

"Not that it matters," Inspector Merriken said, "but I've got a handful of men on their way. It'll take them some time to get here, so in the meantime I'm going to take a look around and see if I find a trace of our man." He glared at me. "Whoever he is."

"I'd advise that your walk take you past the nearest telephone line," James said, "and that you find a way to keep an eye on it if you can."

Merriken turned to him. "You think he'll cut it?"

"I would," James replied.

# CHAPTER THIRTY-ONE

James walked at my shoulder, rifle in hand, as I exited the back door of the house. I felt jangled, uncertain, as if I'd been transported somewhere entirely unfamiliar with strangers. The isolation of this house was complete; I could not see or hear the road far up the shaded drive, nor could I hear or see any neighbors. We were in the bottom of a soft hollow cupped by gentle hills, with no vantage point of the surrounding countryside. It was peaceful and undoubtedly beautiful, but in my state of mind it was almost suffocating.

I walked through the neat garden, tended by yet another person who was mysteriously absent, and into the green expanse beyond. A footpath had been created with large, flat stones set into the green earth, and I followed it. The sun lowered toward the hills and the air grew chill with a premonition of twilight.

"Why the telephone lines?" I asked James, when the silence stretched too long.

"It's a common tactic," James replied. His voice was tense, the words clipped. "Cut the communication lines if you can. We did it all the time at the front."

I stopped on the path, turned to face him. His expression was bleak, the strain heavy in his eyes. "James," I said, "you are not at war."

"Aren't I?" he asked. "I'm carrying a rifle and I'm looking at the landscape, wondering where the enemy might come from. You were nearly shot by a sniper. It feels like war to me."

I put my hands on his face, feeling his rigid jaw. I couldn't stand it anymore. I wanted my familiar James back, the man I knew, the man who had taken me only last night, surrendered to me in passion as the rain had drummed on the windows. I reached up on my toes and kissed him.

He jumped at first, startled, and then cautiously gave in. I went slowly, exploring him, letting him feel his way back. He put a hand to the small of my back, his body warming to mine by degrees, his chest pressing against my chest, his arm sliding up and around my waist, pulling me to him. He was almost tentative at first, as if he hadn't kissed a woman in years, but then he remembered, and he kissed me harder.

I let him do it. His touch was ragged and almost needy, his arm hard with the power of his thick muscles, but the harder he was, the softer I became. I ran my hands gently over his shoulders and the tense line of his neck, and then I broke the kiss.

"*That* did not happen on the battlefield," I breathed.

He relaxed ever so slightly. "No. It did not."

But he did not drop the rifle.

We crossed through a thin rope of trees, the smell of water growing stronger, and when we came through to the clearing beyond, we found the pond. I had pictured some sort of wild place in my mind, but this pond was anything but; it was large, obviously man-made, its edges immaculately cut, the grassy verge trim and the water smooth and reflective. A tangle of cattails and tall grass had been allowed to grow along the far edge, likely to add to the pleasing rustic aspect, and three large stone ornamental frogs were placed in a group in the center of the water, two crouched and one leaping, their faces blank and grinning. The sun was lowering behind the hills now, and the air had a decided chill. I tried not to shiver.

"So this is the place," said James.

I stared at it in a strange sort of dismay. Gloria's body had been carried—or dragged—here, dumped in this water. She had vanished, and at first no one had even known she was dead. The wind blew again and this time I crossed my arms. The cold was biting, crawling down my neck and chilling me through my clothes. Something dark crossed over my vision, as if a cloud had blotted out the sun.

"Ellie?" I heard James say.

I recalled Octavia's face as I'd last seen it in front of her house on Harriet Walk, the account she'd given me of that last séance. Gloria weeping, saying, *I had no idea.* Saying, *Good-bye, darling.* Octavia saying, *I was afraid, because Gloria was afraid, and Gloria was never afraid.*

She had left that séance, and then she had left the note for me at George's hotel. And then she had gone to her death. It had ended here, the strange chain of events, in this quiet body of water.

I felt the chill again, and this time it felt wet. Ripples moving. I blinked. Were there ripples moving in the water?

"Ellie," James said. "Are you all right?"

Far behind us, back at the house, Pickwick barked. Four quick times in succession, a note of surprised alarm.

James put a hand on my arm, turned me silently to face him. He put a finger to his lips. My heart pounded, but I nodded, telling him I understood. He stepped in front of me and raised the rifle to his shoulder as footsteps approached us through the trees.

"Don't come any further," he said, his voice icy calm.

The figure of a man paused at the edge of the trees, startled when he saw the gun. The man raised his hands, palms out, and walked farther into the fading sunlight. His expression was as grim as the first time I'd seen it, days earlier in my sitting room.

"Miss Winter," George Sutter said to me. "I came to apologize. This is all my fault, you see. Gloria was not supposed to die."

Still James did not lower the gun; in that moment I was glad of it. The sight of George Sutter was sinister and unwelcome, even though he was not armed.

"Why are you here?" I asked, moving to James's shoulder.

George's expression did not waver. "My man did not check in," he replied. "The last I heard from him was after you boarded the train for Kent at Victoria Station. I knew something was wrong."

"He saw me board the train?" I said. "I didn't see him."

"Then he was doing his job for once, because you weren't supposed to."

"How did you know to come here?"

"I checked with Scotland Yard," Sutter said. "I was told that Mr. Hawley here"—he nodded briefly toward James—"had been taken for questioning by the chief inspector due to an inquiry he made at the War Office, and that the questioning had ended when Inspector Merriken took over. That both men had disappeared from the Yard shortly after. That the inspector had made a request to send manpower to Kent, and the request was delayed. I'm rather good at educated guesses."

James broke in. "Are you alone?"

"Yes."

The shadows were falling now, and I felt an unreasonable grip of fear. "Why did my dog stop barking? Did you hurt him?"

Now Sutter looked puzzled. "No, of course not. I surprised him when I came through the house, but I patted him on the head and told him to go back to sleep."

I sighed. So much for Pickwick the guard dog. I ran a hand

through my hair, which felt thick and tangled despite its short length. "Your man is dead," I said bluntly. "Your brother Colin killed him."

George Sutter's expression fell. He gave a long sigh, one of such worldly sadness that I wondered why he had never shown such emotion over the death of his own sister. "I'm sorry to hear that," he said. "He was a good man."

"So it is your brother, then," said James. "Colin is alive."

George turned his gaze to the trees, seeing nothing, his mind working, turning something over. "Put down the rifle," he said at last, "and I'll answer your questions."

Reluctantly, James moved his thumb over the safety and lowered the rifle from his shoulder.

"Very good," said George, letting his hands fall. "Shall we talk inside?"

"No," I said, wanting to stay near the pond. I could feel Gloria close by, just a whisper of her. It was fanciful, perhaps, but I didn't want to leave. "We can talk here."

George shrugged. "Where would you like to start?"

"With the Black Dog," I said.

Surprise rippled over his expression, settling into the same wonder I'd seen when I'd found his long-lost toy soldiers. "You never cease to amaze me, Miss Winter. Where did you get that name?"

"Where do you think?"

He looked avid with burning curiosity for a moment, but he quickly tamped it down. "The Black Dog," he said, "is a terrorist and saboteur who has been operating since just before the Armistice. We've known from the first that he was British, and that he was very, very good. He was recruited, initially, by the Kaiser's government before it fell. Afterward, he was dormant for so long that my intelligence contacts believed him dead. But he resurfaced in Spain in 1922 and has been active ever since."

"How did you know he was your brother?" James asked.

"Truthfully," George said slowly, "I didn't, not until Miss Winter told me just now. I only suspected. One of our agents saw him in Spain, and although there is no photograph, he managed to make a reasonably detailed sketch. It was all we had before that particular agent was killed. The sketch looks . . . uncannily like my brother, and the records at the War Office align with the dates." He gave us a bleak look. "Colin was always an idealist, thinking he could change things. It made him fragile. I don't like to think of my brother as a madman, but he wouldn't be the only one whose mind was unbalanced by war."

"He murdered his own sister," I said. "He killed Ramona in her own flat in the middle of the day with a garrote. He shot at me like I was a piece of game."

"Colin is very intelligent, Miss Winter. Intelligent men, in the right hands, are always the most dangerous. Take an intelligent man and find a way to mold him, and you have an extremely effective weapon."

I thought of the woman with the dark eyes, the razor blade, the shrill of the telephone.

"So who's molding him now?" James asked.

"As far as we can tell, anyone with money. The Black Dog has become a free agent, as it were, working for anyone who will arm him, pay him, and give him papers. His only agenda seems to be that he's willing to do whatever harms his home country. He's been working on the Continent for the past few years, damaging embassies and making attempts on visiting dignitaries. He nearly killed our ambassador in Greece when he shot at his motorcar; it was a very near thing, and we had a hard time keeping it quiet. And then I received intelligence that the Black Dog was on his way to England."

"What for?" said James.

George shook his head. "Our information was incomplete. We'd had warning of his movement, but that was all. Presumably someone had hired him to do damage on home ground, since he's a born

Englishman and can blend in more perfectly here than he can on the Continent. It would have taken some time to get him false papers that would stand up, but they must have come through. And then I read an article in the newspaper about my sister, and I found myself making one of my educated guesses. The wildest one I've ever made in my career."

Beside me, James stiffened perceptibly. "My report."

"Yes. Dissected in the newspaper, for the public to read. I usually avoided the gossip coverage of Gloria, but that article was impossible to overlook. I admit, the first thing I thought when I read it was, *Does she have the power to find Colin?* And then I thought, if it had occurred to me, why couldn't it have occurred to him?"

"You think—you think he came here because of the article?" My throat had gone dry, my fingers cold. "To kill her before she could discover him?"

"I had no idea. I only knew that if Colin was here—if he was in fact the Black Dog and she had the power to expose him—then she may have been in danger. I contacted Gloria by telegram. I told her to be careful, and I gave her my telephone exchange. I said I wanted to meet."

"Let me guess," I said. "She was not agreeable."

George sighed. "She telephoned the exchange, which was more than I expected. The message she left was not repeatable and nearly caused my assistant to resign."

"You didn't exactly treat her well over the years."

"I realize that now," he said to me. "If I had played my part differently, if I had communicated with Gloria regularly, I would have had more influence." He looked at my face. "I suppose that seems cold to you, Miss Winter, as she was my sister. I assure you, I deal with issues on a daily basis that have much larger consequences than whether or not my family is offended."

"Fine," I said. "What did you do when she refused you?"

"I wanted to leave it. I did. It was more fanciful than a hunch—it was a wild guess. But it kept coming back to me. If there was even the faintest chance that her powers were as real as the tests seemed to reveal . . . If she could be persuaded to help us, to find the Black Dog and prevent more deaths . . . If there was even a chance that Colin had read that article and had her in his sights . . . I had to get to her before he did."

The wind picked up again, as if in response. It was cold now, and the sun was almost gone, making George Sutter hard to see against the background of the trees. "Why here?" I said. "Why the elaborate ruse to bring her here?"

"She would never have agreed if I'd approached her directly," George said. He stood unmoving, and I could not tell whether the cold affected him. "I'd seen that already. I made contact with that odious drug-peddling lover of hers, and had him set it up. I wanted her to come here because this is a safe house, Miss Winter. It is set up for the use of any of our agents who need it. Agents who have come back from assignment and require debriefing, agents whose cover has been compromised, agents who have been . . . injured in the line of duty. We've had this house in place for years."

"Who are the Dubbses?" James asked.

"Agents, of course," was the reply. "We use a man and a woman, we give them a cover story that keeps them frequently in London, and we have them come and go from time to time so the neighborhood and the few live-out servants we hire don't get suspicious. The location gives us the utmost secrecy without appearing out of place. The cover doesn't hold up well under expert investigation, which was part of the reason I read Inspector Merriken's reports so closely. He missed it at first glance, probably because there were so many other potential suspects to sift through. But I think he would have figured it out rather rapidly, even if Miss Winter hadn't prompted him, and then I would have had to decide how to keep him under control."

"He wouldn't have liked that," I observed.

"He wouldn't have had a choice. In any case, I thought Gloria would be safe if she came here. The agents were to collect her from the train station, and I'd arrive myself, and then Gloria would have no choice but to talk to me. I'd persuade her to help, to become one of us—after she'd come under our protection, of course. If my wild hunch was anywhere close to being correct, I did not want her to go home." He shook his head. "That was when everything went wrong. My motorcar broke down, and I was delayed. At the train station, my agents discovered that Fitzroy Todd and that odious fortune-teller had decided to tag along and wouldn't leave. All of them were drinking, and Gloria was in an uncontrollable mood. Before my agents could handle the situation, Gloria was dead."

James's hands were clenched into fists at his sides. My own bewilderment was turning to anger, swift and heated. "You knew from the very beginning," I said to George. "You knew who killed her, and you knew why. Why in the world did you recruit me and bring me into this? Why did you set him on me?"

"Miss Winter, I'm telling you, I didn't *know*. Even after she was killed, I had only a paper-thin theory. I'd had to improvise the entire meeting, because my superiors would have had none of it. I'd have been locked up in Bedlam. I told them I wanted to interview Gloria as a potential recruit because of her client list—nothing about the Black Dog at all. It was an incredible risk. And when it all went wrong, I still didn't know. Fitzroy Todd could have killed her, or that drug addict he brought along, or someone else entirely—a lover or a customer. I needed you, Miss Winter, to go where I couldn't go, and ask questions. To find out if my gamble was correct."

"And if Colin came after her next, so much the better." James's voice was rough, furious.

"What do you want me to say?" George's composure cracked finally, and he let loose a flare of pure anger. "It was a possibility. I met with Miss Winter in the middle of Trafalgar Square so that if Colin was watching, he could easily see us without being seen. Then I had one of my men tail her everywhere she went."

"Oh, my God." My headache throbbed again. It had all been a lie, even that meeting in London. "And I lost your man right before I stumbled on Colin murdering Ramona."

"We could have had him then." George's voice still simmered with anger. "We were that close. My methods may not meet with your approval, but they work. I don't know if Colin knew how close he came, not then. I'd lay my bets that he knows now."

Something twigged at me, something not quite right. James's paper had listed my powers as unproven, and the newspaper article, obsessed with Gloria, had not mentioned me at all. Why would Colin pursue me if he thought my powers were fake? What interest could I possibly be to him? I opened my mouth to ask the question, but I never got the chance.

Far off to the west, past the pond and the trees, a single shot sounded. I flinched, but James only turned. "That's a rifle," he said.

Two more shots followed, echoing in quick succession.

"And that's a handgun," James said. "Merriken."

Twilight had fallen now, the line of trees like charcoal in the darkness, and a breeze came off the pond, bringing a smell of green dampness. *Gloria, is that you?* I thought wildly before I turned to see James shouldering his rifle.

"Stay here," he said to me.

"Wait."

It was George. He came closer, and I could see the urgency in his face. "Don't do it," he said to James. "It's what he wants—for you to come to him, so he can pick the vantage point. Make him come to you—he will, if you have what he wants. Pick your ground, Mr. Hawley. What is the best place to meet the enemy?"

"The house," I said.

George raised his eyebrows at me. "And what if he throws a

bomb through the window, or a grenade, or a stick of dynamite? Colin is very well armed."

The motorcycle sidecar, I thought. And the glimmer I'd traced through Colin's mind: *No reason to look in the sidecar. None at all.*

James glanced around. "The trees," he said finally. "They provide the best cover, if I know which way he's coming." He glanced at me, and my heart broke by a sliver. James's eyes were dead, his emotions gone. This was the officer who had led his men into those woods in France, watched them die in the space of a moment. The man who had lain next to Fenton's ripped-apart body, smelling the blood, listening to the agony. *Some days I wonder if I'm going to wake from a dream and find myself in the trenches again.*

I swallowed. I could not touch this man before me, could not reach him. There was no way, but I had to try. "What about Inspector Merriken?" I asked. "What if he's shot, injured?"

"Merriken is a soldier," said James. "He'll understand." He turned to George. "The shots came from the east, but there's no guarantee he'll come that way."

"I wouldn't if I were him," George replied, his words fast and clipped. "The ground is wet between there and here—it became waterlogged when they put in the pond. He'll have to skirt it, and the best way that doesn't lead him blind is from the south."

Over the treetops came two more shots, a fast staccato.

"This way." James took my wrist, his grip icy, and pulled me toward the trees. He still wore his jacket, though he had left his hat in the house, and as I followed I could see the bulk of his shoulders beneath the fabric, the strong, graceful line of his body as he pulled me. I could not have removed myself from his grip if I had tried; I could do nothing but stumble along behind him on my sore, exhausted legs, trying to keep stride in my low heels. I thought of James sprawled on his sofa only this morning, laughing. *I don't intend to go around shooting people*, he had said.

Behind me, I could hear George's footsteps following us. "James, please," I said.

"Ellie, be quiet. This is the only way."

He stopped us at the bottom of a rise, motioned us to silence, and climbed it slowly in the darkness, peering through the trees. My head was throbbing. I blinked soddenly, panicked and terrified. Someone was going to be shot, killed, if Inspector Merriken wasn't dead already. It wasn't the only way; it wasn't. It couldn't be. *Darling,* came a voice in my head, and I caught a whiff of perfume.

There was one thing I could do, and suddenly I knew how to do it.

I turned to George Sutter, who stood nearby watching James and waiting. He saw me turn and raised his eyebrows.

"I'd apologize for this," I whispered to him, "but I don't think you've earned it."

He frowned. "Apologize for what, Miss Winter?"

I reached out, grasped his bare hand, and held it between mine. "Hang on," I said into the darkness.

# CHAPTER THIRTY-TWO

Cold and wet. Darkness. She wondered whether she looked beautiful, suspended in the murky water, whether her hair flowed and her skirt pressed against her thighs like a siren of the sea. *I'm finally a mermaid,* she thought, *though I have no tail.*

It had been wrong from the beginning, and she'd known it. She should never have come, except that she didn't care anymore, aside from a hardened, cynical curiosity. She told herself she'd said yes for the money, but almost from the first she'd known there was something wrong. Fitz had been sweating, his handsome face almost gray, and he was in deep with that drug-addled girlfriend of his. Besides, when had she ever trusted Fitz?

The headaches were explosive, like shells landing in her brain, and she'd begun to wake in the night, her hands on her scalp, moaning. Gin killed them only for an hour or so. The sessions, which had always come so easily, came harder and harder. She'd spent months under waves of anger and euphoria and denial and an abject terror that held her in a grip so hard she could barely breathe, but deep down she'd known it was almost over and the shade was being pulled down over the window. She got sentimental, which she never did, and she wanted to see her brothers one last time.

What a humiliation to discover that she couldn't summon them by herself, that she needed that fool Octavia to help her. After Ellie was gone—Ellie, with her blond hair and innocent-wise eyes, who missed nothing, who asked questions of everything, whose emotions played across her face so easily—Octavia had seemed like a replacement, but she'd been nothing except a disappointment. You couldn't replace Ellie with a girl like that. It turned out you couldn't replace Ellie with anyone.

But she'd swallowed it and called Octavia, squeezing money from her at the same time—it was ridiculously easy—and at first the session hadn't worked. She'd faced the possibility that that was it, she would never see her brothers again, and then—and then she saw Tommy. He was just *there*, not some shambling semblance of him but the real man, wearing his army uniform with his hair cut short and combed down, so unlike his usual unruly self. He'd seen her, and she'd felt a swell of pain in her head that was unlike anything she'd ever felt before, and then Harry was there, making it worth it. Harry was in uniform, too, and she heard a rasping cough (*gas—my brother was gassed before they patched him up and sent him back to the front*), but she'd been able to inhale him in, his handsomeness and sweetness and confidence. Seeing them was worth everything. Octavia had been saying something shrill, and through the fog she had summoned Colin, looking for his serious face.

She saw Colin all right, but he wasn't in the room. He was standing outside across Harriet Walk, watching the windows of Octavia's apartments with an intent look on his face, as if he could see through the drawn blinds. Colin and yet not Colin, not really, because his near-comical seriousness had turned to cold and hatred. He moved away and disappeared, vanishing into the streets of London, and Gloria remembered George sending her a telegram—a bloody *telegram*—telling her to be careful, that he wanted to speak to her. And suddenly she understood. Colin wasn't even dead. They'd all been fooled, all these years—even all-knowing George.

She said good-bye to her darling brothers and found she was crying. She remembered nothing about the next few minutes, about getting rid of Octavia and leaving the house; all she remembered was standing on the sidewalk, looking for a figure that had already disappeared, and thinking, *I might be in danger.* Octavia's father had pulled up in his Alvis, sitting in the seat behind the driver, and given her a disapproving look. She had no time for snobbery, not much time left at all, so she simply walked up to the motorcar and leaned in. *Get her out of England as soon as you can,* she'd said to his surprised face. *If you love her at all.* Then she'd walked away. Either he'd take her advice or he wouldn't; it was out of her hands.

She'd gone home and gotten into bed fully dressed and drank until the headache faded. Lying there with her dress wrinkling and her makeup smearing onto the pillow, she could no longer see Colin's strange new face. Davies had knocked, but she hadn't answered, and eventually Davies had gone away. She'd stared at the wall and thought about what she could do, who she could call on. George knew something about this, but as always he wanted to play games, games in which she was the loser. But there were games she could play, too.

The next morning she rummaged through her things until she found an old handkerchief of George's. It took nearly half an hour—sitting cross-legged on the floor, wearing only a man's shirt she'd found under the bed and a pair of drawers, the handkerchief clutched in her lap—before the information came, but finally she picked it out of her throbbing brain. Davies knocked on the door again, the sound like gunshots in her skull, but she ignored it. Then she wrote a note and got dressed.

A little sleight of hand trick, leaving the note at George's hotel. She could simply have sent the note to Ellie, but Ellie might not have opened it, or she might have read it and thrown it away. It was always difficult to predict what Ellie would do.

No, she had given the note to George instead. George would be furious that she'd pulled such a trick after turning down his offer to talk, and he would go to Ellie and push her into action. That would be one good thing—Ellie in action. Besides, it amused her to imagine Ellie and George having a conversation.

But most of all, no matter what happened, eventually Ellie would come. And that made the rest of it almost bearable.

I opened my eyes to the smell of smoke.

George Sutter pulled away from me, staggering, his mouth open, his face sagging in shock. "What was that?" he hissed. "What did you do?"

"I found Gloria," I said, part of me wild with sharp, triumphant joy. "I called her. That's what you hired me for, isn't it?"

"My God," he said. "I saw things—heard things—"

A rifle shot cracked through the trees, and then another. Above us on the rise, James fired his own rifle, then lowered it and scrambled down. "Something's burning," he said.

He was right. Through the pulsing in my head—slick and powerful, out of my control, the way it had been at Ramona's séance—I could feel the pungent sting of smoke in my nose, though I couldn't see any flames.

George tried to pull himself together, looking from me to James. "Colin," he said. "Instead of coming for us, he's burning us out."

"This way," said James.

More gunshots sounded through the trees. Was Inspector Merriken still alive? Or were the men he had called for reinforcements shooting? There were shouts, but I couldn't tell what direction they came from. I followed behind James and George, moving as fast as I could as they led me through the still, quiet woods.

"Not the house," I heard George say. "He'll burn that, too."

"I know," James replied. He was barely out of breath while I was staggering, the smoke growing stronger in my throat. "Do you smell that? Petrol. He's using accelerant."

They said something else, their words moving back and forth in sharp measures, but I no longer heard. We changed direction and I followed, watching James's bent form ahead of me, George's tall frame loping easily. I started to lag, caught up, lagged again.

We crested a rise and at last I saw the flames. An entire section of the woods was on fire now, the flames sweeping beneath the trees, their light swirling into the darkened sky. The clouds of smoke were thick, and I could feel a wall of heat. We had come the wrong way.

"Goddamn it," I heard James say. "He's started it here, too. He's too bloody fast!"

George said something; then more shots came through the trees. And in a single instant I turned and found that I was alone.

"James!" I cried.

There was no answer, no sound but the crackling of the oncoming fire.

*Darling,* Gloria said.

I limped back the way I had come, trying to remember the path we'd taken, lost almost instantly. I had a few moments of hideous panic, gasping for breath, before I caught myself and used the tattered remains of my logic. Not the house; George was right about that. But where to go in a fire? To the water. If I could find my way to the pond, I could stay safe from the fire.

I followed the direction I'd heard Gloria's voice come from. The wound on my knee opened and fresh blood trickled down my shin, but still I kept moving. I saw shapes in the shadows, someone taking even strides, but when I cried out I heard no answer. It wasn't until one of the shapes passed near me—and I saw he was dressed in full army uniform—that I realized why.

"No," I said as Harry Sutter walked past me, his handsome face intent on something I couldn't see. "Gloria, what did you do?"

There were more shouts, alarmed now, more gunshots, and in my ear a sharp bark of laughter. I hadn't summoned these shapes; Gloria had. I'd summoned her and she'd summoned the ghosts, her power mixed with mine, using it, amplifying it, opening the door to the other side. Someone else walked through the trees—a woman. Davies? Ramona? Who else had she called? I ran and ran, hoping beyond logic that I was going in the right direction as I choked on the smoke and felt the heat rise at my back.

I broke from the line of the trees and found myself in the clearing by the pond. I was at the other side of the water now, staring into the cattails and the tall grass, opposite where James and I had stood earlier. Somehow I had gone all the way around, probably a quarter mile, without knowing it. The woods to my left were ablaze, the flames licking up into the sky, like a nightmare I'd never dreamed could happen, inescapable and obscene.

"Ellie!" came a voice from the woods.

"James!" I cried, my throat tearing, my voice barely audible to my own ears. My eyes watered from the smoke and I could hardly breathe. "I'm here! By the water!"

"I'm coming for you—," he said, and then he was silent. I screamed his name again, but my voice was no more than a whisper. I started through the high reeds into the water, the shocking cold of it rising to my ankles, the mud pulling at my shoes.

I had gone only a few feet when I sensed someone behind me.

I turned and saw a figure emerge from the woods. A man wearing farmer's clothes and heavy boots, his cloth cap gone from his dark head. Coming toward me, walking, taking his time, inexorable. In his hands he held a long, thin wire. A living man. Colin Sutter. Coming for me.

"Stop," I tried to say, but nothing came from my mouth anymore. I sloshed backward in the water, the reeds tangling around my legs and ankles, my hands up as if I could stop him, thinking, *This is it—he started the fire to separate me from the others and he succeeded. I was a fool ever to think I could get away. Of course he'd find me— of course.* And still he came toward me, not a single word on his lips, because that was how he killed—fast and silent, without a good-bye.

Footsteps sloshed in the water behind me, and Colin stopped.

Something moved to my left, and there was a horrible smell. Another shape moved to my right, coming from deep in the water, making a rhythmic *slosh slosh slosh* sound. Colin's face froze in a sort of horror, the shadows of the flames flickering over his features. He gazed behind me in disbelief.

I turned. Harry Sutter stood next to me, tall and still in his uniform, looking at his brother. On my other side Ramona emerged from the water, the drops vanishing off her like air. Her face was sick and intent, her eyes like holes in her skull. Behind her, coming up from the depths, came the man in the houndstooth jacket.

I froze where I was. None of them seemed to see me; all were intent on Colin, who still stood at the edge of the water, the wire drooping in his hands. "It can't be you," he said, the first words I'd heard him speak; his voice was raspy with smoke, but beneath that it was deep and melodious. I did not know who he was talking to, as Tommy Sutter had come out of the water now, too, his face so much like his brothers' but different, wider, with its own kind of handsomeness. Like the others, he made no noise.

I turned back to Colin. I wanted to say something, but suddenly nothing would come. Because there was another shape approaching Colin from behind.

She looked nothing like she had been—and everything like it. I would have known her anywhere, even across the divide of life and death, the divide that she and I had been able to travel, that we now traveled together. She was in the shadows, but still I knew. My mind was sure, and my heart—all of me was certain.

Colin became aware of her as she stood at his back. He stiffened, his expression rigid with new alarm. The ghosts in the water with me stood and watched as a flawless white arm reached out and around Colin's neck, draped like a lover's. Another arm came from the other side, the pale hand with its long, perfect fingers touching the side of his cheek, tilting his head. Colin gave a low groan of helpless terror.

Gloria Sutter whispered in her brother's ear.

Colin dropped the wire.

There was the slick sound of a bolt being drawn, and James was there, leveling his rifle at Colin's temple. "Don't move," he said. He thumbed off the safety, his finger on the trigger.

"No!" George Sutter stumbled from the trees, his knees nearly buckling as he ran the few feet to the water's edge. "*No!*" Never had I heard such anguish, seen such pain on a human face. "Hawley, *stop!* He's my brother! Tommy, Harry—my God! *Stop!*"

James blinked, shifted, his fingers flexing. A muscle in his cheek rippled and something moved through his body, something like terrible pain. His gaze flickered to Gloria, still in the shadows, her arms around her brother, and then to the figures in the water. He looked at all of them with a grim knowledge, free of surprise, as if they were part of something he understood all too well. Then he swallowed and lowered the gun.

I was crying, I realized, the hot tears stinging my face. There were more voices, shouts, coming from the trees. I was looking at Gloria's arms, her beautiful white arms, fading now. Or perhaps it was I who was fading; I couldn't tell. The world seemed to be closing in on me, becoming a strange, dark circle, a window through which I couldn't see. I couldn't breathe, and my body went numb. I saw the flash of her dark hair in the firelight, and I thought, *Good-bye, darling,* and then the water came up to meet me and I knew no more.

# CHAPTER THIRTY-THREE

Iawoke in a hospital room. I was dry and warm, a sheet and a knitted blanket tucked over me, and watery sun was coming in the window.

I pushed myself up on my elbows, blinking.

"Good morning," said a voice.

Inspector Merriken was sitting next to my bed. He was folded into a wooden chair, one ankle crossed over the other knee. He was wearing a suit and his black overcoat, and dark stubble showed on his jaw.

"You're alive," I said to him, glad to be saying it.

"I am," he agreed, glancing at the clock on the wall. "And so are you, though you've been out cold for about twelve hours. Hawley is going to be upset; he just left to get a drink of water. But that's fine by me, as I get my chance to talk to you. How do you feel?"

My mind was sluggish, my throat sore. "James is here?"

"Of course he is." The inspector frowned. "He's been some little

293

use, I'll grudgingly admit. He got you out of the water seconds after you passed out, and he was strong enough to carry you from the woods unaided. But with you here unconscious, I haven't been able to get rid of him, and he's going to evict me the minute he comes back. So you're going to answer my questions until he does."

I looked down at myself. My clothes were gone, and I was wearing a hospital nightgown beneath the bedcovers. I ached everywhere, my muscles throbbing, my knee torn. "The fire—what happened?" I pushed myself up farther, ignoring the way my head spun. "Oh, my God—where's Pickwick?"

"Stop worrying," Inspector Merriken ordered. He made no move to assist me. "The local brigade fought the fire all night, and it's almost under control. Nobody died, at least not yet. And one of my men has your dog. He's become rather enamored of him, and says he wants to keep him."

"He can't," I snapped.

"Very well. Will you answer my questions now?"

"Where were you?" I asked, ignoring him. "We thought you were dead."

"I found Colin Sutter by the telephone line, preparing to cut it, just as Hawley predicted. I did my best to shoot him, but he got away. He lit the fire while I was still trying to track him. He was very, very good. I really did try to shoot him, even through the smoke and the flames." He shrugged. "My men arrived and found me, and we made our way to the water's edge, thinking Sutter—Colin Sutter—might go for the same place. When we got there, we found Hawley in the process of not shooting our suspect. So I obliged George Sutter, since he seemed to think it was important, and I kicked Colin over—forcefully, I admit—and handcuffed him."

I swallowed, my throat dry. "What about the ghosts?" I said. "You must have seen them."

Inspector Merriken looked away, and for a moment he looked

very tired. "You have no idea," he said, "how much I hate ghosts. No idea at all." He turned back to me and changed the subject. "Colin Sutter is alive and in custody, but he isn't talking. Did he speak to you? At the pond?"

I shook my head, the motion setting my brain in a queasy spin. "No." He had spoken to the ghosts, but I wasn't going to repeat that part.

"Nothing?"

"No."

"It's very frustrating," he admitted. "We have a good number of the pieces, but not all of them. With the help of your testimony, we can likely make a case for his murder of Ramona and George Sutter's man—whose name was John Richmond, by the way. But we have no eyewitness linking him to Gloria's death. That would have been Ramona's job, since she saw something from the trees when she left the house that night with Fitzroy Todd—according to the testimony of Todd himself, who turned himself in to us. But Colin murdered Ramona before she could confess. Until I have a clearer case, my original murder investigation will have to stay open."

"What about Davies?" I asked.

Merriken frowned at me as he watched me struggle to sit up. "What about her?"

"Did Colin murder her?"

"I should say not, since she's alive. I just talked to her on the telephone from Paris."

"*Paris?*"

"Yes. It seems George Sutter sent her there. With Gloria dead, he thought Davies may be in danger, so he gave her fare for passage and told her to leave England for her own safety."

I shook my head. I'd been sickened, worried she'd been murdered and her body stuffed somewhere. The man who had come to get her at Marlatt's Café had been George. "Terrific," I said. "What a prince. I almost got killed, and Davies got to sit around in Paris, all expenses paid."

"She is rather odious," the inspector carefully agreed. "It does gall a little."

I swung my legs over the side of the bed and put my bare feet on the floor, flexing my toes. "I'd like to help," I said, "but I don't know what I can do for you. I don't think I'll be much use."

He sounded almost amused. "You won't get rid of me so easily, Miss Winter. Scotland Yard is far from finished with you, I assure you."

I looked at his tired face, a good face, an intelligent face, and on impulse I reached out and grabbed his wrist. "Thank you," I said to him.

He glanced down at my hand, then politely raised his eyebrows at me.

"Fine." I sighed. Then I looked at him again, surprised. "Your name is Drew. And she's not your fiancée. You haven't asked her yet, because she's at Oxford and she hasn't finished her degree."

Inspector Merriken blew out a put-upon sigh. "God save me from intelligent women. Good day, Miss Winter." He pulled his wrist from my grip and stood.

"If you ask her," I called to his retreating back, "she'll say yes."

"Who will say yes?"

It was James, coming through the doorway, glancing warily at Merriken and then looking at me. Merriken only touched the brim of his hat and disappeared.

James looked rumpled and exhausted, his jaw dark with an incipient beard, his clothes stained and smelling of smoke. He was in his shirtsleeves, and as I watched he plunged his hands into his pockets and leaned on the doorframe, his gaze careful and shuttered.

"Never mind," I said to him. "It doesn't matter."

He blinked and gazed past me, out the window. "Are you all right?" he asked.

"I think so, yes."

"You were unconscious for a long time."

"It was the smoke, I think. And my mind had . . . exhausted it self." I rubbed a hand over my hair, suddenly self-conscious, wishing for a bath. "Did you carry me out of the woods?"

His gaze flicked to me and away again, and he shrugged. "You don't weigh very much."

The air seemed heavy, unbearable. I wanted to touch him, but I wasn't sure I could stand, and I could tell he didn't want me to. "James," I said.

"Listen." He seemed to be gathering his courage. Still he stood in the doorway, not coming inside. "Ellie, you are . . . You know what you are. To me." He raised a hand from his pocket and rubbed his jaw. "But I think I've proven that I'm a bit of a mess right now."

"You were brave," I said quietly. "And wonderful."

He shook his head, making a sound of disgust.

"And you're hurt," I continued, "and you went through terrible things. But it doesn't mean—"

"It does," he interrupted. "It does mean it. I nearly blew his brains out, Ellie. Right in front of you, in front of his own brother, in front of everyone. I was this close." He shifted, his body moving as if he was uncomfortable in his own skin. "It doesn't matter that he was a criminal and a murderer. Don't you see? I nearly blew his brains out when I knew the police were coming, *while you stood there watching.* I should probably be locked up in one of those hospitals you hear about in the newspapers."

I pressed my knees together, rubbing one aching foot over the other, silent.

"The drinking didn't work," James said. "Working for Paul and the Society didn't work—chasing ghosts. I thought it helped, but it turns out that if you put a gun in my hand, I'm the same old barbarian."

"What are you saying?" I asked, my voice rising in panic before I could stop it.

Finally he looked at me. His eyes were sad, his jaw tight. "You know what I'm saying."

"No. I won't accept it."

"Ellie, you should find somebody else. Somebody—"

"Somebody what? Normal?" I laughed, a bitter sound. "James, I just identified an international terrorist by touching a cigarette, and then I summoned my dead friend. I don't want normal. I want *you*." My voice had risen, but I ceased to care. "Besides, you're forgetting something important. You *didn't* shoot him. You stopped."

"I was so close, Ellie. So goddamned close."

"Yes, you were. It's true. And you stopped."

He looked so exhausted. "God, I'm going to have to fight you on this, aren't I?"

"I don't accept it, James. You may as well know it now. I never will."

He was quiet for a long moment, his eyes closed. I held my breath—quite literally held it, as my heart hammered in my chest. I had made a good show, but a show was all it was. If he turned away now, I would fall to pieces.

The silence stretched on. My fingers clenched in the bedspread.

Finally he let go a slow breath. He came into the room and sat on the end of the bed a few feet away, his back to me, his elbows on his knees.

A small sobbing sound escaped my throat. I scooted over and slid in behind him, putting my arms around his waist. I wrapped my legs around him, hooking them over his thighs, my feet between his knees. I pressed my cheek to his back, between his shoulder blades, feeling the thick tension that ran through his body, listening to his breathing and his blood pulsing. We stayed like that for a long moment.

"You saw her, didn't you?" I said in a whisper.

"Yes," he whispered back. "I saw all of them. What did she say to him, when she whispered in his ear?"

"She said, *No*," I replied softly. "I saw her lips move; I heard it. He was coming for me, and she stopped him. She said, *No*."

"Jesus."

"Don't leave me," I said into his shirt. "I can't do this alone."

He was quiet for a moment. The muscles of his back softened only slightly beneath my cheek. And then he put a gentle hand on my leg, his thumb tracing a line on the back of my bare calf.

"Yes, you can," he said.

"Fine, then," I replied, my arms still around his waist. "I don't want to."

His hand gripped the back of my knee, and in a single movement he'd turned himself around, pressing my knee into the bed, pushing me back, pulling himself over me. He was so incredibly strong. He looked down into my face and brushed my cheek with a brief touch.

"If you're in, then you're in," he said roughly. "For all of it."

I ran my hands down his chest. "So are you," I reminded him.

He kissed me, in that way he had, soft and possessive at the same time. When he pulled away, his eyes had gone dark, his breathing as ragged as my own.

"I'm in," he said.

# CHAPTER THIRTY-FOUR

### THREE WEEKS LATER

The seams of my stockings weren't straight. I bent and fixed them, then brushed smooth my best skirt, its hemline decorously falling to the middle of my calves. I buttoned the matching jacket, then unbuttoned it again. It was wool serge, protection against the early October chill, but as I stood in this small room in Whitehall, I felt myself dampening with sweat.

"Are you finished?" George Sutter asked from beside me.

I glanced at him. Long gone was the man who had begged for his brother's life as the woods burned behind him. Instead, he was once again the calm, powerful cipher in a suit pressed by his invisible wife, watching me with an unreadable expression in his eyes.

"I suppose so," I said, glaring a little at him.

"Good." He ignored my expression. "Remember what I told you, the information we are specifically looking to retrieve. Try to keep control of the conversation."

"Assuming there will be a conversation," I said.

"That is up to you, Miss Winter. In any case, you have been briefed extensively and should have an idea of what questions to ask." He paused. "And remember, someone is watching and listening at all times. He will be bound, and there is a guard just outside the door. He cannot hurt you."

"I shall try not to expire in fear."

George sighed. "It would be beneficial if you would take this with a degree of seriousness, Miss Winter."

I shrugged. The sweat trickling down my back belied the gesture, but I didn't let on. "Just open the door."

The interview was to take place in a small room with a high window, furnished with a single table and two chairs. On the wall was a pane of smoked glass, through which I presumed someone would be watching us. Colin Sutter was already there. He sat at the table, wearing pale prison linens, his hands cuffed and chained to the chair, having been brought from whatever private cell he was kept in as the great minds of British government tried to get him to confess.

His eyes flashed with interest when he saw me; he obviously had not been given any warning of who he had been brought to see.

I pulled out the chair opposite him and sat. He did not move; I tried not to let his resemblance to Gloria rattle me. His dark hair had been combed back and slicked to his head. He was clean shaven, well fed, relaxed. His presence was like that of a snake in the room.

"I may as well tell you," I said to him, glancing at the smoked window, "that I've been briefed about what to ask you. I believe your brother told his superiors that sitting opposite one of your victims would have the chance of unnerving you. That's how he got clearance for me to be here."

Colin regarded me blankly and said nothing.

"But it's a lie," I said, loud enough for whoever was listening—however they were listening—to overhear. "And I think we both

know why. You know why your brother wants me here, and so do I."
I shifted in the uncomfortable chair. "Everyone, quite frankly, wants
to know what I saw that day when you shot at me, but no one in the
official government wants to admit it. They don't want to admit
they're curious about the vision of a psychic."

Colin glanced away. It took me a second to realize that he, too,
was looking at the smoked glass. There was no sound, no interruption. No one came in to take me away. Colin, according to his brother
George, had resisted all attempts at interrogation. He had answered
only the most basic questions, refusing to give names of those who
had hired him, to confess to the bombings or the murders, even to
speak for himself. He was well on the way to being hanged for treason for the bombings, and behind his immaculate exterior, even I
knew that George was afraid his brother would go to the gallows
without answering a single question that hung over the last seven
years of his life.

Colin looked back at me, and his gaze flared with curiosity. In
that second, I knew I had him. Finally, he spoke.

"It was the cigarette, wasn't it?" he said, his voice rasping a little,
as if he didn't use it often.

"Yes," I said.

He leaned his head back and stared at the ceiling. "I knew it. I
knew. It took me too long to remember it—too long. By then, it was
too late."

I shrugged, hoping it was convincing. "You made a mistake," I
said. "It cost you."

"What did you see?"

I didn't want to be in this room with him any longer than I had
to, so I told him. "I saw *her*."

The chains gave an abrupt clang against the table leg as he moved,
and for a second I nearly jumped out of my chair. But he was only shifting, jolting with surprise and suppressed emotion. "*What* did you see?"

"Look," I said. "We can sit here all afternoon and talk of bombings and false papers and shootings of ambassadors, or whatever you've been doing, but I don't want to. Perhaps because I'm a woman. All of that, I think, is secondary. What matters is the woman I saw. She had dark hair and dark eyes, and she was terrified of something. I couldn't see what it was." I stared at him, my chin up, unblinking. "I think she's the key to everything. Am I wrong?"

He closed his eyes briefly, and then there was anger in his face, real anger. "I met her in Belgium. She was helping soldiers to escape, English soldiers, to help smuggle them back through the borders and home to avoid the slaughter. She wasn't the only one; it was a network. We were everywhere. She and I worked together. But someone betrayed her." He looked at me with empty eyes. "She was convicted of treason and executed by firing squad."

I swallowed. "You loved her. And that is why you hate your country. That is why you've done all of this."

"I went to war for my country," he said, his gaze vanishing backward into memory, "and I believed in it. I had dreams, plans. And the first day I went into battle, I saw a man get the top of his head blown off, just"—he raised one chained hand as far as it would go, touched the fingers together—"so. The top of his skull hung down by a flap of skin, dangling, while he screamed and his brains were open to the sky." He looked at me. "People who are shot by firing squads often shit themselves when they die. Did you know that?"

My stomach turned and my head spun. I hadn't been able to eat before coming here; now I was glad. "Give me your hands," I managed.

"What else did you see?"

"I have questions first."

"What could you possibly want to know?"

"How you knew about me," I said. "You read the article about Gloria, didn't you?"

Colin shrugged. "She'd always claimed she was psychic. But yes, when I read it, I realized. She could do a séance, try to reach Harry and Tommy and me. And then she'd know."

"But me," I said. "The article didn't mention me. The tests said my powers were unproven. Why did you come after me?"

He looked thoughtful, and then he decided to answer. "I questioned the fortune-teller before she died. Or I should say, she offered me information."

"What do you mean?"

"When it became clear what my business with her was, she told me that Gloria wasn't the only one. That you had powers, too. That she'd seen you summon the dead."

I put my hands on the table and gripped it. Ramona had tried to sell me in exchange for her own life. How terrified she must have been, trying to think of something, anything, that would placate her killer and convince him to show mercy. "But you knew who I was before that," I guessed.

"I knew you were working for my brother, yes. I'd seen you in Trafalgar Square. But until I visited the fortune-teller, you had stayed largely out of my way. It was only afterward that I understood you were an obstacle. And there you were, just as she finished talking about you—there you were, coming up in the elevator." He almost smiled. "Life has a great many coincidences sometimes."

I wanted out of there, in that moment, more than I had ever wanted anything in my life. But I took one breath, and then another, and I held on. "How did you do it?" I asked, remembering the shreds of the briefing George Sutter had given me, the questions he wanted answered. "How did you convince the Germans to falsify your death, give you a new identity?"

"Oh, come now," he said. His voice had grown easier with use, more melodic. "You can't possibly be confused about that. After she died, I got myself captured by the German army. I demanded to see the prison commander, and I made him an offer to take to his superiors."

"And they welcomed you? Just like that?"

"They were worried I was a double agent, of course, but I was convincing. I no longer cared about my life, and they knew it." He leaned forward over the table, though his restraints did not let him move very far. "Now tell me. What else did you see?"

I cleared my mind, thought about the images that had gone through my head that sunny day on a green hilltop in Kent. "I saw what you were wearing, your motorcycle, the sidecar. I saw you throw a suitcase through the window of a factory." I shook my head. "I saw men at a table, four of them. I saw the woman's face, and I knew that she was dead, that that was what drove you. You wanted to kill yourself with your razor, but she was the reason you stopped. Because you hadn't finished." I looked at him. "And then the telephone rang, and you put the razor down and answered it."

His face was slack, and I suddenly realized that I was heartily sick of that expression, the one of wonder that I had seen on so many faces. I never wanted to see it again. "Impressive," he said after a moment. "I thought that summoning my sister and my brothers was well-done already. You are rather amazing, are you not?"

*Not for long,* I thought. I looked at his hands.

I was supposed to take his hands, to gather information. Names, dates, faces, details. I was to use myself as a conduit, to absorb as much as I could and transmit it to the authorities, like a human radio. Those were my instructions, and they had been clear.

And suddenly I wanted none of it. I pushed my chair back.

"I'm leaving," I said loudly to the pane of smoked glass. "You're going to have to get the rest of your answers yourself."

I banged on the door, and after a moment—there was quiet consultation on the other side, male voices deliberating—the guard opened it.

It was over. I was quits. I did not look back at Colin Sutter. I walked out the door and went back to my life.

* * *

James was dressed in an overcoat and hat in the golden October sunshine. He watched me approach him, standing at the gates to Hyde Park, his hands in his pockets, his gaze warm with appreciation.

"Well?" he said when I drew close.

"It's done," I replied.

He raised his eyebrows at me.

I reached up and brushed an imaginary speck from his coat with my gloved hand. It was an excuse for me to touch him, and he knew it, but he stood still and humored me. "I talked to him," I said. "That was all. I didn't have the heart to do a reading."

He caught my meaning immediately, which was why I loved him so. "It was that bad, was it?"

"Worse." I tried to say more, but the words stuck in my throat. Instead I said, "I'll tell you about it later. If I can."

"All right," he said, but I knew he was watching me carefully.

I shrugged. "Anyway, while I was there, I made a decision. No more readings, ever again." I looked up at him. "It seems I'm out of work."

That made him smile. "I know the feeling." He'd left his job at the New Society, telling Paul Golding that he could no longer work with ghosts. Going back to the law was out of the question, and he'd been at loose ends for the past three weeks. It hadn't bothered him, since we'd spent part of that time selling my mother's house and as much of the rest of it as possible in bed. "Though I may not be out of work for long."

"Why not?"

"I got a letter this morning. An acquaintance of Paul's, referred by him. This fellow has a bit of a problem, and he needs someone discreet to look into it for him. For a fee."

I smiled. "An investigator."

"It's a thought," he said. "I always was good at it."

"No ghosts?" I asked.

"None at all."

I thought it over. "Will you answer him?"

"Tomorrow, perhaps."

"I like it," I said. "You can work while I study." I'd sold my mother's house and moved into James's flat, complete with Pickwick. His landlady was beside herself. She said we could keep the dog, but we couldn't stay in her house unless we were married. James told her to be patient and she'd get everything she wished. In the meantime, I had enrolled, embarrassing as it was, in courses. It had always bothered me that I'd never been to school. I didn't know what I wanted to do with my schooling yet, but just the idea of learning made me think of possibilities.

James leaned down and kissed me, gently, right in front of the Hyde Park crowds, as if reading my tumbled thoughts. "In the meantime, we have a free afternoon," he said. "What will we do with it?"

The leaves were falling in Hyde Park, the trees turned gold and gently preparing for winter. The sun made the colors vivid, and we joined all the other Londoners strolling in the quiet, taking in the fragrant air under the trees. We made it partway down the first path before he put his arm around me, and pulled me to him again, and kissed me, warm against me in the autumn chill. I laughed, and I didn't care whether anyone was watching.

## AUTHOR'S NOTE

The years before and after the First World War saw a wave of interest in spiritualism and the occult, fueled by those grieving for their loved ones lost in battle. With such a large market of customers, fakes and frauds made an excellent profit.

The New Society for the Furtherance of Psychical Research is fictional, but it is loosely based on the British Society for Psychical Research, a group that gathered scientific minds determined to prove the fact or fiction of psychical phenomena; a well-known member was Sir Arthur Conan Doyle. The actual society performed extensive tests on those who claimed psychic ability, and at times those tests included tying the subject's hands and legs to a chair in order to prevent toe or finger taps. They also attempted a countrywide census of the supernatural, encouraging the populace to write in with its experiences in hopes of compiling usable data.

The slang words used in the world of psychics, including *skimmer*, *showgirl*, and *fortune-petter*, are my invention. Many psychic frauds did (and still do) use audience plants to appear trustworthy. The "rules" of séances, including using a round table and staying in one's own environment, are of my own making but are an extension of the kinds of tricks con artists have always used.

Many Americans associate the flappers of the 1920s with the USA, but the flapper culture in 1920s London was deliciously wild. The media called them the Bright Young Things and breathlessly reported their exploits.

The woman Ellie envisions while seeing from Colin's point of view is fictional but was inspired by Edith Cavell, a British nurse who was convicted of treason by the German (not the British) government for helping Allied soldiers escape German-occupied Belgium. She was executed by firing squad in 1915.

Read on for a preview of Simone St. James's haunting new novel. . . .

In England, 1921, a young woman hired as the companion to a wealthy matriarch, and grieving for her husband killed in the Great War, begins to believe that something is not right about the family she is working for . . . or about her husband's death. . . .

## LOST AMONG THE LIVING

Available in April 2016 from New American Library
in paperback and as an e-book.

# CHAPTER ONE

## ENGLAND, 1921

By the time we left Calais, I thought perhaps I hated Dottie Forsyth. To the observer, I had no reason for it, since by employing me as her companion Dottie had saved me from both poverty and a life robbed of color in my rented flat, the life I was failing to live without Alex. However, the observer would not have had to spend the past three months crisscrossing Europe in her company, watching her scavenge for art as cheaply as possible while smoking her cigarettes in their long black holder.

"Manders," she said to me—though my name was Jo, one of her charms was the habit of calling me by my last name, as if I were the upstairs maid—"Mrs. Carter Hayes wishes to see my photographs. Fetch my pocketbook from my luggage, won't you? And do ask the porter if they serve sherry."

This as if we were on a luxurious transatlantic ocean liner, and not on a simple steamer over the Channel for the next three hours. Still, I rose to find the luggage, and the pocketbook, and the porter, my stomach turning in uneasy loops as I traveled the deck. The Channel wasn't entirely calm today, and the misty gray in the distance gave a hint of oncoming rain. The other passengers on the deck cast me brief glances as I passed them. A girl in a wool skirt and a knitted cardigan is an unremarkable English sight, even if she's passably pretty.

I found the luggage compartment with the help of the porter, whose look of surprise turned to one of pity when I asked about the sherry, and from there I rummaged through Dottie's many bags and boxes, looking for the pocketbook. I didn't think Mrs. Carter-Hayes, who had been acquainted with Dottie for all of twenty minutes, had any real desire to see the photographs, but despite the pointlessness of the mission, I found myself lingering over it, taking longer than I needed to in the quiet and privacy of the luggage department. I tucked a lock of hair behind my ear and took a breath, sitting on the floor with my back to one of Dottie's trunks. We were going back to England.

Without Alex, I had nothing there. I had nothing anywhere. I had given up my flat when I left with Dottie, taken the last of my belongings with me. There wasn't much. A few clothes, a few packets of beloved books I couldn't live without. I'd sold off all our furniture by then, and I'd even sold most of Alex's clothes, a wrench that still made me sick to my stomach. The only fanciful thing I'd kept was the case with his camera in it, which I could have gotten a few pounds for but simply hadn't been able to part with. The camera had come with me on all of my travels, on every boat and train, though I hadn't even opened the case. If Dottie had noticed, she had made no comment.

And so my life in England now sat before me as a perfect blank. We were to go to Dottie's home in Sussex, a place I had never seen. I was to stay on in Dottie's pay, even though she was no longer traveling and my duties had not been explained. When she had first written me, declaring starkly that she was Alex's aunt, that she'd heard I was in London, and that she was in need of a female companion for her travels to the Continent, I'd imagined playing kindly nursemaid to an undemanding old lady, serving her tea and reading Dickens and Collins aloud as she nodded off. Dottie, with her scraped-back hair, harsh judgments, and grasping pursuit of money, had been something of a shock.

I tried to picture primroses, hedgerows, soft, chilled rain. No more hotels, smoke-filled dining cars, resentful waiters, or searches through unfamiliar cities for just the right tonic water or stomach remedy. No more sweltering days at the Colosseum or the Eiffel Tower, watching tourists blithely lead their children and snap photographs as if we'd never had a war. No more seeing the names of battlefields on train departure boards and wondering if that one—or that one, or that one—held Alex's body forgotten somewhere beneath its newly grown grass.

I would have to visit Mother once I was back; there was no escaping it. And I did not relish living on another woman's charity, something I had never done. But at least at Dottie's home I would be able to avoid London, and all of the places Alex and I had been. Everything about London since he'd gone to war the last time had stabbed me. I wished never to see it again.

Eventually I gave up the musty silence of the luggage department and returned to the deck, pocketbook in hand. "What took so long?" Dottie demanded as I approached. She was sitting in a wooden folding chair, her cloche hat pulled down against the wind and her feet in their practical oxfords crossed at the ankles. She looked up at me, frowning, and though the cloudy light softened the edges of her features, I was not fooled.

"They don't serve sherry here," I said in reply, handing her the pocketbook.

Dottie's eyes narrowed perceptibly. I thought she often convinced herself that I was lying to her, though she could not quite figure out exactly when or why. "Sherry would have been most *convenient*," she said.

"Yes," I agreed. "I know."

She turned to her companion, a fortyish woman with a wide-brimmed hat sitting on the folding chair next to hers and already looking as if she wished to escape. "This is my companion," she said, and I knew from her tone that she intended to direct some derision at me. "She's the widow of my dear nephew Alex, poor thing. He died in the war and left her without children."

Mrs. Carter-Hayes swallowed. "Oh, dear." She looked at me and flashed a sympathetic smile, an expression that was so genuine and kind that I almost pitied her for the next three hours she'd have to suffer in Dottie's company. When Dottie was in a mood like this, she took no prisoners—and she'd been in this mood more and more often the closer we came to England.

"Can you imagine?" Dottie exclaimed. "It was a terrible loss to our family. He was a wonderful young man, our Alex, and I should know since I helped raise him. He spent several years of his childhood living with me at Wych Elm House."

Her glance cut to me, and in its gleam of triumph, I knew that my shock showed on my face. Dottie smiled sweetly. "Didn't he tell you, Manders? Goodness, men are so forgetful. But then, you weren't together all that long." She turned back to the bewildered Mrs. Carter-Hayes. "Children are life's greatest joy, don't you agree?"

It would go on like this, I knew, until we docked: Dottie speaking in innuendos and double meanings, cloaked in polite small talk. I moved away and stood by the rail—there was no folding chair for me—and let the noise of the wind blow the words away. I hadn't bothered with a hat, and I felt my curls come loose from their knot and touch my face, my hair tangling and my cheeks chapping as I sightlessly watched the water.

This wasn't her only mood; it was just one of them, though it was the most vicious and unhappy. I had learned to navigate the maze of Dottie's ups and downs over the last three months, not finding the task unduly hard as I was well versed in unhappiness myself. She was fiftyish, her frame narrow and strangely muscular, her face with its gray-brown frame of meticulously pinned-back hair naturally sleek, with a pointed chin. She looked nothing like Alex, though she was his mother's sister. She was not vain, and never resorted to powders or lipsticks, which would have looked absurd on her tanned skin and narrow line of a mouth. She ate little, walked often, and kept her hair tidy and her shoes practical. All the better for chasing and devouring her prey.

I glanced back at her and found that she was now showing the photographs to Mrs. Carter-Hayes. She kept six or seven of them in her pocketbook, on hand for occasions in which she had cornered a stranger and wished to show off. From the softening of Dottie's features I could tell that she was showing the picture of her son, Martin, in his officer's uniform. I had seen the photograph many times, and I had heard the accompanying narrative just as often. *He is coming home to be married. He is such a dear boy, my son.* The listeners were always too polite, or too bored, to question the fact that the war had ended three years ago, yet Dottie Forsyth's son was only now coming home. That she still showed the photograph of Martin in uniform, as if she hadn't seen him since it was taken.

I turned back to the water. I should quit. I should have done it long ago. The position was unpleasant and demeaning. I had been a typist before I married Alex, before my life had fallen apart. My skills were now rusty, but it was 1921, and girls found jobs all the time. I could try Newcastle, Manchester, Leeds. They must need typists there. It wouldn't be much of a life, but I would be fed and clothed, with Mother's fees paid for, and I could stay pleasantly numb.

But I would not quit. I knew it, and, I believed, so did Dottie. It wasn't the pay she gave me, which was small and sporadic. It wasn't the travel, which had simply seemed like a nightmare to me, as if I were taking the train across a vast wartime graveyard, the bombed buildings just losing their char, the bodies buried just beneath the surface of the still-shattered fields. I would not quit because Dottie, viperish as she was, was my last link to Alex. And though it hurt me even to think of him, I could not let him go.

I had last seen him in early 1918, home on leave before he went back to France and flew three more RAF missions, the final from which he did not return. His plane was found four days later, crashed behind enemy lines. There was no body. The pack containing his parachute was missing. He had not appeared on any German prisoner-of-war rosters, any burial details, any death lists. He had not been a patient in any known hospital. In three years there had been no telegram, no cry for help, no sighting of him. He had vanished. My life had vanished with him.

*He died in the war,* Dottie had said, but it was just another sting of hers. According to the official record, my husband had not died in the war. When there is a body, a grave, then a person has died. But no one ever tells you: When you have nothing but thin air, what happens then? Are you a widow when there is nothing but a gaping hole in what used to be your life? Who are you, exactly? For three years I had been trapped in amber—first in my fear and uncertainty, and then in a slow, chilling exhale of eventual, inexorable grief.

As long as I was with Dottie, part of me was Alex's wife. He still existed, even if only in the form of Dottie's innuendos and recriminations. Just hearing someone—anyone—say his name aloud was a balm I could not let go of. I had followed her across Europe for it, and now I would follow her to Wych Elm House, her family home. Where Alex had lived part of his childhood, something he had never thought to tell me.

I stared out to sea, uneasy, as England loomed on the horizon.

Photo by Adam Hunter

**Simone St. James** is the award-winning author of *The Haunting of Maddy Clare*, which won two RITA Awards from Romance Writers of America and an Arthur Ellis Award from Crime Writers of Canada. Her second novel, *An Inquiry into Love and Death*, was shortlisted for the Arthur Ellis Award for Best Novel from Crime Writers of Canada. She wrote her first ghost story, about a haunted library, when she was in high school, and spent twenty years behind the scenes in the television business before leaving to write full-time. She lives in Toronto, Canada, with her husband and a spoiled cat.

CONNECT ONLINE

simonestjames.com

facebook.com/simonestjames